D0458700

THE ANOMALY

THE
ANOMALY

MICHAEL RUTGER

GC

GRAND CENTRAL
PUBLISHING
New York Boston

Copyright © 2018 by Michael Rutger

Cover design by Brian Lemus. Cover image © Cultura Exclusive/Manuel Sulzer/Getty Images. Cover copyright © 2018 by Hachette Book Group, Inc.

Grand Central Publishing
Hachette Book Group
1290 Avenue of the Americas, New York, NY 10104
grandcentralpublishing.com
twitter.com/grandcentralpub

First Edition: June 2018

Grand Central Publishing is a division of Hachette Book Group, Inc. The Grand Central Publishing name and logo is a trademark of Hachette Book Group, Inc.

The publisher is not responsible for websites (or their content) that are not owned by the publisher.

The Hachette Speakers Bureau provides a wide range of authors for speaking events. To find out more, go to www.hachettespeakersbureau.com or call (866) 376-6591.

Book design by Marie Mundaca

Photograph on page 71 © DesertUSA.com. Used by permission.

Names: Rutger, Michael, author.
Title: The anomaly / Michael Rutger.
Description: First edition. | New York: Grand Central Publishing, June 2018.
Identifiers: LCCN 2017053130| ISBN 9781538761854 (hardback) | ISBN 9781478999430 (audio download) | ISBN 9781538761847 (ebook)
Subjects: LCSH: Archaeologists—Fiction. | Suspense fiction. | BISAC: FICTION / Suspense. | FICTION / Action & Adventure. | FICTION / Fairy Tales, Folk Tales, Legends & Mythology.
Classification: LCC PR6069.M5225 A55 2018 | DDC 823/.914—dc23
LC record available at https://lccn.loc.gov/2017053130

ISBNs: 978-1-5387-6185-4 (hardcover), 978-1-5387-6184-7 (ebook)

Printed in the United States of America

LSC-C

10 9 8 7 6 5 4 3 2 1

For my father,
with love, and with thanks for his
unrelenting belief and support.

What we wish most to know, most desire,
remains unknowable and lies beyond our grasp.

—James Hollis, *The Archetypal Imagination*

THE ANOMALY

PROLOGUE

He went back.

As he ran, he felt a reverberation under his feet, the shudder of something very heavy landing on the stone floor. Close by? Impossible to be sure.

He hesitated, almost ready to give up, but some impulse kept him moving forward. "Samuel!" he shouted, voice cracking.

And this time he finally gained a response. A strangled attempt at speech, half-choked with a sob. On the left. Only yards away in the darkness.

"Get the light."

Maqk—one of only two natives left, the others all dead or deserted or lost—grabbed the candle from the floor and followed George as he felt his way along the wall in the direction of the sound, keeping his rifle in position, trying to hold it steady, though his arms were exhausted and his nerves shot.

There.

In the dying glow of the candle.

Samuel. Slumped on the ground. Something in his hand, which he scratched against the wall. A knife. Blood on the handle. Blood over his shirt and face, too.

"For God's *sake*," George said. "I told you to *follow*."

The man didn't seem to hear. He kept at his bizarre, pointless task.

"We leave now *or we die*."

Maqk, too, pleaded with Samuel to move. He got no more of a response.

Another scream, from deep within the cave. A long, fading, and even more horrific sound than the one before, a sound that said who-ever made it would not be capable of a noise of any kind for much longer.

Losing patience, on the edge of outright panic, George gestured to Maqk and they lunged forward, each grabbing one of Samuel's arms. They pulled, tugging him to his feet.

"No!" Samuel shouted. "I *must finish it*."

They ignored him, yanking with failing strength, hauling the man back the way they had come. They stumbled together along the cor-ridor, using each dim candle like a rung on a ladder.

Finally they were able to see a faint glow ahead—narrow, dark blue, a sliver of dawn from outside.

But they could hear something, too.

"Go," Samuel said brokenly. "Just go. Leave me."

George grabbed the man's arm tighter and yanked him into some-thing like a run. Maqk kept shoving him from behind—but cried out. A shout, and then a scream.

George glanced around and saw the man suddenly disappear—yanked back into the darkness, eyes and mouth frozen wide.

George and Samuel ran as fast as they could toward the light, putting their souls in the hands of God.

PART ONE

It's the loss of the Grail that sets us out
on the Quest, not the finding.

—Martin Shaw, *The Snowy Tower*

The Lord saw that the wickedness
of man was great in the earth,
and that every intention of the thoughts
of his heart was only evil continually.

—Genesis 6:5

CHAPTER

1

It took six hours to get to the Grand Canyon from LA despite the fact that Ken drives like a crazy person, and by the time we arrived at the hotel it was late afternoon and everyone was very hot and extremely ready to not be in the car anymore. The Kenmobile is a big old Lexus SUV bought in better times, but with five people's bags and Pierre's extensive collection of camera and lighting equipment—the majority of which, I'm convinced, is superfluous for any function unrelated to Pierre's ego—four of us spent the long, hot drive in moderate discomfort. Ken's insistence on playing loud progressive rock from the 1970s did not make the time pass any faster, though I'll admit there was an hour of unrelenting desert toward the end when it lent the experience an epic Kodachrome grandeur.

The hotel was twenty miles from the canyon, and pretty new and perfectly okay. Two wings of identical rooms on three floors, open-plan lobby in the middle with a half-decent restaurant and airport-style bar, surrounded by parking lot and desert. Ken defaults to this kind of place—it's Molly who arranges the bookings, but with anything involving expenditure you can bet he made the judgment call—because they're cheap and have loyalty programs that feed points back to the company credit card. Ken's chief skill as a producer/director is to pinch each penny until it begs for mercy. Without this talent the show wouldn't have made it to the web in the first place, and it was even more crucial now that we had the steely eye of a cable network overseeing every aspect of production, and so I'm grateful, I guess. I'm also glad this kind of crap isn't my problem, because I'd be hopeless at it—but that doesn't stop me wishing that, once in a while, we could base operations somewhere with views over something other than asphalt.

We tumbled out of the SUV into the lot and stretched and muttered and burped. The team:

Ken—late fifty-something (and pointlessly evasive on the precise number), paunchy, face like an old pug, thinning black hair. Came over from England way back (quite possibly on the run from the authorities), punched his way up through commercials and music videos and produced a few horror movies in the early '90s that made some actual money. These days *The Anomaly Files* is all he does, and he does not stint in making comedic play over how far this shows his star has fallen.

Molly—assistant producer—twenty-eight, confidently attractive in generic Southern California style, destined for better things. Surgically attached to her iPhone, never without a binder, usually smiling in a way that says it really will be better for all concerned if you just do what she says.

Pierre—midtwenties, pointlessly good-looking, our cameraman. I don't know why he's called Pierre. He's not French. His parents aren't French. He can't speak French and (I checked) has never even been to France. It's annoying. Pierre is convinced he's on the fast track to Hollywood and one night when he's annoyed me even more than usual I'm going to tell him I've been there and it's not as much fun as it looks. But not yet, as the most annoying thing about Pierre is that he works hard and is genuinely talented, certainly a lot more so than the past-it journeymen who'd normally accept this type of gig. Plus he has rich parents and comes with his own high-end gear and so Ken loves him, insofar as Ken's capable of loving anyone who isn't actively handing him either money or a drink.

Finally, a temporary addition to our merry band, a woman I'd met for the first time that morning when the Kenmobile picked her up from a bland little house in Burbank. Mousy, pale, a neohippie type in floaty multilayered clothes with hemp shoes and an ankh necklace. I was still struggling to address her as Feather, though that appeared to be her actual name.

And then yours truly, of course.

But that's enough about me.

Molly led the way into the hotel and supervised check-in. Ken went first, naturally. Once processed, he told Molly to get his bag sent up to his room and announced that he'd see us all in the bar in an hour—at which point he marched straight over to it, to do an hour's predrinking. His dedication in this regard is legendary.

Pierre and Feather went next, and wandered off toward the elevators together, Pierre draped in black canvas tech bags. Theoretically he brings them inside to stop people stealing the gear from the car, but I suspect the primary intention is to show off his gym-muscled arms as he hefts them to and fro.

I finally stepped up to the desk next to Molly and smiled at the registration clerk. "Hey, Kim," I said, reading the name from her badge. "How's your day?"

She frowned, which was not the desired effect. After a moment, however, it became clear she was trying to place me, and then that she had. "Whoa," she said. "You're that guy."

"That guy?"

"Yes," she said. "You are. The YouTuber. That archeologist guy. Unsolved mysteries and stuff."

This, I should note, seldom happens. My grin in response was charming, and the accompanying shrug could have been used as a Wikipedia illustration of "self-deprecating."

"Guilty as charged," I said. "I am indeed Nolan Moore."

"Wow. My dad *hates* your show."

"Oh. Why?"

"He's an actual archeologist. Or was. Now he's a professor at

7

NAU in Flagstaff. He's real smart. I tend to go with what he thinks."

"Good for you. Well, I'm sorry he doesn't like the show. Can I check in now?"

She clattered on her keyboard, peering at the screen. "Actually, I don't seem to have a reservation under the name Nolan Moore."

"It'll be under Roland Barthes."

"Why?"

"Long story." Actually, it was a fairly short story. A very successful movie actor I used to go drinking with in a previous life told me that one of the ways he'd made it seem like he was, or might soon be, famous—in the early days—was checking into hotels under an assumed name. For the mystique. Every now and then I experimented with doing the same. This encounter was not the first evidence that it was a really dumb idea, certainly outside Hollywood.

"I'll need to see ID in that name."

"I don't have any."

She looked up with an unapologetic half smile.

"Molly," I said, "sort this shit out, would you?"

I stomped back outside to have a cigarette.

CHAPTER

2

Having showered and tweeted and replied to the few nonasinine comments on the show's YouTube channel, I spent an unedifying half hour wandering the parking lot, smoking diligently and looking at the view—360 degrees of desert, sporadically enlivened by stunted shrubs; the lights of a gas station twinkling in the distance as dusk settled in. At seven I walked into the hotel bar, ready for refreshment.

Ken was holding court at a center table, Molly on the couch beside him. They stick together like glue while in production, mainly so they can shout "No" in unison every time I suggest some cool unplanned thing we could do. Feather perched on a chair opposite, looking enthusiastic in a nonspecific way. No sign of Pierre yet; presumably he was either in the gym or meditating in his room, two habits he's mentioned multiple times and for which I have not yet, miraculously, slapped him.

Ken saw me enter and held up two fingers. I glanced at the women but Molly shook her head and Feather merely smiled, not understanding the question. Of course, there was waitress service, but when Ken wants another large vodka he kind of wants it *now*, and though I'm theoretically the star of this thing, I'm generally the one expediting it. Molly is Ken's bitch for anything to do with work, but drinks aren't work, so when it comes to those she's adamant that she isn't. The complexity of the interacting hierarchies within a small group is beyond the scope of my tiny mind. I mainly just do what I'm told.

As I waited at the bar I checked out the other patrons. A few couples making plans for the next day's excursions to the canyon, a family of four peaceably chowing down on identically vast burgers, a scattering of singletons frowning at their smartphones to prove they totally weren't lonely and bored—and a trim redhead with a perky ponytail at the other end of the counter, hammering away on a laptop. She favored me with an amused smile and then pointedly looked away. I sternly ignored her while I signed the drinks to my room, so that showed *her*.

When I got back to the table, Molly was out in the lobby, pacing up and down and barking into her phone. In the run of things she's unflappably affable, but experience has shown that supply companies who get on her wrong side will come to regret it in profound ways.

"Fuckup with the boat," Ken said.

"Oh. What?"

"The last bunch of tourists sank it. The issue is under discussion."

"So I see."

"You sorted on your bits of shit?"

I spread my hands in a gesture of quiet confidence.

"Okay," he said patiently. "But really?"

I tapped my temple. "It's all up here."

He sighed. "That's wonderful, mate. But I'm going to suggest to you, not for the first time, that I'd prefer to see it in an actual *script*."

"Not how I roll. As you know."

"Sadly, I do. But remind me why?"

"I'm done with scripts."

"Plus you're an arsehole. So there's that." He chinked his glass against mine. "Cheers. Here's to the successful and within-budget hammering of another nail into the coffin of received wisdom and the dastardly agenda of Them."

"I'll drink to that," Feather piped up, with surprising vehemence. She raised her glass and I tapped mine against it.

Pierre arrived in the bar looking annoyingly serene. Ken, Molly, and I waved at him as he approached. Pierre understood this wasn't a greeting and dutifully changed course toward the bar. I noticed the ponytailed laptop lady glance at him as he arrived, checking out his form in a way I can only describe as "appreciative."

Meanwhile, Feather was beaming at me. "I don't want to sound like a fangirl," she said, "but...okay, let's face it, I'm a total fangirl. I *love* your show. What you're doing is incredibly important, Nolan. And I want to thank you for it."

"Well, we should be thanking *you*," I said, disliking the heartiness in my voice.

"Happy to be able to help," she said. "*So* happy."

"I'd love to hear more about what the Palinhem Foundation actually does," I said, trying to imply that I was on top of all but the finest details. In fact I had no clue. Our new sponsors had come directly to Ken and he'd handled the negotiations. Or more likely said yes without a second thought. He'd take cash from the NRA if they promised to keep out of his face during filming. And gave him a gun. Without the Foundation's cash injection—and their controlling stake in the NewerWorld cable network—there's no way we'd have this chance of the jump to a real TV show. Being conspicuously nice to Feather was high on my list of priorities over the coming days—as Ken had reminded me, many times.

"Truth," she breathed. "That's what we're about."

"Absolutely. But, uh, in what way?"

"The way *you* mean it, Nolan. What you've shown us time after time in *The Anomaly Files*. We need a compelling voice to fight the way scientists, the government, and the liberal autocracy have painted a misleading picture of the world and a false narrative of human history, stomping down on anything that doesn't fit their agenda."

I wasn't sure what the "liberal autocracy" was supposed to be—

and actually it sounded like something I should probably not be against—but smiled warmly anyway. "Right on."

"Yeah, but seriously," Ken said. "Where's the money come from? Don't think I'm not grateful, love. I'm just curious."

"Seth Palinhem was a successful industrialist," Feather said. She used the term as you might say "violent alcoholic." "He died ten years back. Thankfully, toward the end of his life he realized there were bigger truths and wider horizons. He set up his foundation to fund researchers who shared his vision. This is my first big project. I'm so excited to be here."

"And it's a pleasure to have you," Ken said, dutifully taking his turn to sound hearty, though I'd been there to witness his reaction when he discovered that a Palinhem representative wanted to do a ride-along on the first shoot of the new season. It had featured foul language of a breadth, inventiveness, and duration that may never be bettered in the course of human history. I wish I had it on tape.

"I only hope you're not going to be bored," I said. "Making TV involves a lot of waiting around."

"I won't be for a second, I'm sure. And I want to be helpful," she said. "Part of the team. So what can I do? When the expedition starts?"

"Don't worry, love," Ken said breezily. "We'll think of something. Just ask Molly."

My suspicion was that "something" was going to be a master class in fetching and carrying objects of zero import, occasionally being asked for an opinion on things that didn't matter, and generally being kept out of the way.

At that moment Molly returned and plonked herself down on the couch, looking satiated. Ken grinned at her. "So—do we have the boat we ordered?"

"No," she said tersely. "We have a bigger and better boat. For the same price."

"That's my girl."

"Different guide from the one I talked to before, but this guy's more experienced, apparently. So that's a win, too."

"Nice. Though who needs a guide when we've got Nolan to lead the way?"

They winked at each other in a way that was doubtless intended to be amusing.

When Pierre arrived with the drinks, I was surprised—and annoyed—to see Laptop Lady from the bar behind him. I'd seen him work fast, but this had to be a record.

"Okay," he said, however. "So, this is Gemma, who's coming with us apparently?"

"Good," Molly said. "But where's *my* drink?"

Pierre rolled his eyes and headed back toward the bar. Laptop Lady held her ground and smiled down at us, apparently unfazed at being abandoned with strangers.

Then it dawned on me. "Gemma," I said, standing and reaching out to shake her hand. "Great to meet you."

"Likewise, Nolan," she said. Her hand was cool.

She was offered a space on the couch between Ken and Molly, but took a nearby stool instead. "How come you didn't say hi when I was at the bar?" I asked.

"Heisenberg."

Ken frowned. "The bloke from *Breaking Bad*?"

Gemma laughed. "No. My being here can't help but affect the dynamic of your little team. I wanted some time to watch you before joining the group. Get a sense of you all."

Ken and I glanced at each other. His face remained expressionless, but his left eyebrow rose a millimeter: Ken-speak for *Careful with this one*.

There was chatting, more drinks, the eating of burgers and club sandwiches and fries.

"All right, you bastards," Ken said when it got to ten o'clock. He stood decisively, a bucket of hard liquor having its customary lack of effect other than making his voice twenty percent louder and causing his body to appear, curiously, ten percent wider. "Tomorrow, the adventure begins. So fuck off to bed now, all of you. Wake-ups are booked for five a.m. Be standing by the car by six or you'll be walking."

Everybody started to leave. "If you're available," Gemma said to me, "it'd be great to start getting some—"

"Not tonight," Ken told her firmly. "Nolan's got more important things to do."

"Plenty of time over the next two days," I said, trying to be charming. She smiled in a way that made it impossible to tell whether I had succeeded, and walked away.

Ken sniggered—he loves playing bad cop—and we headed out for a cigarette. "Still think that's a stupid idea," he said as we emerged into the parking lot.

"And I still think you're wrong. An article about the show, on a site with a bazillion readers—what's the downside?"

"Not all publicity is good, Nolan."

"I've got final approval."

"Of course you haven't. All Gemma has to do is press a key on her laptop and a hatchet job will be up on the site in two seconds. By the time we get her editor to pull it down it's already been read and retweeted."

"By the five people who give a shit."

"It's more like ten these days," he said. "You're moving up in the world, Nolan. And I couldn't care less about the fans. For our loyal conspiracy nuts, *The Anomaly Files* being ridiculed by a proper news site is just further proof we're onto something. It's a no-lose. And hardly the first time. Remember that *MediaBlitz* piece on you last year?"

"Not after all the therapy I had afterward, no."

"Exactly. And we survived. But what I *do* care about is not fucking up the deal with Palinhem."

"It'll be fine," I said.

"It needs to be a lot better than fine, you muppet." He was looking at me seriously now. "For reasons I don't understand but am trying not to question, the universe has thrown us a major bone here. We've got this one shot at cable. Blowing it is not an option. I'll be honest, Nolan. We get bounced back to webcasts, I'm done."

I tried to shrug this off, but he saw the look on my face.

"Sorry, mate. It's been fun, but it's barely keeping me in vodka and porn. I'd insist on me or Molly riding shotgun whenever you talk to that Gemma woman, but you'd ignore it. So repeat after me: 'I will not fuck everything up.'"

"Ken—"

"Repeat it, you tit."

I mumbled. "Won't fuck it up. Dad."

He sighed. "Go do your thing—and make it good. Then get some sleep. Lots of on-camera time for you tomorrow on the hike down. It'd be good if you didn't look deceased."

As I headed for the stairs to go up to my room, I passed Gemma and Feather waiting at the elevator.

"For the record," Feather was saying, "Heisenberg proposed the uncertainty principle. I think you meant the observer effect. Hope that helps."

Gemma blinked. Feather smiled sweetly.

I decided that I could come to like Feather.

FROM THE FILES OF NOLAN MOORE:

THE PHOENIX GAZETTE—APRIL 5, 1909

Oldest Paper in Phoenix—Twenty-Ninth Year.

GAZETTE, MONDAY EVENING, APRIL 5, 1909

EXPLORATIONS IN GRAND CANYON

Mysteries of Immense Rich Cavern Being Brought to Light.

JORDAN IS ENTHUSED

Remarkable Finds Indicate Ancient People Migrated From Orient.

The latest news of the progress of the explorations of what is now regarded by scientists as not only the oldest archaeological discovery in the United States, but one of the most valuable in the world, which was mentioned some time ago in the Gazette, was brought to the city yesterday by G. E. Kinkaid, the explorer who found the great underground citadel of the Grand Canyon during a trip from Green river, Wyoming, down the Colorado, in a wooden boat, to Yuma, several months ago. According to the story related yesterday to the Gazette by Mr. Kinkaid, the archaeologists of the Smithsonian Institute, which is financing the explorations, have made discoveries which almost conclusively prove that the race which inhabited this mysterious cavern, hewn in solid rock by human hands, was of oriental origin, possibly from Egypt, tracing back to Ramses. If their theories are borne out by the translation of the tablets engraved with hieroglyphics, the mystery of the prehistoric peoples of North America, their ancient arts, who they were and whence they came, will be solved. Egypt and the Nile, and Arizona and the Colorado will be linked by a historical chain running back to ages which staggers the wildest fancy of the fictionist.

A Thorough Investigation.

Under the direction of Prof. S. A. Jordan, the Smithsonian Institute is now prosecuting the most thorough explorations, which will be continued until the last link in the chain is forged. Nearly a mile underground, about 1480 feet below the surface, the long main

fect ventilation of the cavern, the steady draught that blows through, indicates that it has another outlet to the surface.

Mr. Kinkaid's Report.

Mr. Kinkaid was the first white child born in Idaho and has been an explorer and hunter all his life, thirty years having been in the service of the Smithsonian Institute. Even briefly recounted, his history sounds fabulous, almost grotesque.

"First, I would impress that the cavern is nearly inaccessible. The entrance is 1486 feet down the sheer canyon wall. It is located on government land and no visitor will be allowed there under penalty of trespass. The scientists wish to work unmolested, without fear of the archaeological discoveries being disturbed by curio or relic hunters. A trip there would be fruitless, and the visitor would be sent on his way. The story of how I found the cavern has been related, but in a paragraph: I was journeying down the Colorado river in a boat, alone, looking for mineral. Some forty-two miles up the river from the El Tovar Crystal canyon I saw on the east wall, stains in the sedimentary formation about 2000 feet above the river bed. There was no trail to this point, but I finally reached it with great difficulty. Above a shelf which hid it from view from the river, was the mouth of the cave. There are steps leading from this entrance some thirty yards to what was, at the time the cavern was inhabited, the level of the river. When I saw the chisel marks on the wall inside the entrance, I became interested, secured my gun and went in. During that trip I went back several hundred feet along the main passage, till I came to the crypt in which I discovered the mummies. One of these I stood up and photographed by flashlight. I gathered a number of relics, which I carried down the Colorado to Yuma, from whence I shipped them to Washington with details of the discovery. Following this, the explorations were undertaken.

The Passages.

"The main passageway is about 12 feet wide, narrowing to 9 feet toward the farther end. About 57 feet from the entrance, the first side-passages branch off to the right and left, along which, on both sides, are a number of rooms about the size of ordinary living rooms of today, though some are 30 or 40 feet square. These are entered by oval-shaped doors and are ventilated by round air spaces through the walls into the passages. The walls are about 3 feet 6 inches in thickness. The passages are chiseled or hewn as straight as could be laid out by an engineer. The ceilings of many of the rooms converge to a center. The side passages near the entrance run at a sharp angle from the main hall, but toward the rear they gradually reach a right angle in direction.

The Shrine.

"Over a hundred feet from the entrance is the cross-hall, several hundred feet long, in which was found the idol, or image, of the people's god, sitting cross-legged, with a lotus flower or lily in each hand. The cast of the

(Continued from Page One.)

which indicates that some sort of ladder was attached. These granaries are rounded, and the materials of which they are constructed, I think, is a very hard cement. A gray metal is also found in this cavern, which puzzles the scientists, for its identity has not been established. It resembles platinum. Strewn promiscuously over the floor everywhere are what people call 'cats' eyes' or 'tiger eyes,' a yellow stone of no great value. Each one is engraved with a head of the Malay type.

The Hieroglyphics.

"On all the urns, on walls over doorways, and tablets of stone which were found by the image are the mysterious hieroglyphics, the key to which the Smithsonian institute hopes yet to discover. The writings resemble those on the rocks about this valley. The engraving on the tablets probably has something to do with the religion of the people. Similar hieroglyphics have been found in the peninsula of Yucatan, but these are not the same as those found in the orient. Some believe that these cave dwellers built the old canals in the Salt River valley. Among the pictorial writings, only two animals are found. One is of prehistoric type.

The Crypt.

"The tomb or crypt in which the mummies were found is one of the

contains a deadly gas or chemicals used by the ancients. No sounds are heard, but it smells snakey just the same. The whole underground institution gives one of shaky nerves the creeps. The gloom is like a weight on one's shoulders, and our flashlights and candles only make the darkness blacker. Imagination can revel in conjectures and ungodly day-dreams back through the ages that have elapsed till the mind reels dizzily in space."

An Indian Legend.

In connection with this story, it is notable that among the Hopis the tradition is told that their ancestors once lived in an underworld in the Grand Canyon till dissension arose between the good and the bad, the people of one heart and the people of two hearts. Machetto, who was their chief, counseled them to leave the underworld, but there was no way out. The chief then caused a tree to grow up and pierce the roof of the underworld, and then the people of one heart climbed out. They tarried by Paisisvai (Red river), which is the Colorado, and grew grain and corn. They sent out a messenger to the Temple of the Sun, asking the blessing of peace, good will and rain for the people of one heart. That messenger never returned, but today at the Hopi village at sundown can be seen the old men of the tribe out on the housetops gazing toward the sun, looking for the messenger. When he returns, their lands and ancient dwelling place will be restored to them. That is the tradition. Among the engravings of animals in the cave is seen the image of a heart over the spot where it is located. The legend was learned by W. E. Rollins, the artist, during a year spent with the Hopi Indians. There are two theories of the origin of the Egyptians. One is that they came from Asia; another that the racial cradle was in the upper Nile region. Heeren, an Egyptologist, believed in the Indian origin of the Egyptians. The discoveries in the Grand Canyon may throw further light on human evolution and prehistoric ages.

CHAPTER

3

U p in the room I drank several glasses of water, tried unsuc-
cessfully to wrestle the air conditioner up from its subarctic
setting, and sat at the desk. I had most of the blog post
drafted already but I like to finesse them at the last minute. People
would see the piece, no question—the newsletter has over thirty
thousand subscribers, and the show has slowly clawed its way up to
93,211 Twitter followers (not that I obsessively check). Hardly stel-
lar, but these were numbers I hoped would increase exponentially
once we started going out on cable. You can bullshit all you like about
how YouTube is the medium of choice for the young and smart-
phoned, but even a professionally produced webcast gets no respect
compared to an actual network.

Ken was right. This was a big deal, and not to be screwed up.
But did people care that the time and date at the top of the blog
post were real? I told myself it gave the material a here-and-now
veracity. And maybe it did. Or perhaps it was a question of kidding myself that I was a real investigative journalist. Either way, it
needed to be done.

I rolled up my sleeves and started typing my last blog post from
the world as we knew it.

DAY 1: THE CALM BEFORE THE STORM

I'm sitting in a hotel room twenty miles from the Grand Canyon. From my window I can see the lamps of the parking lot, and beyond it, darkness shrouds mile upon mile of the great desert: a forbidding environment that deflects mankind's gaze—and, I believe, cradles secrets waiting to be told.

It's been a long day getting here. And now, as always at the start of an expedition, I'm filled with both excitement and a sense of responsibility. I know how many of you share my conviction that the world is a far larger place than we're allowed to believe—and that access to the facts will open our eyes to the wonders of our land, our species, the entire planet . . . with its curious corners and extraordinary secrets.

So let's look at some of those facts.

On April 5, 1909, the *Phoenix Gazette*—at the time, one of Arizona's leading and most respected news sources—ran a front-page story under the headline EXPLORATIONS IN GRAND CANYON. The article details how a hunter and explorer named G. E. Kincaid came to the newspaper with a story. He told how a recent expedition—conducted under the auspices of the Smithsonian, and directed by one Professor S. A. Jordan—traveled to a spot Kincaid had previously come upon while cruising down the Colorado River (and that "down" is important, as you'll see over the next two days), prospecting for minerals in the Grand Canyon.

There, halfway up the sheer 3,000-foot wall of the canyon, Kincaid had spotted an opening. He'd clambered up and discovered that a cave lay beyond, a passageway into the rock, nearly a half mile below the current desert level. He'd explored a little, finding a few relics. These he dispatched to Washington. His finds were enough to inspire the Smithsonian to fund the expedition led by Professor Jordan.

There are other crevices in the Grand Canyon. Stanton's Cave, for example, is home not only to some striking big-eared bats but also to four-thousand-year-old twig figurines, shells, and beads, and ten-thousand-year-old remains of giant condors and mountain goats. Though inside this cave, the Kincaid Cavern, they didn't find mere twigs and bones.

They found . . . *wonders*.

But . . . it's getting late, and we've got an early start tomorrow. So for now I'll just urge you to read the original article (linked here), and read for yourself what they discovered. What they *claimed* to discover, at any rate— claims that have been ignored or derided by the archeological establishment ever since.

Try to decide whether this article is a piece of idle make-believe, or if it's possible these brave and inquiring men of yesteryear uncovered evidence that North America was visited in eldritch times by another culture. Consider the question of whether the idols, artifacts, and crypt that Kincaid and his colleagues claimed to have explored in 1909— which, admittedly, no one has ever been able to locate in the century since—are mere figments of imagination . . . or if there is a great truth here.

A truth we're not being told.

I'll admit it's curious that the Smithsonian claims to have no record of Kincaid. No record, either, of this Professor Jordan. But as we've seen in previous episodes of *The Anomaly Files*, the Smithsonian has a long record of being tight-lipped—perhaps even of being prone to "counterfactual statements"—when it comes to any idea that contradicts the consensus the museum was established to maintain.

Questions. Doubts. A fog between us and the truth. I don't want to live my life in a fog—and from what you tell me in the comments section, and via Twitter and our Instagram page (links at the bottom), you feel the same. And so tomorrow we're going to once more cut through all this smoke and try to find evidence of the fire beneath.

We're going looking for Kincaid's cavern.

It won't be easy. We will be breaking the law, entering the canyon via a route that's closed to the public (and why, you might well ask, should that be?). I have spent many hours conducting my own analysis of the original account, and as a result I'll be leading us toward a location that's quite different from where others have tried before.

Will we find the cavern? I don't know. But I *do* know this: In the search for truth, it matters not whether we find.

It matters only that we continue to seek.

I'd better turn in. Tomorrow the expedition starts in earnest. We'll start by hiking down to

I stopped typing and rubbed my eyes.

The fog/smoke mixed metaphor wasn't great. It needed a stirring final paragraph, and stardust sprinkled over it. It was hokey and below my usual standard. When you're selling a sense of wonder, you need to feel it.

I wasn't feeling it.

For that I needed coffee and a cigarette. The latter meant schlepping downstairs, which I decided would be a more appealing prospect if I made the coffee first and could take it with me. Let it not be said that I am incapable of long-term planning.

While I waited for the coffee to brew I corrected a few typos and then flipped over to Twitter and spent a couple of minutes replying to comments. There weren't many, because I'd done this before heading down to the bar earlier. There hadn't been many then, either.

But that was going to change. Right?

The coffeemaker started to cough like a consumptive dog, indicating it still had a minute left to go. This unfortunately gave me a little spare time. In it I did something I'd been determined not to.

I typed in a Twitter username.

The relevant homepage loaded quickly. I flicked down, feeling like an intruder, glimpsing tweets in her distinctive, direct style. I told myself that I had a very different audience but the fact was that Kristy was simply better at concentrating her messages down to tweetable length. Better at writing in general, if the truth be told.

The header image was different from last time I'd yielded to this impulse, a few weeks before. It showed her standing somewhere wild and cold, looking dynamic and committed—yet also down-to-earth and vulnerable.

There was a link to a recent blog post on her main site, from two days back. I couldn't face reading it, but cached the post to my phone for later, or more likely never.

I flicked back to her Twitter homepage and looked at the most recent pictures in the timeline. They were also of somewhere cold. The accompanying tweets doubtless explained where she was, and why, but I didn't read them.

I didn't need to know.

I took my coffee downstairs and stood in an especially uninteresting section of the parking lot. As a smoker you often get to see the backs of places, parts other people don't notice, the secrets hidden in plain sight. I once tried convincing Ken this was kind of a metaphor for *The Anomaly Files*, but he just stared at me for a while and then walked away.

It was very cold now, and it occurred to me that a smarter guy would have brought along a thicker sweater for the night we'd be spending in the canyon. Too late. I wish I were that guy. It must be great being him.

Halfway through the smoke I realized I could hear voices, low tones in what was otherwise silence. Sounded like a man and a woman, around the corner. She was doing most of the talking. I couldn't make out the words but the cadences sounded familiar.

It struck me that it might be the receptionist I'd encountered when we checked in. I regarded that as an unsuccessful human interaction, and I'd had enough to drink over the course of the evening that it seemed like a good idea to stroll around the corner and be affable at her.

As I walked in their direction, however, the voices suddenly stopped, as if they'd heard me coming. There was silence for a moment, then two sets of footsteps, rapidly receding.

By the time I'd turned the corner there was no one there. No telltale smell of smoke, either, or butts on the ground. Some minor hotel-based intrigue, most likely, and none of my business. It still left me feeling vaguely rejected and alone.

I went back upstairs, fixed my post, and submitted it. Then I went to bed and listened to the air conditioner until I eventually fell asleep.

CHAPTER
4

Very early the next morning Ken strolled pugnaciously out of the hotel lobby, steaming cardboard cup in hand.

"Fuck are you looking so smug about?" he said.

I'd been there ten minutes, long enough to discover that a desert lot at 5:45 a.m. is no warmer than it is at midnight. "It's not smugness," I said. "I can't move my face."

"Bollocks. This time of day you normally look like you've been exhumed. By an amateur. But this morning it's like you think you've discovered a reason to keep on living. Which is an illusion, incidentally. Heed the tiny demons and their wheedling voices. End it all."

"Ken, I'm not killing myself so you can claim the insurance. We've discussed this."

"Never been a team player, have you, mate."

"I guess not."

"Seriously, Nolan. Spill it."

I'd been intending to keep it quiet but he clearly wasn't going to let it go. "Got an email."

"From?"

"The publisher."

Ken raised an eyebrow. "'The'?"

"My."

He grinned like a kid and cuffed me on the shoulder, hard enough to spill half the coffee out of my cup. "Fucking fantastic, mate. Top news."

It actually kind of was. The two books I'd produced in the last year—accounts of *Anomaly Files* investigations, featuring stills from the show along with archive photographs—had been self-published, cobbled together by yours truly and thus looking like they'd been assembled by a reasonably talented sixth-grader. The email that had arrived before I came downstairs confirmed both were being acquired by a real-life publishing house and would be coming (fairly) soon to a bookstore near you.

"They paying much?"

"Almost nothing. But that's—"

"—not the point. I know, mate. Congrats. Great boost for the show, too. Blimey. So I guess we'd better try to find this bloody cavern, then, eh?"

"Can't do any harm."

We clinked paper cups and stood in companionable silence, sipping very average coffee and watching the sky start to bloom as we waited for the others to arrive.

Molly had somehow organized a humongous thermos of much better coffee to warm up the cold, sleepy faces inside the SUV—and there's a good atmosphere at the beginning of one of these things, when it all seems possible and exciting, the tiredness and bad temper haven't yet set in, and you haven't started to really quite hate each other. Ken spared us the prog rock and there was joking and laughter along the highway, early-morning sun slanting through the windows. Feather proved good at going with the flow. Gemma seemed distant, though as her hair was still shower-wet it's possible she wasn't awake enough yet to participate. Or else this was her Observing Journalist face.

Eventually we turned off the main road and went rattling along a dusty track between twisted trees, following instructions from Molly and her trusty GPS unit. We were going to need it. Partly to navigate the very precise requirements of the planned route—which, though

I'd admittedly borrowed freely from online sources, genuinely did involve original thinking from me—but also because when we were down in the canyon itself, the phone signal would be weak at best, nonexistent most of the time. And no data coverage at all, thankfully, which meant Ken couldn't make me do one of the excruciating "live" updates that I was confident were watched by three people and a cat.

Half an hour of desert later, the road abruptly came to an end and Ken parked in a cleared area that evidently passed as a lot. Pierre jumped out of the SUV first, camera on shoulder. Molly followed with the boom mike. I shoved my hands through my hair, waited until Molly nodded, and opened my door.

I stepped down and took a slow look around, then started walking across the scrubby plain in the direction of the canyon, doing my best to appear thoughtful and committed, picking my intrepid way through gnarled clumps of low juniper, pinyon, and cottonwood trees. Pierre and Molly kept tracking while I got closer to the canyon—Ken holding Feather and Gemma back out of shot.

When the canyon revealed itself properly I found myself slowing down, losing awareness of my job in front of the camera, genuinely taken aback by what I was seeing.

It doesn't matter how many times you're told that nothing will prepare you for your first look at the Grand Canyon; the fact is nothing will prepare you for your first look at the Grand Canyon. It takes all the superlatives you've encountered before—words like "vast," "inconceivable," and "mind-blowing," and drains all the color from them.

It seems to stretch forever. The riot of reds and oranges and ochres in the rock walls is almost beyond credibility. The drop to the river defies comprehension, too, like an optical illusion, or something discovered on a distant planet where they built everything on a more expansive scale, under the direction of gods with a bigger budget.

I reached for an appropriate response, something stirring enough to capture the emotional resonance of the moment. I walked to the edge, stared out across the landscape, and—after a long, pregnant pause—said:

"Huh."

"Christ," Ken muttered. He waved to Pierre to stop filming. "Moll, let's feed Nolan a lot more coffee and a cigarette . . . and then we'll try that again, shall we?"

The second take was fine. Centered by doses of my two key food groups, I stood in silence for a moment and then started to talk, gazing out at the astonishing landscape beyond.

"They say nothing prepares you for your first glimpse of the Grand Canyon," I said with a wry smile. "And it's true. Mankind may build towers to the sky and circuits too small for the naked eye, but only Mother Nature has the ability to truly take your breath away. I'll give you a moment to let her do that."

I stepped to the side. Pierre had the sense to stay on the view for a few seconds and then pan slowly to my new position, by which time I was facing him in to-camera presenter mode.

"I'm sure you'll agree it's not surprising so many stories have grown up around this extraordinary place," I went on. "When mankind is faced with something wondrous, we have a tendency to reach for the stars— for the *gods*. As we embark upon our expedition, it's important to guard against that. We have plenty of secrets of our own, and we're going to look for one of them now. Come along with us . . . and let's see what we find."

I left a beat, then turned and walked along the rim of the canyon with the blithe and confident air of someone who had the faintest idea of where he was going.

"It'll do," Ken said. "Log it, Pierre. And now let's go look at this trail."

Having been born and bred in California I could hardly have avoided hiking. But though I am a native there and to the manner grudgingly reconciled, I've always favored hiking in the sense of a "nontaxing wander through some pretty woods." It was quickly obvious that get-

26

ting down to the river from the rim of the canyon would involve hiking of a wholly different stripe.

I'd told Molly where I thought we needed to get to, down at the river thousands of feet below, and she'd sorted out the rest—establishing that there were a couple of little-used descent trails from this area. The one we were intending to use was technically on the Navajo reservation, and so we kinda weren't supposed to be here without permission.

"Seriously?"

A narrow and uneven trail clung to the edge of the crumbly, rocky cliff face, winding back and forth through striated fissures in the rock—looking down into a vast open space into which a sizable town could be dropped without touching the sides.

Ken whistled. "Now would be a bad time to reveal you get vertigo, mate."

"I'm more worried about Pierre having to do it with the camera."

Pierre jumped off the rim and landed neatly six feet down the "path." He trotted along it, then back, casting an annoyingly professional eye at the route farther down. "It's fine," he said. "I go trail-running on worse than this."

"Of course you do," I muttered.

Ken smirked. "Okay, camera boy, get yourself in position twenty yards down and we'll do a walk-to-you. Molly, mike Nolan up. Nolan, walk toward us and say something very interesting. And try not to fall off."

"What should I do?" Feather asked.

"To be honest, love, what I mainly need from you and Gemma right now is to stay out of my way. So hold the fort up here until someone shouts up that we've got the shot done. If any Red Indian braves show up, tell them we're with the government."

"Really?"

"No," he said. "*Obviously* don't do that. Just...look, just stand there, okay? Both of you. And keep quiet."

Pierre and Ken headed down the trail. I waited until they were in position, while Molly threaded the lapel mike into my billowy off-white shirt and dropped the transmitter in the back pocket of my jeans. Then she picked her way down the path toward Pierre and Ken, looking sure-footed and confident despite the awkward boom mike. I suspect her family hikes don't all start at Starbucks and end in a bar.

When they were all together, Ken raised his hand.

I stepped down onto the start of the trail, gazing out across the eerie multicolored moonscape. Then I started walking, looking at the camera and trying not to think about the enormous drop only a couple of feet to my right.

"A long time ago," I said, "there was a soldier, geologist, and explorer by the name of John Wesley Powell. He led the first passage through the Grand Canyon by Europeans, and went on to direct the Smithsonian's ethnology department. His influence on the study of America's prehistory is far-reaching, admittedly not always in positive ways. But whatever his bias, he's responsible for recording a few of the Native American legends about the canyon."

I indicated the gorge. "There's a Hualapai legend which said all this was created after a great flood, when one of their heroes, Pack-i-tha-a-wi—and no, I'm not sure that's how you pronounce it—stuck a great knife into the land, and moved it back and forth until the canyon was formed, allowing the waters to flow back out to the Sea of the Sunset."

By now I was within a few yards of Pierre and the others. Ken motioned at me to keep going, however, and Pierre continued to film, walking steadily backward.

"Another legend claimed the canyon was created to solace the grief of a great chief, after his wife died. The god Ta-vwoats created a trail to a beautiful land—heaven, in effect—and the chief visited his wife there. Ta-vwoats made him promise never to tell of what he'd seen, in case people wearied of the tribulations of life and tried to get there early. The chief agreed, and Ta-vwoats caused water to flow over the trail, barring access to the other land forever. This is a sacred place. Powell said he'd been warned by local tribes not to enter the Grand Canyon, that it was disobedience to the gods and could bring down their wrath. It didn't stop him. And it's not going to stop us— though we'll be visiting with due respect to the local tribes and their beliefs, of course."

I was pretty much done now, but Ken and the others kept moving away from me down the path.

"So," I said, with enough emphasis to communicate that if they didn't stop backing away soon I was simply going to stop talking, "two different perspectives—and the advantage freethinking researchers have is that we *listen*. We also consider things like the fact that within the canyon are massive rock formations with names like the Tower of Set, the Tower of Ra, and the Isis Temple. The official story is the early explorers simply happened to like Egyptian-sounding names, which were fashionable at the time—and maybe that's true. But let's keep an open mind. And now I'm going to stop talking, and concentrate on getting down to the river in one piece."

"And...cut," Ken said. "Bit esoteric for the clickbait crowd, but history dorks will love it. Good work, everyone. Except you, Nolan. You were shit."

"Thanks."

"You're welcome. Okay, slackers, let's head back to the car and gather up our crap. It's time to boldly go."

CHAPTER

5

I was just saying," Molly said to me, meaningfully, as we started the walk back to the SUV, "how useful it is to have Feather with us."

"Hell yes," I said. And to be fair, Feather was quickly adapting to being asked to carry things and/or stay out of the way, doing both with unflappable good cheer. "You're part of the team already."

She grinned like a schoolgirl. "Ooh, ooh," she said, handing her phone to Molly. "Before we get out of signal. Can I get a picture with Nolan?"

We posed while Molly took a shot. I tried, as usual, not to look like a craggy middle-aged man who exercises but not quite enough.

Feather grabbed the camera back and fired the picture off in an email. "To my husband," she explained. "He's a huge fan, too." She flicked through her photos and held the phone out so Molly and I could see. A shot of a hipster-looking guy, standing grinning at the camera with a small boy.

"Cute," Molly said dutifully. "What's his name?"

"Perry. He's five."

I took a look, too. "So...how old's the kid, then?"

It took her a moment, but then she laughed her head off. Molly caught my eye and winked.

Good job, Nolan.

*　　*　　*

As the team unpacked things from the SUV and distributed them for carrying down the trail, I walked a little way off to grab a cigarette. After a few minutes, Gemma wandered over to me. "So, Nolan. Is now good? For that little bit of background?"

I smiled broadly. "Now is *great.*"

"I must say, you're a better actor than I realized."

"How so?"

"Your reaction to seeing the canyon. You made it look like it was genuinely your first time."

"Well," I said, "actually, this is my first time."

She stared at me. "What?"

"I live in LA," I said defensively. "So if I want a vacation, I tend to go farther away."

"You're leading an expedition to look for this alleged cavern, for which no one's ever found a shred of evidence, and you've never even *been to the Grand Canyon before?*"

"I've never been to Egypt, either," I said. "Does that invalidate my views on the pyramids?"

"Well...maybe, yeah."

"Scientists say a bunch of things about Mars. None of them have ever been there."

She was looking at me in a curious, baffled way. "That's...different. You can *see* that, right?"

"Being too entrenched in the consensus can stop you from spotting what's in front of your eyes," I said, wondering if I might be better off heading back to the SUV to help. "Everybody agreed for years that the out-of-Africa diaspora of Homo sapiens happened sixty thousand years back, for example. But then in 2015, excavators at Daoxian in southern China found teeth in a cave floor, sealed below stalagmites that were uranium-dated to eighty thousand BC. Slam-dunk proof that the teeth *have* to be older—possibly as old as a hundred and twenty-five thousand years. Did you know that?"

"I did not."

"And you don't care. But my point is, sure, it got reported. Eventually. In journals nobody reads. But all the independent researchers who'd been ridiculed for years? It's 'Run along—the grown-ups have finally found evidence for what you've been saying. So *now* it's real. But we're controlling the story. Oh, and that other stuff you say? That's still wrong.'"

"But you didn't *know*," she said.

I blinked. "What do you mean, 'know'?"

"On this and everything else. You were just making shit up, or repackaging other people's made-up shit. You didn't actually *know* this stuff."

"I'm hazy on your qualifications as an epistemologist."

"Is that to do with bugs?"

"No. It's the branch of philosophy that concerns the nature and scope of knowledge. Kant burned his entire life on it. Shoulda waited to talk to you, evidently."

"Throwing in a long word every now and then doesn't make you smart."

I was trying to keep my tone light but finding it a struggle. "Neither does a lot of short ones. And a *next page* button. And Google ads for diet pills."

"Cheap shot. And may I also point out that it wasn't *you* who found these teeth? This is all secondhand information—like every single thing I've heard you say."

"Discoveries like that don't come along often."

"Right. Hence your mantra that 'it matters not whether we find, only that we continue to seek.' Very zen. And super convenient, too. Because you've made kind of a specialty of *not* finding shit, right?"

"Were shit easy to find," I said, "shit *would already have been found*. It would be part of the consensus, instead of buried and denied."

"Neat sidestep. But seriously. I think my favorite was that episode where you marched up to the Smithsonian in Washington, DC, and demanded to see all the skeletons of giants hidden in the vaults. That was priceless. You in pouring rain, in the street, demanding they stop covering up the secret history of America. And that poor guy from the museum repeating again and again that the skeletons didn't exist."

"There are," I said, "many reports from the 1800s mentioning huge skeletons. Even the 1891 Report of the Smithsonian's own Bureau of Ethnology—at that time directed by John Wesley Powell himself, as conventional a scientist as you'll find—details skeletons over seven feet tall found in Dunleith, Illinois, and Roane County, Tennessee. I've got a PDF of the original right here on my phone if you want to look. There are a *ton* of similar stories, in some cases found in deposit levels suggesting they predated the Native Americans."

"Wow. You're prepared to go *there*? That way lies 'the tribes weren't the first people in North America, so they should stop whining about their land rights.' You really want a piece of that? You're braver than I thought."

"Of course not. Some of the reports could have been concocted by settlers who were trying to undermine Indian claims to be the most significant inhabitants. Which a number of Native American myths also do, by the way—consistently mentioning red-haired, fair-skinned 'culture bearers' in prehistory. Though naturally," I added quickly, "it's hard to tell how reliable our records of their oral histories are."

"Nicely dodged, again. Carefully not saying anything. *Again.* I'd love to ask whether you wanted coffee or tea. My guess is you'd wind up with both. Or neither."

"Look, screw this," I said. By now my voice had gotten loud, and I saw Ken glance over in our direction. "You said you wanted to do a genuine piece of journalism about the show. This kind of bullshit isn't how you deal with a fellow professional."

"But you're *not* a professional," she said calmly. "Except in the limited sense that you eke a living out of it. No, I'm not an epistemowhatever-the-fuck. And you have zero qualifications in archeology or anything else. You're a cut-and-paste merchant who qualifies every assertion with 'Could it possibly be that...' or 'This has led some to wonder if...,' so in the end you never actually *say* anything."

"I'm just—"

"And I don't think you even *believe* any of it. That's the worst part. You don't really think there's an alien spaceship in Area 51. You don't think we're ever going to find Noah's Ark. You just know a good fairy tale when you see one, and you've developed the knack of selling secondhand snake oil to the drooling imbeciles of the interwebs."

"And how does that make me different from you? Your stuff's hardly Pulitzer bait, is it? 'Ten Reasons Why Nobody Hires Jessica Biel Anymore.' Classy, important think pieces."

This evidently hit a nerve. "I'm writing material of greater substance these days."

"A couple of unpaid op-eds in the *Huffington Post* make you neither Woodward nor Bernstein."

"Noted," she snapped. "And now we're speaking of *real* journalists, does it bug you that Kristy's doing so well?"

"Kristy who?"

She hesitated. Then rolled her eyes. "Ha ha. You know which Kristy. Your *ex-wife* Kristy."

"Define 'well.'"

"Seriously? Everything she types immediately syndicated across the world before she lifts her dainty hands from the keyboard. One of the most-viewed TED Talks of all time. Just listed in the Top Fifty Female Opinion Formers in the USA—okay, only at number forty-three, but still. Over a quarter million Twitter followers. Off at the moment doing something super-worthy about permafrost in Alaska. So petite and skinny-fit that she vanishes from sight when she turns to the side. *That* kind of doing well."

"Certainly sounds like it bugs *you*. So much for the sisterhood, huh."

"You're really kind of an asshole, aren't you."

"It's been said."

"Seriously. Does it bother you?"

"Being an asshole? No. I'm used to it."

She just looked at me and waited. "Not at all," I said. "Kristy deserves every success. She has real and valuable opinions. She has integrity. She's the smartest person I've ever met."

"So how come you split, if she's such a peach?"

"Because none of those things are true of me." Everybody was standing now at the SUV with backpacks on, ready to roll and clearly waiting for us. "It's time to go."

She smiled at me, head cocked. "I'm surprised. I thought you'd be harder to knock over than this."

"No, I fall down easy," I said, suddenly feeling very tired. "My trick is I generally get back up."

FROM THE FILES OF NOLAN MOORE:

GRAND CANYON, PAINTING BY THOMAS MORAN, 1916

CHAPTER

6

Twenty minutes later we'd started the descent. After the steep initial section—during which I'm not ashamed to admit I kept one hand on the wall most of the time—the path gradually snaked back and forth as we headed slowly downward, the team soon a straggling line along the trail. We all wore backpacks and were carrying additional weight in the form of equipment, notably a shit-ton of camera batteries, and so everybody was pretty focused on their feet, looking up only occasionally to gawk at the extravagant beauty of the canyon.

I was some way behind the rest of the group, walking by myself. I wasn't being a prima donna. I just didn't want company. I wasn't fuming or nursing bad thoughts about Gemma, either. I knew perfectly well that she was right. In some ways, to some eyes. Including my own.

Though I've been interested in weird history and the unexplained since I was a kid, I'm not an archeologist. Until three years ago I was in the movie industry. Or near it. I was a screenwriter, which is to "being in the movies" what waiting tables is to attending the party. I worked hard and earned some money and jumped through all the right hoops. I tried. For years.

I just wasn't any good. Or not good *enough*, anyway. I finally bailed on the industry after a year writing and rewriting a surefire winner. It was TV on this occasion, the long-cherished pet project of a guy near the top of Fox, and thus Totally Guaranteed to Get Made. Then one day he suddenly wasn't there anymore, for reasons I never established—it was like he was abducted—and his successor followed the standard procedure of setting fire to any project that had consumed conspicuous resources before she arrived.

I took the meeting, was polite and professional and did not stab her with a pen, and walked out sanguinely considering which of my spec scripts I'd return to, phone in hand to inform my agent I was back in the ring and he should put me up for every open assignment in town. Then I stopped walking.

People tutted as I stood on the sidewalk and stared down at my trusty phone. It looked like an alien artifact, and I realized that the promising ideas on my laptop were destined to remain that way. Empty promises.

I shoved the phone back in my pocket and walked Pico Boulevard all the way to Santa Monica. This, in case you're unfamiliar with the geography of LA, is a very long way.

By the time I got to the ocean I was hot and tired, perplexed and a little concerned to find my face wet with tears I hadn't noticed shedding. I was exhausted, frustrated, and bored to death. I lay on the beach, trying to doggedly rekindle the phoenix of my mojo as I had so many times before, acknowledging that I should take a break—the Fox guy had been a smart producer but excessively focused, and I'd been working long, long days for a long, long time—but basically telling myself to get on with life as I knew it.

Neither of these things happened.

My soul was empty.

I was done.

When the light started to fade I called Kristy and she came and picked me up. We went out in our neighborhood and sat in a bar with our arms around each other and she told me how talented I was and how I'd find my thing eventually and everything would be great and that she loved me.

We were like that, then.

*   *   *

I became aware of footsteps approaching, and looked up to see Ken falling back to join me. The trail had temporarily widened enough for two people to walk abreast.

"So," he said. "I'm pleased to report that morale up front is high. Pierre is getting good stuff, and that Feather girl turns out to be a cheerful little love who's causing me no grief whatsoever. It's all fabulous, basically, apart, I'm sensing, from within what passes for the soul of Nolan Moore."

"I'm fine."

"Bollocks you are. I overheard the closing stages of that little 'interview' up there. Voices got loud."

"If you say that you told me so, I will slay you."

"No need. And fuck it. I don't say this often, because I don't want to encourage you. But you're good at what you do, Nolan. That's nothing to do with talent, because you have none. But you find stuff worth saying and then you say it, nice and clearly. Whether you believe any of it doesn't matter."

"I think it does."

"That's because you're a tosser. Bit of history for you, mate. As you know, the most successful movie I ever made was called *The Undying Dead*."

"I . . . still haven't seen it."

"Good. It's still a piece of crap. *But* it got great word of mouth and we were in profit before it even went to DVD. The Kenmobile came out of that movie. And the wife's tits. Her choice—I was perfectly happy with the ones she had. Anyway. The movie was by-the-numbers vampire bollocks, and the director was the biggest wanker I ever had the misfortune of working with. Nick, his name was, Nick Golson. *What* a cunt. But I ran into him six months ago during a party at a horror convention down in San Diego—he's churning out zombie shit for cable these days—and I joked with him about how fucking poor *The Undying Dead* was. He listened, and when I was done, he crooked his finger. I followed him across the party to this woman. He tells her I was the producer on *Dead*, and asked her to tell me what she'd just told him. I won't bore you with the details but basically her mum died a month before the movie came out, and there was a chunk of dialogue—which I wrote, information that Golson was man enough to volunteer, amazingly—that helped her move on, come to terms, all that. Nearly twenty years later, she's still grateful. Quoted the entire speech, word for word."

"That's nice."

"It is. And so I did not tell her that I'd written most of it while taking a shit. My point is neither you nor I know what will matter to the audience in the long run. The *truth*? Who gives a fuck? The Bible's full of utter cock and there are ten thousand wankers out there using it as an excuse to behave like total fucking arseholes. Same as the Koran and the Talmud and probably whatever the fuck it is that Buddhists get their spells out of. But on the other hand there's been *millions* of people, over *thousands* of years, who've got through the day because of that bullshit, or had their heart lifted, or looked at the world differently for ten minutes."

"*The Anomaly Files* is not a spiritual enterprise, Ken."

"Isn't it? You say one thing in each episode that makes someone see the universe as a bit less tedious, or makes them ask questions about the world, it's job done, mate. Whether it's 'true' or not, or what that snide Millennial bitch Gemma thinks…*who cares*? The truth is for teenagers and hippies. We're too old and ugly for that crap. 'Wake me up, make me think, or buy me a drink. Otherwise, fuck off.'"

"You have unexpected depths, brother."

"No, I'm a twat. So are you. Now get your head straight and let's go find this fucking cavern."

"We're not going to find it, Ken, you know that."

"It matters not, mate. Isn't that what you always say?"

He picked up the pace, and I followed him and the others down into the canyon.

CHAPTER

7

T*hat's* the boat?"

It was well after midday now and very hot. You could have lit a match off the inside of my mouth. The trail had remained manageable, though increasingly narrow and broken-up, slowly winding down through a series of gullies for much of the time, at others a more precarious progress along sheer wall.

The first hour or so had felt glorious and intrepid. The air was still cool and the experience of slowly descending into the canyon—stretched out like a painting of Mars on the jacket of a 1960s science fiction novel—was genuinely magical.

It is, however, characteristic of the human mind that custom will stale life's infinite variety. The next several hours had gone on a bit, if I'm honest. I've always been of the opinion that if a hike takes longer than, say, forty minutes, there's an argument you should have parked closer to your destination.

The final section perked up again as we wound closer and closer to the river. Now, only a hundred yards away, we'd turned a corner around a huge outcrop—and there, on a beachy area below, lay a large pastel-blue craft. The front quarter consisted of low rigid structures in white plastic. The rest was inflatable. A much smaller dinghy was lashed to the back.

"Well, yes," Molly said.

Ken peered down. "It's got no fucking *engine*, Moll."

"No. It's a rowing raft. For rowing."

"Are you having a laugh?"

"No," she said patiently. "I explained this the other night. We were supposed to have a boat with an engine. That's what I booked. But now we've got this instead, which is twice as big, and means as well as sleeping bags, it comes with several small tents. Which is a *bonus*."

"But it has no *engine*. Is my point."

"You win some, you lose some."

"So we have to *row* it?"

"It'll do you good."

"Fuck's sake."

Twenty minutes later we stepped off the end of the trail down onto the rocky bank of the river.

"Wow," Feather said, turning in a slow circle, looking up. "Unbelievable. Awesome. *Wonderful*."

The walls of the canyon had been towering over us for most of the morning but reaching the bottom multiplied the effect a hundredfold. Nearly a mile of rock face above, and down here, a river only a hundred feet wide. You felt as if you were somewhere secret, strange, and old—an environment that predated human expectations, and a place where unusual things might be true.

A man came striding toward us from where he'd been waiting in shade. He was immediately identifiable as one of those gung-ho guys who's so brim-full of testosterone that he's going bald at thirty. He introduced himself as Dylan, and appeared to be South African, for some reason.

After shaking hands with everyone he turned to me. "So you're the Indiana Jones figure, hey?"

"Something like that."

"Awesome. One thing, though. On the river, *I'm* boss. We'll get most of the way this afternoon, camp tonight, and should make it to your target area after a few hours tomorrow. It's plain sailing apart from a stretch of rapids later today, which are bouncier than usual because a tremor pulled some rocks down last year. But even when it's calm we don't mess around when we're this far from civilization, okay? Do you have a lot of experience in boats like this?"

"Not much," I said, aware of Gemma's eyes on me.

He cocked his head. "So how much experience would that be, *exactly*? Just to be clear."

"Exactly? None."

"Best do what I tell you, then, and we'll all have a ball. Okay?"

"Sure," I said. I didn't bother to explain that if he felt the need to establish dominance he should have been addressing Ken, or Molly. He'd find that out soon enough. I could, however, have done without seeing Gemma pull out her notepad. I was confident that, whatever else her piece might eventually contain, this exchange would make the final draft. Probably as a pull quote.

Dylan spent the next half hour demonstrating how to stow our stuff in the waterproof lockers, wear life jackets, and use rowing gloves to prevent blisters; explaining the relevance of oars in relation to the waterborne propulsion process; and generally patronizing us as thoroughly as possible. Pretty soon he antagonized Pierre sufficiently that Pierre started dropping in references to annoyingly intrepid experiences he'd personally undertaken in watergoing craft. I wandered off to have a cigarette while they waved their penises at each other.

Ken joined me, glaring at his phone. "Barely a single bar of signal," he muttered. "It's the fucking Dark Ages down here."

"Excellent," I said. "Because who knows what secrets our forebears cherished, the deep spiritual insights they shared, when not enslaved by technology's endless grip upon our—"

"Shut it, you tool."

Eventually we got in the damned boat, which was big enough that the process didn't feel especially perilous or result in someone falling amusingly into the water. Once we'd worked out where and how we were going to sit, Pierre and Ken and I clambered back out again.

Naturally when we started heading downriver we'd be doing most of the shooting so it looked like I was on a solitary quest, but audiences are savvy enough these days to realize the guy who yaks to the camera can't also be pointing the thing, and Ken felt there was an argument for letting it be seen that a team of people were involved—on the grounds it made the expedition seem more of a big deal, not just me screwing around in a canoe for my own amusement.

So the others got to work fastening ropes that had already been fastened once, and taking off their life jackets and then putting them back on again, while Pierre lined up a shot that situated this activity tastefully to one side of frame while focusing on a wide angle across the river, me standing on the beach in the foreground. Ken lofted the boom mike and nodded at me to start talking.

"We're not the first to go looking for Kincaid's cavern," I said in my most thoughtful voice. "Something that strange, that game-changing...there have been other attempts. All unsuccessful. Kincaid's account is quite specific in some regards, frustratingly vague in others. And perhaps not accidentally so. One of the first things he's quoted as saying is—and these are his exact words—'I would impress that the cavern is nearly inaccessible.' He goes on to state that 'the entrance is 1,486 feet down the sheer canyon wall.'"

I half turned to indicate the canyon wall on the other side of the river, and Pierre neatly shifted angle to reinforce this, slowly tilting back to show the mile-plus of rock face dwarfing us. "Then he says it's on government land. And *then* adds that anybody found there will be prosecuted for trespass. Bear in mind this article was published back when just getting to the canyon was a feat of endurance. There were no roads or trains or air-conditioned cars. To then track down a hidden cavern halfway up a vertical rock face, along mile after mile of canyon? Forget it. That's what Kincaid's saying, and that—to me—is extremely interesting. Because to *me* it suggests that these explorers knew what they'd come upon was of extraordinary importance. And that suggests to me that this thing is *real*. And out there to be found."

I left a beat of silence, so it'd be easy to cut at that point, then gestured to Dylan. "I'd like to introduce you to Dylan," I said. "He's experienced on these waters, and he's going to be our guide for this part of the expedition."

Dylan strode over, squaring his shoulders to look even more butch. "Hey."

"The spot I've asked you to head for—have you had anybody ask to go there before?"

He shook his head. "Nah. It's a new one on me, to be—"

"Great," I said. "Can't wait to get started. But before we do, I've got to ask something that I know a lot of our viewers will be keen to know."

"Fire away."

"What's the precise water displacement of the raft, in cubic inches?"

He blinked at me. "What?"

"Or centimeters, if that's easier."

"I don't . . . know."

I laughed. "And who cares, right? But something we really should be aware of, as we set off—that first European voyage down this section of the Colorado River. What year was it?"

"Um," he said.

I let the pause settle deep, and stood looking at him, an expression of immense serenity on my face.

After five very long seconds of this, Pierre sighed and ostentatiously stopped filming.

"It was May 24 through August 30, 1869," I said. "John Wesley Powell. No biggie. Might be a nice fact to share with your next group of tourists, though, right? What with re-creating part of Powell's landmark journey being . . . your actual *job*?"

Dylan coughed. "Can I try another question?"

"No," Ken said curtly. "We need to get on the water. And we're a one-take style of operation, mate. Something that Nolan nails time after time."

"Sorry."

"Don't worry," I said, clapping Dylan on the shoulder and smiling kindly. "You'll get used to it. Probably."

He slunk off toward the boat. Pierre discreetly gave me a fist bump, and Ken winked.

Let it be known that I can wave my own penis around, should the need arise.

CHAPTER

8

One of the things I like about my so-called job is that it makes me do things I normally wouldn't. Most writers (and even ex-writers) are lazy asses, physically at least. Sure, there are exceptions, like Hemingway, who'd leave the house to shoot something or get macho on a big fish, but I'll bet even he was far happier back at home propping up the bar or on the porch communing with his cats in short, declarative sentences.

As discussed with Gemma, I somehow hadn't gotten around to visiting the Grand Canyon before. And now I was not only here, but cruising along the Colorado River more than a mile below the rest of the world, wearing a life jacket and periodically rowing and generally doing the thing. We sat in three rows, Ken and I at the back like a pair of schoolboys. I could tell that Dylan felt the team wasn't taking the process seriously enough, but he was still sufficiently cowed by the filming incident that he didn't seem inclined to give anyone grief. Yet.

It was already midafternoon and the sun was turning the jagged walls of the canyon some pretty glorious shades of red, orange, and brown. Much of this was organized in horizontal striations, but there were patches of mineral staining across it, and vertical lines, too. The lower stretches were sparsely dotted with shrubs and small, gnarled trees. Broken rocks led down to the river, about sixty feet wide at this point, and thirty feet deep. It truly felt like being on another planet.

Later I'd be doing another to-camera segment concerning our route, but I'd keep it short. Partly to maintain the air of mystery—and pay lip service to Kincaid's circumspect description of his expedition, which genuinely did strike me as intriguing. Also because frankly I couldn't remember why I'd decided this was where we should be looking. I'd mapped out the general area by triangulating five different articles I'd found on the web, all written with the brain-searing turgidity of people who find detail very interesting indeed. I have many fine qualities (I imagine) but a rigorous attention to detail is not one of them.

So far, so good. To complicate matters, however, I'd gone on to de-cide that the researchers/speculators whose work I'd been collating/stealing had missed further subtle references in the original text, which to me (under the influence, I'll confess, of a certain amount of alcohol, along with some killer pot sold to me by the Latvian woman who cleans my apartment, which is a story I'd prefer not to get into) implied that Kincaid had been sowing a false trail. I had in my pos-session (in a virtual sense—I'd photographed it and kicked the pics up to my Evernote database) the huge piece of paper on which I'd sketched and calculated and diagrammed until I had my own specu-lative location for the cavern. It looked like the kind of thing the cops discover nailed to the garage wall of some guy they've just arrested on suspicion of multiple grisly homicides over a decade-long campaign of terror, but it made sense at the time. Sort of.

I had it narrowed down to a four-hundred-yard stretch of the river—an unremarkable portion of backwater up a side canyon that had attracted no interest from anyone whatsoever—where the water was both unusually wide and unusually deep.

But first, we had to get there.

After an hour of gently cruising, the raft started to go far more quickly, for no obvious reason, at first.

"Are we getting close to the rapids?"

"Ya," Dylan said. "You all might want to hold on."

The raft jumped another notch in speed and was whipped around a bend, and suddenly the river looked very different. Instead of an open, calm course, it had narrowed to less than a third of the previous width and was strewn with big rocks, the current varying markedly as it cut around them—but all going very fast.

Before any of us had time to get used to this we were being thrown chaotically from side to side, the raft briefly airborne, slapping back into the water with a bone-juddering thump—and then there was another huge bounce that took the right side of the raft two feet higher than the left.

And suddenly Feather wasn't in the boat anymore.

"*Shit!*" Dylan shouted.

He started bellowing instructions, trying to get the raft to a calmer section toward the left side as he stared wildly around for Feather. He seemed extremely disconcerted—which didn't help the rest of us.

"Where is she?" Molly shouted back. "Where—"

But then we saw her. Swimming alongside us, cresting the currents easily, deftly avoiding a big boulder's attempt to flip her over, and then cutting back through the water toward the boat with strong, measured strokes.

Pierre reached a hand down and she grabbed it and was back in the raft in a moment, grinning from ear to ear.

"Again, *again*," she said.

After a few more minutes of extreme bumpiness there were no more rocks. The river widened and the water slowly returned to a more normal pace. Feather looked disappointed.

"You okay?" I asked.

"Okay? That was *awesome*. Dylan—are there more rapids coming up today?"

"No. And look, when I say hold on tight, *hold on tight*. I'm here to make sure you don't die, ya?"

I winked at Ken. "Ah well. Shame not to get the shot of *me* falling in that I suspect you were hoping for."

"Yeah," he said. "But there's always next time. You can run, mate, but you can't hide."

CHAPTER

9

T his is a bit more like it."

It was early evening and Ken and I were sitting in rickety camp chairs on a small patch of beach, fifty yards long and half that deep, in a portion of the canyon where the wall sloped gently before shooting back up into the sky. The opposite side was sheer right down to the water, but the fading rays of the sun bounced off the rim, far, far above, hazing out the sky and setting the walls alight.

It was a heck of a view. Adding to our sense of comfort was the fact we were pretty full. In addition to the camp chairs and three tiny tents stowed on the boat—immediately allotted, without recourse to speech or discussion, to the women present: I could see Gemma considering whether this constituted gender fascism of a virulence worth resisting and deciding nuts to that, it would get cold in the night—Dylan had unpacked a portable grill. Once we'd settled in and gotten the tents up he started wielding tongs and spatula and produced skewers of lamb and chicken from a cooler, and the smell of these cooking in the pure air was enough to provoke audible noises of anticipation from people's stomachs.

Of course, that kind of food always tastes better in the outdoors and when you're on something of an adventure, but it turned out Dylan had spent a year as a personal chef somewhere in the Mediterranean and genuinely knew what he was doing. Even Feather, who was—naturally—vegan, seemed satisfied, as there were containers of non-amateur salads available, too. She was still chowing down on kale and quinoa, her nose and forehead glowing red from the day's sun, long after the rest of us had staggered away from the table.

It further transpired that Ken had firmly stipulated that this not be a dry expedition, and so a number of bottles of vodka had found their way into a dedicated cooler. He and I were, therefore, slowly getting blasted.

"It's not crap," I agreed.

"What's the deal with the colors?"

The view was changing minute by minute, the last rays of sun highlighting striations of red, orange, and brown in the walls and the boulders, large and small, strewn over the slope on either side of the beach. "Mineral deposits."

"I know that, you tosser. I meant, isn't there something we're supposed to be looking for tomorrow?"

"A lot of the wall up and down this stretch of Marble Canyon is made up of an aggregate called Vishnu Schist, two billion years old and originally ten miles underground. So in the process it got heavily compressed and is therefore relatively dense, and a darkish brown color. That's not what we want to be seeing. Kincaid mentioned sedimentary layers near the site of the cavern, and specifically refers to 'stains' about halfway up the wall. Along here, that basically limits us to a five-mile section."

"Five miles is a lot of rock to stare at."

"I narrowed it down to about a quarter of a mile, and that's the location Molly passed to Dylan. He reckons we'll get there late morning."

He winked. "Big day tomorrow, then. Should be exploring the cavern by lunchtime."

"Ha, ha."

*　*　*

Later, having successfully said things while Pierre pointed a camera at me, I was sitting by myself on a rock, drinking coffee and smoking a contemplative cigarette, when I heard someone approaching.

"Don't worry," Gemma said. "I'm not wearing my investigative journalist hat. Just looks like you've found a good spot to sit."

I moved up so she could perch a couple of feet away, and for a while we looked along the dark canyon together, listening to the sound of cold water.

"I did want to ask something, though," she said.

"How confrontational is it, on a scale of one to ten?"

"Only about a two. Mysteries. What's the appeal? To you, I mean. And don't feed me that 'it matters only that we seek' crapola. Most of the stuff you cover—let's face it, there's never going to be an answer. Isn't that kind of frustrating?"

"No," I said. "Once you're in possession of a fact, you're done. Case closed. Mind closed, too. Unresolvable mysteries *expand* the mind."

"I don't see how. Truth is what shows us new things."

"But there's never just one truth. You threw Noah's Ark at me earlier—so take flood myths as an example. They appear all over the world with remarkable consistency. You can't just ignore that. You need to try to find an explanation."

"So try one on me."

"I'll give you three. First, you could claim it's evidence of historicity, a real flood in ancient times—a catastrophe on a scale so massive it was recorded in oral histories all over the world, histories that gradually morphed into myth."

"But for which people have found zero evidence, right?"

"Actually they have, but only ones outside the mainstream— because it makes you sound like you're trying to prove the Bible, which consigns you straight to nut-job status. But sure, ignore their decades of research, though at least acknowledge that the end of the last ice age affected sea levels worldwide, wiping out coastal villages and covering previously inhabited regions like Doggerland in the North Sea. So instead you cite these localized rises in water level—for which there is demonstrable, science-friendly evidence in places like Iraq and the Persian Gulf, the heart of civilization ten thousand years ago. On the back of which you speculate that the universality of a flood myth suggests ancient migrations caused the movement of legends around the world. You don't get the global superflood, but you *do* get the idea that the peoples of prehistory were far more mobile than conventional archeology is prepared to admit."

She appeared to consider this idea seriously.

"Worst case," I went on, "you go Jungian and speculate that the idea of a flood (always framed as a result of mankind's behavior provoking divine retribution—as in the Bible, the Epic of Gilgamesh, the Koran, and the Mesopotamian Epic of Atrahasis) represents an archetypal fear universally resident in the human psyche. That it's a metaphor for the cyclical collapse of societal forms, followed by a period of chaos, and the gradual establishment of a new paradigm in the aftermath. And why are you grinning like that?"

"When you're on a roll, you're not too dumb-sounding. It's disconcerting."

"My point is any or all of these explanations might be true—and reveal something eye-opening about humankind. Yet 'science' downgrades Noah's Ark and all other myths to the level of 'made-up shit from before we had computers.' *That's* what pisses me off. Science is supposed to be the revealer and leveler—but it's become a religion. 'Shut up and believe *our* "truth"—even if it flies in the face of long-established traditions, and half of it is funded by vested interests or dictated by fashion. Oh, and we reserve the right to change our mind next year. And then again the year after that.' Because . . . science."

"But people in the past got stuff wrong, too," she said. "Like thinking the Earth was flat until the Middle Ages."

"Nope. Herodotus was kicking holes in that idea back in 500 BC. The flat-Earth idea was a fake put about by science fanboys like Washington Irving and Andrew Dickson White—to 'prove' religion's dogmas needed defeating."

"Ah, the dreaded conspiracy at work once more."

"Make fun if you like. But to me it's the height of arrogance to dismiss thousands of years of folk knowledge through an evangelical adherence to scientific paradigms that remain theories rather than facts. Our species didn't suddenly start being smart a hundred years ago."

There was a sound from behind, and we turned to see Feather standing on a rock close by, feet neatly together, clapping.

"Bravo," she said.

I shrugged modestly—wishing only that Ken or Molly had been there to see me Conspicuously Pleasing Our Sponsor.

And that I could remember what I'd just said.

FROM THE FILES OF NOLAN MOORE:

MARBLE CANYON, EARLY PHOTOGRAPH (DATE UNKNOWN)

CHAPTER

10

Holy *crap* it was cold in the night.

The sleeping bags just about made it bearable, so long as you curled up like a grub and stayed absolutely still long enough for trapped body heat to build. I drifted off quickly—the day had featured a level of exercise wholly alien to what I like to think of as my "lifestyle"—but woke within an hour to anxious bleating from my nose and cheeks.

When I woke for the third time I sat up and smoked, giving my eyes enough time to adjust to the darkness, and realized that Pierre and Dylan had taken the obvious step of pulling their heads down inside the sleeping bags. Ken hadn't, but he was carrying a ton of vodka inside him and likely feeling no pain.

So I tried the head-inside technique, and managed to get a couple of fitful hours. I was awake again at four thirty, waiting for the sun to rise and turn the walls of the canyon three-dimensional. In the meantime I looked up at the stars, so sharp that their light seemed almost blue.

Just before the dawn I realized I wasn't the only person awake. It's strange how you can tell. I turned my head, expecting to see Molly up on her feet, getting an early start on the day in the organized and can-do way she has.

But she wasn't.

56

Nobody was, in fact. I could see all the other members of the team, either still zipped up inside mini tents or curled up in sleeping bags.

And yet it felt strongly as if I wasn't alone.

I looked around again, slowly panning my gaze across the small beach and over the rocky areas on either side. Nobody there. Of course. We were a long way from anywhere. It wasn't possible for another person to be here.

Here, and watching me. Watching us.

I remembered a final Hopi legend, one that I hadn't included in my spiel to camera before we started down the trail. A story that somewhere within the Grand Canyon lies a deep, hidden cave that is home to their god Maasaw, the "keeper of death"—and that's why portions of the canyon have long been associated with accidents and anxiety attacks.

I hadn't included this tale because I was sure—as Powell himself had been—that it was their way of keeping people out of a sacred site, and there was no truth in it beyond that.

Nonetheless, I was glad when it was properly light.

Eventually other people started to stir. Dylan first, who nodded in my direction and got on with filling the cold air with the smell of cooking bacon. A little banter around the grill the night before had improved relations between the males in the group, and I was considering giving him a few nontaxing moments on camera at some point today.

Hollow eyes among my fellow crew members told me I wasn't the only person who'd suffered a patchy night. The tents the women had slept in hadn't helped much with the dead-of-night temperatures. Ken looked the same as usual, but he usually looks like shit—albeit a robust type of shit that stands up and holds out his hand for a cup of coffee and starts dealing with the world as if waking with sand in your hair at the bottom of the Grand Canyon is business as usual.

We ate and drank coffee and struck camp and got in the boat and paddled gamely off down the river, ready for adventure.

*   *   *

But by three o'clock something was clear.

There was nothing here.

Nothing over and above the outstanding natural beauty, that is, but that wasn't what we'd schlepped all this way for. We'd come for the cavern.

And it wasn't there.

We'd cruised for four hours—as it got hotter and hotter—including navigating another short stretch of mildly turbulent water, then a further hour of calm. Eventually we reached the stretch I'd outlined, determining its position via GPS.

We then rowed slowly along it with great anticipation, each member of the team instructed to focus their gaze on a specific level of the towering wall.

When nothing was spotted, we gamely paddled back upriver, still watching.

Then floated down again, everyone staring at different heights of the wall this time, to keep eyes fresh. Nothing.

Then, at Molly's suggestion, we laboriously maneuvered the raft over to the far side of the river—it was about eighty feet wide at this point, and very deep—in case the change in viewing angle made a difference.

It did not.

We went back upriver again, then down again, then paddled back up until we were in the middle of the search area.

Nothing. Merely a lot of striated rock, pitted, pocked, and striped and—after a while—really not very interesting at all. This whole process took over two hours, most of it conducted in harsh sun.

And there was no damned cavern.

Usually when this happened there was a sense of the team being thwarted together—shucks, well, we tried: Onward and upward. I don't know what was different this time but it felt like it was only *me* being proved wrong, in the company of people who were being fairly patient about it despite noses and foreheads now sunburned to crap.

I stood on the last attempt, so Pierre could film me gazing up at the towering wall. This just made me feel even more like I was out on a dumb limb by myself.

We finished, and Ken asked if I wanted to go again. I shook my head, sat down, took out a cigarette, and lit it.

"Don't start, Dylan," I said. He'd already stopped me doing this on several occasions. He elected not to this time.

The already precarious morale in the boat dropped further as people accepted it was also clear that we weren't getting back to the hotel tonight. Some of the team seemed to regard the prospect of another night in the canyon with equanimity, even enthusiasm in Feather's case. Others less so. Molly, usually stoic in the face of adversity, was suffering disproportionately from the ministrations of mosquitoes. She viewed the prospect of more of the same with zero joy.

"There's simply no way we can get back to civilization today?" Ken asked.

Dylan shook his head. "Not a chance."

Ken nodded decisively. "In that case I have adjusted my goals, as follows. I need a drink and a piss, and then several more drinks. You're either with me or against me. Bearing in mind I sign the checks, I'd advise you all to be with me."

People muttered assent and made an effort to cheer up.

"Hey, we tried," Pierre said.

"I know," I said. "And thanks."

Ken clapped me on the shoulder. "You know what we need before we call it a day, mate. And do it in one take, eh? I really do need a piss."

Ken and Pierre swapped positions so Pierre could shoot sitting down, keeping the camera low so the canyon wall looked even more gargantuan behind me. Molly knelt on the next bench and held the boom mike over my head. Her forehead looked like someone had taken a blowtorch to it.

"So," I said to camera, with my best oh-well-never-mind smile. "It seems this is another of those mysteries that will remain unsolved—at least for now. Regular viewers will know that's the way it goes sometimes."

"Pretty much always," Molly muttered. Gemma sniggered from the front.

I ignored them. "And that's okay. It really is. Because what matters most, what empowers us to grow and develop not just as individuals but as a culture, is never the *finding* of things. The finding isn't important. It's that . . . we continue to seek."

By now I could see, out of the corner of my eye, that Gemma was actually mouthing along to the words. I wondered if there was any chance I could get away with shoving her off the boat. And whether it might be worth doing anyway.

"I've shown you the original newspaper report," I went on doggedly. "You've heard the story of Kincaid's cavern. It's up to you now. I can't tell you what to think—but I can ask you *to* think. To keep asking questions. Do you believe you're being told the truth about America, and the prehistory of mankind? Are you happy about the way conventional science dismisses any idea that doesn't fit a neat and tidy narrative? If not, let me know via Twitter and Facebook. And most of all—"

"Wait," Pierre said.

I looked up from the lens and stared at him furiously. If he'd screwed something up technically it meant a redo on this whole embarrassing piece-of-crap sign-off, and I honestly wasn't sure I could be bothered.

He'd raised his head from the viewfinder, however, and was looking at something behind me. "What's that?"

"The same shit we've been staring at pointlessly all afternoon," I said. "Fuck is wrong with you, Pierre?"

"No," he said, pointing. "Up there."

I turned and tilted my head to follow the line of sight indicated by his finger. High, high up on the striated rock face of the wall of the canyon was . . . more rock.

"Seriously, Pierre. If you're trying to be funny you're missing it by a country mile. Screw this. We got enough. I'll cap it with something when we're back on dry land."

"Hang on a sec, though," Ken said, standing. "Oi, boat bloke—try to keep us steady."

"Ken, I'm having something of a sense of humor failure here, in case you hadn't noticed, so—"

"Shut it, Nolan. *Look*."

I turned around. Ken was pointing at the rock wall, toward an area about a quarter of the way up, to the side of a long splatter of stain across the layers of sediment—a patch that looked as though someone had thrown an enormous cup of coffee across the canyon wall.

And there, for a moment, smack in the middle, was a very small darker patch.

"It keeps disappearing," Pierre said. "It's very small. And as the boat moves, the light changes on it."

"I don't see anything," Molly said, squinting against the slanting sun. "Are you sure...Oh, okay. Huh."

Everybody else stood and looked, too. Dylan did something with the front oars, and for thirty seconds the boat was relatively still on the water.

"I don't know about you, mate," Ken said quietly, "but that, to my untutored eye...looks a lot like a fucking cavern."

CHAPTER

11

The beach was smaller this time. It was nestled in a bend twenty minutes downriver from where we'd made the sighting, semiprotected by an overhang. It was angled so as to catch the last of the afternoon sun, too, heat the rock would presumably hold for at least some of the night. Molly was, dare I say it, mollified. It wasn't clear yet what we'd found, but we'd found *something*—and the mood was cautiously buoyant.

Once all our stuff had been taken off the boat, Pierre found a shady spot behind a boulder and Ken and I crouched there together to take a look at the footage of the canyon wall. Maxing out both optical and digital zoom, and the rocking from the boat made it blurrier than Pierre's usual rock-steady work, but it was enough to confirm there was a small opening in the cliff face, less than a quarter of the way up.

This was only about three hundred feet above the river, far lower than Kincaid's description, thus validating (I hoped) my suspicion that he'd seeded misinformation into his account. Three hundred feet is still pretty high. The opening wasn't large, and looked even smaller from below because a lip of rock obscured it from view except within an extremely narrow angle of vision.

"Heck of a job, Pierre," I said. "That would have been easy to miss. Well, we did miss it, for a couple hours."

"I got lucky," he said. "Plus you took us to the right place. That's got to be it, right?"

"It's definitely something," Ken said. "Worst case, we've found a feature that other people don't know about. The question is how we're going to get up there."

Pierre scrolled back through the footage. He played a section, then stuttered forward with a few pauses before letting it run again. "We can climb that," he said.

"Fuck off," Ken said. "Have you *met* me?"

"It's not a walk in the park," Pierre admitted. "But there's a consistent concave in the wall, and a ton of crevices and hand-holds. We can use the rowing gloves. If we take it slow, it's totally doable."

"Maybe for you," I said. "But we're not all you."

"So I'll go first," Pierre said. "Establish a route. If it can't be done, it can't be done, and you can figure out a plan B. But I know Molly's done some bouldering, and from the look of her in the water yesterday Feather's pretty athletic, too. I don't know about Gemma, but my guess is she can hack it."

"Great," Ken said. "I can ride on her back."

The three of us laughed and looked at each other.

"Okay," I said. "Let's do it."

Midevening found Gemma and me sitting on opposite sides of the fire down by the water. Molly was applying liberal quantities of aloe vera to her face—and muttering darkly when it turned out her little pot of lip balm was empty. Feather was doing yoga. Pierre was cycling out batteries on his equipment and making backups of the footage he'd taken onto portable hard drives. Dylan was reading a book, weirdly. Only Ken was nearby, resplendent in a camp chair, looking up at the stars and smoking one of my cigarettes and sipping what was—by his standards—a remarkably small vodka.

Gemma looked at me. "Congrats," she said.

"Everybody gets lucky once in a while, huh?"

She rolled her eyes. "I didn't mean it like that. I meant you should be feeling pretty good about yourself."

"Not yet."

"You do take all this stuff seriously, don't you."

"Yes. Because not all of it is just made-up shit," I said. "It's remarkable how much of it ties together, too. Take Tutuveni, as a relevant example."

"And that would be?"

"A collection of a hundred sandstone boulders in a nearby corner of Utah. 'Tutuveni' means 'newspaper rock,' and on just one of them there are five thousand petroglyphs, engraved into manganese-iron deposits on the surface. The official story says they're clan symbols, carved by young Hopi men on a ceremonial rite-of-passage pilgrimage, over the course of a thousand years. Their way of proclaiming 'I'm here, in honor of my tribe and the gods, as my forebears were before me.' And there are plenty of images that do look like coyotes or cornstalks or other traditional symbols. But there's weird stuff, too. Footprints, and most look right. But a couple with four toes, and a few with six—which look a lot more like fingers. And if there's one thing a person who takes the time to chip something in rock tends to know—however 'primitive' their culture—it's how many fingers and toes we have."

"So they're some kind of paw symbol."

"Name me an animal with six toes."

"Elephants," she said. "And giant pandas."

"Seriously?"

"I kid you not."

"Huh. Okay, well, neither are indigenous to the American southwest, can we agree on that?"

"Or were they?" she intoned mysteriously. "Perhaps the authorities are covering up the existence of roving flocks of pandas in American prehistory, the better to keep us woefully ignorant of—"

"Shut up. Because what's most striking is . . . hang on."

I got out my phone and kicked up the Evernote app. It bleated at me about not being able to contact the server. Gemma moved around the fire to see what was on the screen, coming close enough that I was suddenly aware that she was not just someone to be convinced but a woman who possessed physical form.

"Good luck with that," she said when she saw what I was doing, raising her hands to indicate a dark and signal-less sky.

"I don't need data. I've got thousands of pages of research cached on the phone. And what I need is…this."

I angled the phone so she could see the picture of Newspaper Rock, then expanded a section. Near the top of the explosion of designs are two figures close together, another a couple of feet above. "Ignore the higher one for now," I said. "It's close to pieces of modern graffiti, so it's possibly not authentic."

"Goodness," she said. "You have a dispassionate scientist side, too. You're *full* of surprises."

"Do be quiet. Check out the other two."

Both drawings showed powerful figures, almost rectangular in the body, with stubby, widely spread legs and arms that were hunched up at the shoulders with big hands pointed down, in classic *I'm coming to get you!* style.

"Spooky," she said. "A bear symbol?"

"Maybe," I allowed. "Except bears don't have horns. And there aren't any bears around here. Though maybe they got eaten by the marauding packs of prehistoric pandas."

She laughed, genuinely—the first time I'd heard her do so. "But wait," she said. She moved her face closer to the screen, frowning with concentration. "One has curved horns. The other's are straight, like stylized antlers. And one's got four fingers on each hand, the other has three."

"Exactly. They clearly depict the same thing and yet every detail is stylistically different. Not like some we-always-do-it-this-way clan icon, but as if two different guys were trying to draw something as accurately as they were able."

"Huh," she said. "But relevant how?"

"Where were all these young Hopi dudes headed, on this sacred pilgrimage, for century after century? A place they called 'Ongtupqa.' Now known as...the Grand Canyon."

"You know a bunch of weird shit, I'll give you that."

"It's a curse. Do you think I enjoy having attractive women thinking I'm a nut?"

She arched an eyebrow. "Are you hitting on me, sir?"

"No," I said. "If that comes to pass then I'll make it very obvious, so you may reject me in the proper manner."

"Oh, come on," she said. "My spider-sense tells me you are no stranger to waking hungover in a tangle of motel sheets and thinking, 'So who the hell is this chick?'"

"Your spider-sense is misinformed."

"Seriously?"

"I was married."

"I know that. But faithful?"

"Yes."

"Good for you. Since?"

"I went through a phase of wanting to prove I wasn't dead yet. Sure. But soon realized that wasn't the way to do it. Not that this is any of your business."

"It speaks to character."

"I don't have any. I seem to remember that being your point yesterday morning."

"I never said that."

"It's what you meant."

She looked away. "Yes," she said. "But I have been known to change my mind. Grown-ups do. You'll learn that one day."

"Jesus. Was it the chance to be openly hostile to everyone that first drew you to journalism?"

She laughed. "No. That's just a bonus."

"Then what?"

"Trying to put the world right."

"Ah, how noble."

She made a face. "Yeah, okay, I know how that sounds. Deep background, and long story short. I was late getting ready for school one day. I was fourteen. My dad lost his temper. So I took my own sweet time and picked a pointless fight and I still don't even have any idea why."

"You were fourteen. That's all you need."

"I guess. Anyway, eventually we leave the house and it's silence the whole way. Normally Dad would do a reset and ask some question and we'd end up chatting. That morning he didn't. We got to school. As I'm opening the car door he looks at me.

"'Know why I wanted to get to school on time today?' he said. 'I mean, more than usual?'

"I shook my head, not caring even a tiny bit. 'I've got a meeting,' he said. 'Kind of a big deal. I was hoping I could get downtown in time to have a coffee first, take a minute, get myself set. That's not going to happen now.'

"And I stared at him, thinking... 'Seriously? You escalated that whole thing'—he hadn't, of course, he'd been calm throughout, or pretty calm—'so you could get a hot beverage?' I said all this. And more. I ripped into him about how it was all about him and Mom, all the time, and they didn't care about me, and on and on and on."

"What'd he say?"

"He listened, and nodded, and said, 'Okay, if that's how you feel.' He told me that he loved me and to have a good day, and I flounced into school aflame with self-righteous ire."

She stopped talking and looked away. I waited.

"Cancer," she said. "He died ten months later. The 'meeting' was to get his results. He had a pretty good idea what was coming."

"Shit."

"Yeah. But all that was okay, weirdly. As okay as it could be. I mean, we had time. I wised the hell up very quickly. I'd been focusing on the shortfalls—he got too wrapped up in his work, could be distant, impatient, blah blah blah. Luckily I had enough time to get that where it counted, he rocked. And I realized he genuinely liked me, too. We parted on very good terms."

"But . . ."

"It's not even the fact that's the day he got the news. It's just, you know, *he wanted a damned coffee*. A half hour to sit while he still hoped he might live forever. I stole that from him. Can't ever give it back."

"Nobody gets through life without being an asshole," I said. "Once in a while you're going to dig in over something and get it wrong and make a scratch on the world you'll never polish off. Those scratches will define you more than anything else."

"Bingo. Because guess what my dad did? He was a journalist. A good one. Important stuff on Big Pharma and AIDS. He did his best to put the world right. He fought for truth. He made a mark on the world."

"Aha."

"So does that answer your question? Including the unspoken one about why I always want facts, not made-up shit?"

"I guess so. How do you get on with your mom?"

She poured herself another drink. "Not at all these days. Something *else* I hadn't realized about my dad was that he was skilled at hiding the fact my mom drank. Our relationship got patchy after. She died in a car accident when I was twenty."

"Christ, seriously?"

"No," she said. "They're both alive and well and I've just been pulling your chain."

She got up and walked away.

Ken watched her go.

"She's fucking with you," he said when she was zipped up inside her tent. "And not in a good way."

I sighed. "I know."

"Hey," Feather said.

Ken and I turned our heads, not having realized she was there, sitting on the sand a little way behind us. She got up and wandered over, looking diffident.

"Could I have a look? At the Newspaper Rock thing?"

I handed her the phone. She clicked on it inexpertly. "Wow. You've got a *lot* of notes. Do you mind if . . ."

"Help yourself."

She scrolled up and down for a while, clicking things, reading, moving on.

"When I was a little girl," she said, "my grandma used to tell me, 'Everyone needs something to believe in.' And that's what you do, Nolan. You give people something to believe in. But I realized years ago that not everyone's like us. Some people are only happy when they've got something to *dis*believe."

She handed back the phone. "I feel sorry for them."

Once again I found myself awake in the middle of the night.

I stuck my head out of the bag and shuffled myself to a position where I could sit with my back against the wall of the canyon. There were no signs of life from the rest of the gang, and no sound but for water slipping by in the river, coursing from A to B as it had for untold years, with a persistence that had gouged out this bizarre environment.

After a while I realized: I was nervous. Partly it was a reprise of what I'd felt the previous night, a sense that this wasn't necessarily a good or safe place to be. There was also the prospect of the climb. I'm not super fond of heights. They can be very high. And there was also the prospect of not failing, for once. Of actually having found a thing, and having to deal with what came next.

I tried to shrug all this off, but then realized there was something I wanted to do about my nerves, something that would have been my first course of action for a long time.

I wanted to talk to Kristy.

My mother died when I was thirty. In the years that followed I realized that in addition to losing her, I'd lost a chunk of myself. My dad simply hadn't retained a lot of material about my early years—so it was now gone. If losing your mother is the burning down of your personal Library of Alexandria, no longer having the counsel of your wife is akin to losing contact with the fellow war correspondent with whom you spent years deep in-country, witnessing the bad times but also the good, together with the long, rich quiet of just-another-day. There will be serious journalistic bias in her notes, of course, and flawed recollection (which you won't be able to prove is flawed, because yours is so much worse), but afterward it can feel like losing the third dimension, or a second soul. With anybody else I'd have to explain what I was feeling, and by the end of that process would have decided it was dumb or unimportant.

Kristy would have just known.

I got out my phone, but of course there was no signal. And just as well: Texting in the dead of night would have been a very bad idea. I remembered that I'd cached a blog post of hers back in the hotel, though, and decided I might as well be a dork and read it.

It was good, direct, concise. Kristy had evidently landed in the far reaches of Alaska with a team of hard-core cryogeologists to investigate the impact of global warming on permafrost by measuring the temperature at various levels of the surface, including deep in some developing fissures. Kirsty is well-known for environmental stuff, being able to spin it in such a way that it doesn't antagonize non-believers. By the conclusion of her piece I was immeasurably better informed on the subject, though not on its writer: She keeps herself resolutely out of the picture (something I'm not great at doing, as you may have noticed). I was pleased for her, too. She'd been trying to get something like this together for a long time.

I was about to turn off the phone and try to get some sleep when I noticed smaller text at the bottom of the article. I turned the phone on its side to enlarge it, and read:

The expedition would like to gratefully acknowledge the support of our sponsor, who made this research possible.

Their sponsor's logo was familiar to me. It belonged to the Palinhem Foundation.

FROM THE FILES OF NOLAN MOORE:

NEWSPAPER ROCK, UTAH (DETAIL)

CHAPTER

12

S eriously?" Feather said, around a toothbrush.

It was a little after eight and everyone was on their feet and getting their breakfast/coffee/ablution needs met quickly. We'd decided not to strike camp, on the grounds that whatever the alleged cavern did or did not hold (assuming we could get to it), we couldn't be sure to have established the lay of the land in time to depart today. Dylan reckoned that so long as we didn't leave anything worth stealing at the site it'd be safe, and that the chances of anybody coming down this side canyon today were around zero anyway. While valuables, camera equipment, bottles of water, and sandwiches were being loaded onto the boat, I'd found Feather sitting on a rock, brushing her teeth. When she was done I showed her the page on my phone.

"Wow," she said. "What a *super*-cool coincidence."

"You didn't know?"

"No idea. The Foundation's kind of big. Or broad. There's not many staff, but lots of little departments in different cities. This is the more science-y end of things. I've never even met someone who's involved." Suddenly her face fell. "Oh, Nolan, I'm so sorry."

"About what?"

"Being dumb. I didn't stop to think—this might feel weird to you. Or hurtful. And here I am just being excited about it."

"It's fine. Just a little surprising to come upon in the middle of the night, that's all."

"I'll bet! But it's a totally different kind of expedition anyway. And kind of boring, don't you think?"

"Climate change is boring?"

She laughed. "Of course it is. Everybody knows it's supposed to be a thing, and they either believe in it or they don't. Whatever they find in Alaska isn't going to change that. But what we might find to-day...that would prove to the establishment—and people like our cynical friend Gemma over there—that the entire human narrative is skewed. And *you* will have done that, Nolan. You, and nobody else."

She smiled brightly and hurried off to go help put stuff on the boat. I watched her go, feeling curiously as if I'd had a chance to talk to Kristy after all.

An hour later we had the raft at the foot of the canyon wall. Over half that time had been spent trying to get it lashed securely in position. Through some fluid mechanics complexity I wouldn't pretend to comprehend, the side of the river up against the wall was seriously bumpy in parts and weirdly calm in others. Dylan, Pierre, and I eventually got front and back ends of the craft tethered to outcrops in a way that Dylan thought would hold.

"Give me your shirt," Pierre said.

"Excuse me?"

He took off his T and held out his hand for my shirt. As always on shoots, I was wearing the billowy creamy-white number. Don't blame me—Ken says it looks the part.

"We're both wearing jeans," Pierre said. "And have brown hair. I put on your shirt, Molly points the camera, and we've got footage that'll make it look like you were the—"

"Christ, Pierre," I said. "I don't need to be the first up there. Or to look like I was."

"You found it," he said, hand still out. "And you're the man."

"Do it," Ken said.

I took off my shirt and swapped with him, reflecting that if Pierre kept being this unannoying I might have to confront the possibility that I found him annoying merely because he was young and affable and unnecessarily handsome. "Thanks."

He conferred with Molly over the camera, then squared up to the wall of the canyon. Timing it for when the rocking of the water brought the boat right up against the wall, he stepped out confidently—landing so his hands and feet were immediately secure, already scanning the climb ahead with the professional gaze of some-one who knew what he was doing.

"Be careful," I said.

"Yes, Dad," he said.

And so we watched. It took a while. It soon became clear that Pierre's assessment of the canyon wall was correct, however, and it didn't rep-resent a technically challenging climb. He moved quickly and surely.

Once in a while he paused and appeared to make choices, some-times avoiding what looked like the straightest route, I presume because there was a longer alternative that would make for a more feasible ascent for the rest of us.

Molly filmed enough of it that the shirt-clad figure slowly getting closer and closer to the opening could be cut into the show to look like me. Especially as Pierre got higher, there was no way of telling the difference. Meanwhile, the real me started to feel queasy and had to stop watching.

"Yeah," Ken said, accepting a cigarette. "I'm simply not seeing this as credible, mate. You, maybe. You jog and stuff. But me? I mean, fuck's sake."

"But so what was the plan?" Gemma asked. "You knew this place was supposed to be halfway up the canyon wall."

"Be honest with you, love," Ken said, "and I don't think I'll break Nolan's heart by saying this: I did not for a moment think we were going to find this thing."

"Mind blown," I muttered.

"And according to the Kincaid article it's supposed to be a lot higher than this. I know Nolan said he thought some of the details might have been changed, but Nolan does talk an awful lot of bollocks. So my thinking was, if we found something, then we'd cliff-hang the show as a 'To Be Continued,' and come back with some proper climbers with ropes and all that jazz."

"So this is great news," Gemma said with a sly smile. "It means you get to go up there yourselves. You must be delighted."

"Yeah," Ken and I said, unconvincingly, in unison.

"Piece of cake," Pierre said as he jumped back onto the boat. He was sweating but not much out of breath. "And the last section is the eas-iest, which is great, because people will be tired by then. I could see a way straight up. So I didn't bother. This really is not hard."

"Are you sure?"

"It's more than hiking but most of it's barely climbing. Which makes sense, right? Kincaid doesn't mention it being tough. Despite claiming the cavern was three or four times higher than this. Kind of a giveaway in retrospect, huh?"

Ken and I glanced at each other. "Seriously," Pierre said. "Nolan, my mom could do it."

"Didn't you tell me your mom once free-climbed El Capitan?"

"Years ago. And she barely got halfway."

"Lazy bitch," Ken said.

"It's actually kind of hard, dude."

"He was joking, Pierre."

"Oh. Well, not my mom, then. *Your* mom could do it."

"I doubt that," I said. "Even before she died."

"Christ, sorry. I'm going to stop talking now."

"So how would we tackle it?" Ken asked dubiously, peering up at the wall.

"We all go together," Pierre said, taking off my shirt and handing it back to me. "Couple yards apart. That way the person behind me can see what I'm doing, which holds I'm choosing. There's a few bits where there's a hard way and an easy way. I'd make sure we all went the easy way."

Ken thought about it. "Fucking hell," he said, turning to the assembled. "Okay, look. Mountain Goat here says he thinks it's a go. Obviously I'm not going to tell anybody they have to do this, or even ask—and that includes you, Nolan—but..."

"I'm not missing it," Feather said immediately.

"Let's do it," Molly said, with the gameness only a sporty Cali girl with two older brothers can muster.

Gemma didn't look much more enthusiastic than I felt, but she shrugged. "Sure. YOLO, right?"

"I'll have a crack at it," Ken said. "But I'll go last. That way I'll only be killing myself if I plummet like a sack of bricks."

So then all eyes were on me.

"Christ," I said.

CHAPTER

13

Pierre went back onto the wall and climbed up far enough to give room for Feather to follow. Then Molly, then Gemma. Then me. I was half expecting to hear Ken shout, "So long, suckers," and see him merrily untying the boat and instructing Dylan to take him back to all the vodka. Within a minute of scooting up out of the way, however, I looked down to see his face a couple of feet below, meaty hands gripping the rock.

"I hate you," he said.

We all wore backpacks, contents disproportionately spread in terms of weight and importance. Pierre had the camera and batteries, Molly the sound gear, and so on. I was allotted the sandwiches. Make of that what you wish.

On Pierre's advice, we took a moment to get settled.

Then we started up the wall.

The lowest portion was barely more than a tough hike, with less margin for error on where you put your feet. After about fifteen minutes this gave way to something more like actual climbing. The surface of the wall was uneven, however, with plenty of extrusions and crevices. Pierre took it slowly, stopping every five minutes to give people a chance to shake their arms and clench and unclench gloved hands.

I'd heard people describe climbing as a kind of physical chess, which doesn't help, as I suck at chess. But yes, for a while, I kind of understood the appeal of choosing which outcrop to put this foot on, and then that, shifting your weight from hand to hand. As we moved higher and higher I even had a chance to revisit the feeling I'd had when we first got on the river—a surprised awareness that I was doing something intrepid and cool that, left to my own devices, wouldn't have made it onto any realistic bucket list.

From time to time I took a few moments to turn from the wall and look out across the canyon, down toward a river that was an increasingly significant distance below, sparkling in the sun. Ken was gamely keeping pace. He let loose with an occasional burst of profanity, but as time went on it became clear that this was part of his process rather than an indication that he felt in imminent danger.

I was glad to have him there, and glad we were effectively climbing together. It helped, for some reason, and not just because he was the most self-evidently unsuited to the undertaking. This probably meant, I realized with something of a shock, that he had become, like, a friend.

That hadn't really occurred to me. I wondered if I should mention it at some point, found it easy to imagine the weapons-grade irony with which the observation would be met—I would do exactly the same, of course—and decided not.

When Gemma fell, I had half a second's warning.

We were more than two-thirds of the way up and my arms and calves were feeling it, but I'd settled into a rhythm and the whole escapade had stopped feeling unfeasible. To be honest, it looked a lot worse from the river than it was when you were in the midst. I still kept checking below once in a while (Ken doggedly replicating my every step and handhold) but had stopped looking around at the view—we were a little too high now to do that with equanimity. Instead, part of my mind had moved toward working out what I'd say to camera when we eventually made it up there. A lot depended on what we found, of course, but I wanted to be at least slightly prepared. I was deep in this train of thought when there was a short, squawking scream.

Then the sound of scrabbling.

Before I'd had time to consciously process these noises, Gemma was sliding back toward me. Fast.

Even if I'd known the recommended response to this kind of event there wouldn't have been time to do anything except what I did, bracing my feet and tightening my grip with both hands.

Gemma had only a couple of feet to build up speed, and was grabbing at rocks on her way down. She still hit me like a freight train. The impact knocked all the air out of my lungs and I felt my lower right back muscle snap straight into spasm.

But there was enough room between me and the wall for her to slide into, and somehow my hands held.

She quickly got handholds on the wall, too, and her weight came off me within seconds.

Then we both just held tight.

I was very aware of the heat of her skin through her shirt, and the perspiration on the back of her neck where she'd tied her hair up. That, and my heart beating like a jackhammer.

"*Shit!*" Molly shouted. "Are you guys okay?"

"Let's not do it again," I said, my voice a little unsteady. "But yeah, we're good. I'm good, anyway. You okay?"

"I'm fine," Gemma said, turning her forearm to look at a long, deep scrape there. Blood was already beginning to bead along it. Her voice was very shaky. "Fucking *fuck*, though."

"Nicely put," I said. "I take back everything I said about the quality of your prose."

I held on while she gingerly climbed back up.

Pierre watched, hanging casually onto the wall above. "Ready?"

We climbed.

About ten minutes later Pierre turned and looked down at the rest of us again.

"Nolan?"

"What?"

"See these little ledges, to my right?"

"What about them?"

"I'm going across there. Moll, Feather, and Gemma—you come this way, too. Nolan, you head straight up."

"Why?"

"I can film you getting to the cavern from here."

"Look, Pierre—"

"Do what he fucking says," Ken said, tersely. "My arms are falling off. And if that thing up there is just a bloody recess, the drinks are on you forever. I mean it."

I waited while people climbed up the remaining ten feet and moved sideways onto the series of small ledges. They were only about eighteen inches wide and sloped markedly, and everybody but Pierre kept their hands firmly gripped to the wall. I saw Gemma rest her head against it, eyes closed, and realized she was pretty much done with this crap.

I then waited until Pierre had carefully extricated the camera from his backpack and gotten it into position in his left hand, holding on to the wall with the right.

"Rolling," he said.

I climbed the last thirty feet alone. It wasn't hard, especially now that the end was in sight. Pierre had been correct about this, too—concavity in this section of the wall made the final chunk a lot easier than the middle portion.

Foot by foot I went up, until the opening was just above me. I am familiar enough with the playful ways of the gods, however, that I made doubly sure every hand- and foothold was secure as I covered the remaining distance.

Then I had a hand on the lip of the opening. I carefully pulled myself up, and a minute later, I was inside.

80

FROM THE FILES OF NOLAN MOORE:

THE CANYON

CHAPTER

14

The opening was an irregular gash in the wall about four feet wide and five tall, with a pile of rock inside. It was immediately clear that what lay past them was more than a mere recess. Daylight illuminated about twenty feet of cave depth—with the suggestion of more beyond—and the same width. I stayed on hands and knees, turned, and stuck my head out.

After withstanding an intense moment of vertigo at the sight of the drop, I called down, "Get up here."

"Is it a cavern?"

"Yes. Yes, it is."

"How deep?"

"Can't see yet. But there's plenty of room."

I moved back and waited. They arrived, one by one: Ken first, then Gemma, Molly, Feather, and finally Pierre. I stood back with Ken while the others came up, looking at the walls beyond the opening. They were rough, variable in color—rock of the type we'd been climbing. At the back was a further gap, narrower, but wide enough for two to walk abreast.

"This it?"

"I don't know yet."

"What are those piles of rocks doing there?"

"Don't know that, either."

"Excellent. Glad you're on top of everything. When Pierre's got his breath, we need some film. And check this out." He ran his hand along a section of the side wall. "Look kind of like chisel marks, don't they?"

"A little."

"Which Kincaid mentioned, yes?"

"He did."

"Fuck me, Nolan. This could actually be the thing."

"Let's not get ahead of ourselves."

Pierre eventually scrabbled up into the space, and had his camera in position quickly. Molly put the boom mike together and the others moved out of the shot, squeezing up against the walls.

"It's been quite a climb," I said to camera, when Molly was ready. "And it wouldn't have happened without the team here. Pierre—pan around."

Pierre looked confused at my breaking the fourth wall, but I gestured at him to do it.

"Molly, Feather, Gemma. And this guy, Ken. Actually I have no idea who he is, but he's here. And the only reason we're here at all is our cameraman Pierre, who spotted the opening, said we could do it, and showed us how. So. Thank you, Pierre."

I noticed Gemma watching this with an odd expression, but carried on. I walked back toward the opening, indicating that Pierre should show how far up we were.

"We're three hundred feet up the wall. Pretty high, but nowhere near the altitude Kincaid mentioned in the *Phoenix* piece. That could indicate we're dead wrong, and this is a different feature that nobody happens to have noticed. But I've talked before about the idea that Kincaid changed some of the details. He couldn't help but reveal the cavern's existence. It's kind of a big deal. Though maybe he wanted to control the information and keep the place safe from prying eyes. I don't know. But it's intriguing. It's all... very intriguing."

I dusted off my hands. "And so I guess now we take a look at what we've found."

*　　*　　*

Pierre stopped filming while we got headlamps out of backpacks and Ken and I smoked. Then we organized ourselves into a line with Molly right behind me with the boom mike, Feather and Gemma armed with flashlights to direct at anything that drew my attention, and Pierre free to move around me.

I walked into the cavern.

Within a few feet it already felt cooler, but also stuffy. The ceiling was about three feet above my head. There was a dry, dusty odor, the smell of time and old rock. Now that we had light on the space, I could see it was closer to thirty feet wide, and perhaps the same deep. The walls on both sides were a little concave, top to bottom and front to back. The rocky floor was far from even. It was hard to believe the space was wholly a result of natural forces, but I didn't know enough about geology to be sure.

"We've already noticed these," I said, indicating the portion that Ken had pointed out earlier. "What *could* be chisel marks— suggesting a natural feature was enlarged and shaped by human hand. I'd want a field archeologist to pronounce before I went there. The shape of the walls…it looks like people widened it. But natural forces can produce things that look man-made— underwater features like the so-called Bimini Road in the Bahamas, and the Yonaguni Monument off Japan. So all I'm saying is…that's the way it looks."

I walked in a slow circle, illuminating the walls with my head-lamp. "I don't see anything else of note. There's no symbols or carvings. If this place is indeed what we hope, then this area seems to be a kind of antechamber. Undecorated, utilitarian."

I ended with the light on an opening at the end. "The aperture at the back of the cave is about six feet wide. Looks pretty rough from out here, like a natural fissure, tapering sharply toward the top. Let's go have a closer look."

I stepped into the passage.

I was aware of . . . a reluctance. Nothing major. Not a big *don't for God's sake go in there* siren. Merely a note of caution, spiraling up from the deep back brain, a little like the feeling I'd had while sitting alone early the previous morning. I was, after all, going where—so far as I knew—no man or woman had boldly gone in a damned long time. And we were a very significant distance underground. There was a heck of a lot of rock over my head, and no way of telling how stable this portion was, or where it led.

And it was dark. Doesn't matter how old you get or how much creeping around you've done in cemeteries or abandoned insane asylums and other places of self-evident spookiness in pursuit of halfway-watchable online viewing; the dark is the dark is the dark.

"Kincaid mentioned a passage," I said. "And he said it was around twelve feet wide. This is narrower. The walls are uneven. There's a strong taper toward the top. The floor is bumpy and slopes a little. This could just be a natural fissure. We're not going to know until we come to the next detail in the account. Kincaid said that fifty-seven feet along a passage from the entrance, he and the other explorers came upon a doorway. That was the gateway to all the strange stuff. So let's go look."

"Or not," Molly said.

"What?"

"Nolan, I don't like this."

Pierre lowered the camera. His face said he was thinking the same as me—that the last person you'd expect to get the jitters was Molly.

"Moll," I said, "it's just a crevice at this stage. I don't even know if it's an actual passage."

"I don't like it," she said stubbornly.

"Okay," I said. "And I respect that. But we're going to head down there anyway, right?"

"I don't want to."

"But . . ." I didn't know what to say.

She stood looking at me, lips pursed. It's funny how, as you get used to being with people, you stop seeing them. You assign them a role and see that instead. Molly had become Moll, to me—fearless scourge of hotel clerks and rental companies, solid and dependable, the person who made everything happen, who fixed the world when things went awry. The mom of the team. Because of this I think part of me had even assigned her a greater age than mine. Moms are older than you. It's the law.

Now I looked at her properly—hair stuck with perspiration to a forehead still angry from yesterday's sun—and remembered that she was fifteen years my junior. And that she was at least nervous, maybe scared, and really didn't want to do this.

"Sure," I said. "That's fine. Of course."

"I could carry the microphone thing instead, if you wanted," Feather said diffidently.

"That'd be great," I said. "And you know what? This is actually great. Duh. We should have thought of it before. Moll—can you stay here, film us heading up the passage? A little bit of phone-quality coverage would be great to use as a teaser on the blog."

"Sure," she said quietly, handing the boom to Feather. "I'm sorry, Nolan. Really. I know I'm being dumb about this."

"Yeah...or else you're the only one of us who doesn't get eaten by the huge monster. Time will tell, right?"

She laughed, and it was okay.

Feather held up the mike. Molly headed back toward the opening, phone out, ready to film us heading into the gloom, and Pierre got the camera in position again.

"So let's do it," I said.

We walked down the passage, Gemma shining her flashlight low to make it easier to traverse the increasingly uneven "floor," Ken now holding Feather's light to point the way. He counted his steps, too, putting one foot directly in front of the other to yield a rough indication of the distance in feet. The passage soon started to narrow, and by forty feet in, it had reduced to the point where I could almost touch both sides at once.

The walls began to taper in more markedly above us, too, disappearing into blackness. I was careful to inspect both walls as we passed. They were very ragged, and did not look like they had been worked or refined at any point. There were no openings on either side.

At about 140 feet into the rock, the passage simply stopped, dead-ending in a slanting wall. This did not look like a designed feature, either. It merely looked like the end of the road.

"We must have missed it," Feather said hopefully.

We trouped all the way back to the antechamber, then turned around and headed in again, more slowly, this time using all available lights to focus on the walls.

There was no doorway.

The passage led nowhere.

CHAPTER

15

Y ou found the cavern, Nolan. Or *a* cavern. That's something."
Ken and I were sitting near the opening. The vista outside was still beautiful, but I wasn't seeing it.

"Yeah," I said. "'Something' is precisely what it is. 'Some thing.'
And not a very interesting thing, at that."

"Don't be a twat, Nolan. It proves—"

"It proves *shit*, Ken. We found a natural feature. It wasn't where
Kincaid said it would be, and it's nothing like he said it was. For all
we know this thing's already logged and the only reason it's not on all
the maps is that it's a tedious fucking cave that isn't worth the effort
of the climb."

"It is what it is. Or what we spin it as."

"Which is *what*? Can we even get a show out of this?"

"Dunno. Worst case, we can throw it into a 'the ones that got away'
bucket show midseason. Or stitch it into a roundup of things you've
proved *don't* exist. You know I think that would help with the haters.
'The Anomaly Files—Your Dispassionate Seekers After Truth.'"

"Yeah—and *you* know I think it's a crap idea. It's hard enough getting people to believe in this stuff without handing them proof of
absence on a plate."

"Nolan's right," Feather said. We turned to see her standing a little
way behind us.

Ken shrugged. "It's your money, love."

"Not really," she said. "I don't get to make the big calls. But I can tell you what I think. I was a psych major and one thing I learned is you're never going to change some people's minds. Some are *born* cynical and suspicious. They don't need our help to carry on being deaf and dumb. Nuts to the disbelievers, is what I say. The point of a charity like Palinhem is to make a difference."

"Fighting talk," Ken said. "I like it. But so what now?"

"You don't show weakness," she said resolutely, "and you never give up."

"Right on, sister," Ken said, and I nodded, but all I'd heard was the word "charity."

Half an hour later I was by myself having a cigarette before it was time for us all to climb back down the wall. By then I was in less of a snit. It's not like I'd disproved the existence of aliens or shown that the Knights Templar were only ever a Little League team. Mainly I was just tired and looking forward to a night in a hotel and several beers and sincerely hoping we were leaving in time to make these things possible. I was nearly done with the smoke when Molly crouched beside me.

"We're good," I said. "Seriously. You don't like tunnels. It's no big deal."

"It is to me. I am not a girl who bails. And to make up for it, I may have something for you."

"What?"

"Don't you like surprises?"

"Depends what they are."

"Just come."

She led me toward the back of the cavern. Ken watched us as we passed. "What are you up to?"

"Dunno," I said.

"Well, don't be long. There is a shower, much alcohol, and a cheeseburger the size of my head waiting for me back at the hotel.

All of these things are critical to my future well-being, and you fuck with the prospect at your peril."

"Yes, boss."

Molly led me right to the back, and spoke in a low tone. "After I did my bugging out thing—" she started.

"Which I've just told you is totall—"

"Shh, Nolan."

"Do you get to tell me to *shh* like that?"

"Yes."

"Oh. Okay."

"After that, I did what you asked. Faded back, took a bunch of pictures. Which I'll sling in the production Dropbox when we return to the wonderful world of Wi-Fi. Then I shot some video of you all heading off into the fissure. I'm no Pierre, but it's HD and usable."

"Great. So..."

"Then you all came back, turned around, and tried again. I was going to stop filming but, you know, always worth having take two, and all that. So I kept going, and came closer to the passage the second time. I even went a little way down. And...well, I'm just going to show it to you."

I waited as she navigated on her phone and pressed the button. Murky footage of us all heading into the inner crevice for the second time. "I'd already covered the basics, so I waved the camera around a little more," she said. "And I was looking through it a couple minutes ago, and...there."

"What?"

"I'll play it again." She held the phone up closer.

"What am I looking for?"

"You'll see Ken pointing the light around all over this place, trying to get you a look at each bit of the walls on either side. In typically chaotic fashion. But what I'm talking about...Look carefully at the end part."

It was hard to make out what I was seeing. The backs of the line of people who'd been behind me. Unpredictable slashes of light and dark as Ken and Gemma waved flashlights around, and we got farther and farther from the camera. But then . . .

"What was that?"

She rewound, pressed PLAY again, then PAUSE. "*That* is what I'm talking about."

The freeze frame caught us at the far end of the crevice, a collection of shoulders and backs of heads, quite some distance from the camera. The phone wasn't dealing well with the low light conditions, and the image was blocky. Toward the top, however, Ken's light had wandered well above head height—and the area captured in the beam was sharper.

And for just a moment, it caught something. Three little outcrops, each about the size of a brick, the last directly above the first, the middle one offset, in a left-right-left pattern. We hadn't been looking up, and so hadn't noticed them.

"Don't those look kind of regular? As if someone at least finished them off a little?"

"Could be," I said dubiously. "Though to be honest, Moll . . . could just be a foreshortening effect. They're a long way from the camera. This . . . is all you've got?"

"Yes," she said. "And probably it's nothing, I know. But if someone way back did smarten up a few little nodules in the rock—that's *something*, at least, isn't it?"

"I guess."

"Come on. This would take it to another level, right? It would prove this cave was known to Native Americans at some point, and they decorated it. Archeologists will want to come look, at least. Worst case, they'll name the damned thing after you, and that's actually kind of cool."

"Okay, okay," I said. "I'll go take a look."

"No," she said. "*We* will."

We got out flashlights and walked to the back of the antechamber.

"You really don't have to do this."

"Yes, I do," she said. "I had some issues back in the day. Anxiety. Panic attacks. Bulimia for a while."

"Oh," I said. "That must have been...well, pretty shitty, I would imagine."

"It was. But it was a while ago and I did a lot of work on it and I'm fully functioning now."

"Huh. You think you know someone, eh? Next thing you'll be telling me you're a Republican."

"I am."

"What?"

"But the point of my oversharing moment is that this 'I'm not going down the passage' crap cannot stand. So let's get to it. Lead on."

"Seriously, you vote Republican?"

"My dad's a GOP congressman."

"Okay then."

We switched on the lights and walked in. With all the others still back in the main cave area, getting ready to climb back down to the river, the crevice seemed different. Extremely still and immensely quiet. Very, very ancient—of course, as it was hundreds of thousands of years old, if not more—and fundamentally inhuman. Molly's breathing was very regular in the semidarkness, as though she was doing something in particular with it.

"Yoga?"

"Yes," she said.

"Cool. Is it helping?"

"Actually, it's making me light-headed. I'm going to stop it now."

I kept a close eye on the walls as we walked farther into the fissure, hoping I'd spot something that had been missed earlier. But there was nothing. Just yard after yard of irregular, natural, uninteresting rock.

We trained our flashlights up toward the ceiling now and then, such as it was; a sharply tapering area, plagued with shadows. There was nothing to see there, either.

Then we were at the end. "Ha," Molly said, voice a little shaky. "In your *face*, dark and claustrophobic tunnel. I win."

"It doesn't look the way it did on the phone," I said, pointing my light straight up at the ceiling.

"There's a lip," she said, peering up. "About ten, twelve feet up. Take a couple steps back."

We did, and I saw she was right. From this angle the beams showed a small recess beyond. "And there are your little outcrops," I said. "One, two, three."

"What do you think?"

"I don't know. I mean, sure, they look even in distribution. Possibly. But...Okay, hold the light."

I put a headlamp on and looked around before selecting a couple of especially ragged sections of side wall. I set my right foot on one, and used the other to pull myself up.

From this elevated position I was able to angle myself so that my back was against the end wall, and then start to inch my way up, shifting feet and hands as required.

"Wow," she said. "It's Spider-Man!"

"Do fuck off, Moll."

It took five minutes of puffing and exertion to grab and yank myself up the twelve or fifteen feet until I could get a hand over the lip. I was stymied for a couple of minutes when it appeared that I was stuck, unable to get the rest of my body up, but I finally found a way to haul myself over.

"It's about six feet deep," I told Molly below. "Kind of narrow, less than four feet."

"What about the outcrops? Do they look like they've been chiseled into shape?"

There was enough illumination from my headlamp to show straightaway that both the frozen image on the camera and our view from below had been misleading.

"They're not outcrops," I said. "They're recesses."

"Like where a stone has fallen out of softer rock?"

I moved up closer. "No," I said. "Not unless the stones were all the same size. And...rectangular."

I slowly tilted my head back, redirecting the beam of the headlamp and revealing that this deeper part of the recess didn't have a ceiling, but was open above my head.

"And there's more. Perfectly regular. Left, right, left, right. Stretching up as far as I can see. Holy crap, Moll."

"What?"

I looked down at her. "This is a ladder."

PART TWO

The highest goal that man can achieve is amazement.

—Johann Wolfgang von Goethe

And the Lord regretted that
he had made man on the earth,
and it grieved him to his heart.

—Genesis 6:6

FROM THE FILES OF NOLAN MOORE:

ENGRAVING OF JOHN WESLEY POWELL'S
1869 EXPEDITION (1875)

CHAPTER

16

K en was trying to sound nonchalant but not carrying it off. "How far up did you go?"

"About twenty feet," I said. "The steps kept going as far as I could see."

"So what's your thinking?"

"Maybe Kincaid wasn't dicking around with the height thing after all, or could be this opening isn't the one he was talking about. It's a lower one, a second way to access a structure way up above. Maybe even the cavern he described."

"So we've got to go look, right?"

"You mentioned something about needing a burger."

"Don't be a twat, Nolan. I'll have two tomorrow."

"It's just a few steps at this stage, though, right?" This was Gemma.

Feather stared at her. "Is that not enough, sweetie?"

"Food will become an issue," Molly said. "If we end up staying in the canyon for another night."

"Half rations," Ken said breezily. "Only eat half our lunch, save the rest for tonight."

"And tomorrow morning?"

"We sup on clean air and sunshine and call ourselves renewed in the eyes of a beneficent God."

"I get it," I said. "You've got a secret stash of food, haven't you. Hand it over."

"More like a thick winter coat to draw upon," he said. "Plus I'll have extra fries tomorrow. And onion rings. It all evens out."

"You play the long game, my friend. I admire that."

"It's got me to where I am today."

"And yet you still do it?"

"Or," Dylan interrupted, from below in the boat: Molly had him on the short-range walkie-talkie, though the sound kept breaking up. "You check this thing out. I'll take the dinghy downriver. There's a spot a few miles down where there's usually a little phone signal. I'll call from there, get a mate to bring another cooler of food. Or worst case I fetch it myself, which just means you'll have to hang around the cave until late afternoon."

"Sounds good," Ken said. "But do not tell anybody. Not a word. Got that? This is ours."

We recorded a brief to-camera with me explaining what we'd found, and then gathered together.

"Okay," Ken said. "Nolan, you're going up first, so Pierre can shoot you heading into the unknown. Also because you're not fit enough to go at a stupid pace. The rest of you can go in whatever order you like, but I'm at the end again. So I can take a break every now and then without someone sticking their head up my arse."

"But wait," Molly said. "Can you even get up to where the steps start, without someone . . . well, without assistance?"

Ken opened his mouth, looked at the obstacle, and shut it again. "I'll go last," Molly offered. "I promise I won't stick my head in your ass even once."

And so, individually, we scrambled up to the higher level and then, one by one, we started up the shaft.

I had a headlamp and once in a while looked up to check what was ahead. Gemma—right behind me—had a lanyard light that was left on the whole time, as everyone agreed that while we wanted to conserve batteries, it might get a little weird and claustrophobic climbing in the dark.

Once you were in the shaft, full-body, it was impossible to deny it was man-made. It was about three and a half feet square. Even if it only went up fifty feet, that was many hundreds of cubic feet of rock chiseled out and carried through the fissure and, presumably, thrown into the river below.

To me that was an inconceivable amount of effort unless something important was involved, though people in ancient times measured time and effort differently. Once they'd caught or picked dinner and made sure the youngsters weren't being eaten by marauding pandas, there wasn't a lot to do except sit around the fire passing deep ancestral wisdom back and forth. And, as I had tellingly observed in *The Anomaly Files'* episode about Stonehenge (conducted via stock footage and diagrams and a terrible 3-D model some cocaine-addled friend of Ken's had concocted), ideas of mobility were different, too. These days if you grow up in town A and are halfway motivated, the first task of postadolescence is getting the hell out to city B, or country C, even if you eventually wind up back near town A a couple of decades later because you've realized there is no Magical Other Place and you're going to remain the same asshole wherever you go—so you might as well be somewhere it's not a pain for the kids to see their grandparents once in a while.

But back in BC? Families stayed in the same place for thousands of years, and so it doesn't seem such a big deal to spend thirty of those years shuffling huge rocks around—because you do it on the unspoken assumption that every conceivable descendant will benefit from your efforts.

Likewise, maybe, this shaft.

After what felt like a pretty long time I paused and turned my head down toward Pierre in the middle of the pack.

"How far have we come?" I was panting pretty hard.

"There's about two feet between each foot- or handhold," he said, not remotely out of breath. "And I've done a hundred and fifteen. So call it two hundred and thirty feet."

"Okay," I said. "Everybody down there okay?" There were murmurings and grunts of assent. "You okay, Ken?"

"Fuck off."

I started up the ladder once more.

When we checked later, we discovered it had taken forty minutes to climb. We had a couple more short breaks, when thighs and arms tightened or started twitching with fatigue, but otherwise we went up and up and up. I fell into a kind of trance, maintaining the repetitive process of reaching up, moving hands and feet, pushing up. I didn't bother to speculate about what—if anything—we were going to find. The thing that has kept me from going crazy at certain periods in my life is the ability to let the future be. This has, naturally, meant there have also been times when life has dealt me a stunning blow to the jaw that I should have seen coming, laying me flat on my back while the gods of foresight laugh and point.

But for the rest of the climb this faded away. Molly had me wrong in thinking I'd be pleased at the idea of this cave being named after me. Partly because if it was what we'd been looking for, Kincaid had prior claim. Mainly because I didn't care. It's never the world at large you want to prove yourself to. It's someone in particular. Doesn't matter how old you get, you're still hoping for Mom or Dad to kiss you on the head.

And yes, that person should ideally be yourself, just as the answers to all our questions and the objects of our quests should most likely be found within our own souls. But they're not. We need more. Someone or something bigger than us. A magical other.

And *that's* why we reach for the gods.

Or for someone to love.

Eventually I looked up to check the next section of shaft and saw there was only another few feet before the handholds stopped, giving way to blackness.

"Okay, people," I said. "I think we're here."

I pulled myself up the last few steps.

CHAPTER

17

It was immediately clear that another passage lay at the top of the shaft. A real one, this time. My headlamp revealed ten feet of floor on either side. It was rocky and covered in dust—some of it dark, almost like soot—but basically level and flat.

Before me, the passage disappeared into darkness. Turning, I saw it did the same back toward the wall of the canyon, running in the same direction as the fissure hundreds of feet below.

I pulled myself out of the shaft. The walls here were also even. Not perfect, but without question worked and man-made. The passage was ten or twelve feet wide and about the same high—much closer to the dimensions Kincaid had claimed in the article.

"Do we come up?"

"Yeah," I said. "You should do that."

I walked a little farther down the passage as the rest of the team completed the ascent. The width remained constant. There were chisel marks on the walls. It was fairly cold, but clammy. The air felt dead. Most of it would have been here for a very long time.

Gemma was out next. "Didn't get a chance earlier," she said. "Just wanted to say, you know, thanks."

"For what?"

"Saving my life, you dick."

"It was an accident. I was busy saving mine. You received collateral salvation."

She shook her head. "You really do have a problem."

"And what's that?"

"No idea. I'm not a therapist. I don't know if it's fallout from your marriage imploding or what, but you seem determined to prove you're an asshole."

"I can't keep up with you. Last night you thought maybe I wasn't, now we're back to it being a done deal."

"I'm serious. Like when we first got up in the cave down there. If anybody else had found it they'd have been all 'I'm the man.' Legitimately, for once. But you get busy trying to pass the accolade on to Pierre." She lowered her voice. "Who's a nice guy and plenty hot but probably can't find his way out of his own apartment without using Google Maps."

I shrugged. "I got us somewhere. Yes. It may still be there's nothing here."

"True," she said. "Well, perhaps you're right. Maybe you are just an asshole after all."

"Fuck me," Ken panted as he climbed laboriously out of the shaft. "So this would be an actual passage, then."

"Yep."

"So what's the plan? I mean, after I've stopped feeling like my heart is going to explode."

"We go that way," I said, pointing along the passage that led toward the wall of the canyon.

"And there's enough air and stuff here, right?"

"I assume so. Presumably it's open to the canyon at that end, and we just didn't spot it because it's too high, or hard to see amid the sediment staining. So I think we should walk that way, stake out the territory. Plus it'll show if there's any openings along the way."

"Not *if*," Feather said. The others were standing in a group now, flicker-lit by the light around Gemma's neck. "*Where*. This *has* to be Kincaid's cavern, doesn't it?"

"You've gotta hope," I said. "But wait and see. And let's only have a couple of lamps burning. We're going to need artificial light all the time. It's a long way back for more batteries, and I've seen all those movies."

"Good thinking," Gemma muttered as everyone but me and Ken turned off their lights. "Because also it's totally not spooky or anything doing it this way."

"Pierre," Ken said. "Start filming."

Pierre tucked in behind me as I started to walk.

"After a long climb," I said, "we're here. Wherever 'here' is. It's certainly man-made. The contrasts between this passage and the fissure below are obvious. This is much wider, there's a more even floor, far greater consistency in the walls and ceiling. Someone put a lot of effort into this. Why? I hope we're about to find out."

We walked farther, seeing more of the same. I turned my head to the right so the light was stronger on the wall. "I'm still not seeing any markings, or anything else of interest, beyond some evidence of chiseling," I said.

Then I stopped. "Well, except...that."

We all looked in silence at the doorway in the wall.

The opening was about four feet wide, sides perfectly straight, curving to a graceful arch at least ten feet from the floor.

"There's one on the other side, too," Molly said.

All heads—and Pierre's camera—slowly swiveled to see. Yes, a matching opening on the opposite wall.

"Nolan," Ken said, "does this tally with Kincaid's report?"

"Yeah. Well, in that he said that fifty-seven feet from the outside wall there were openings on either side. With curved passages leading from both." I moved the light from side to side and peered into the doorways. "Which does appear to be the case."

"You want to check if these are about that distance from the entrance?"

"Let's do that."

And so we walked farther along the passage, marking out the distance with our feet. "Shouldn't we be able to see light from the opening to the outside by now?" Gemma asked after a minute.

"Yes," I said. "Well, maybe. Soon."

But after another twenty feet the light from my headlamp showed why we weren't seeing anything. The passage didn't end in an opening. It ended in a wall.

"That makes no sense," Molly said, with a trace of anxiety. "This passage is straight, isn't it? We must be at the canyon wall by now."

I went right up to barrier and bent down to get a closer look, and finally put two and two together. "It's been sealed," I said. I ran my finger along a joint. "Chunks of rock, joined with some kind of rough mortar."

I turned to Ken. "*That's* what the rocks were inside the opening below. Dylan said there'd been a tremor in this area last year, right? And it dislodged rocks into the river?"

"Yes," Gemma said. "Hence those rapids yesterday being more hectic than they used to be. He did say that."

"And it was enough to crack the bricking-up below, too. That's why nobody has spotted the opening in the last hundred years: *It wasn't there.* Last year the fill-in fell apart, leaving what we found. Up here it survived. Did anybody keep counting as we walked?"

"Yeah," Ken said. "We're now about twenty yards from those doorways, so call it sixty feet. Or fifty-seven, near enough. I'm bored with being judicious and 'maybe, maybe not,' Nolan. This is Kincaid's cavern. Face it."

"I think it must be. So the only question is . . . what do we do now?"

"Meaning?"

"There's a strong argument that we should retire in triumph and hand it over to the grown-ups."

"Nolan, we *are* grown-ups."

"You know what I mean, Ken. Qualified, experienced, by-the-numbers and write-it-all-down archeologists. People who won't inadvertently screw up the site."

"But Kincaid and the bloke from the Smithsonian already stomped all over it a hundred years ago."

"That just means there's *two* layers of archeological evidence to protect. We've found the thing, and that's awesome. So let's not turn a small gain into a huge loss."

"*Small* gain?" Feather said. "Nolan—you found Kincaid's cave! You've proved thousands of people wrong, including *the Smithsonian itself*. This could change . . . *everything*."

"So let's protect the win. And I'm not only talking about *The Anomaly Files*, Feather. Your foundation doesn't want to be associated with a monumental screw-up. It's somewhat illegal to enter a cave in the Grand Canyon without permission. And when I say 'somewhat' I mean 'totally,' in a 'this is an actual criminal offense' sense. And that's going to count tenfold for a cave nobody even knew was here. It's not just the archeological establishment we'd have to worry about, or radical Native American groups. The science fanboys of the Internet will *crucify* us."

"So what are you actually worried about?" Gemma asked. "The integrity of the site, or losing your cable show?"

Ken and I turned to her. "Both," we said, together.

Pierre stopped filming and lowered the camera. "So what are we going to do?"

Everyone turned to Ken. Molly might be Acting Mom, but nobody's in any doubt about who's the daddy.

Ken thought it over, but not for long.

"Annoyingly," he said, "the twat in the billowy shirt is correct. We have not often been forced to confront the problem of actually *finding* something. Or ever, really. So I'm thinking on my feet. But the bottom line is we've already done enough to make a few headlines. Let's make sure they're good ones. Having said which, I'm not leaving without taking a peek down one of those side passages. We've earned that, I reckon. And if we trample some old dust in the process, well, sue me. Okay, Nolan?"

"Fine by me."

"All right, team. So let's all get back there and we'll film Nolan going in." He looked at me, unable to suppress a grin. "Well done, mate. I *told* everyone you weren't a total loser."

"Did they listen?"

"No. But they might now."

He led the others back up the passage while I took another look at the sealed-up opening. Gemma lingered.

"Congrats again," she said. "Seriously. But you got one thing wrong."

"What's that?"

"You said the only question was what we did next."

"Well, it is."

"No. I'd like to know the answer to another one."

"Which is?"

"Why Kincaid went to so much trouble to brick this place up."

CHAPTER

18

S o what's supposed to be down there?" Ken asked.

We'd gathered around the doorway on the left side of the passage, backpacks piled against the other wall. Pierre experimented with Feather and Gemma to find the best way to hold their lights so he could hope to get usable film. It wasn't going to be easy. The darkness had an inky quality, only reluctantly yielding to the glow of a flashlight, quickly reclaiming its territory as soon as the beam moved on.

"Didn't you read the original article?"

"Yeah. Well, some of it. Come on, Nolan, neither of us thought we were going to *find* the thing. I may have skimmed the later sections. And earlier sections. Okay, all of it."

"He didn't say much about these passages. Just that there are rooms along them."

"Ready," Pierre said.

"Okay," I said, to camera. "I can assure you that we're mindful of the respect due to this ancient site, and aware that the first thing that needs to happen is a thorough investigation by archeologists with the expertise to rigorously analyze what's here, and place it within historical and anthropological contexts. But as regular viewers know, we've spent a long time seeking. Having finally found something, it's hard not to allow ourselves a peek."

I started into the side passage. It was narrower than the main one, but still about eight feet wide. The floor was just as flat, and the walls even more clearly worked. As soon as I entered, it bent to the right, then carried on straight.

After about ten feet I saw something in the wall. A recess, six inches deep. I ran my finger over the lower surface. Dust, again dark, like soot.

"This looks like it was designed to hold a torch or lamp," I said. "And whoever lived here, or spent time here, would have been in constant need of artificial illumination. It's really, really dark. There's no natural light. Never has been. And of course there's the question of why someone would want to live this far under the ground. Because though we got here by climbing, that's where we are. There's some precedent for Native American tribes living in cliffs. The Anasazi inhabited an area known as the Four Corners, where Colorado, New Mexico, Utah, and Arizona meet. Other tribes referred to them as the 'ancient people,' and they established cliff dwellings in places like Chaco Canyon, New Mexico, and Mesa Verde, Colorado. But those were constructed into existing overhangs, in large, open cave mouths. They didn't involve forging tunnels into solid rock. Why would you go to the unfathomable effort of building a passage like this, so deep in the earth?"

After ten feet my flashlight revealed a doorway on the right-hand side. Six feet wide, again curved at the top.

"So—is this another passage?" I stood in front of the opening. "It appears not."

I walked into the space, holding the light up in front of me. Pierre tucked in behind and shot over my shoulder, as close to my POV as he could. The others followed.

It was a room, oval, about twenty feet long. The ceiling was a little lower than in the passage we'd entered from. The floor and walls had been worked to the same standard. Both sides had three of the niches we'd seen, all empty. At the far end, off-center, was what looked like a table or plinth. A portion of the wall hadn't been carved back to meet the curve, but instead left as a level platform three feet wide, three feet off the ground, like a cube partially embedded in the wall.

I walked around the room, holding the light up to the walls, and then down toward the floor. No markings, nothing on the ground except for more of the dark dust. Assuming the room had ever been used for something, no traces of activity remained. It felt dead.

"The plot thickens," I said to the camera. "Clearly this room had a purpose, but it's impossible to tell what it might have been."

When I moved the light again I noticed something I hadn't seen before, on the other side of the room. A portion where the floor hadn't been leveled—where, in fact, a small and very regular four-sided pyramid shape remained, about two feet high. The sides were even. Its purpose was even harder to guess at. It was not level with the "table" on the side, nor positioned in obvious relation to it. You don't realize how used you are to seeing symmetry in man-made structures until you're confronted with blatant asymmetry, nor how much being a member of a culture enables you to immediately make informed guesses about something's purpose.

I said something to this effect to the camera. "And that makes you all the more prone to ask 'What the heck was it for?' If not decoration, it must have had a function. What was it? I don't know. Maybe an archeologist will."

I wandered back through the room slowly, giving Pierre a chance to pick up some nonspeaking footage for intercuts, and then went back out into the corridor passage.

"Well," I said.

Everyone remained silent, even Ken. This place did that to you. It was very heavy. Very quiet. In the outside world, real or virtual, there's such a clamor that you feel you have to make a sound. To establish yourself as part of the crowd, make sure that you are added to the reckoning, to stick up your hand and claim the attention that proves you're alive.

In a silence this profound you felt different. Some deep, rusty, older part of your brain urged you to remain quiet, to avoid being noticed.

"Let's go on a little farther," I said.

We spent the next hour exploring the passage. There were more rooms on both sides. Most about the same size, others larger, including one perhaps three times as long, in more of a lozenge shape. There were a few smaller ones, too. All but two of the rooms we entered had an example of the wide, semicuboid ledges, and most also had a small pyramid. Their location was unpredictable, and it's not as if they could have been shoved to different places and left there by accident: they'd been hewn out of solid rock. The one thing it did remind me of was the curious unfinished chamber found under the Pyramid of Cheops. Small, low-ceilinged, divided into different levels and sections, its purpose yet to be established.

"So what's the deal with those things?" Gemma asked me when we were in one of the larger rooms. We'd stopped filming a while back, and were exploring the passage in pairs.

"No idea," I said. "And I don't understand the variation in placement, either. Native American art is generally pretty formalized. Like I said the other night: There's a way of representing something, and that's the way it's done. So I'm assuming these probably aren't art, but utility structures."

"For doing what?"

"Your guess is as good as mine."

Ken popped his head into the room. "Nolan, come and have a look at this."

We followed him forty feet down the passage. "Dunno if it means anything," he said. "But it's different."

He led me into a room that was smaller, about ten feet across, and circular. Neither the ledge nor a pyramid structure was present, though there was a rectangular depression in the floor. I noticed the rock within it was darker than usual, and then I realized that the walls were, too.

"Looks almost like that was a fire pit," I said. "Though..."

I raised the lamp and looked at the ceiling. No sign of a concentration of carbon material, as you might expect above a fire. And no hole. "Who'd light fires underground? The whole place would get choked with smoke in seconds."

"What about a whatsit?" Ken said. "One of those ceremonial things."

"A kiva," I said. "Yeah, maybe." Gemma was looking uncomprehending. "Some of the southwestern tribes had underground circular spaces called kivas. About this size, sometimes larger. You see them at Chaco and Mesa Verde, to which, yes, I have actually been. In real life."

"Ha ha. What are they for?"

"Rituals, and for guys to sit around making laws and being sexist and stuff. Usually had a fire pit in the middle. Often built-in banquettes in the walls, too, which this doesn't, but maybe it had wooden benches or something. Kivas have a hole in the ceiling, so in this one you're still going to have a serious smoke problem, which might explain the dark dust, but...who knows."

Ken stood, hands on hips, looking around. "Well, it's all very much of a something," he said. "And I think we can assume we're hell-yes going to get another season on the back of this. But right this moment there's a more pressing concern we need to attend to."

"What?"

"I'm hungry."

CHAPTER

19

We went back to the main passage and got out the sandwiches and water. We all stuck to Ken's suggestion of eating only half, in case Dylan hadn't managed to score additional food for tonight. Pierre wandered off down the opposite corridor with his sandwich and came back twenty minutes later.

"Same down there," he said. "Same rooms, similar sizes, same pyramid things. There was a doorway that seemed like it'd been blocked with a single sheet of stone. Couldn't move it."

"How far's the passage go?"

He shrugged. We didn't know how far the other one went, either. When we'd turned around to head back for lunch, after seeing about twenty rooms, the passage was still leading out into the darkness. "Didn't Kincaid claim there were statues and urns and hieroglyphics and stuff?"

"Yes. But not in this part."

"So where?"

"Well, bear in mind he doesn't even mention the shaft we came up from the fissure. But I think after about another hundred and fifty feet the main passage is supposed to open out into a large circular space. With a big statue in the middle. Then rooms full of gold urns and mummies and Lord knows what else."

"So we're going to go have a look, right?"

"I don't know," I said.

Pierre wandered off to sit next to Gemma.

I'd been firm about not trampling the site earlier, but so far there'd been nothing to disturb. I knew that what we'd seen and filmed was enough. But it didn't *feel* like enough. And that wasn't an ego thing. What we'd found was weird and interesting and would have a bunch of academics scratching their heads and muttering "Huh." Maybe even the father of the woman running reception back at the hotel would be forced to consider the idea that amateurs without tenure knew stuff. Or sometimes accidentally turned out to be right, as Gemma would doubtless have phrased it. We were guaranteed a spread in *Ancient American* magazine, and maybe a mention in *Obscure Academic Quarterly About Indigenous Peoples* (circulation: 151 copies worldwide, hidden in college libraries where no one under the age of forty goes except to make out).

But that wasn't *getting it out there*. That wasn't jamming stuff in front of the eyes and into the minds of the people with a lock on the historical narrative, nor the millions content to regard what's trending on Twitter as the burning issue *de nos jours*. And this wasn't Chaco or Mesa Verde, somewhere tourists could come look, ferried in buses and wandering down nice, easy paths. It was some distance up a rock face in a minor and restricted back section of the Grand Canyon. Once the archeologists had done their thing, this place would be shut off and forgotten and nothing would have changed. That wasn't enough. Not if there was more.

I checked the time. Twenty after two. I turned to Ken, who was sitting a few feet along the wall, gazing up at the ceiling and smoking.

"Ken," I said.

"I agree."

"With?"

"What you're about to say."

"We both argued to the contrary earlier."

"We need more than this, Nolan. Okay, not 'need.' Want. Deserve. What we've found is great. But if there's slam-dunk evidence we can get on film by taking a five-minute walk past that shaft, we'd be mental not to get it in the bag. Unless we've got the money shot in our grubby little hands, we can't hope to own the story. You know that as well as I do. I was just sitting here waiting for you to realize it."

"And if I hadn't?"

"I would have found a way of gently pointing it out."

"I see."

"So what's supposed to be down there?"

"A big round room. With a bunch of passages leading off, like the spokes of a wheel. That's where Kincaid claimed they saw the really zany stuff—golden urns, mummies."

"And there's a statue in the main room?"

"So he claimed. Massive, lots of arms."

"You don't believe it, do you."

"No. That whole section always read to me like he just started making shit up. It could be that he had the same experience we've had. He'd found something amazing. Something that *should* have been enough. But he knew it wouldn't get the man on the street to raise his head from the trough. Kincaid was a guy who'd spent his whole life in the wilderness, back when America was genuinely wild. He wanted the folks back east to understand what an extraordinary country it is, how deep and unexpected its history might be. So he embellished. A *lot*."

"So there's a chance there's nothing down there?"

"Such is the disappointing fate that oftentimes befalls impartial questers after truth."

"Don't I know it. All right—let's have a look. Then we'll piss off. There's a cold bottle of Tovaritch on that boat with our names on it. And for once, you've earned it."

Ten minutes later we set off, heading back up the main passage. We walked carefully around the hole down into the shaft, and then we were into new territory.

After another hundred feet or so the design of the passage abruptly changed. The walls—previously straight—became concave on both sides, more like a tunnel. The passage widened by a couple of feet. There was also a slight upward slope. The overall effect was far more finished and noticeably grander. It seemed clear that we were heading in the right direction, getting closer to the heart of a ceremonial structure.

Though Pierre filmed me heading onward, I didn't say much. I pointed out the change in the design of the passage, and speculated that the slope might be part of a form of emotional architecture, signifying upward spiritual progress. I wasn't sure if this made sense within local culture and frankly it could have been they simply messed up keeping it level, but saying this kind of thing is what I get (minimally) paid for.

Otherwise I kept quiet, until suddenly something changed. The air became noticeably cooler, and the walls on either side disappeared.

"Okay," I said. "Everybody—lights on."

One by one, the people behind me turned on their headlamps. There was a long moment of silence.

"Holy crap," Gemma whispered.

CHAPTER
20

Slowly we spread out into the space.

The room was very large. Far bigger than anything we'd seen before, well over a hundred feet across. It was hard to be sure of the full extent because light struggled to penetrate the darkness, but as people walked out into the room the glow of their lamps seemed to reveal a perfect circle, rising up toward a dome.

In the middle, directly in line with the main passage we'd come up, was a cube of stone, three feet to a side. This had been carved out of something other than the bedrock surrounding us. It looked harder and much more finely worked than anything we'd encountered before. It had already struck me that the small structures we kept seeing in the rooms down the side corridors—the embedded table/ledges and the randomly placed four-sided pyramids—seemed notably geometric. This took that stylization to a whole other level, and would have been remarkable even were it not for the thing sitting on top of it. It wasn't a statue, a Buddha-like god rendering of the type Kincaid had described.

It was a sphere. Carved out of stone, utterly perfect. And about— I estimated by comparing it to Pierre, who was approaching it as he filmed—twelve feet across.

"What the actual fuck?" Ken said, staring up at the sphere as we walked around it.

"I know."

"You seen anything like that before?"

"No. A bunch of granite balls were discovered in Costa Rica back in the 1930s. Maybe some in Bosnia a few years ago, too, though the word is those are likely concretion artifacts, natural phenomena. The Costa Rica ones seem genuine, but the biggest is under six feet high. And I don't think any of them are this perfect."

"So there's nothing like this?"

"Nowhere in the world, ever. Certainly not buried over a mile underground. Propped on an equally perfect cube."

"So this would be the money shot?"

"This is the shot of our *lives*, Ken."

Molly called over from near the wall. "There's markings here. And a doorway."

We went over. There were indeed markings on the wall, chipped into the rock, made visible by sooty deposits. It was impossible to tell what they were supposed to represent. The doorway was six feet wide and maybe twice that tall. Beyond, utter darkness.

"Why'd they make the passages so high?" Ken said.

"No idea."

"There's more doorways over here," Feather called. She and Gemma were exploring around the bottom of the room, close to the main entrance.

"Spokes of a wheel," Molly said. "Isn't that how Kincaid described it?"

"He did."

"Good," she said briskly. "So we've found his cave. And we've found that thing in the middle, too. Which is truly awesome. We rock. If you'll excuse the pun. And so now, I'm hoping, we're going to leave?"

Her voice sounded the way it had when it'd been just her and me in the lower passageway. Tight, overmodulated. I didn't think it was merely claustrophobia, though, or whatever it had been about earlier. We were tired, after a few nights of patchy sleep and a lot of exertion—but it wasn't that, either. However much you know that an archeological site is no big deal, its inexplicability a function of cultural ignorance, it has a strange atmosphere. A sense of passing and loss and things gone by. When you are far separated in time from its creators, and divorced, too, from their lives and motivations, they feel stripped of humanity—especially when total lack of ambient light means that you're effectively there in the middle of the night.

"Yeah," Ken said, and even he didn't sound his usual self. "We need twenty seconds of Nolan talking in front of that big stone ball, and then we're out of here. Nolan, make it good. Or just stand there and point. It kind of speaks for itself, mate."

I walked with him over to the sphere, and Pierre told Ken how to hold his lamp to back up the light attached to the camera. I was aware of the others wandering around the periphery of the room, but any flickers of light from them would only add to the atmosphere. They'd all know to keep quiet.

"So," I said, to camera. Something was supposed to come after that, but I wasn't sure what. I started again. "As you can see, we've found something else. Something that makes the rooms earlier seem...less of a big deal."

I gestured up at the sphere. Pierre slowly tilted back to take it in, then followed me as I started walking around it.

"I don't know what type of rock this is, but it's different from what the passages are carved out of. Different from the canyon as a whole. This looks more like granite. Something hard enough to be precisely worked and shaped. And then, somehow, they got it here."

I stepped back a few paces. "And to make matters stranger, it's balanced on top of a cube. Well, not 'balanced'—you'll see it fits neatly into a shallow depression which has been carved to hold it in position. I don't even know how you'd start doing something like that."

I turned from the ball and spoke straight to camera. "I'll be honest with you, viewers. I don't know what to say about *any* of this. I've never heard of anything like it, anywhere in the world. Kincaid said they found a big statue here. Why did he lie? I have no idea.

Or, maybe, one idea. In his day people were still discovering extraordinary things about this country—the Native American mound complexes, natural features like the Devils Tower in Wyoming, vistas like Bryce Canyon. Maybe Kincaid didn't think a stone ball would be big enough news.

"But he was wrong. That other stuff? It's amazing, but we now know what it is, and why it's there. The object behind me is something that conventional history has *no* way of explaining. This, my friends, is an honest-to-God anomaly. And you've been with us every step of the way. This is yours. So now we're going to beat a graceful retreat, and hand this mystery over to the experts. Thanks for coming with us on this remarkable journey."

I winked, to show I was done, and stepped back from the sphere. Pierre lowered the camera.

"Good enough," Ken said. "So now let's—"

"Hey, guys." This was Gemma, calling from the darkness on the far side of the room. "Before we go, you should come see this. There's a—"

The grinding noise was not loud.

It came from under the floor, but was such a deep tone that it was hard to tell from which direction. It was a gentle sound, and wouldn't have been at all unnerving except for the fact that the room was so quiet.

Then, suddenly, the cube disappeared, dropping through a neat square hole that had appeared beneath it. It didn't plummet, but descended at a measured rate, until the top was flush with the floor.

This was so very surprising that there was a one-second delay before I processed the inevitable consequence.

The stone ball descended, too, landing on the ground with a crash.

Then the ball started to roll.

"Everyone—get out of the way!"

Pierre threw himself to the side. Ken and I backed hurriedly away. I knew Gemma was out of range on the far side and Molly's squawk confirmed she was well clear, too.

But then I saw Feather.

She was down near the entrance from the main passage, frozen in place, eyes wide, staring at the ball as it came toward her, unable to comprehend what was happening.

"Feather!" I shouted. "Move!"

The ball was gathering speed, rolling down the indentation of the path, and still she appeared rooted to the spot. I started to run, but I was on the wrong side to get around to her and I knew all I could do was keep shouting in the hope that I'd break through to her.

Finally her eyes snapped back to awareness.

She moved. But she darted the wrong way.

Instead of getting out of the path of the ball, she seemed to get confused, or...I don't know what went through her head, and unless you've stood in the path of a massive stone ball rolling toward you like a movie come horribly to life, you don't realize how the mind and body can part company, explode in an instant into a level of fear where it's impossible to make rational choices, or any decision at all.

Ken and I shouted at her, and she realized what she'd done. But by then the ball was nearly upon her and so she started backing away from it instead—and then turned and ran down the passage, the only way she could go.

The ball rolled right into it.

Ken and I ran after but by now the ball was going so fast we couldn't keep up. We were shouting and screaming at Feather but I can't tell you what we were trying to say.

There was a crunching impact that nearly knocked us off our feet. At first I couldn't work out why the ball had stopped but then I remembered the passage had gotten wider as we'd walked up it, about the point where the slope had kicked in—a slope I now realized was not an error, or architectural conceit, but there to cause the ball to roll.

The impact reverberated through the earth like a tremor, and then everything was quiet.

CHAPTER

21

Two seconds later, a cacophony of people yelling and screaming and running. Only Ken and I had been in a position to clearly see what had happened—the others blindsided by the ball, or too far back in shadow. Everyone was screaming at everybody else, all at the same time, trying to check if people were okay, and gradually—once they realized her voice wasn't among those echoing in the tunnel—specifically shouting for Feather.

Ken was the first to rein the chaos back into actual words. "What the fuck?" he bellowed. "What the *fuck*?"

I had nothing. I was standing blinking at the stone ball. It was extremely hard to process what had occurred, not least because it seemed ridiculous, too absurdly Indiana Jones to have happened in front of our eyes. My mind kept ricocheting between a conviction that it had only been a seen-it-all-before special effect—and a horrified awareness that no, it had just actually happened *in real life*.

I finally got stuck between the two in a state of momentary calm, or indecision about how exactly to freak out. I turned from the ball and in the flickering and swirling of flashlights was able to run a quick internal roster and establish that everyone else was here, in the passage, and they all seemed okay. Physically, at least.

I shouted for quiet. It took ten seconds to get through to everyone. Then there was silence.

I held up my hand to keep it that way. And after a few seconds, we heard something.

"Nolan? Ken?" It was Feather's voice.

"Feather—are you okay?"

"Yes, I'm okay," she said. Her voice sounded shaky but clear, and surprisingly close. Though the stone ball fit snugly in the passage it had rolled down—the concave walls making terrible sense now, too—the point where the tunnel narrowed had square corners, meaning the ball didn't plug it like a cork in a bottle. "Are you all okay?"

"We're fine," I said. "Well, unharmed. Are you okay?" I was dimly aware I'd asked this before. Once didn't seem enough.

"I fell down," she said. "I scraped my leg. And face, I think. But...basically I'm okay."

"Have you got a light with you?"

"Yes—a headlamp. Though it's a bit weak."

"What can you see from there?"

"There's gaps around the ball," she said. "But...they're really small. What...Nolan, what are we going to do?"

"There's only one thing I can think of," I said. "There may be some other way out of here, but...it could take a while to find it. I'm going to have to ask you to go back down the shaft. Get down to the river. Hopefully Dylan will be back by now. Tell him what happened. And go get help."

I turned to Molly and Ken. "Unless one of you has a better idea?"

"No," Ken said. "There is no other idea. But Feather—be very careful. Do *not* rush down that shaft, or down the canyon wall once you get outside. Look after yourself. Be safe. We're not going anywhere."

And it was only when Ken said these words that we started to truly understand the position we were in.

Fifteen minutes later we were all in the middle of the big central room. We'd spoken with Feather a little longer, making sure she was as calm as could be hoped for, and telling her again and again to take it easy on the two descents. Then she left. I couldn't help thinking that in an ideal world it would have been Pierre setting off to do this, as he'd be able to do it twice as fast, and more safely—but it was already evident that we weren't living in an ideal world.

Molly and Pierre were taking inventory of what we had with us— food, water, camera batteries—getting the key stuff out of the backpacks and putting it in piles so we knew what we were dealing with.

Meanwhile I took Gemma to one side. "What happened?"

"I'm so..." She was fighting back tears.

"Gemma, it's okay. I'm not giving you a hard time. Nobody's going to do that. It could have happened to any of us. I'm amazed it wasn't me. I'm the team klutz. We just need to know what made it happen so we can avoid doing it again."

She looked at me gratefully. "There was a...Come. I'll show you."

Ken saw where we were going and joined us. Gemma led me to an area of wall close to one of the passages leading into darkness. There was a rectangular patch of floor, about a foot wide by two feet long, that looked different from the rest. It was now half an inch below the rest of the ground.

"I was actually trying to tell you about this," Gemma said, indicating a portion of the wall next to the passage. Something had been carved into it. The letters *D O*, and what might have been an *N*, or part of an *M*.

Ken grunted. "Classy. One of the previous guys chipped his name into the site."

"Right. It distracted me, and that's how I ended up..."

She stopped talking. I patted her on the back, feeling awkward. "It is what it is. What happened to your arm?"

She glanced down at the smear of blood along her right forearm, thick enough that it was dripping onto the ground. "Oh, nothing. It's the cut from when we nearly fell down the wall earlier. I must have knocked it."

"Okay," Ken said. "Either a couple of us need to grid-walk this room, checking there's nothing else like it, or else we all go sit in the middle and stay very still."

"That's assuming there's anything else in here to trigger," I said. "There may not be. That ball did the job pretty effectively already, don't you think?"

"But what job? Stopping whoever gets in here from leaving again? Why?"

"I have no clue," I said. "And . . . we don't actually know there's no other way out."

"We haven't proved it, no. But why block that passage if there is?"

"Gemma, do me a favor—go tell Pierre and Molly to turn off their phones. You too. As in complete power-down."

"Why?"

"There's no signal in here, so they're pointless. Except that if all the other batteries run out, we can use them as flashlights. So let's start saving power."

"Oh. Yeah. Good thinking."

Ken watched her go. "That's smart, but you just freaked her out a little, Nolan. Nobody wants to think about sitting around in this place with no light."

"I know. But I wanted to talk to you in private. Because I don't think we *should* be sitting around. What time is it?"

"Coming up for four."

"So Feather's not going to get down to the raft until after five. Even assuming Dylan's ready and waiting, it'll be hours before they can get to park officials or the police or whoever the hell they can find. Who are probably *not* going to immediately leap into action on the say-so of a hippie chick and a random boat guy with poor interpersonal skills—especially as we're not even supposed to be here in the first place."

"We're spending the night. I understand that."

"Longer than that, Ken. Even if they get right on to a rescue tomorrow morning, they're going to have to source drilling equipment or dynamite. Which will likely take hours to get together and transport to the canyon. And then it's all going to have to come up here the way we did—which will take further hours. Not to mention there could be delays from people saying no one's allowed to blast holes in an archeological site just to rescue some assholes who got themselves stuck in it."

"Don't be a twat, Nolan. They have to get us out."

"Of course. But it's going to be twenty-four hours, minimum, thirty-six—possibly more. And never mind the food or batteries. We can live without those. It won't be fun, but we can do it. It's dehydration that will mess us up. How much water do you have left?"

He made a face. "Half a bottle."

"I'm about the same. I thought we would be out of here soon. And we're physically depleted already from making two big climbs, one of them with the sun on our backs."

"You're making me feel very thirsty, Nolan."

"This would be my point. Don't suppose you snuck a bottle of vodka into your backpack?"

"I wish."

For a moment we watched the others, who stood in a little pool of light in the center of the room. Even from here you could see how little water there was in the pile they'd made. "We may have no choice but to sit it out," I said. "But we've got to take a look down these side passages, just in case."

"Looking for what? Another shaft?"

"That, or could be one of the passages winds back out toward the canyon wall. Or *something*. We're going to have a lot of time to kill, Ken. Be dumb not to check if there's another way out. And keeping busy is probably a good idea."

"How are we for cigarettes? And yeah, that's a hint."

I lit one for each of us. "Well under a pack."

"Christ. Run out of those and we're really going to see a downturn in the situation. People could get hurt. By me."

He thought for a moment.

"You're right," he said. "Let's go have a look around."

FROM THE FILES OF NOLAN MOORE:

THE HIDDEN CHAMBER UNDER THE
GREAT PYRAMID OF CHEOPS

CHAPTER

22

After long and thoughtful consideration, Molly declined the opportunity to come looking down pitch-dark passages with us. I think her exact words were "No."

Pierre managed to say he wanted to remain in the big room without looking like he was doing so for her sake, continuing a long run of failing to be annoying in a way that meant I was close to having to recategorize him as "actually not annoying after all." Gemma wanted to come with us. We each took a mouthful of water, left the other two holding position in the middle of the room and—pretty much at random—headed toward the passage at the ten o'clock position in the room.

"So what did Kincaid say about these passages?" Ken said.

"A bunch of stuff," I said. "But to be honest, he lost all credibility for me the moment he failed to mention the great big rolling stone ball. We're better off investigating using our own eyes than relying on made-up shit."

"So how do we know there's not more of those things up these passages?" Gemma asked, looking dubiously into the darkness beyond the doorway.

"We don't. But in everything we've seen so far there's been an elegance of design. Simplicity. That ball has already blocked the main way out of here. Why duplicate, when it means thousands more man-hours' work?"

"That's very now-centric," she said. "These guys didn't think like the Apple design department. Why build the pyramids that high, when half as high would do? Because they could. Because Pharaoh told them to. Because they felt like it."

This was sufficiently in line with things I'd thought while climbing the shaft that I couldn't come up with a reply.

"She's right," Ken agreed. "Plus, if you're saying this is the only entrance they had to block, you're also saying there's no other way out. So why risk it?"

"Whose side are you on?"

"The side of not getting killed. For future reference, that's the side I'm always on."

"Me too," I said. "And look. Feather's not a bad climber. Better than me, definitely. But not like Pierre or Molly. If she hurries or loses her hold and slips and falls down that shaft, then we're here forever. And we won't even know it's happened until we've already run out of water. Yes, going up this passage is a risk. But so is *not* going up it."

I was holding the light. I stepped right up to the entrance to the passage. "We'll do it this way. I'll go in. You stay back. Nothing happens, you follow."

"Nolan, you tosser—we don't want you killed, either."

"I'm immortal," I said. "Didn't I mention that?"

And I stepped into the passage.

Nothing happened.

I stood very still for a moment, then moved back into the main room, and out of the way. We all listened carefully for grinding or rolling sounds. There were none.

"One step doesn't prove anything," Ken said.

"I know." I'd also known what taking that single step would do, however—halve the tension by breaking down a mental barrier. "But that's how we'll do it. In sections. Walk a little way up, using the light to check the floor for anything that looks weird. Then a little farther. And so on."

"Fine," Gemma said. "But I'm going first."

"Bollocks you are," Ken said.

"Why? Because I'm a woman?"

"Since you ask, yes. And you can report me to social media all you fucking like."

"Have you forgotten who got us stuck in here?"

"That was an accident," I said.

"*My* accident. I did it. And right now, I'm doing this."

She snatched the light and stepped into the passage. Like me, she stayed motionless for a few seconds. Then took a careful step onward. She bent at the waist, looking carefully at the floor, directing the light in a slow sweep from side to side. Then took another step, doing the same. And then another.

"How's it look?"

"Just like rock. I'm going to keep going."

"Be careful."

"Thanks, Nolan. Otherwise I'd have started jumping up and down."

She was methodical. She didn't, as I might have done, lose patience with the process and start speeding up. She diligently kept her pace slow and consistent, one step at a time. Ken and I stood meanwhile with heads cocked, one ear toward the passage. Neither of us heard anything untoward.

"There's a doorway here," she said. She was about thirty feet up the passage now.

"What's it look like?"

"A dark and scary-ass doorway. I'll keep going."

And farther she went, until the glow from her lamp was a bare flicker in the blackness, saying little as she walked but for a mention that she'd seen another doorway, on the other side, and then another.

She went far enough, in fact, that I started to notice something about the light. I took a step into the passage myself. I walked ten feet along, against Ken's foul-mouthed protestations, and got out my phone.

"I thought that was supposed to be turned off," he said.

"I forgot. I'll do it in a minute."

I found the app I'd been thinking of and loaded it, then laid my iPhone on the floor. Gemma came back toward us, still keeping her light pointed at the ground but now walking at a normal pace. "What are you doing?"

"It's a spirit level. Look."

We all squatted down around it. "There's a slight tilt downward as it leads away from the main room. Same as the main passage, in fact. Maybe not quite as much."

"And you think that proves nothing's going to come rolling this way and squish us like bugs?"

"Doesn't prove it, no. It could slope in the other direction, way down there, like a parabola, and there's probably someone smart enough to say what the angle and distances would need to be depending on the size and weight of a hypothetical stone ball, but it sure as hell isn't me. I'm just suggesting that the downward slope makes it a little less likely that we need to worry."

We straightened up. Looked at each other. And started walking together, very carefully, down the passage.

We weren't measuring but I'd say it was about a hundred and fifty yards long. At the end it stopped in a wall: flat, neatly worked, final. I hadn't really been expecting a set of stairs with an illuminated EXIT sign, but it was still extremely disappointing.

"One down, seven to go," Ken muttered.

"We passed a bunch of doors on the way," Gemma said. "You never know—could be something leads off one of them."

"Maybe," I said. "It's worth looking. And make sure we keep checking the ceiling of the passage on the way back, too. That's how Molly spotted the entrance to the shaft."

"Yeah," Ken said. "Not feeling quite so proud of her for that now, if I'm honest."

"But that's how you found this place," Gemma said. "Okay, being trapped here for a while is sub-awesome, but it's still good, isn't it?"

"Ask me again when I've got a pint in one hand and a large piece of food in the other."

So we walked back up the passage, Gemma shining her light at the ceiling, revealing only a smooth, consistent arch.

The first room we encountered was on the left. It was different from ones we'd previously seen, in that it was sternly oblong, walls, floors and ceilings meeting at right angles. It was about twenty feet long and ten wide and high and completely empty. The floor was thick with the dark dust we'd seen in other places. The end wall was entirely covered, floor to ceiling and wall to wall, by symbols neatly chiseled into the rock.

I hesitate to call them hieroglyphics. I'd be lying if I pretended to be fluent or even competent in that writing system, but I've spent enough time looking at photographs to be able to dependably recognize it. There was a superficial resemblance, in that some of the symbols looked as though they could represent real-life objects—corn, a mountain, a river—and groups of them were neatly arranged so as to suggest they had an aggregated meaning. But there the similarity stopped, and despite the pictograms dotted along the lines, to me it actually looked more like some kind of cuneiform.

"We're waiting," Gemma said.

"Huh?"

She looked at me, eyebrow raised. "This is the moment where you trace your finger over those symbols and—at first haltingly, and then with increasing breathless fluency—tell us exactly what it all says."

"You'd be thinking of a real archeologist."

"Good. Because in the movies, most of the time it turns out to be a curse that raises an ancient demon or something, and to be honest that's kind of the last thing we need right now."

"No idea what it says?" Ken asked.

"None," I said. "I'm sure this is what Kincaid described as hieroglyphs. But that's not what they are, at least not Egyptian. Egypt was big in popular culture back then, and they leaped to conclusions.

I don't know what this actually is. Phoenician. Ancient Anasazi. JavaScript, for all I know."

We left the room and walked to the first door on the other side of the passage. This led to another, narrower passageway.

"Ha," Ken said. "This heads toward the canyon wall, doesn't it?"

"Well, yes. Though it's a long way from here."

"Still worth checking out. And look—more of that writing."

This time there was a single row of the composite characters, running along the wall about four feet from the ground. I lagged behind the others as we walked deeper into the side passage, and yes, I did even trace my finger along the carvings, as if that might help. The symbols in the previous room had been a seamless, orderly mass; these came in clumps, about three feet long, with a gap of a few inches between each section. Like sentences, perhaps, or observations or instructions. Somebody more learned than I was going to have a field day with this stuff.

Assuming they got to see it.

"Christ," Gemma said suddenly. She sounded some distance away. I realized they'd gotten twenty or thirty feet ahead of me, and hurried to catch up.

"Careful, mate," Ken said.

They were standing close to a side wall. At first I couldn't see why. Then I realized the passage stopped abruptly right in front of them.

CHAPTER
23

Gemma's headlamp wasn't cutting it so Ken pulled out his light, too. Together they shone them into the blackness.

"Hell is this?"

Water, appeared to be the answer. A lot of it. It started nine inches below the ledge we were standing on. It was clear and still, and shining light down through it revealed a flat rock floor three or four feet below.

I maneuvered myself carefully to the edge of the drop. The walls on each side were flat and smooth and disappeared into blackness.

"Well, that's our fluids problem solved," Ken said.

"Seriously?" Gemma said. "I'm not drinking that."

"Why? Looks clear to me."

"But where's it come from?"

I took Ken's light and shone it upward. The roof of the room was about six feet above my head. It, too, had been worked—of course; this was hardly a natural feature—but was cracked and uneven. "Above, maybe," I said. "Some of it, at least. Dripping down through the rock, very, very slowly."

"Filtered, in other words," Ken said. "Nice. Shame we don't have any single malt with us."

"I'm still not drinking it," Gemma said. "We don't know how long it's been sitting here. It's got to be full of bugs and microbes."

I squatted and looked at the water. Even close up, it seemed very clear. Strangely clear, in fact—as you would indeed have thought that standing water would become infested with algae and microscopic creatures.

I sat on the floor and took off my shirt and shoes and socks, putting phone, lighter, and cigarettes safely to one side. I discovered a battered and bent matchbook in my back pocket that I hadn't even realized was there, and added that to the pile.

Ken watched this process. "Fuck are you doing, Nolan?"

"Taking a closer look."

I swung my legs over the edge and down into the pool. It was not cold, though below body temperature.

I eased myself down into it. The water came about halfway up my chest.

"There's no lifeguard on duty, dude," Gemma said.

I turned my headlamp on and walked out into the pool. The rock underfoot was smooth. The water stretched around me, the far edges hidden beyond the glow of the light, the surface fading into darkness as though it went on forever.

I started moving diagonally, in the hope of finding its extent, and I kept a close eye on the floor as I went. After about twenty yards I started to make out a wall.

When I got to it I saw there were small square openings in a line along it.

"See anything?"

Ken's voice was surprisingly clear. I looked up and saw now that the space was domed above, in a low curve.

"Holes in the wall," I said. "I assume that's what keeps the level constant. Water drips in, then slowly pours back out of these holes. Keeps it from ever getting high enough to flood the rest of the passages, I guess."

"Does that also explain why it isn't manky?"

"I don't know. Maybe. Though it's going to be a very slow process." I dipped my hand into the water and brought it up to my face. "No smell at all."

I turned from the wall and took another diagonal course, this time heading right. After a few yards my foot met resistance. I looked down and saw why.

"There's some of those pyramid-shaped rock things in the water," I said. "Sticking up from the floor."

I had in mind to make it over to the opposite wall, but then something else caught my eye.

"Nolan," Gemma said, "maybe you should come back now?"

"In a minute."

I changed direction and waded straight toward the end of the room. I'd been assuming the pool would stop at a wall there, too, but soon saw this wasn't the case. Instead there was a lip about the same height above the water as it had been at the entrance, and an open area beyond.

I sloshed up to the edge of this and stood looking for a full minute—silent long enough for Ken to call out.

"You okay?"

"You might want to come see this," I said.

By the time they'd made it across I'd hoisted myself up out of the water and was sitting on the edge. I shone my light so they could see where they were going. Gemma moved quickly and confidently, still regarding the water with great suspicion. Ken looked sufficiently ridiculous as he doggedly waded toward me out of the gloom that I couldn't help laughing.

"Fuck's up with you?"

"No longer shall I use the expression 'a duck out of water.' Going forward, I shall think of 'a Ken *in* water.'"

"Fair enough, mate. Much as I have abandoned use of the term 'wanker,' because I've found saying 'a total Nolan' does the same job."

Gemma ignored us, staring at what I'd already seen on the platform beyond. She put her elbows up on the edge and scrabbled out, then turned to help me with Ken.

135

We stood together and looked. "Okay. This is just taking the piss now," Ken said, as if personally affronted.

The ledge, platform, was thirty feet wide and ten deep. It sloped a little, a few inches higher at the back than the front. In the perfect center of the space was a standing stone. That's what it looked like, anyway—the kind of thing you see in tilting rings in Europe, or at the edges of Stonehenge. A lump of hard, old rock, maybe four feet tall and two wide.

All around it, arrayed in three neat rows, were cubes of rock. Ten behind the standing stone, ten in front, eight in a row that included it as the centerpiece. Twenty-eight perfect cubes. But that wasn't the end of it.

On each of these stood a sphere. They were different sizes, ranging from about six inches in diameter to three feet, and each was subtly different in color.

"What is this stuff? Metal?"

"Looks like it. Or minerals." The sphere in the middle at the front looked a lot like copper. One a couple of cubes away could have been iron. The others were various types of ore. One was a cloudy, translucent shade.

As we wandered among the spheres I spotted another at the back, previously hidden in shadow. This was much larger, perhaps five feet in diameter, and stood in a depression on the floor rather than on a cube. It was very dark, almost black, with a matte surface. Like the smaller examples it looked like it had been stamped out of a mold, or poured into one.

Ken appeared next to me. "So what's all this?"

"I have no idea," I said. "Some kind of ritual pantheon thing, maybe—one representing each of the key gods. Or a stylized model of the solar system, complete with comets. Someone's rock collection. I don't know."

"Look at this."

Gemma was standing at the stone in the middle. The top of it had been smoothed off, leaving a surface that looked as though it had been sliced with a sharp knife. The resulting plane was smooth and polished. Into it had been carved more of the hieroglyphics we'd seen along the corridor. This time they were arrayed in a neat grid, ten by ten.

"There's a hundred," Ken said. "Does that mean anything?"

"Not to me. I should know whether the local tribes worked a decimal system, but I don't. I mean, we've got ten fingers and ten toes, so it's possible. But this is something else for the smart boys and girls to figure out."

This time it was Gemma who ran her fingers over the carvings, as if they were an ancient form of Braille, waiting to reveal their secrets. I noticed she'd managed to scrape the cut on her arm again when lowering herself into the pool, and it was bleeding freely.

"When we get back to the main room," I said, "see if Molly's got a first aid kit in her backpack. That's not going to heal if you keep scraping it."

"Yes, Dad."

"I'm just saying."

We stood looking impotently at the pictograms. They were extremely neat, far more precise than the ones we'd seen on the walls of the passage approaching the pool and in the previous room. About half an inch square, each an intricate combination of symbols, some of which appeared in more than one pictogram. Presumably it worked on a similar principle to Egyptian or Chinese, each of the component glyphs being picto- or ideographs representing constituent things or ideas, but to get anywhere with interpreting the overall designs you'd need to understand the meaning of the component parts. One looked like the short curved horns on a dung beetle; another could have been a big hill, a pair of eagle wings, or an evocation of a welcome breeze on a summer afternoon, for all I knew. The pile of things I didn't know or didn't understand about this place was now so high that I wasn't tall enough to keep adding more to the top. I was also tired and very thirsty.

"We should get back," I said. "The others are going to be wondering where we are."

They nodded distantly—Gemma still tracing her fingers over the carvings; Ken standing with hands on hips, glaring at the stones as though hoping to intimidate them into confessing their purpose. I've seen a similar look work immediately on barmen and hotel clerks and very senior people in the film and TV industry, but the stone balls weren't talking.

I stepped down off the ledge into the water, not bothering to be gentle about it.

"Christ, Nolan!" Gemma yelled as she took a big splash up her back.

I pushed away from the edge, deciding the hell with it and going fully under the surface. When I surfaced I tentatively licked my lips. They tasted fine. A little metallic, like mineral water—and who knows, maybe that's what it was, sourced out of a hidden spring rather than drips from above—but perfectly drinkable.

"Come on in," I said. "The water's lovely."

Ken stepped back in, and Gemma followed, and for a while we swam back and forth, silent but for quiet lapping sounds, in a pool of water a thousand feet underground.

CHAPTER

24

W hen are you going to say it?"

"Say what?"

We'd been back in the main room for a couple hours. Investigations into two of the other passages had revealed similar nondescript rooms. Pierre had now gone to scout up one of the remaining passages by himself. The rest of us were sitting in a circle. I'd taken two small mouthfuls of the remaining half of my sandwich. I'd left my water bottle alone for now, and was monitoring my guts for signs of unruliness after ingesting liquid from the pool.

"The bleeding obvious," Ken said. "Look, Nolan. I yield to no one in my respect for the red-skinned man—both in his achievements in wiseness and his *or* her rights of precedence in your chaotic farce of a so-called country—but there's no way Native Americans built this place."

"I know."

"So? Who did?"

Everybody looked at me. And it's a curious thing. You think it'd be awesome to be the guy who gets to intone, "Maybe it was *aliens...*" You think that'd be cool, especially if you're right there on-site, one of the people who's discovered the evidence. But in reality it's not something you want to say. It says all bets are off. The walls of reality come down. It's like someone asking, "Hey—did you just hear a disconcerting sound from the cellar of this abandoned house deep in the woods?"—and having to answer: "Uh, yes. Yes I did."

But also, as I have said countless times on camera, aliens are never the answer to any sensible question. There is nothing on Earth that can't be explained by the actions (however surprising and anomalous) of Earthlings. If you look back through the history of the idea of extraterrestrial contact, with few exceptions it's always proffered by an opportunist, a lunatic, a religious nut, or some magic-is-just-science evangelist one step away from a padded cell. Where once we reached for God and his angels, now we grasp for beings in spaceships. Both are merely attempts to explain that which we cannot explain, by bailing preemptively from the discussion by means of the magical other or an unverifiable deus ex machina.

"This structure does not," I agreed carefully, "seem likely to be the work of local tribes. Even the Anasazi, who did some pretty zany stuff."

"And so?"

"I'm wondering about the Romans."

"The *Romans*? Seriously?"

"It's not as dumb as it sounds. People have this picture in their head of America as a young place. The 'New World.' But it's as old as anywhere else. It's been here as long as Europe or Africa. It's a contentious subject but there's people who think there were populations here before anybody made it over the land bridge. And others have asked how the Romans could have failed to make it to North America."

"Because it's a long way from Rome, you tool. You're not telling me they sailed right across the Atlantic."

"They wouldn't need to. They were in your neck of the woods for nearly four hundred years. Ran the place, as I recall. From the United Kingdom you can make a series of shorter hops around the top of the North Atlantic, via Iceland and Greenland and Newfoundland, each of which was well within the capabilities of the Roman navy. If they chained those together they could totally have gotten here."

"Coulda, sure," Gemma said. "Any evidence they *did*?"

"Some, perhaps. A very Roman-like sword found off Oak Island in Nova Scotia. Coin hoards here and there. It's said the Micmac language includes maritime terms that are remarkably similar to vernacular Roman equivalents, and the tribe carries a rare DNA marker that's been tentatively traced to the Eastern Mediterranean. And no, Gemma, I can't point you to officially sanctioned documentation. Certainly not in the current circumstances."

"But even if you could, even if we buy that—Nova Scotia is *thousands of miles* from here."

"Right—but this is the Romans we're talking about. The most can-do nation of all time. Their soldiers routinely marched well over twenty miles, day after day, in full armor. At that rate they could have come this far in, what—four, five months? It would have taken longer in reality, of course, because they wouldn't have come in a straight line and would have been exploring the unknown rather than heading for somewhere in particular. But they were tough, resilient guys who knew how to live off the land and find or make everything they needed to survive—backed up with the experience of having conquered most of the known world already. These are people who brought not only food crops with them to new environments but medicinal plants, too, so they'd have their traditional remedies and salves on hand after taking the place over. They had serious colonizing game. Like a team of a hundred Rambos, without the colorful psychological issues. It's not out of the question that an exploratory force could have made it this far."

"Kind of makes sense," Ken said. "And I'd credit Romans with knowing how to build that pool. Smelting and metalworking techniques for those spheres, too."

"They're not the only group rumored to have gotten here before Columbus," I told Gemma. "The Vikings, of course. Irish monks—with alleged examples of ogham script found here and there. Maybe the Egyptians, or Phoenicians or Minoans, too. I'd call those long shots, but the Romans? Maybe. You've seen what we're dealing with. The Romans are the best I've got."

"But the writing we've seen isn't Latin."

"That is, I'll confess, a disappointing hole in my hypothesis. Though, wait."

I got up and walked over to the passage with the pool. Ken came with me. "What?"

I pointed at the three letters Gemma had found. "They could be Roman, I guess?"

Ken shook his head. "Nothing else we've seen here presents like their writing. And look." He pointed just to the right of the N or M. "Little nick there, like someone was about to do another letter and didn't have time to finish. It's just 'Dominic,' mate, or 'Donald' or something. Like I said—just one of the previous bunch who was here, leaving a mark."

"Yeah, you're probably right."

"How long has it been?"

This last was from Molly, who'd been sitting quietly at the edge of the group, arms looped around her knees, looking toward the main passage. Listening, but not participating.

She'd been sitting exactly like this when we got back from finding the pool. While we'd been in the passage she had divided all of our resources—the remaining sandwiches, water bottles, a couple of tiny bags of peanuts, and a handful of granola bars—into neat piles. Spare batteries for the flashlights and Pierre's camera were in another.

None of the piles was as large as I would have liked.

Molly had efficiently bandaged Gemma's arm with gauze from her kit, then gone back to sitting. She listened while we told her what we'd found, but made no comment. She seemed calm. Too calm, I thought, but then I realized she was simply waiting. She was done being here. She had no further interest in this place or anything we might discover about it. She wanted out.

"Four hours," I said. "A little more."

Molly glanced at me, and then went back to looking down the main passageway.

A while later Pierre came back and told me he'd found something different. I asked Ken if he wanted to come see but he said no, though to shout for him right away if it turned out to be a fully stocked bar or a lap-dancing club.

I followed Pierre down the passage that ran out from the three o'clock position in the room.

"How're you holding up?" I asked.

As soon as the question was out of my mouth it seemed a strange one. Unguarded, and unlikely to be helpful. It could only remind someone of our situation.

He shrugged, however. "Good. I mean, I'm totally ready to be somewhere else, but you know, it's all still awesome."

"Do you think Molly's okay?"

"Oh yeah. She's just—I think she gets kinda claustrophobic in the dark. Plus that girl is half-woman, half-smartphone. She's had no signal for two days. That's got to be driving her nuts, right? Her Facebook is going to explode."

I laughed. "How are you doing for camera batteries?"

"Okay. But I'm running low on disk space. That's why I stopped shooting everything in sight. I figure you and Ken can tell me what you want me to pick up before we leave, and I'll do it then. Worst case, I can trim some of what we already have, though I don't want to lose much. I don't expect I'll get to film something like this again."

After fifty yards it was evident that this tunnel was different, in that it bent markedly to the left—deeper into the rock—rather than heading out straight from the main room. I observed this.

"Yeah," Pierre said, stopping and pointing up the passage. "Plus it's longer. Though it still ends in a wall. This is what I wanted to show you, though."

He gestured through a doorway, and I went into the room beyond. "*Yi*," I said, immediately.

"Right."

The odor was insidious rather than strong, dry and old—but no-ticeably more powerful than the general smell of dust and charcoal that hung around the rest of the tunnels. My initial reaction was due to the fact that it was implacably unpleasant, even in small doses—like the smell that lingers around the corner of a building near rat traps.

The room was big, too. I couldn't see how big, because after walk-ing ten feet—the smell getting a little more forceful with each step—I retreated to the doorway.

"What's causing that odor?" Pierre asked.

"No idea," I said. "But Kincaid did mention a room they'd found that smelled bad. He described it as 'snaky,' I think. I don't know what snakes smell like."

And then we heard the sound of shouting.

Sudden, urgent—and coming from the main room.

CHAPTER
25

Pierre and I ran in to find the central space deserted. This was extremely disconcerting until we heard voices from the main passage. By the time we got into it, Ken, Molly, and Gemma were together down at the end, up against the stone ball.

"What's up?"

Ken gestured to me to come forward. "We heard a noise," he said. "Scared the crap out of me. But then she called out and we realized who it was."

"Feather?" I said.

"Yes."

He stood back so I could get closer to the wall, near where the small gaps were. "Feather? Are you okay?"

"I'm okay," she said, though she sounded exhausted.

"Is Dylan with you?"

"No. He's not there. He's not anywhere."

"What...do you mean?"

"He's not there! He wasn't *there*."

"Not back at the raft? Why didn't you wait?"

"I didn't wait because the *raft isn't there, either*."

"What? Feather, look—tell me slowly, okay?"

There was silence as she gathered herself. "I climbed down the shaft," she said. "I tried to go quickly but not too fast, like you told me. It's a *lot* easier going down. Then I dropped into the passage and went back out to the opening in the wall. And I looked down, and...the raft wasn't there. It's *gone*. A storm's come in and it's raining and windy. And the boat just *isn't there*."

Ken blew out his cheeks. "So what did you do, love?"

"I waited," she said. "I didn't know what else to do. I figured maybe he'd taken the raft after we left, instead of the dinghy, for some reason. Maybe the water got too rough to stay there. But could he do that? Could he manage the raft by himself?"

"I don't know. Probably, if he had to."

"That's what I thought. So, I waited. I lay on the ground and looked down from the opening, because I thought there's no point climbing down if he's not even there, and I could shout when he got back. But then I thought, maybe the raft came untied accidentally or something. But if that happened he'd still come back, right? He'd come back in the dinghy?"

"I'm sure he would have," I said. I was trying to think through the possible scenarios and rank their odds. For some reason Dylan left in the raft, and had trouble getting back upriver. Or...was running late. Or...he came back, then went away again. Any of these was possible. "So what did you do?"

"It got dark," she said. "I didn't know whether he'd be able to see me up there. Or hear me, because it's a long way down the wall and the river's loud. I thought maybe I should climb down to where we got onto the wall from the river, but then I'd just be hanging there, in the dark, and cold. So...So I climbed up the shaft and came back here. I hope that was okay, Nolan—I didn't know what else to do."

"You did exactly the right thing," I said. "We'd have started to worry soon if we didn't hear anything from you."

I was aware of Molly turning from the ball and walking back up the passage to the main room. I looked at Pierre and gestured with my head for him to go after her.

"But *now* what?" Feather said.

"Now...look, it's eight o'clock. I don't know what happened to

Dylan. Maybe he freaked out because we were gone a long time, and went to get help. And because of the weather, he got stuck somewhere."

"Do you think?"

"Probably. Either way, there's nothing we can do tonight. There's no point you spending the night hanging out of the opening staring into the dark. So we sit tight, and try again tomorrow morning, okay?"

"Okay," she mumbled. She sounded strung out and very tired.

"I'll be back in a minute," I said.

I trotted up to the main room. Molly had returned to sitting in the same way she had been earlier, though now she wasn't looking down the main passage. She was looking at the floor.

"You okay?"

She didn't respond. I grabbed the remaining chunk of sandwich and half bottle of water from my pile and went down the passage again. I dropped to my knees close up to the wall and stuck my hand through the small gap there.

"Feather—can you see my hand?"

"Where? Oh, yes, okay."

"Can you get to it?"

I heard her moving down to the floor and shuffling forward, wedging herself into the narrow space between the far side of the ball and the wall and floor. Then the sound of a grunt as she stretched toward me. A light touch, when her fingertips brushed mine.

I pulled my hand back, transferred the sandwich to it and stuck it back through the gap. "Take this."

"Nolan...I can't."

"Yeah, you can. We have other stuff in here, you don't. And you've climbed down and back up the shaft. Just take it."

After a few seconds I felt the sandwich go. I did the same with the water.

"Thank you," she said. Her voice was quiet.

I stood up. Ken was looking meaningfully at me, and I nodded. Gemma caught the look.

"I'll hang here awhile," she said.

We left her there talking to Feather and walked halfway back up the passage together.

"This is not good," Ken said.

"Dylan wouldn't just have bugged out, would he?"

"No. He's a dickhead, not an arsehole."

I'd worked with Ken long enough to understand the distinction. And I agreed with his take. "So what?"

"Fuck knows. The river's pretty bumpy down there. And probably a lot worse now if there's a storm. So maybe it's beached somewhere downriver. We're just going to have to hope he comes back tomorrow morning and waits."

I felt something turn over in my stomach. A liquid sensation. Not a repercussion of drinking water from the pool, but a beat of low, intense uncertainty. A recognition that it wouldn't take much for our situation to morph from *not great* to *really very bad indeed*.

I stomped down on the thought. "What's plan B?"

"The only one I've got is..."

"Asking her to swim it?"

"Yeah. Which is a big ask. But she could get down to that beach we camped on, and wait. Scream her head off at the next boat to come down the river. And yes, we have no way of telling how long that could take. But unless you've got something smarter up your billowy sleeve..."

"Yeah, right. You're the brains of this operation."

"That's what worries me. Because I have my limitations, and there's a danger this situation is about to get shitty, Nolan."

He looked at me. "As in, not very good *at all*."

CHAPTER

26

I don't know what time it was when I woke. I'd finally remembered to power down my phone and didn't want to turn it back on for fear of waking someone. I lay on my back for a while in the darkness, remembering a story I'd heard once about a guy who'd been on one of the moon missions and had a dream while he was there. In it he was driving the moon buggy and started to realize he could see something coming toward him. Gradually he understood that it was another buggy. He kept watching, warily, and eventually he realized that the guy driving it . . . was him.

I remembered hearing this story and thinking how mind-melting it must have been to undergo that dream, and wake up and think . . . *Ah, okay, it was just a dream.* But then to remember moments later: *Wait, Christ—I'm on the* moon.

Waking to find myself trapped inside a prehistoric artifact created by a culture (or cultures) unknown—our only hope of escape being a South African raft captain, whereabouts also currently uncertain . . . it felt kind of the same.

We'd stayed up a couple more hours after Feather's return. Talking about this and that, speculating about the purpose of what we'd found, remembering previous expeditions. Ken spent a while reminiscing in lavish detail about some of his most memorable cheeseburgers, until everyone turned and looked at him. We each took half an hour sitting down by the stone ball, talking with Feather on the other side.

It was during my stint that she fell asleep, or at least stopped responding. I'd like to think it's because I have a nice voice and a soothing, reassuring manner. It could be that I'm unbelievably dull.

By then everyone else was beat. And hungry and thirsty. It was agreed that sleeping was the obvious way of trying to ignore those facts, and of bringing on tomorrow more quickly.

We each took our own backpack for a pillow and stretched out in a patch of space in the main room. You might think it'd take a while to get to sleep in such circumstances. Not for me. It was dark, and very quiet. I was exhausted. And there wasn't anything else that could be done. I am a shambles of a human being in many ways, shackled with a personality that's at best a rough first draft, but I've always been able to ignore problems over which I presently have no control. Which admittedly often includes "life in general."

After subsequently waking and lying there for twenty minutes, I became aware of a quiet sound off to my right. I'd made a guess at who it might be before I heard the steady cadence of her breathing—a rhythm interrupted every now and then by a quiet hitching sound as she started to hyperventilate and had to bring it under control again.

I sat up. Patted my hand around until I found the small lanyard light I'd placed nearby. Crawled over, taking my time and not trying to be super quiet, to give Molly a chance to realize I was coming her way. When I was up close I reached out in the darkness and by chance found her hand.

"Come with me," I whispered.

I guided her by the shoulder toward where I thought the doorway would be, and missed by only a few yards. When we were in the passage I walked for thirty feet or so before turning on the light, keeping it low and in front.

Molly blinked and squinted against the glow. "What are you doing? Why are we here?"

She'd kept her voice low, and I did, too. "Want to show you something."

"I don't want to go up there."

"You should at least see," I said.

"Really, Nolan. I don't want to."

"Well, I'm going. If you want to go back and sit there fretting in the dark, be my guest."

I started walking again. After a few seconds, she followed.

I led her along to the last doorway on the left, and then into the narrower passage beyond. "Careful," I said, when I knew we must be getting close.

I turned the light to the floor and stopped walking when I saw it abruptly disappear. Then raised the light so it shone across the pool.

She looked out over the water. With only this single, weaker light, it looked less clear than earlier. And without being able to see the sides, like nothing more than a pool of standing water in a cave, of a type she'd doubtless encountered any number of times as a kid on road trips with Californian parents. She gazed out at it nonetheless.

"And that other stuff—it's at the far end?"

"Yeah."

She reached down to pull her T-shirt over her head.

"Excuse me?" I said.

She undid her jeans and pushed them down, too. "I'm not trying to sleep in wet clothes afterward."

"Okay then."

"I am wearing underwear. You'll cope."

I stood there dithering, wondering whether to do the same. It'd taken a long while for my clothes to dry off after the last time. By the time I'd decided, she'd already launched herself off the edge and into the pool, in a practiced shallow dive.

I transferred everything of importance to my shirt pocket and let myself gently down off the edge, still fully clothed, feeling like her granddad.

"Did you notice every one of these is different?"

We'd walked around the spheres. She agreed that each looked like it was a different type of metal or mineral. She was now standing at the rock in the middle and talking about the pictograms carved on its top surface.

I joined her. She was right. It didn't leap out at you because each of the composite forms was somewhat complex, a combination of between four and six individual symbols. At a guess I'd say there were thirty or forty of these component images. Some simple geometric signs, others that looked like a sheaf of wheat, or an oval with six tiny lines coming out of it—a stylized sun, or perhaps a sacred bug or something, as I'd speculated last time I was here. The human mind seeks patterns, so when you look at the surface you tend to see uniformity—the repetition of the constituent symbols. It took a little longer to appreciate there was uniqueness within the bigger picture. Each of the hundred icons was different.

"Huh."

"There's a smear on it."

A small brown smudge across the top. "Gemma was dripping blood from that scrape on her arm," I said.

"So what is this thing?"

"I don't know. A dictionary. A galactic genesis myth. A grain inventory. Somebody with tenure will work it out."

"Assuming anybody else ever sees it."

Even though I'd thought this myself earlier, I gently trod on the idea. "Which they will, Molly. Obviously."

"Nolan—how are we going to get out of here?"

"Tomorrow morning Feather will go look for Dylan again. If he's not there . . . I talked to her about the idea of climbing down and waiting there all day, or maybe swimming downriver. She's willing to do either."

"But where the hell did Dylan *go?*"

She sounded petulant, betrayed, and young. That and the fact she was standing there in wet underwear made her seem very unlike Molly Mom.

"He went to organize more food. It took longer than expected. In addition, possibly, the raft was too hard to work by himself in more hectic waters. He will, maybe even as we speak, be resolving one or both of those problems. He'll be there bright and early tomorrow morning, and our situation will rapidly start to improve."

She looked up at me hopefully. "You think so?"

"You met the guy, Moll. He has a great big ego, and with that comes pride. He's not just going to bail."

"I hope you're right."

"Molly—what's the deal here? I mean, you don't have to tell me. But you can if you want."

She looked away, at the symbols. Then pushed back from the stone and wandered to the edge of the platform. She sat down, pulled her knees up, and wrapped her arms around them.

I came and sat cross-legged a few feet away. Took out a cigarette. Eleven left now. I frugally lit up with a match from the book I'd found, reasoning that it was a good idea to conserve my lighter as much as possible. As I did so I noticed the book was from a bar in Santa Monica—the one Kristy and I had finished up in, the night I bailed from the movie industry, in fact. I know the owner a little and he's a bad-tempered asshole, prone to fight any form of opposition—and signs of "progress" in particular—with both fists. Hence still printing his own matchbooks, years after you were last allowed to smoke in a bar in LA. I realized there were probably drinkers in their twenties now who simply didn't understand why bars had match-books. It'd be like having menus in places that had never sold food. We live among fossils and rock paintings and ancient signs, wherever we are.

I sat smoking for a while, Molly looking out at the water.

"You know…" she said eventually, "I don't even *know*. I mean, I know what it's supposed to be. The issue. I've been over it. With people whose job it is to know how to get to the other side of that kind of thing. And I have. And it's not like it's so terrible. It's really, really not. It's barely anything. And nothing lurid. This is not NSFW material."

"That's a relief. Not a Bad Uncle story, then."

"My uncle's awesome," she said. "He taught me to surf. But actually...he is kind of relevant. Though he doesn't know it. Look, bottom line, there was this night. When I was a kid. I was seven years old. And I woke up."

She stopped. Breathed in, breathed out.

And then she told me.

CHAPTER
27

ormally I'd just go back to sleep," she went on. "I was good like that. My brothers had already worn out the needing-to-be-nursed-back-to-sleep routine. By the time I came along my parents were done with that crap. On this night I'm talking about, I tried, but it didn't feel right. Something about the house, about the world...it *just didn't feel right*.

"So I got out of bed. I figured I'd go to my parents, get one of them to come tuck me in. Though when I was on my feet I remembered it would have to be Mom, because Dad was away in San Francisco. Which was fine—she was better at it anyway. So I left my room and padded along the corridor and into their room. Went up to her side of the bed. I got real close to it before I realized...she wasn't there.

"The bed was mussed up—my dad's a bear for remaking the thing every day, and I'm the same now. Takes two minutes, and it's so much nicer. But when he was away, my mother didn't bother. So I couldn't tell whether she'd been in bed and gotten up, or hadn't made it there yet. She had a little clock radio that my brothers and I bought her for Christmas. It said it was 1:20 a.m. Which was very late. I knew sometimes she'd stay up when Dad was away, though, watching a movie. So maybe that was it. But it meant going downstairs to get her. I kind of didn't want to do that. I was awake enough now that the house felt big and dark and weird. And awake enough that I'd remembered my brothers weren't at home, either. One was at a birthday sleepover, the other on a seventh-grade trip to Yosemite. So it was just me and Mom. Earlier, at dinner, that seemed cool, and we'd joked about being girls home alone. But now...I really wanted her to be there in her bed. I didn't want to have to go find her by myself in the dark. But I also knew I wouldn't be able to get back to sleep now without being tucked in. You know how it is when you're a kid. Things like that become nonnegotiable. So...I went downstairs.

"They've downsized now, but our house back then was a big place. And very quiet. I went down the stairs anyway. There was a little light to see by because they always left a couple small lamps on. I went to the living room. She wasn't there. I went to the kitchen. She wasn't there. And then I thought, duh, she'll be in the family room, watching TV. But she wasn't."

She looked at me. "She wasn't anywhere."

"You mean...What do you mean?"

"She wasn't in the house. At all. I looked in every room. She wasn't there. I even looked in the garage, though I found it pretty scary even in the daytime. She wasn't there, either. She wasn't anywhere. I was alone in the house."

"Christ. So...what did you do?"

"What could I do? I freaked the hell out. But very quietly. I checked every room again. Upstairs and down. I started crying. I kept searching, getting more and more scared. I tried to work out what I'd done wrong. I finally wound up sitting halfway up the stairs, curled in a little ball. Knowing I was alone now, and she was never coming back. That none of them were.

"Dad had gone first. Then my brothers—they were part of it, too. Part of some plan they'd kept secret from me. Then tonight, my mom had left. What I'd thought had been my family was not. They had all gone. And so I sat and cried as quietly as I could so nothing would hear and come get me, feeling like I was in a dark and lonely cave, wondering what was going to happen. Because slowly I realized maybe they hadn't abandoned me after all, but something had come and gotten them—or gotten my mom, at least. A monster in the dark. Who'd taken her, and sooner or later would come back for me. After a while I even thought I could hear it. Smell it. Coming closer. And closer. Hidden in the darkness. Standing over me."

She hugged her arms more tightly around her knees. "And then . . . I heard a sound outside the house and the door unlocked and my mom walked right in. I didn't move. *Couldn't* move. I stared down at her. She didn't look like my mom anymore. Because she hadn't *been there*, you know? That world was dead and gone to me now. That world and those people. This was something that just *looked* the way my mom used to. Some stranger, letting herself into the house.

"*Maybe this was even the creature*, I thought, *in disguise*.

"But then she saw me sitting there and came running up the stairs and I said I thought she'd gone forever and she hugged me so tight it hurt and said she'd never ever leave me and then made me warm milk and took me to my room and tucked me in and slept there in bed with me, right through the night."

"Where had she been?"

"My uncle—he's my dad's brother—lived ten miles away up the coast. He'd gotten home late, and only when his ride had driven away did he realize he'd locked himself out. My mother didn't have to explicitly explain that he was drunk. Didn't happen all the time, but, well, it did once in a while. We kids were used to it. He was fun when he was drunk. And responsible enough to stay away from his car. So he walked back down to the highway and found a public phone and she drove up there with spare keys to his house, and came back. She considered waking me before she went, thought she could get away with it, decided not to. She called it wrong. That's all."

"Christ, Moll. I'm sorry."

"For what? I survived a nonevent."

"It evidently doesn't feel that way."

She smiled. "And that's what therapy boils down to in the end, right? Plus . . . there's a little more. A few days later it was all but forgotten. Mom and I agreed next morning the rest of the family didn't need to hear about what happened, because my brothers would make fun of me for getting upset and thinking I'd been abandoned. They could be assholes about that kind of stuff, call me a baby, you know. And they were home now, my dad was back, and the universe had been restored to its proper functioning, so whatever.

"And so I'm out playing in the yard on this particular evening, and I hear Mom and Dad chatting in the kitchen while they're fixing dinner, those sounds that make you feel comfortable and at home and as if everything is good and simple and always will be. And Dad is telling her how he met Uncle Pete's new boyfriend in the city and they all had a few after-dinner drinks together, and he seems really nice, and Mom said that's great, Pete deserves to be with a kind person for once, and eventually the conversation moved on to other things. And I stopped playing, and sat there. And thought for a while. And then I started playing again, and life rolled on."

She turned her head and looked at me, eyebrow raised.

"I don't get it."

She waited.

"The fact he was gay?"

"God, no. That was a known thing. Uncle Pete was stridently homosexual, always had been. Nobody ever tried to hide it or acted like it was a big deal."

"Okay, so?"

"My folks live in San Diego now. But I grew up in Santa Cruz."

"I know it well. I'm from Berkeley."

"Right. And so you'll also know that if you live in the Bay Area there is one place—and one place only—that you'll hear referred to as 'the city.'"

It didn't take long for me to get it. "Your dad was talking about his recent business trip to San Francisco."

"Only time he went to the city overnight that year."

"And if your uncle was up there with his new guy, it seemed unlikely to you that your mother could simultaneously be letting him into his own house, alone, sixty miles away."

"Yes."

"Huh. So?"

"I don't know. I never found out. I didn't ask, obviously. But I thought back and I realized it had been her idea not to mention her being out to the rest of the family. She'd been subtle, and loving—she knew how my brothers made fun of me for every little thing—but still, it was her idea and she was unusually firm about it. I don't know where she was that night. But she went out, and I don't think it was just for a moonlit drive, because she could have said so. She went to see someone."

"Who?"

"I don't know."

"Do you have a theory?"

"A few months later I started to overhear arguments between my parents, late and loud and long, and they were snippy with each other for a year or two, and my dad seemed very distant sometimes, unhappy, distracted. But eventually that passed. They're still together now and they're super happy with each other and so whatever happened during that period, they held their course and navigated those rough seas and came out the other side stronger. Which is awesome. But from then on..."

She shrugged.

"You knew something your dad didn't," I said. "Or your brothers. And you also knew your uncle had been used as a fake alibi, but couldn't tell him even though you loved him. Plus your mom's suddenly a lot more complex than you realized, and you're the only other woman in the household, so you wonder if *you* are, too. Goodbye, simple world—hello, secrets and lies."

"You're not bad at this," Molly said. "Right. Precisely that. All of which has been discussed with strangers who charge a hundred and fifty bucks an hour, and with all of which I have made my peace. And, come on, Christ, all that oversharing boils down to: Girl gets left alone in a dark house, is subsequently wary of dark places? That's embarrassingly direct."

"As my grandmother used to say, human beings are very basic cakes. We just have a lot of fancy icing on top."

"She really said that?"

"No. She was a nice woman but she couldn't bake for shit. I just made it up."

"Ha. But the truth is that the event itself was really not that big a deal."

"And so what is?"

"The other things. That other information. Learning that there's always something going on that you don't know about. And that people will lie to you, even if they love you. And that nobody can be trusted, no matter how much you love *them*. And also that sometimes you'll know in your heart that something's wrong about the world, like I did when I first woke up that night. And you know what? You'll be right."

She looked me full in the eyes. "I'm right now, too, Nolan. About this place. There's something very not-okay about it. Something bad. I wish I'd never spotted the way up into that shaft. I wish we'd never found this."

I held her gaze and I tried to come up with the words to tell her no, it was okay, it'd all be fine.

But I couldn't.

We made our way back across the pool. As I stood on the other side waiting while Molly dressed in her nice dry clothes—wishing I'd had the sense to do the same—I noticed again that the water in the pool wasn't as clear as I'd thought. And then that, around the edges, there were tiny little aggregations of what looked like algae.

I realized either I hadn't spotted these before, or that we'd changed things, somehow polluted the water, compromised this place, by bringing in stuff from the outside world.

By being here.

CHAPTER
28

I wasn't especially hungry when I woke the next morning to find our area already dimly lit by a flashlight on the ground. I was cold—my clothes were still a little damp from the time in the pool—and I was sure as hell thirsty. It has long been my practice upon rising to imbibe a quantity of coffee equal to (or greater than) the volume of my own body. Ken operates a similar policy. I would, in fact, pity the fool who tried to out-caffeine us before noon, if we ever teamed up and went pro. Realizing there was no coffee was therefore an ominous start to the day.

I stood, creaking, rolling my shoulders to try to get the kinks out. The spasm in my back from Gemma's slide down the canyon wall had faded to a dull ache. I got a measure of my thirst and informed it that what it was about to receive was all there was for now, and to be grateful. I took a sip and sluiced it slowly and thoroughly around my mouth before swallowing. I saw Ken do the same, then look dubiously at the scant third of a bottle that remained.

"Going to need a top-up trip to the pool before long," he said.

"I don't know whether that's still a good idea."

I told him what I'd noticed there in the night, though not about what Molly and I had discussed. She got up and stretched as I was updating him, and strode off by herself down the main passage toward the stone ball. I hoped this meant the talk might have helped, a little.

Ken shrugged. "If it was there last night, then it was there when we found the place," he said. "Nothing grows that quickly. Except bamboo. Or a bar bill in Vegas with an all-female crew. Seriously. I'm still paying that one off. Plus, if you'd seen some of the shit I've eaten over the years, then you'd know a few single-celled organisms don't stand a chance of fucking me up. And your gut's been all right, hasn't it?"

"Fine."

"Well then."

"On that subject," Gemma said. We turned to find her standing with unusual diffidence a few feet away.

"What?"

"I was wondering. Should anybody require to divest themselves of waste products of the digestive process, quite soon, what's the protocol? I'm...asking for a friend."

"Eh?" Ken said.

"Pick a room," I said. "And we'll designate it the latrine. The archeologists will hate us but it'll limit site damage. And, you know, fuck 'em. They're not here."

"Roger that," she said, and set off toward one of the corridors with her backpack.

"Oh," Ken said after a moment. "That's what she meant."

"Yeah. And it makes me realize we're already dehydrated. I haven't personally divested myself of even liquid by-products for a long time now."

"Me neither. You really think we ought to avoid the pool?"

"I'm not drinking it again unless things get desperate. In terms of water loss, the absolute last thing you want is explosive diarrhea."

"I do enjoy our chats, Nolan. Always have."

Molly came running back into the room. "Guys," she said. "Feather's gone."

"Feather?"

It was the fifth time Ken had called. I'd tried multiple times, too. And Molly, and Pierre.

"So where the hell is she?"

"Maybe she got an early start on going back down the shaft," Molly said. "It's seven thirty. It will have been light for an hour or two out there."

"She wouldn't have gone without telling us. Would she?"

"Maybe she tried, and we were all asleep."

"Doubt it," Pierre said. "I've been awake since four."

"Seriously?"

He looked embarrassed. "I thought I heard something, like a thud. A couple of times. Just bad dreams. But then I couldn't get back to sleep."

"Or she got confused about the time?"

"She wears a watch," Molly said. "She showed it to me."

"Maybe she's exploring," Pierre said. "Gone to the canyon wall to see if she could dislodge those rocks. Or to check if we missed anything in the side corridors. We never actually got to the ends of those, right? Could be they're super long and she hasn't heard us calling."

I thought about it. "I could buy the idea of going back to the canyon wall. Not the side corridors. Would you? By yourself?"

"If I had to."

"But if you didn't? With a little flashlight? And if you didn't know how long the batteries would last?"

"Probably not."

"She has her phone as a backup," Ken said.

"No, she doesn't," Molly said. "It's in her backpack. Which is with us."

"Either way," I said, "I find it hard to believe. But if she went to the end wall, it's a straight shot down that passage. She would have heard us calling, and called back."

"So what, then?" Molly said. She was scratching her arm, back and forth, in what looked like a nervous reaction.

I called out Feather's name one more time, very loud. Everybody listened. Nothing came back.

"Who was the last person to talk to her?" Molly asked.

"Me. She fell asleep," I answered.

"How do you know?"

"She stopped responding."

Molly looked at me.

"What? What the hell else could have happened to her?"

She shrugged.

"No, seriously, Moll. Nobody else knows this place even *exists*. What the hell are you suggesting?"

"Easy, Nolan," Ken said.

I took a deep breath. I hadn't even realized how I was sounding. "Okay, yeah. Sorry."

Molly shook her head and smiled to show it didn't matter. But it kind of did. Not to her, but to me. At that moment Gemma came walking down the passage. We all turned to look at her, wondering how to describe the situation.

"What?" she said. "Oh, for God's sake. Jesus. Yes, I just took a crap, okay? Women crap, too. Get over it."

"Feather's disappeared," Molly said.

"Oh."

Back in the main room we appeared to reach a universal unspoken agreement to assume the best. Pierre speculated about whether Feather would go with Dylan to get help, or send him off and come back to reassure us it was in hand. The consensus was she'd likely do the latter. And that if she'd left *really* early, hopefully there wouldn't be too long left to wait. We discussed this cheerfully, in quiet, confident voices. Everything was cool. Nobody was starting to panic. Not a bit.

Most took a bite of what remained of their sandwich. Ken offered me some of his, but I shook my head. "I almost never eat before lunchtime, so I won't miss it. Save it for later."

There was a sudden tiny but sharp point of pain on my left arm, and I swung my hand and slapped. When I lifted it there was a little splotch of blood. "Mosquito."

"Hell is a mosquito doing here?"

"They're everywhere, dude."

"No, but seriously. What's it doing here? Until yesterday there was fuck-all here for it to eat."

"Could have come up the same shaft as us. Maybe on our clothes. Or there's a tiny gap somewhere."

"Gap to *where*, Nolan? There's at least a quarter mile of rock in every direction."

"Ken, I don't know. It's dead now anyway."

"I saw a bug," Pierre said. "In the night. I was lying awake and after a while I wanted to know what time it was so I turned on my phone. There was a bug on the screen."

"A mosquito?"

"No. Little buggy thing."

I looked at Gemma. "You're smart. What do bugs eat?"

"I don't know. Plants. Smaller bugs. Bug food."

Ken was looking at me. "What's on your mind?"

"I'm not sure," I said, scratching the back of my neck. "But. Yesterday afternoon Pierre showed me a room up that passage over there. It smells bad. I mean, really rank."

"Sorry to have missed it."

"We got pulled away because you called when Feather arrived back. But thinking about it—what makes a room smell like that?"

"Like what?"

"Dry and fusty but with a kick to it, a kind of meaty undertone."

"Sounds like half the Merlots I've ever drunk."

"It's an organic smell, is my point. I just realized—maybe it's something rotting. Or something that rotted a very long time ago, and the smell hasn't had a chance to escape. Could just be some plants. Or *maybe* . . . a small animal."

"And you're speculating that if it's animal, then in order for it to die there, it had to get in from the outside somehow."

"That is precisely my thinking. And I don't see an animal climbing all the way up that shaft like we did."

"Could it be something that got in here through that opening in the wall that's now bricked up? How long do smells last in confined conditions?"

"I have no idea. But Kincaid talked about a bad-smelling room. And that's a hundred years ago. It can't have lasted *that* long. And he talked about the smell being so bad, and the room so dark, that they didn't explore it further."

"And you're hoping there's some shaft or tunnel in the back and once in a while a coyote or something falls down it, and we might be able to get out that way?"

"I don't have anything else. Do you?"

CHAPTER

29

We left Pierre and Gemma with our phones and with instructions to come running if Feather reappeared, took the biggest flashlight, and headed up the passage.

"Whoa," Molly said as we entered the room. "You're right. That's skanky."

"I kinda like it," Ken said.

"That's because you're a disturbing human being with no redeeming features."

"There's some truth in that."

We walked in together, Molly in the middle, directing the light. The room was reminiscent of the one with the end wall covered in symbols, in that it had been cut as a precise oblong, right angles between floor and walls and ceiling. These walls were bare, however.

We advanced slowly, taking time to try to become accustomed to the odor. As I'd noted the day before, it didn't start strong, which made the degree of its unpleasantness all the more surprising. It remained low, insidious, irrevocable, but got more intense as we progressed into the room. Breathing through your mouth helped a little, though not enough. After a while it seemed to coat your tongue.

"I'm ready to bail on this," I said.

"Oh yes. Check this out before we go, though," Molly said. Her voice was muffled because she was holding her hand over her nose and mouth. She lowered the beam of the light so that it shone on the floor.

"What?"

She moved the beam back in an arc so it illuminated the patch we'd just walked over. "Compare and contrast."

The floor ahead was darker in color than the portion behind. The demarcation was uneven, like a tide mark. As we walked farther the effect intensified. At first it was a faint stain. Slowly it began to thicken until you couldn't see the rock through it anymore. The color distribution was uneven, varying from dark gray to nearly pitch-black.

I squatted down and got up close, wet my finger and ran it over the surface. "It's smooth," I said. "And very hard. Like it's been baked onto the rock."

"Is that where the smell's coming from?"

"I'm not sure. It could be." I smelled the finger I'd run over it. "Actually, yes. I think so."

"That's not great news," Ken said.

"Why?" Molly asked.

"Couple of mummified rats, maybe we're onto something. But if it's some nasty fossil fuel gunk that's seeped out of the rock over the years and dried out, we're no better off."

"We don't know for sure that's what it is," I said. "Let's keep looking."

We moved on, taking a diagonal course toward the right wall. The stuff on the floor continued to become thicker. The gray patches disappeared and it became unrelenting black, almost glassy.

"Look at the walls," Ken said.

Molly redirected the light. There was discoloration there, too, but a different kind. More like smoke damage, deeply ingrained soot from an intense flame. It was also on the ceiling.

"Sorry, Nolan," Ken said. "But I think we're on a loser. Something burned up in here a long time ago. Whatever it burned or melted or baked onto the floor is what's causing that smell, I reckon."

It felt strange to be standing in a place where at some point—

168

hundreds or thousands of years ago—there had been an intense fire and great heat. That was gone now, along with any hope of understanding what had caused it. All that remained was an unpleasant olfactory echo. And us, stuck, with no way out.

"Yeah," I said. "I think you're right."

He and I waited together as Molly wandered farther into the room, taking the source of light with her. I had a headache, and it was getting worse. My stomach made a sudden and protracted growl.

"Eat some of that sandwich when we get back," Ken said.

"I will. But when that's gone, we've got a few peanuts and a couple granola bars and that's the end of it."

"Nolan, this is not good. And you know what's weird about this place?"

"Seriously? How about 'everything'?"

"True. But also, apart from those spheres in the pool room, there's nothing here. It's totally bare. Not even any rocks lying on the ground. Completely empty."

"Maybe Kincaid and his crew took it all."

"Every single thing? That's pretty shitty archeological practice, even by the standards of the time. But my point is now this room's turned out to be a bust, I'm wondering whether our new goal should be finding something—*anything*—that we can use to bang against rock."

"Because...?"

"I don't know how else we're going to get out of here."

"You're kidding, right?"

"I'm not talking about hacking out a tunnel. I mean trying to make the gap around that big stone ball bigger. So that somebody slim, like Gemma, can get out."

"It's *rock*, Ken. If we had chisels and hammers and dynamite we could get somewhere. But banging a pebble against it is just going to be a waste of energy that we can't afford."

He opened his mouth, but closed it again. Nodded. "Yeah. I know. But...then what?"

More than anything else so far, the fact that Ken had been semi-seriously talking about trying to bang a hole in the passage around the ball made me realize how screwed we were. When you're in a bad situation there's always part of your mind that carries blithely on, assuming you merely haven't thought of The Thing yet—that there's some obvious solution you simply haven't fallen upon. *Sure, it looks bad right now,* this voice murmurs, comfortingly, *but it won't when you've come up with The Thing That Solves It All.*

But what if there's no Thing? What if the situation is actually as bad as it looks? Or worse?

"Shit, Ken," I said. "I'm sorry I got us into this."

"Don't be a twat. And look, I'm only being a producer and coming up with a plan B for the sake of it. Feather will come back. And the longer she's gone, the better."

"How do you figure that?"

"Because it implies she's hooked up with Dylan and gone with him to get help. Yesterday she was only gone a few hours, right? Because he wasn't there, and so she came back. If she's *not* back in a couple hours it's because it's all in hand and stuff's happening. Or that's what I'm telling myself."

"Is it working?"

"Fuck off. By the way—are you aware you keep scratching the back of your neck?"

"What?"

He pointed at my hand—and only then did I realize that yes, I was scratching there again. And had been for a while.

"You were doing it on your arm earlier, too. I've seen Molly scratching as well."

"I feel kinda itchy. Probably dried sweat."

"Except you've had two swims in that pool. In fact, you and Molly were the only ones who had one in the night, right? When the water looked cloudy, according to you. And now you and her are the people scratching like cats with fleas."

"What are you saying?"

"Just pointing out a correlation, mate."

I wasn't at all sure what he was getting at. My headache was getting steadily worse, and my mouth felt very dry.

"Hey, guys," Molly called. She sounded a long way away. "There's an opening back here."

CHAPTER

30

The room was deeper than I'd realized, and it was twenty yards before we got to Molly. The back wall hadn't been shaped and smoothed and right-angled like the others, and looked like a remnant of an originally natural space, a cavern deep underground. In the middle was an opening. It, too, looked natural, a crack in the rock, tapering sharply at the top and bottom and about two, three feet wide in the middle.

Molly shone the light directly into it, revealing a rough, slanting, and narrow passage beyond.

"Now we're talking," Ken said.

"Should we tell the others before we check it out?"

"No," I said. "We're here now. And we need someone holding the fort back there for when Feather gets back. If it looks like this is going a significant distance, someone can go fetch them. Bummer we didn't bring a headlamp, though."

Molly handed me the light. I stepped up into the "passage," which in reality—this became clear when you got into it—was a very ragged fissure. Despite the hundreds of thousands of man-hours spent chiseling and shaping nearby, it seemed like nobody had done anything to this part.

"It gets kind of tight up ahead," I said.

"What are you implying?" Ken asked.

"Nothing, you ass. Just I'm wondering why they never worked it, made it like the other passages."

"Is it possible it happened after this place was built? Earthquake damage?"

"Maybe. I'm not a geologist. But I'm thinking not, because the end wall was uneven, too. It's more as though this thing was already here when they built the rest of it, and they decided to preserve its natural state for some reason."

I moved along the fissure, carefully. The floor was very uneven and had cracks big enough to twist your ankle in. Once I was a few feet down Ken followed, with Molly at the back.

After a while the crack jagged to the left, and got narrower. Narrow enough, in fact, that we had to move sideways along it. And then stoop.

"Are we even sure this is going anywhere?" Molly's voice was tight. "By which I mean anywhere we want to be?"

After another twenty feet I stopped. The top of the crevice was getting lower and lower, though thankfully the smell had abated. "We're nearly going to have to crawl through this next part," I said. "If anybody wants to bail...this is probably the moment."

"Just keep going," Ken said.

I hung the light around my neck and lowered to a crouch. Took a deep breath. I don't have a particular problem with confined spaces, but this was very confined indeed. A low, insistent voice in the back of my mind wasn't happy, and was toying with the idea of panicking. If Molly managed to make it through this section, she was a hell of a lot braver than me. Assuming this wasn't merely the beginning of the end of the fissure, of course, the point where it dwindled to nothing. The light wasn't showing far enough to tell.

We kept going. I thought there was a slight upward trajectory, though not one that would make a difference. A matter of degrees. To get to the surface at this incline would take several hundred miles. I moved one foot forward, bracing against the walls to the side and above my head, then shifted the other foot after it. Repeat.

It was very slow and tiring, the space thick with the sound of our panting and grunts of exertion. The only upside was that we were now out of range of the smell from the room. The crevice smelled like dust, and was like being in a coffin made of rock.

We progressed like this for ten minutes. I was close to giving up but then there was space over my head again. Room to move my elbows, too.

This caught me by surprise and for another yard or so I continued to shuffle, crabbed down in a crouch. Then I straightened, cautiously.

"Are we there yet?" Ken's voice was muffled.

"I don't know. But you can stand up, at least."

"Thank Christ for that."

I held the light so he could see his way as he scrambled from the fissure, like an ungainly and bad-tempered champagne cork. He was red in the face and sweaty. Molly emerged a minute later with a little more grace but didn't look like she'd enjoyed the experience even a little bit.

"Okay," Ken said. "You may now turn and reveal the express elevator full of beer, which the temple-builders of antiquity thoughtfully installed for our convenience."

I turned and directed the light into the inky darkness.

We were in a long space, maybe fifteen feet wide. The sloping ceiling was a couple of yards above our heads. The floor was still uneven but looked like it had been given at least some attention to level it out a little. It was impossible to tell how far the cavern went, because the light wasn't strong enough to penetrate more than twenty feet.

The wall on the right was rough, natural. On the left it was smooth and flat—but it was hard to tell whether it had originally been that way. And within a moment of turning your attention to it, you didn't care.

"Fuck...me," Ken said.

This wall was covered in paintings.

They started almost immediately after the fissure widened into this bigger space. They were large, each a couple of feet tall, and rendered in a loose style. Some had been minimally shaded and filled in, but most were confined to simple flowing lines evoking shape and movement, like sketches.

I couldn't tell what the first was supposed to be, but the second looked a lot like a bird, or perhaps an insect, as it seemed to have more than two legs—though it was hard to be sure because of the degree of stylization.

Then there was something that looked like a condor or eagle, though the head was oddly shaped. The next was a rodent or other small mammal.

And they kept on going. There were lines in what looked like charcoal, others that were white, like a chalk. Completely protected from the elements and the sun, they were as bright and strong as the day they'd been put there.

I turned and redirected the light, slowly revealing a line of more paintings stretching into the darkness. If you'd come upon this in a cave in France or Germany you would have no doubt what you were seeing. The resemblance to the kind of work that had been discovered in the caves of Lascaux—paintings made nearly twenty thousand years ago—was striking and undeniable.

We stood staring at it for several minutes. I honestly didn't know what to say. Ken, naturally, did.

"Nolan, this is Neanderthal. And I mean that in a good way."

"Not Neanderthal. Upper Paleolithic. But it can't be. That era of Homo sapiens were never *in* North America, or barely. Certainly not the cave-painting kind."

"Says who?"

"Literally everyone. Even the woo-woo crowd doesn't go there. There's never been the slightest evidence."

"Well, not until we just found a huge great wall of Neolithic cave paintings."

"Kincaid never made it this far?" Molly said.

"No," I said. "They bailed at the beginning of the room that smells bad."

"This is *immense*," Ken said. "We are in new and uncharted territory, Nolan. The first white people ever to see this. Maybe the first people *since the stone age*. This rewrites the entire history of fucking everything. You know it does."

"Yeah," Molly said, her pretty, open face tilted back to look up at the pictures. "It's going to be a bummer if we end up dying without being able to tell anyone."

Ken and I turned to stare at her.

"Sorry," she muttered.

We progressed along the line of paintings, looking at each in turn. They got rougher and more hurried as the line progressed, as though this project hadn't been finished, or the artist or artists had run out of time. There were further birds, bison, a fish, something that looked like a big cat with long teeth, a spiderlike creature with legs that were wavy and all pointing in the same direction. Others were harder to identify. Maybe a wolf. A mammoth, possibly. Something like a species of antelope, but on its rear legs, the front ones much shorter than the back.

"Nolan," Molly said. "Check that one out."

At first glance it looked like another kind of deer, though much bulkier, again portrayed either up on hind legs or frozen in midleap. When I moved the light, however, I got what she was getting at. It clearly wasn't a deer, when you looked properly. It was bulky and powerful across the back. Its head was bulbous and very large.

"Looks like one of the things on that Newspaper Rock in Utah you were telling Gemma about."

"It does. Which makes this further proof of the idea of the Hopi braves making pilgrimages here. And also maybe that they'd been happening for...a really, *really* long time."

"And what's after it," Ken said. "What's that about?"

There was no picture to the right of the bear-like creature, at least not in the sense we'd become accustomed to. Instead there was a patch of black, ochre, and white handprints. Most were left hands, suggesting the painters were right-handed, but I saw one right hand, too.

"Humans," I said. "All the animals were illustrated. But when it came to humankind, they made handprints instead. Maybe like a signature. To say 'We're different. We're the animal that paints, instead of being painted. And we made this stuff, and this place.' The question is—how long ago?"

Lascaux has been dated to around 15,000 BC. There are other illustrated Paleolithic caves twice that old, however, and recent discoveries suggesting more basic Neanderthal decoration of underground locations as long as 170,000 years back.

"Except, there's a human," Ken said. "Huge one."

I was turning to shine the flashlight to see what he was talking about when the illumination it provided suddenly dimmed to a low, dirty yellow. And flickered.

And then went out.

FROM THE FILES OF NOLAN MOORE:

CAVE PAINTING FROM LASCAUX

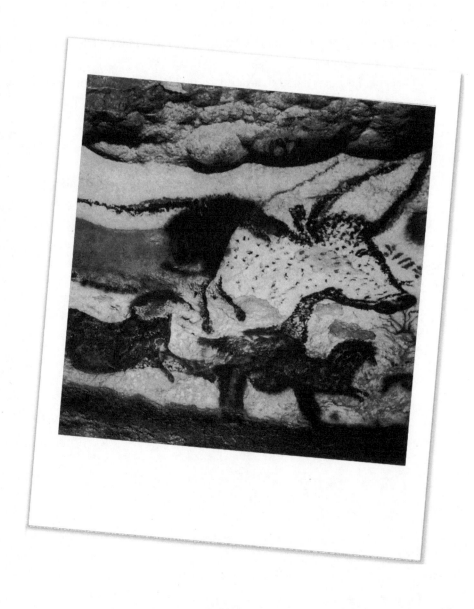

CHAPTER

31

I flipped the switch on the flashlight back and forth. All this achieved was another dim, dying flicker as the batteries gave their last. Then blackness again.

"Bollocks," Ken said.

"Anybody got another light?"

"Nope," Molly said. Her voice was flat.

I was waiting for my eyes to adjust, but realized this was dumb. These weren't low-light conditions. These were conditions of no light at all. No sunlight had fallen here, ever. None. Since the dawn of time. All my eyes could come up with was sparkles in the blackness as my brain tried to make sense and patterns from random retinal firings.

"Okay," I said. "Okay. This is . . . not great, but it could be worse."

"I'm looking forward to hearing how, Nolan."

"We know where we are, and how to get back."

"Fuck," Molly said, suddenly and very loudly. "Fuck fuck fuck fuck *fuck*."

I'd never heard her swear before. The words rebounded in the cavern and then it was very quiet again.

"It's all right, love," Ken said. "Nolan's right. All we've got to do is retrace our steps."

I reached out in the dark and found Molly's shoulder. It was shaking. "It's going to be fine, Moll."

She didn't say anything.

"Nolan," Ken said. "You're going at the front. Moll, stand behind him and grab hold of that ridiculous shirt. By the way, Nolan, have I ever mentioned that you look like someone playing Hamlet in amateur dramatics in that shirt? Or like a waiter in a really gay restaurant? In 1982?"

"Several times. You even emailed me to that effect once."

"Did I? I don't remember that."

"You may have been drunk. You misspelled your own name."

"I like the shirt," Molly said quietly.

"There you go," I said, relieved that our little double act seemed to have achieved its goal. Or what I assumed had been its goal—it's possible that Ken really had just wanted to be rude about my attire. "And either way it's what I'm wearing, so yes, Moll, grab the back of it."

"And don't be alarmed if you feel a hand on your shoulder," Ken told her. "For it shall be mine."

We got in a line and readied ourselves.

I steered us toward the side opposite the paintings, so we didn't mess them up by running our hands along them while following the wall. I walked slowly and steadily, knees bent, sweeping each foot out to tap the way with my heel and check for unevenness, lowering the front of the foot, then repeating with the other side. This mode of locomotion came to me without thinking, and it took a moment to remember where from. For my birthday one year Kristy got me a couple of months' private Tai Chi classes. I'm not sure why—I'd never expressed an interest—but I did kind of enjoy it. I didn't practice enough in between sessions to improve much, though it did change the way I moved. And here I was, a decade later, walking that Tai Chi walk, in a cavern, in the pitch dark, and not falling over or banging into anything, like a total stealth ninja.

I was just glad that Ken couldn't see me doing it.

It took ten minutes to get the length of the cavern. Ken swore quietly, twice, presumably having stubbed his toe. Molly said nothing but kept a firm grip on the back of my shirt. The wall finally started to bear in toward me and I used my left arm to keep myself at a consistent distance while flapping out with my right, trying to find the end wall. When I felt it under my fingers I stopped moving.

"Okay," I said. "Time to shuffle to the right and find that passage. Then the fun part starts."

"Christ," Molly muttered.

It took only a minute to find the fissure. I felt around the opening with my hands, then stepped up into it while crouching. I did this slowly and carefully but still managed to crack myself on the top of the head.

When I was properly inside I paused.

I hadn't enjoyed this part before. Having no light shouldn't make it worse. Not rationally, anyhow. I'd feel my way. Probably I'd end up scraping my elbows or knocking my head, but otherwise, what difference?

All the difference in the world. In the same way that anybody can walk along a single line of bricks, but if you build that single line up to a hundred feet high, then almost everyone will fall off within a few feet. It's no harder, for the body anyway. But for the brain . . . that's different. The panicking, consequence-aware mind will interfere with the body's innate ability to balance.

Pushing yourself into a confined space in pitch blackness is similar. The mind has a whole lot of things to say about the prospect, and none of them are "Bring it *on*."

I got myself into as tight a crouch as possible. I'd already reconciled myself to bangs and knocks—and tried to relax myself about the prospect. I did as I had when coming in the other direction, inching each foot forward, using hands and elbows to brace against the passage walls. I kept my eyes shut, against the retinas' attempts to interpret sensory deprivation in misleading ways. A couple of inches at a time.

I focused on the sensations in my fingers and feet, the feel of the rock, the smell of the dust. Every step was hard, but thank God we were going back rather than forward. I knew it would end. If you're patient, one step at a time will take you as far as you need to go. I submerged myself in the process, blanking out everything else.

But then I became aware of fast, uncontrolled panting behind me. "Moll? Are you okay?"

"I can't do this. I can't. I have to get out."

"That's what we're doing, love," Ken said. "Getting out. Just keep going."

"I can't. I can't do this. We're going to die down here and that's okay, but I can't die in this tunnel. I *can't die here*. I have to get out. I HAVE TO GET OUT."

I stopped trying to move forward. "Moll. Shout it again. Shout it one more time. Get it out."

"I . . ." But her voice cracked, and she started crying.

"Moll, come closer. Come right up behind me."

She shuffled up. I felt her forehead on my back. It was slick with sweat, and her entire body was trembling.

"You're wrong, Moll. We *are* going to get out of here."

"No, we're not!"

"We are. We can rely on Feather. She will get down to the river. Or she's there already. Dylan will be there, and he's a big macho bundle of testosterone who will get right on to turning himself into the hero of the day—which *involves saving us*. You met the guy. He's going to be all over that. No save, no hero, no parade. Don't you think?"

She mumbled something.

"And you know what else?" I said. "Even if he *has* bugged out or sunk the raft or gotten abducted by aliens, I trust Feather to swim it. I trust her to get to the beach and wait until she sees someone and shout her head off. Someone will come, Molly. Today or tomorrow or soon. Depend on it. All we have to do is keep our shit together until it happens. It will not be easy and it will not be fun, but we will do it. And step one of that is getting out of this crevice. Because it sucks in here. This is the place and point and time from which the rest of our lives start. There is a path from here. And so we need to move along it. We have to go on, and keep going. Okay?"

"Okay," she said, very quietly. Then, a little more strongly, "Okay. Sorry."

"Don't be sorry. You're amazing. In your position I would have exploded by now. Literally exploded. It could still happen. Which would be gross. I'm not enjoying this process either, and that's because it's *shit*. So let's go."

I started to shuffle forward. After a moment, I felt her follow, still holding on to my shirt.

We kept moving. Slow yard after slow yard.

And then somebody screamed.

CHAPTER

32

The sound wasn't loud or close but it was sudden and very penetrating. We froze in the blackness. A second later we heard it again.

"Fuck was that?" Ken said.

"Gemma," I said.

I told myself to keep it slow but it was impossible. Not when you'd heard something like that. And so I scraped and banged my way down the remaining yards of the confined section, hearing my breath start to become ragged and constrained, trying not to panic. Then I reached above my head and found we were back in the section where we had to go sideways but could straighten up. The smell was back, too.

"We're nearly there."

The scooting-sideways section was longer than I remembered but at least I could stand upright. I nearly turned my ankle on the cracked floor and had to keep forcing myself not to start running, recalling only at the last minute that we'd had to step up into the fissure—and so there'd be a drop into the room when we finally got there.

And there it was. "I'm out," I said.

My stomach rolled over, and I gagged. The smell was even stronger than I remembered. I took a couple of steps into the room, mouth firmly shut and hand over my nose, trying to picture the direction we'd need to aim in. Molly and Ken dropped down behind me.

"You worked out the angle?" he asked.

"I think so." I reached out with both arms and gathered one of them on each side.

We hurried together into the blackness. Within a couple of steps I noticed something was different, but Molly was faster to articulate it. "Are your feet sticking?"

"Yeah," Ken said. "That black stuff on the floor—it's tacky. It wasn't earlier."

"We must be walking on a different part," I said. "Whatever—just keep moving."

We missed the door but only by a couple of feet. We shuffled sideways until we found it. Then we were out into the corridor and could see a glimmer of light from the main room. I've never been so pleased to see something so basic.

I let go of the others and we ran.

When we made it into the main room Gemma and Pierre were together in the middle. Each had a lamp. They were standing back to back, panning beams of light around the space.

"What *happened*?"

Gemma was whirling in circles, slashing her light around, high and low. Molly walked toward her slowly, holding out her hands in a calming way. Given that ten minutes previously she'd been on the brink of losing it, I thought her powers of recovery were pretty remarkable.

Pierre hurried over to us. "Gemma. She..."

"I *felt something*!" she shouted. "Something *brushed against my leg*."

I looked at Pierre. He shrugged.

"Did you see what it was?"

"We were sitting in the dark," Pierre said. "I thought, only the two of us here, we should conserve power."

"Good thinking," I said. "Our light just died on us. In fact, you might want to turn yours off now."

"Oh, right." He did so, leaving Gemma's, which she was still waving around like a light saber. Molly placed her hand on her arm and said something to her quietly.

"So, we were sitting back to back," Pierre said. "On the floor in the middle of the room. Talking. We've been waiting there, except for going down to the stone ball and shouting out once in a while. Nothing. And you'd been kind of a long time and it was a little bit of a struggle for us to not, you know, freak out. Anyway, Gemma was telling me about other stuff she's written about, and suddenly she leaps up and she's screaming that she felt something brush against her in the dark."

"Did *you* feel anything? Or hear anything?"

He shook his head. "No, but we were facing opposite directions. Did you guys find anything in that room? Like rats or something? Could it be that?"

"No," I said. "We found stuff, but nothing living."

"So what the heck?"

I shook my head. "I have no idea." I left Ken with Pierre and went over to where Molly had now managed to calm Gemma down a little.

"I *felt* it," she said. "I *did*. Don't tell me I didn't. I felt something brush against my leg."

"You're sure it couldn't have been a breeze?" I said. "Or...and I'm only being thorough...it couldn't have been Pierre's hand? Accidentally? Or...otherwise?"

"No," she said indignantly. "We had our backs to each other. And he's not like that. And, come on, seriously, fuck off, Nolan. I'm not dumb. I know what I felt."

"Okay," I said. "So...Okay. Did you get a sense of how big it was? Or what kind of thing?"

"No. But it wasn't small. Definitely not a mouse or something. I was sitting..." She dropped down to the floor and sat, knees up, arms folded. "Like this. And it brushed against my shin. It had, like, fur. Not soft fur like a cat, but bristly. Like a dog. Or maybe a raccoon."

"I don't think there are raccoons in the desert."

"A coyote, then. How big are coyotes?"

"Not huge," Molly said. "When I was a kid we got them in our yard all the time. They're the size of a small to medium dog. Though skinnier. But I really do not see how a coyote is going to get all the way down here. Or up."

"No. There's no way," I said. "They're smart and they're decent jumpers but I just don't see it."

"Well, *something* did," Gemma insisted, standing up again. "Something's trapped in here with us, Nolan. Seriously. You have to believe me."

"I do. I just don't know what to do about it. We could go looking and maybe we will, because however it got in here could be a way out. But for now we have to chill about it. If it wanted to bite you, it would have."

"But what if it fetches more of them? Coyotes do that, don't they? Separate to explore, and then get the pack if one of them finds something worth attacking?"

"That is kind of their MO," Molly admitted.

"That's not what's happening here," I said. "I don't know what *is*, but I don't believe it's that."

Gemma shrugged angrily and walked off. Molly and I looked at each other.

"What do you think?"

"There's an eighty percent chance it was just a disorientation effect," I said. "From dehydration. They were sitting in total darkness. We know what that's like. You lose perspective. Feel things you're not really feeling."

"But that leaves a twenty percent chance."

"She seemed...very convinced."

"But what does that mean?"

"It means I'd really like Feather to come back with the news that everything's going to be okay. Soon."

"Or *now*," Molly said.

"Yeah. Now would be good."

We all sat together in the middle of the room, one of the smaller lights in the center. Everybody took a little of their sandwich. Ken held his out and looked at me until I took a bite. I took my time chewing it. The bread was dry and stale. The processed cheese was very hard. This left everyone with a single bite remaining. After that there would be a few nuts and half a granola bar each. And then, nothing.

My headache had settled into a sharp horizontal line between my temples. I saw some of the others screwing up their eyes, or rubbing them, and knew I wasn't the only one suffering.

Ken and I shared another cigarette. After that, there were only seven left.

Pierre said he wanted to go shout out for Feather again. Gemma and Molly went with him. Gemma lurched as she stood, as if dizzy. All walked slowly. Listlessly.

Ken and I looked at each other, and Ken nodded.

CHAPTER

33

When the others had gone down the main passage, we poured the remaining couple of inches of water from my bottle into Ken's, left it with the backpacks, and set off with one of the small lights. When we were halfway along the passage to the pool—and out of hearing range—Ken turned to me.

"So how are we going to do this?"

"I'll be the guinea pig," I said. "My stomach's tough."

"I doubt it's seen the action that mine has."

"I doubt anybody's has. But I mean specifically when it comes to bugs. Years ago Kristy and I went on a cheap vacation in Ensenada. Too cheap. She lost eight pounds and spent three days in the bathroom, even though the motel and the nearest restaurant—both owned by the same guy—provided bottles of mineral water for guests. They made a huge deal about it. Then one evening I caught him filling them up from the rusty tap around the back of the motel. That I had previously seen being licked by a goat."

"Arsehole. Not the goat. The guy."

"I thought so, too. So on the last morning we stole the ice bucket, two blankets, a lamp, and every towel we could find. I've still got the lamp. But my point is my stomach was fine, though Kristy and I were literally sharing the same bottles. So I'll have a few mouthfuls now. If there's a problem, it generally takes a couple hours to show. Hopefully Feather will be back by then. If not, I'll ask Gemma which room she used. And hope I don't end up crapping my actual brains out."

"There is that risk. But we've got to try it, right?"

"You saw how everyone's looking. Hunger is uncomfortable. But like I said yesterday, lack of water will fuck us up *fast*. And not only physically. This situation is bad enough without people losing it or starting to imagine things."

"You think that's what happened with Gemma?"

"I don't know. But it'll start happening to all of us if we don't find something to drink."

Ken nodded. "Speaking of Kristy, how are things?"

Ken and I became acquainted when I was still married, in the year after I said farewell to the movie business. Like many farewells it wasn't a clean break, and once in a while I got sucked back. One instance of this was an uncredited rewrite on a pilot for HBO, as a favor for a friend. Ken was being paid a consultancy fee to keep an eye on its young showrunner during preproduction, as a favor to a different friend, because the showrunner's sole claim to expertise was being related by marriage to a senior exec. Ken's role in the show was summarily curtailed after he punched out the showrunner one afternoon (and by God the entitled little prick deserved it), but by that point we'd started to grab an occasional beer together in the afternoon—and this eventually led to *The Anomaly Files*.

"There are no things," I said.

"At all?"

"Brief email exchange a couple months ago."

"Still a mystery to me," Ken said.

"You know what happened."

"I do. But you two were tight, Nolan. And it's not like it was that big a deal in the general scheme of the shambling chaos of human relationships. I'm surprised you couldn't bull through it, come out the other side battered and scarred but still on the same journey, all that New Age bollocks."

"Yeah, well, we didn't."

"Sorry. Shouldn't have brought it up. Still, makes a change from talking about diarrhea."

"True. By the way—do you really hate this shirt?"

"'Course not. I've got a semi on, just looking at you."

"How about you stop saying things, and we go find some water?"

"Right you are, squire."

I'd had enough of being the leader for one morning, so I gave the light to Ken and he led the way down the narrower side passage. I'd had enough of being in darkness, too. After twenty-four hours—and it felt like a hell of a lot longer—it had ceased to be surprising. For better or worse, I adapt fast. If a ceiling light goes out, then within a day or two I live in a world where there was never a lightbulb there in the first place, to the utter exasperation of the few people who've tried to live with me. This felt different, not least because in here darkness was not merely a state of affairs but a statement. Light meant being out in the world. Dark meant we were not. The darkness said we were trapped.

We got to the end of the passage and squatted down at the lip over the pool. Ken held up the light so I could fill the bottle, but I didn't even begin the process.

"Okay," Ken said. He sounded very tired. "What the *hell* is going on now?"

The water was no longer even remotely clear. Where you could see it at all, it was brown and murky and looked like the kind of pestilential crap you would be drinking at your peril.

But stranger still was the fact that two-thirds of the surface was now covered in some kind of algae. It was predominantly green, iridescent, like the back of a fly or pool of gasoline seen in low light, shot with blues and dark purples.

I took the light and lowered it down near the surface. The algae was a quarter of an inch thick in places. The water also had tiny motes within it, sparkling in the light.

Then, raising the lamp, I spotted something a long way into the pool, down on the bottom. One of the metal balls.

"And what the *fuck* is that doing there?"

I held the light up and out as far as I could, moving my arm in a slow semicircle. On the right-hand side, a little farther from us, I caught sight of another of the balls.

"This morning," Ken said. "Pierre. Didn't he say he'd woken in the night—thought he'd heard something?"

"Yeah. Some thuds. But how?"

"Those things were up on pedestals, those cubes. Like the huge stone ball in the main room. We've seen how that could drop, and what happens afterward. And there was kind of a slope on that platform down the other end, wasn't there?"

"Yep."

"So the cubes were lowered, and now all the balls are in the water."

"I assume. I'm disinclined to go check. I think you were right earlier—that itching was because Molly and I were in here last night. And whatever is now growing in there, we got some of it on our skin."

"Still itching?"

"No."

"Could you have touched something down at the end when the two of you were here, stood on something to trigger this?"

"I don't think so. Nothing that I'm aware of, anyway. We looked at the spheres, and that thing in the middle. But the water was already clouding. So I'm thinking the process had started before Moll and I even got in the water. Maybe when you, me, and Gemma found it in the afternoon."

"What process?"

I shook my head. There was no point in continually repeating that I didn't have an answer.

"Something's happening here, Nolan. And not only this. Do you really think we happened to come along a different path in that room that stinks? Or could it be that the black crap on the floor is melting, loosening up?"

"But how would that *work*? It's not like it's getting warmer. It's pretty cold in here."

"I don't know. But if I lift the hood of the Kenmobile and look at what's inside I don't know how any of that mechanical crap occurs, either. I don't have a clue how my phone works. Shit still happens on it. Endlessly."

"We need to stop doing stuff," I said. "Stop exploring, stop touching things. Something's happening. Something that wasn't happening before we got here. We need to stop making it worse."

"I think it's too late, mate."

"I hope you're wrong."

"For once, me too."

We took a last look out over the pool and then walked back to the main room. When we got there everyone was standing together in the middle.

Molly turned when she heard us coming. "Gemma's found something," she said. "It's . . . a little weird."

CHAPTER

34

Gemma was holding a phone. A white iPhone in a teal case, to be precise. I recognized it.

"So," she said. She sounded tired but fired up. "We went down the passage to the big ball and shouted. No response, still. So we came back in here and Molly was talking about how your lamp had run out. And it struck us maybe we should try to get a sense of exactly how much light we have left."

"Good idea. And?"

"We've got a lanyard and another of the small lights still working. One of the bigger ones. Only one headlamp, and it's really dim."

"That's it?"

"Yes. And there's no way of telling how much juice is left in any of the batteries. Could be a couple hours, could be ten minutes. There's the more powerful light on the camera, too, and Pierre reckons he's got like maybe two hours of batteries for that. Which is cool. But we're being thorough, so we decide to check how much power is left on everybody's phone, too. Which is...not much, unfortunately."

"Okay. But..."

"Then I remembered that we've actually got another phone here, if we need it. Feather's. I took it out of her backpack." She handed the iPhone to me. "Take a look."

"Isn't there a pass code?"

"Well, yeah. It's 6115."

"And you know that . . . how?"

"I'm observant. It's my job. Just look at it."

I pressed the button. A scant home screen of standard apps, arranged in no evident order. "Okay, so?"

"Notice anything?"

"Not many apps."

"Right. In fact, just the ones that come preinstalled on the phone. She hasn't added anything. Not even Facebook."

"Not everybody's on Facebook, Gemma."

"But over a billion people are. Especially women. And Feather? She's totally the type. She's going to be all over liking pictures of her friends' spawn and wishing people love and light on a daily basis. Trust me."

"So she does it on a computer instead of her phone."

"Maybe. But now check the photos."

The Photo app was on the top row of the home screen. I clicked on the most recent picture, feeling like an intruder. It was a not-great shot of everyone getting ready to board the raft yesterday morning. "So?"

"Scroll back."

I rolled up through the pictures, going back in time. There were a few more of the group in various locales, some shots of the canyon, the river, the raft. Typical *this is what I'm doing and seeing* shots from someone basically on vacation. Then the one of her and me posing near the trailhead, and finally the picture of her husband and kid she'd shown us.

"I don't get it, Gemma."

"I only looked at her photos because the Facebook thing intrigued me. Like you say, there's no actual law that people have to be on social media, or have the apps on their phone. But it seemed weird to me. So I snooped. And the first one on there, well, you've seen it."

"Yes. I've seen it before. She showed it to Molly and me. So what?"

"Okay, two things. Apart from trip photos and that one of you and her, that's the only picture."

"So it's a new phone, Gemma. And that's the first picture she took because she wants her family with her at all times. That's the least surprising thing I've ever seen. It's how moms roll. And that's also maybe why there's not a bunch of other apps. Either she didn't have time or it's her first smartphone—or whatever, and who cares?"

"Look at the picture properly."

I tapped and it filled the screen. I saw what I'd seen before. A blandly good-looking guy with a hipster beard, laughing with a kid. "Just spell it out, Gemma."

"Doesn't it look kind of posed?"

"Of course they posed."

"But don't their clothes look very well matched?"

"Well...kinda."

"And aren't they unusually well lit?"

I inspected the photo more closely. It had been taken in late afternoon, and you could tell where the sun had been in the sky from the long shadows. But yes, it seemed like there'd been a second light source, too, because there were no hard shadows on the subjects' faces.

"So she got lucky. Or used fill-in flash."

"Judging by how crooked all her other shots are, I'm not sure she's at the fill-in-flash level, Nolan."

"Someone else took it, then."

"Christ, have it your way. But here's the real thing. I know that guy."

"You know Feather's husband?"

"Aha." She held up a finger. "I didn't say that. And I don't *know* *him* know him. But I've seen him before. Several times. And we were at the same party once."

"Seriously? When?"

"When I covered fashion. He's a model, Nolan."

"So..."

"Who lives in San Francisco."

"But—"

"For God's sake, Nolan. He's *gay*. He's a gay model who's gay and that's not a family photo. It's a magazine fashion shot."

"Are you *sure*?"

"Yes. I'm actually eighty percent certain it would be for the Sundance collection, because the fabrics look familiar. And there are no contacts on that phone, Nolan. No texts. No emails. No recent calls."

"No emails? She said she'd sent the picture of me and her to her husband. Molly—you were there."

"Yes," Molly said. "I was. And she did say that."

"Fine. But this really doesn't prove anything. Maybe she's actually single, and embarrassed about it. Or..."

Ken was standing apart from the group, staring into space—or, rather, into the blackness that surrounded our small pool of light in the center of the room. "Ken? What do you think?"

He didn't speak for a moment. Kept staring into the dark, absentmindedly chewing his lip. "I saw you right after I got the call about Palinhem wanting someone to do a ride-along on a show. Yes?"

"Well, yeah," I said. "You were, uh, unenthusiastic. We went drinking in Santa Monica."

"And I ranted on. I remember. And you were all Californian about it and kept buying drinks and saying 'It is what it is' and you were right and eventually I got it out of my system and we moved on to other things and further alcohol. And so I don't think I even told you about the other part."

"What other part?"

"One of the things that came with the bump to cable was network oversight. Which also pissed me off, but we needed this. So I was asked to submit a list of subjects we were hoping to cover. Kincaid's cavern wasn't even on the first page of ideas, because, well, I didn't think there was a chance in hell that we'd find it, plus it would be a more expensive trip than usual and involve serious hiking, so fuck that. But an email came smartly back saying how much they liked the sound of that one, and we should do it first, with a Palinhem ride-along."

"Why didn't you tell me this at the time?"

"Because it didn't seem to matter."

"And it does now?"

"I don't know, Nolan. But Gemma's right. That picture doesn't look kosher to me."

"Shh," Molly said suddenly.

Ken and I fell silent. And then we could all hear the sound of the slow handclap.

It stopped almost immediately, but it was clear where it had been coming from.

We walked together down the passage and stopped a couple of yards short of the stone ball.

"Feather?" I said. "Is that you?"

"Yes."

"Good. I'm glad you're back. Funny thing...we were just talking about you."

"I know. I heard."

"Weird...that you got back just as it was happening."

"Oh, I've been here the whole time, Nolan."

"You've...what?"

"I've been sitting here quietly."

"Didn't you hear us shouting for you earlier?"

"Of course."

"So how come you didn't answer?"

"Nothing to say."

Ken took over. "Okay, love. So...did you go down the shaft and try to latch up with Dylan?"

"No. There's really no point."

"Why?"

"Dylan's dead, I'm afraid."

"*What?*" I said. "What...makes you think that?"

"The fact that I killed him yesterday."

CHAPTER

35

Nobody moved.

"Feather...if that's supposed to be a joke," I said carefully, "you missed the mark. By a very long way."

"It's no joke," she said. "He was waiting down at the river like a good and faithful servant. He'd met up with some guy and got extra food and water, and came back just as fast as he could. So I climbed down and got on the raft and, well, events ensued. A necessary fatality occurred."

"Feather," Ken said, "this isn't funny."

"No, I can imagine."

"So then what?" I said. "You climbed back up and pretended he hadn't been there? Why?"

"Well, first I took the raft down to the beach where we'd been staying. Which was *not* easy, by myself. Landed it and put up a couple of tents and tables and chairs. It's pretty realistic, I think. After that, yes, I came back in the dinghy and back up the shaft. Heck of a day, exertion-wise. I did bring some water, but only enough for me. Sorry. I was tired."

"The dinghy's still down there?"

"Yes. But it's well hidden."

A large part of me was still trying to believe this was a very poorly judged attempt at humor. The human mind is fiercely protective of what it believes to be true about the world, especially if those beliefs are unspoken or taken for granted at a deep level. It's like the moment when you learn someone you love has died unexpectedly, or you find out your wife has been having an on-off affair with someone you thought was something like a friend, a man you'd had a convivial lunch with only a couple of days before. Our minds can't immediately process reversals of that magnitude. They will do everything they can to make the evidence—the phone call from your crying father saying your mother had a heart attack, or the "I thought you should know" email from your wife's best friend—fit somehow with the previous narrative, in which those inexplicable things aren't true and never could be.

But your soul knows. Your soul most likely had an inkling long before the events you're struggling to comprehend had even occurred, sensitive as it is to currents and changes too subtle for the conscious mind to observe, and responsive as it can be to the futures shaping themselves in front of you.

And so your soul sits waiting for you to catch up.

And in the moment when I stood there, not knowing what to say, I had a flash recollection of Feather's face when she'd gotten stuck on the other side of the main room in the seconds after the big stone ball was unleashed. The way she'd been frozen in fear, or so I'd thought. Some higher-level function of my brain, late to the party but suddenly full of insight, now made a belated but forceful cross-reference to how she'd responded when bucked out of the boat into the hectic rapids on the first day: the fast, decisive, and athletic way in which she'd dealt with both the physical and mental challenge.

I looked again upon my internal picture of her face and wondered whether instead of fear and confusion, I could see calculation—the making of a quick judgment call that needed to be followed by a convincing display of apparent flight.

I wondered this, and immediately knew the answer.

"You said 'necessary,'" I said. "Why?"

"Dylan was a dick but basically a decent guy," she said. "When you guys didn't return, he was always going to go and get help."

"And why didn't you want that? What's going on, Feather?"

"You've found something very important, Nolan. Possibly the most important thing that's ever been found. I wasn't lying back at the hotel, when I said I'm a big fan of yours. I really am. We *all* are, at the Foundation. We have other irons in the fire. Other people out looking for us. They don't know that's what they're doing, either, naturally. Not even Kristy, and she's *famously* smart."

"What," I said slowly, "are you talking about?"

"The permafrost crack in Alaska. There was speculation there might be something of interest to us deep down in it, another example of what we believe is here in this canyon. It's a long shot, but you never know. I don't know what's happened with that one yet. You've got my phone, of course."

"Feather," Ken said. His face was composed and his voice extremely calm. I'd seen him that way once before. A bar fight broke out soon afterward. "How about you stop being a cunt and tell us what the fuck is going on."

"That's not a nice word, Ken."

"I know. But unless you're a fantasist having a mental breakdown then you've murdered the one bloke who could get us out of here. Deliberately fucking us up. So pardon my fucking Anglo-Saxon, love, and just tell us."

"I'm not going to do that," she said. "My instructions are to let events unfold. To wait, and hope."

When she spoke again her voice was quieter, as though she'd moved farther away. "But out of respect, Nolan, I'll tell you that you already *know* what you've found. Or could work it out, at least. I wish you were on this side with me. There's so much we could do together. You're cleverer than people think, and you've got all the pieces in there. You've just got to put them together. It won't save you, unfortunately. But it might be satisfying to know you've been right all along."

"Feather..."

"You're going to change the world, Nolan. Forever. Be proud."

And then she was gone.

PART THREE

"Then why do you want to know?"
"Because learning does not consist only of
knowing what we must or we can do,
but also of knowing what we could do,
and perhaps should *not* do."

—Umberto Eco, *The Name of the Rose*

So the Lord said,
"I will blot out man whom I have created from
the face of the land, man and animals and
creeping things and birds of the heavens,
for I am sorry that I have made them."

—Genesis 6:7

CHAPTER

36

We walked back up to the main room and sat in a circle. For a while, nobody had anything to say. After we'd heard Feather's footsteps receding, Pierre called out to her. The sound rebounded flatly in the passage. And sounded dumb. It wasn't Pierre's fault. It was the fact that this name—the name each of us had called out many times in the last twenty-four hours, out of concern for her safety and in the increasingly urgent hope that she was on her way back with help—now conjured a very different picture. She'd never needed our help, and she had never gone to seek any for us.

I could see several of the others struggling through the mental process I'd undergone, reframing everything Feather had done. Pierre and Molly were the most withdrawn. Gemma had been a few steps ahead of us, of course. She'd rapidly jumped to conclusions after going through Feather's phone—and she'd been right. She too, though, seemed extremely tired and drawn.

Ken's face was unreadable, but I knew he was capable of getting his head around a dark new world faster than any of us. He was a pragmatist, used to rolling with punches, from actors being airlifted to rehab in the middle of expensive shoots to being fired the day before principal photography on what would have been the biggest movie of his life, a career game-changer, because the studio felt like it.

205

And me? I was there, pretty much. Certainly there enough to know anything that had happened before this didn't matter.

All that mattered was what we did next.

One of the advantages of being a smoker is you are never in doubt as to the most appropriate response to any circumstance, whether it be good or...really, really bad. I lit up a cigarette and passed it to Ken. He smoked half of it without looking at me, and then passed it back.

"What'd she mean?"

"When?"

"When she said you had all the pieces."

"Don't know. She's obviously been sitting on the other side of that rock the whole day, listening. And we all talked to her last night, told her what we'd found up to that point. So she knows everything we know. Presumably it's a piece of that information, or a combination of pieces adding up to something bigger."

"So what *do* we have? List it."

"A bunch of passages and tunnels, with rooms, most of them completely empty. The pool with the metal spheres, which have now moved."

"*Moved?*" Gemma said.

Ken told everyone what we'd found just before the phone thing with Feather blew up. He did not need to explicitly explain it meant that any hope of additional water had vanished.

Then he nodded at me to continue.

"Plus there's a room with black stuff on the ground that smells bad and may be loosening up. And a fissure out the back that leads to that cave beyond. Then there's Gemma thinking something brushed against her in the dark."

"It *did*."

"Okay."

Ken nodded thoughtfully. "That's it?"

"And it adds up to zip so far as I'm concerned. I'll kick it over to the boys in the back brain and see if they can connect the dots, but right now . . . I got nothing."

"So what do we do?"

"First, accept that we're not getting any help from Feather. Which means anybody else either. Nobody's coming." I saw Molly start to blink rapidly. "Sorry, Moll—but that's the deal. No point pretending otherwise."

"I know," she said. "It's my head. It really hurts."

Mine did, too, and my mouth felt like it was full of old cardboard. "It's down to us to try to find a way out. But we're obviously changing the conditions here by exploring. That's already lost us our water supply. I don't want to make things any worse. So . . ."

"There's no choice," Pierre said. He spoke slowly, and then paused to blink, scrunching his eyes up tight. "If we don't do anything then it's going to get worse anyway. I don't know about you guys but I feel like crap. Headache. Weak. Fuzzy. Doing nothing is not an option."

"That's exactly where I was going," I agreed. "We need to get on it, and fast."

"Okay then." Ken stood up decisively. Staggered. "Ooh. Nice little head rush. So. What's the plan?"

I shrugged. "I have no idea."

"Shame," he said. "You were on a roll there for a while. Okay. We haven't looked up all the passages yet, have we?"

"I've done all but two," Pierre said. He turned and pointed to doorways at the nine and twelve o'clock positions.

"All right, so job number one is we do that." He peered at Gemma. "You all right, love?"

Gemma was crouched with her head over her knees. "I'm okay," she said. "Just nauseous. It's been coming on awhile, but whoa, suddenly it's a lot worse."

"We need to eat," Molly said. She grabbed her backpack—which had become the de facto storage place for sustenance—and took out the carefully wrapped final scraps of sandwich. "I know there's not much left but there's no point saving it for when we're dead."

She unwrapped each fragment in turn, handing one to Ken first, probably unconscious of the way the traditional hierarchies were still operating. Then one to Pierre. Broke her little chunk in two, and handed half to me.

"My turn," she said. "Kind of wishing you hadn't been so gallant with yours yesterday, to be honest."

"Trust me. Henceforth hungry womenfolk will have to pry the crumbs out of my cold, dead hands."

She held out the last piece to Gemma, who accepted it without enthusiasm. We all took our bites, chewing slowly. The bread was even drier and harder now. The cheese tasted exactly like plastic. Swallowing wasn't easy.

"Lovely," Ken said. "My compliments to the chef." He hesitated a beat as he remembered that the chef had been Dylan. "So. Moll and me will go check that passage, and Pierre and Gemma look at the other."

"What am I doing?"

"Going down the passage to the stone ball."

"Why?"

He lowered his voice. "Because I wouldn't be at all surprised if Psychobitch is still on the other side, listening. And so you should go down there and talk to her. See if you can get her to respond. You're the only person she seems to take seriously, Nolan. Get something out of her. Find out what the fuck's going on and if there's anything we can do about it."

"I'll try."

"Do better than that, mate." He looked at me seriously. "This would be the moment for your very best work."

CHAPTER
37

I watched the others head off. It occurred to me, too late, that maybe they should all go together, so they only used one light. But then I realized it would take twice as long that way, so probably no power would be saved.

My mental processes felt like they had lead boots on, wading through thought-treacle: with the exception of sudden sharp, disconnected ideas that burst out of the fog like lightning and just as quickly disappeared. For a rare moment I experienced my mind as fully part of my body, and inhabited the exhausted, arid sluggishness of the whole.

I ran my tongue around my mouth and across my teeth but it didn't help. It just made my gums feel big.

I hauled myself to my feet, turned off the light, and walked toward the big stone ball.

It was very dark. Perfectly dark. And perfectly quiet. I felt my way to the ball and sat down next to it, hearing nothing but the soft sound of breath going in and out of my body.

Nothing from the other side of the ball, either. I didn't actually think Feather would still be there. Her farewell had sounded final, and she'd seemed confident that she'd heard enough to confirm that the situation on our side—whatever it might be—was heading in the direction that she, and whoever she was aligned with, wished it to go. Assuming there genuinely was anybody else involved, of course.

"It's uncertainty that'll kill you," I said after a long pause. My voice sounded strange in the silence. Tired, lonely—the way it sounds inside your head when you're lying on your bed in the dark, reliving old mistakes. "Not hope, like everyone says. If you can blindly hope, that's what you'll do. But if you don't *know* ... That's poisonous. It's impossible to commit. You're unable to throw yourself in one direction and follow that path. I have no idea why I'm even saying this."

No sound from the other side.

I didn't know what Ken thought I was going to be able to find to say. There didn't seem to be anything worth articulating. But I decided I may as well think aloud, try to talk myself through the story, as I had often done years ago: pacing around the study in the house Kristy and I shared, walking miles along the beach promenade, wandering the backstreets of Santa Monica and Venice Beach—talking aloud, coaxing a movie plot to emerge by forcing it to manifest in words.

"You're not dumb, so I'm going to flat-out admit that Ken thinks I might be able to find something to say that'll change your behavior. I think that's unlikely. You're locked on course. The only question is what that course is. And why you won't simply tell us. You said you weren't allowed. But if we're never going to make it out of here, who cares what we know? Who's going to find out? Corpses keep secrets very well."

I thought about that for a moment. "But there's *you*, I suppose. *You'd* know you'd done something you weren't supposed to. Which could imply that you're worried someone would get that information out of you sooner or later. So ... fear of future punishment is a possibility. Or else you know yourself well enough to understand that guilt would be bad for you. That it would eat away. Undermine whatever you'd achieved here, even if it stayed your dirty little secret forever. Yeah. I think that's it. And God knows, I get that."

There was no sound from up the corridor, nor any sign of light. I guessed the others were still exploring the passages, being thorough. And slow, probably, moving sluggishly, supporting themselves with a hand on the wall, blinking in the darkness. Either that or they'd all been sliced into slivers by some huge swinging ax-knife and I was here all alone, talking to a woman who wasn't even there.

"I broke my life in half that way," I said. "By not wanting to have a secret. Kristy...turned out she was having an affair."

Only when the words were out of my mouth did I realize how seldom I'd articulated the fact out loud. To Ken, yes. To a couple of mutual friends who needed an explanation for why Kristy + Nolan suddenly wasn't a thing anymore. To most, I just shrugged and said, you know, shit happens.

"I'm not even sure it was that big a deal. I mean, of course it's *something* of a deal. You're married to someone and they become intimate with someone behind your back, that's a deal. But a *big* deal, once you get past the betrayal and hurt pride and all that crap? Depends. Tying two people together for life is a hell of an ask. People change, inevitably. Even if most of the time you walk in the same direction, there'll be times when one of you wanders off the path. I wouldn't even have known about it if a friend of hers hadn't emailed me. And after I got that note...I could have let it go. Trusted that it was part of life's mysterious process. I'm not dumb. I could guess what the affair involved. Afternoons in motels. A feeling of connection and engagement and gleeful surprise. The kind of guilt that bonds. Sex that felt fresh and new and real. The promise of different horizons, however illusory. The fever dream of novelty. Secrets. Liking the smell of someone's skin.

"So there would be all that, of course. But for all I knew...Well, the guy she was seeing was kind of a friend of mine. He's smart, funny, good-looking. He's talented and committed. He gives a shit about the environment. For all I *knew*, he could actually have been the one for her, right? In the grand scheme of things I could just have been a step on Kristy's path to him. The old love isn't necessarily better or more important or real than the new one. He could have been where she was destined to be. Who knows?

"So I didn't know what it *meant*, and that's where uncertainty kills you. I could have chosen to hope it'd all turn out okay. I wanted to believe that. But I didn't *know*. I couldn't be sure this was merely a tough stretch of road, and not the end of it. The guy I am, two years later... Now, I would have the sense to let the thing run its course and see what happened. We loved each other. I'm pretty sure that would have won in the end. And if it didn't, well, that would have proved or at least suggested we didn't love each other *enough* anymore, which would have been information we could have done something with. But instead... instead, one night, after a couple too many drinks, I stopped by her friend's house.

"My only intention was to double-check the source. Make sure that *she* was sure. And she let me in and we talked, and yes, she was certain, and a couple things she said convinced me, too. Things I should have noticed myself, but... My mind was always on some script or other, and after a while you just take things for granted. And I know what you're thinking—an hour later, me and the friend are having sex on the couch, right? But no. We had a couple glasses of wine, agreed that life sucks sometimes, and I got a cab home.

"Couple days later over dinner I asked Kristy if there was something going on. She froze. She asked why I was asking. I said I had a weird feeling, had picked up on a couple things. She admitted to the affair.

"There was a *lot* of talking that night, and straight through to the next day. The kind of talking that makes you think, when you're done, that you don't ever want to talk again. But over the next weeks we started to make headway.

"Except, and this is the dumb fucking thing, the fact that *I'd* lied was picking at me. Not because I'm an angel. I've lied before and survived. It was more that the *sole thing* I had to feel good about in the situation was inhabiting the moral high ground. She was the bad guy here, and I was the good. But the tiny little lie I'd told undermined that, and so it pecked at me. If we were going to get to the other side of this thing, I thought, then everything needed to be out in the open. I was asking her, all the time, to be honest. But I wasn't being honest. And so I told her. And *that's* what fucked us up."

"But that's not fair," Feather said.

I blinked. Hesitated. Realized I should keep talking.

"Actually, it is," I said. "Because she'd asked me, several times. She'd asked what specific things had made me start to suspect. And I'd had to make some up, back-fitting things I'd only put together since it came out in the open. That first lie trapped me into others. There had been a lot of brutal honestly flying around. I'd asked for it. *Demanded* it. She'd provided, even when it made her look bad and feel terrible. And meanwhile I'd been lying to her face. It wasn't even the fact that her best friend fed me the tip, though that was not ideal because suddenly that woman's motivations were called into question and eventually there was a very loud phone conversation between Kristy and her. They've never spoken since.

"But that wasn't the real thing, the bad thing. The bad thing was the lies. A small lie is just as much a lie as a big one. And like one of those smart dead guys said—it's not the content of the particular lie you told me that's the problem; it's that I can't believe you anymore. That's what destroys everything. Suddenly, instead of being one of the closest couples I'd ever known, we were people who'd been prepared to lie to each other, time after time. We'd built separate worlds out of things that weren't true, and were living in them alone—rather than inhabiting the real world together. That breaks a spell. Over the next few months we spiraled slowly in opposite directions. I tried to pull us back. She did, too. We really tried. But we were through."

"It's still not fair."

"It is what it is, and what's done is done. But my point is I get how corrosive lies become. I understand the need to be able to live with yourself, to not have something lurking back in the dark of your mind, stopping you from being at peace. Are you going to be able to live with that?"

"Nice try," she said. "Yes, Nolan, I will. It is what it is, as you would say. It's been nice talking, but I really am going to go now. I've got things to do."

"What things?"

"They don't concern you. So—did it help, sharing all that with me?"

"Not really."

"That's a shame. But I wouldn't want Ken to think you've lost your touch, so here's a little information in return. The paintings you saw are fifty thousand years old—so, yes, a long time before humans are conventionally agreed to have gotten to this continent—and they're part of the jigsaw I know you're smart enough to put together. Kincaid did. Well, Jordan was the brains on that part. He wrote a paper when he got back to Washington, and submitted to the Smithsonian right away. They buried it. Immediately, and very deep. We have that paper. We always knew what they'd found. It was only a matter of waiting until the time was right. And all we needed was the one thing they kept secret, the thing you were smart enough to work out—where this place actually *was*.

"And you've also got the building blocks to figure out what they figured out, but they're not all in those rooms, and they're not all in your head, either. There's a big story here, Nolan—a *huge* story. An arc. Don't let me down. I believe in you. You're going to want to know, and you deserve to."

"Just tell—"

"That's it, babe. I'm done."

I didn't get up for a while. She'd gone, for real this time. I could tell, somehow.

I didn't try to get anywhere with what she'd said. I wasn't sure it meant anything and I was worn out, my head fuzzy and broken. I didn't feel bad for having told her what I'd told her. It's old news.

And I hadn't told the whole truth, either.

Of *course* I had sex with Kristy's friend that night. I really am that fucking dumb. It was a drunken mistake and I admitted it. It was what killed us in the end. You could argue that event B wouldn't have happened without event A, which is true, but all that would prove is you've never been in a long-term relationship. Logic is never the issue and there is no court of appeal. And as Molly had said, it's not like it's big stuff. None of it's big stuff. Unless you were there.

Unless it's your stuff.

I think I fell asleep for a few minutes, or at least nodded into a half doze.

Then I heard something coming toward me in the darkness.

It wasn't coming fast, but it wasn't slow. It was approaching at its own pace. A soft padding sound, with little clicks that sounded like claws on rock.

I didn't move.

There wasn't anywhere I could go.

The sound got closer, and closer. Then it stopped.

The thing, whatever it was, felt as though it was only a yard or so from me now. There was a faint, visceral odor, like wet fur. A noise, like a sniff, then another.

A quiet, moist sound, like jaws opening.

I did my best to make my peace with God, the world, and everything and everybody within it.

Then I heard it trotting away.

CHAPTER

38

They arrived back in the main room soon after I did, the dim glow from their lights approaching out of the two tunnels. In the darkness it was like watching some creature's face, in which one eye was getting bigger than the other. Then for a moment I was convinced it was instead a pair of cars on a highway in the fog. My desiccated brain was playing, exhaustedly coming up with interpretations of the scant information presented to it. Ken and Molly eventually emerged from their passage well ahead of the other two.

Ken shook his head.

"More of the same?"

"Empty rooms," he said, "but with those pyramid things we saw on the other side of the ball. I put my hand on one and it felt warm, which is weird. Or I'm starting to lose it. But the passage ends in a flat wall. And yeah, I watched the roof on the way back. No shafts. So—you got any news?"

"You were right," I said. "She was there."

"And?"

"Nothing helpful. She implied again that there's pieces we could put together. Said the paintings were fifty thousand years old."

"And?"

"That's it."

Ken looked at me.

"Okay," I said. "I'm also convinced Gemma actually did feel something brush against her leg earlier. The same thing just came and had a good look at me in the dark."

Molly was very unhappy to hear this. "What was it?"

"I don't know. It was, like I say, dark. But I'm pretty sure if it had decided to attack, it would have won."

I watched Ken think this over. Dimly lit from below, he looked like he'd lost weight in his face. Okay, only an ounce or two, from dehydration, but I still didn't like seeing it. Most of the time our culture tells you skinnier is better. It doesn't take long in adverse conditions for that to change. The brain flips back to the old, tougher days, a mind-set in which seeing a member of your tribe reduced stirs a fear that the same will soon happen to you. That things are running out. That they may soon be gone.

"That is," he said, thoughtfully, "actually the best news we've had in a while."

"Yeah," I said.

Molly frowned. "How do you figure that?"

"Because it didn't try to eat him," Ken said. "Which means either it's got good taste or it's not desperately hungry. It got in here somehow. And either recently, or via a route it's confident it can escape through."

"Oh. Right."

"Let's wait and see if the others found anything," Ken said. "If not, then..."

"Yeah, we'll try that. I can't think of anything else."

"Can I join the hive mind, please?" Molly said. "Or is it invite-only?"

"The room with the paintings," Ken said. "We didn't get to the end. The light ran out and so we turned around."

"Oh, screw that," she said. "I'm not—"

"You're not invited, Moll," I said, deadpan. "You were a pain in the ass before."

"Ha ha." She stuck her tongue out.

We turned at the sound of Pierre and Gemma emerging from the other passage, then hurried over when we realized Pierre had his arm around Gemma's waist, half carrying her.

"She's really not feeling good," Pierre said. "That's why it took us so long. Sorry. We didn't find anything anyway."

We got Gemma to the middle of the room and onto the ground. She sat there hunched up, arms tightly crossed. Molly laid the back of her hand against Gemma's forehead.

"She's got a temperature."

"Christ," Ken said. "Gemma—what's the problem? Is it the flu or something?"

"I don't know. Maybe, yeah. I ache all over. But..."

She moved her hands away from her stomach, revealing how bloated it was. "I've got terrible gas, too. It's tight like a drum. And really painful."

"Your sandwich was the same as ours, right?"

"Yes."

"And you haven't eaten anything else?"

She looked up. Her face was drawn, eyes cloudy. "*No.*"

"Gemma, look—it's no big deal. If you had something stashed in your bag and kept it to yourself, it doesn't matter. We just need to figure out what's wrong with you."

"Fuck you, Nolan. Of course I didn't."

"Okay."

"I..." Abruptly she turned her head and threw up.

Nothing much came out, but the smell was sour and rank. Molly pulled a spare T-shirt out of her backpack, helped wipe around Gemma's mouth. Then it happened again. Three strong retches, subsiding into dry heaves.

"Oh shit," Gemma said, her voice guttural and clogged. "I really do not feel good."

"I'm pursuing this for one reason only," I said. I knew I was sounding like an asshole. It didn't matter. "If this is the flu or something, chances are we're all going to get it. It'd be better to know ahead of time."

Gemma took the T-shirt from Molly and wiped ineffectually around her chin. Her hair was hanging in rats' tails over her forehead and down her cheeks.

She breathed in, out, in, out. Looked like she was going to retch again, but didn't. She winced, long and painfully, and crossed her arms back over her stomach.

"Okay," she said. "I had no food. But."

"But what?"

"When I asked you about where to go this morning?"

"You needed to go to the bathroom."

"Right. I went. And when I was done, I was thinking I didn't know how much longer I could go without a drink, and I was already halfway there. So."

"Halfway where?"

"The pool," Ken said glumly. "Fuck. She went and took a drink from the pool. Christ, Gemma—didn't you see the way the water was?"

"I didn't really look. I just scooped some in my hands and drank it quickly."

"How much?"

"I don't know. Half a pint? Maybe more."

"What'd it taste like?"

"Not good. Muddy. Metallic. But I was so thirsty. And Nolan drank some when we found it, and he seemed okay."

"Why didn't you tell us earlier?"

"Because I felt okay then." She stopped talking suddenly, as if about to throw up once more, but stifled a belch instead. "I do not feel okay now."

"So," I said. "I guess that means it's not the flu. It's a stomach bug from contaminated water. You are going to feel like utter crap for a few hours, Gemma. But then it'll be done. Moll—how much water do we have left?"

"Just over half a bottle. Between all of us."

"Feed her a third of it. A mouthful at a time, five minutes apart. If she vomits again, stop immediately."

"What are you going to do?"

I grabbed the bigger light. Then, as an afterthought, my phone as a backup. I really didn't want to get stuck without light in that tunnel again. "I'm going to try the cave we found—see if there's an exit at the other end."

"Be careful."

"Of course. Oh, and Gemma—you were right."

She looked up at me blearily. "About what?"

"There's something in here with us."

"Awesome."

I turned to Ken. "You ready?"

"Nah," he said. "Take Pierre. He'll be twice as fast. And that fissure is no picnic for the fuller-figured gentleman."

"Okay. Keep a light on in here. If you see anything...shout."

"Bollocks to that, mate. If I see anything, I'm just going to eat it."

A couple of us laughed, but it sounded hollow in the darkness.

CHAPTER
39

We could tell before we got to the room that the smell had become worse in the meantime. Much worse. We started to get a taste of it while we were still twenty yards away. Once inside, it was so acrid that it made your eyes sting.

"What the heck?" Pierre had pulled his T-shirt up to cover his nose, and his voice was muffled.

I did the same. It didn't help a whole lot. "Something's changing here, too. Earlier we found a cave at the far end, with some paintings on the walls. In the time we were there, it seemed like the floor in here loosened up a little. I wasn't sure about it then. But yeah, it's clearly happening."

"But how? And how can a layer that thin smell so bad?"

I walked into the room, feeling as if I was having to physically fight against the stench. Within seconds my feet were sticking to the floor, and the farther I went, the tackier it became. After a few yards it was half an inch up my shoes and like trying to walk in old molasses.

"Christ," I said, giving up, stepping back. "That's why. Because the floor isn't level. It slopes like in a swimming pool, getting deeper toward the other end. The surface only seemed flat because the liquid in it was solid. And now it's not."

"Are we really going to wade into that crap?" Pierre and I were close together now, huddling, as if that would somehow help. He was squinting, his eyes streaming. "I mean, I'll do it if we have to," he said. "Of course. But—"

"No. We have no idea how deep it gets. That's going to have to be a last resort."

Pierre was blinking rapidly against the stinging. "Aren't we kind of at the last-resort stage already?"

"Not quite. And I'm not embarking on it without warning the others what we're doing." I nodded back toward the door. "Come on. Screw this."

"So what do we think that stuff is?" Ken asked quietly.

He'd come and taken a look. We then returned to the main room, and were sitting in darkness, twenty feet from the others.

"I've been assuming it's some kind of fossil fuel, crude oil or something. Which could have explained why it caught fire at some point. But I say that in total ignorance of what that kind of material looks and smells like, and where it's found. I don't actually care what it is. What I don't get is why it's liquefying."

"A chemical reaction."

"Okay, obviously, but what's causing it?"

"We walked across it a few hours ago," Ken said. "So I'm thinking it's probably us. Again. As with everything else."

"We're going to have to grit our teeth and tackle it anyway. You know that. There's nothing else to try."

"But if it's ten feet deep at the other end, then we're fucked, mate. We can't swim in that kind of gunk—not even Pierre. And if you walk into it until it's up to your neck, then you're never going to be able to get out of it again. It's too viscous."

"We need to float something on top."

"Right. But you've forgotten that whoever designed this game didn't give us any props, Nolan."

"*Fuck.*" I stuck my head in my hands. My brain felt as if it were splitting down the middle. "If only that light hadn't run out when we were there before. At least we'd know if there was anything worth trying to get to."

"'If only' a lot of things," Ken said. "And none of them are any bloody use to us now."

There was a groaning sound. We watched as Molly moved out of shadow into the dim glow around Gemma, and put her arm around her. There was the sound of dry retching, a rasping croak in Gemma's throat, and then another louder moan.

"She's getting worse."

"Yeah," Ken said. "The first mouthful of water came straight back up, so we stopped. She's going to have to let the bug pass through her system, however dire that makes her feel, and however long it takes. Right now, even if we did find a way out, I don't think she could move."

I lit one of the ever-dwindling supply of cigarettes and we passed its red glow back and forth in silence. Toward the end I looked at Ken. He met my gaze and held it.

"I wasn't going to tell you," he said as we finally looked away, "but I ran into Kristy a few weeks back."

"Okay."

"She was sitting outside the Peet's on Third. By herself. I said hi. We chatted. I asked if you two had talked recently. She shook her head. Said: 'It's over.'"

"Gee," I said. "Thanks, Ken. Fuck's sake. Why would you even *tell* me that?"

"Because she said it the same way you do."

"Which is?"

"Like it's not over."

I stared at him, unsure whether to be angry or very sad.

"We're dead when we're dead, Nolan," he said, reaching over to pat me on the cheek. "And not before."

*   *   *

223

We sat in silence for a while after that. Generally you get a reliable sense of the passage of time, but my mind was working so much more slowly than usual. I couldn't be sure how long it had been before there was a sudden noise—a groaning cry, much louder than the ones before. Louder, and more urgent.

Pierre and Molly were leaning over Gemma by the time Ken and I got over there. Gemma was on her knees, bent double, arms wrapped tight around her waist.

She made a dire croaking sound, the noise of someone whose stomach is in spastic revolt but has nothing else to give.

"This isn't getting better," Molly said. "I don't know what we're going to do with her."

"She *has* to be getting out the other side by now," I said. "She's empty. The water she drank this morning is long gone from her system. Maybe this is just a final—"

The croaking sound came again, morphing this time into a harsh, jabbering belch. It had extraordinary force and didn't sound like it was the tail end of anything.

I crouched next to her. Put my arm around her back. The heat coming off her skin was intense. She was making a continual low moaning sound, and seemed to be trying to screw herself up as tightly as possible, as if every muscle in her back and limbs was contracting.

"Gemma," I said, "it's going to be okay."

She belched again, a long, rasping bark, releasing an appalling smell.

She jerked her head up. Her cheeks and forehead were soaking with sweat, hair matted. "Oh," she said.

It wasn't to me, or about me. At first I wasn't sure she even knew I was there. But then she said my name, twice. Her voice sounded like an old woman's.

"Gemma, let it out." I remembered that I'd already said those words to someone, at a point earlier in the day. "Try not to cramp. Let it out."

I went to pry her hands away from her abdomen, only then realizing how incredibly swollen it was—bulging so much it was straining the buttons on her shirt.

"The gas is putting her gut muscles in spasm," I said. "She's got to get it out." Gemma was strong enough to pull her hand back, returning it to her stomach. I had a flash memory of being a child, in bed, with gut pain—and how nothing but the feel of my mother's cool hand on my stomach had seemed to help.

So I put my hand on her belly, as gently as I could. She screamed. Her head was right next to mine and the scream was so loud I thought my eardrum would burst.

"Sorry," I said. I pulled my hand away but she screamed again. And again. It wasn't me that had made her scream. It was something else.

I looked up at the others but saw only blank faces. None of them knew what to do about this, either, how to relieve this pain. None of us had children, and so we didn't even know how to pretend we could make it better. When it came to this kind of thing we were all still children ourselves.

She opened her mouth to scream again but another of the barking belches came out instead. The smell was even worse than before. The noise tailed off into the most dreadful sound I've ever heard from a human being, an animal mewl of agony.

She toppled over, knocking the light away and flipping it over, making everything dark.

I reached for her, feeling her burning skin against mine again. Found the light and turned it. Gemma was on her side now, face screwed up tightly. She was hyperventilating.

Then her eyes opened wide. Her breath was hitching—uneven. A bubbling sound leaked out of her throat. She was staring at me. Her mouth was moving but I didn't know what she was trying to say.

A clot of dark blood gushed out of her mouth.

Her eyes grew wider.

Her arms tensed, hands knotting into claws. More blood belched

225

up into her mouth, but without the force to break clear, leaving her gurgling as she tried to scream.

I hurriedly pulled her onto her side, into the crash position. I stuck my fingers in her mouth to try to clear the backlog, but it kept coming. It just kept coming.

She choked.

She died.

CHAPTER

40

I tried everything I knew, everything I'd seen on TV. I pumped her chest, rolled her over, pumped again. It made no difference.

What do you do when that happens in front of your eyes? I stayed there, kneeling beside Gemma, feeling like I was in some kind of bizarre and dreadful play. Her body was sprawled as if she'd been hit by a car, neck twisted by her final spasms.

I gently rolled her onto her back.

Her eyes were open, staring flatly into the darkness. Her chin and throat and chest were covered in blood and bits of tissue that she'd vomited up. The smell was terrible, a combination of a bloody, metallic tang along with something richer and much worse, presumably something torn inside.

I finally knew what it seemed I should do next. It felt absurd, but I did it anyway.

I laid my fingertips on her eyelids, feeling the warmth of them, and pulled them down. One moved more easily than the other, and for a moment she was caught in a grotesque wink. Then they were closed.

I got up. It seemed inconceivable that the thing at my feet could have housed the smart, determined person we'd known.

We stood around Gemma's body in silence and then Pierre picked up the light and we all walked to the side of the room and sat there in a row, our backs against the wall.

My head hurt like it was going to burst. I assumed that after a while Ken would ask for a cigarette, but he did not. This was beyond even that source of comfort.

"What are we going to do?" Pierre asked eventually.

"About what?"

"Gemma. What are we going to tell people?"

"Nothing," Molly said. She turned to look at him. "Don't you get it? We're not leaving this place either."

It was later. Five minutes, ten, maybe more. Perhaps a lot more. I was aware of being hungry, of stomach muscles cramping in protest. It felt like a distant concern. Water was the issue. There were a few mouthfuls left, but when it was gone there'd be nothing to hold out as a carrot for getting through the next few hours. Plus I don't think any of us wanted to return to Gemma's body, not yet, and that's where the backpacks were.

I felt desiccated, two-dimensional. I was aware of Ken sitting a yard away, eyes open, head nodding. Then my vision seemed to white out, and I couldn't have told you whether I was awake or asleep, where I was, or even who.

Some time later, Ken lifted his head.

The movement was obscure in the dimness, but enough to focus me back. I blinked, eyelids gummy, and turned my head, assuming he was looking at me.

He wasn't. He was staring into the room, frowning.

The other two were curled up asleep against the wall. The glow from the lamp—which should have been turned off, we were wasting power we couldn't afford—reached ten feet into the room. Maybe twelve, though by that point it was a warming of the darkness rather than real illumination.

That darkness sparkled softly, its blackness a challenge the retinas couldn't handle, seeming to billow like a curtain caught by a soft breeze.

Something moved in it.

I blinked, hard, assuming at first that it was illusion. And when I opened my eyes all was darkness once more.

But then there was another movement. There was a shape standing there. For a split second I thought it must be Feather.

But it wasn't. It was an animal.

It took a faltering half step into the low light.

It wasn't like anything I'd ever seen. It was the size of a big cat, a puma, and moved like one, but its head was more canine in shape, mouth and eyes open wide. A very large tooth curved down from each side of its upper jaw.

Fully awake now, I glanced at Ken. "Are you see—"

"Yeah," he whispered. "I am."

We weren't quiet enough. The animal's head snapped toward us, as if sensing danger. Or prey.

Then it stepped back into the darkness, vanishing as if it'd been erased.

We were on our feet quickly and quietly.

"Are we doing this?" Ken said.

"Yeah."

We moved cautiously toward where the animal had been. Or had *seemed* to be. Only moments after it had disappeared, it was hard to believe it had ever been there. I realized we didn't have a light with us but I had my phone in my pocket. As we hurried toward the nearest passage I turned it on. We paused at the entrance and waited for the phone to boot.

"This is the one with the stinking room, right?"

"Yes."

"What else?"

"I don't know," I realized. "Pierre scoped it out early yesterday. He was all about the room that smells. I'm not sure he even said what else was down here. He didn't get to the end."

The screen of the phone flickered to life. I held it up above my head—revealing eight badly lit feet of tunnel.

Ken and I spread out across the passage. We drew level with the stinking room but kept going, on the unspoken assumption that nothing would go in there if it had a choice.

Ken kept his gaze on the passage ahead while I peered into the doorways as they coalesced out of the darkness. All were empty, further examples of the anonymous rectangular spaces we'd seen down passages on the other side of the main area, with the small rock pyramids.

"Hell did it go?"

"We're not finished yet. And however it got in here..."

"I know."

We kept pushing forward, and a couple of minutes later came across a doorway that was narrower than the others, opposite one final room.

"Doesn't that look a lot like..."

"Yes," Ken said. We quickly headed into the narrow passageway. Off the passage on the other side of the main room was a line of the hieroglyphs chiseled into the wall.

After fifty yards the floor stopped abruptly. A foot below was crystal-clear water.

"Oh, thank Christ for that. It's another pool."

"Back away, Nolan. We do not want to kick a single grain of dust into it. And given what just happened to Gemma, I'm not sure I'd risk it anyway."

We turned and hurried back up the tunnel into the passage. "Okay, so it's got to be in the room opposite."

"How do we do this?"

"Block the doorway together so it can't get out."

"And then what?"

"Ask it politely how the fuck it got in here."

"Ken..."

"If it feels cornered, it's going to run back out the way it came."

"Or it could just *attack* us, Ken."

"Yeah. There's that."

We were halfway across the passage when Molly started shouting Ken's name from the main room.

Shouting it like a siren.

"*Shit*," Ken said. "It got around us."

But when we reached the room, Molly and Pierre were in the center, near Gemma's body. Molly turned. Her eyes were wild.

"Where *were* you?"

"Just...looking," Ken said. "What's up?"

She pointed down at Gemma's body. "We heard something. Like a...I don't know. Look at her."

At first Gemma just looked like she had when I'd last seen her. Deader, but otherwise the same. Then I saw what Molly meant. Her abdomen was even more swollen.

"It's gas, trapped inside...her," I said. The shape on the ground really didn't seem like a "her" anymore. "I guess...I guess even though she's dead, it's still increasing. It does that postmortem. As the...processes of decay start to take place."

"That *quickly*? And shouldn't it be able to escape?"

"I don't think so. The autonomic nervous system..."

I stopped. For a second there, in the low light, it looked as though the surface of her belly moved. The buildup was continuing, very fast. "I don't know much about what happens to bodies after death. But I think it's going to keep..."

Then it happened again. A bulge, more on one side of her stomach than the other, strong enough to strain the buttons on her blood-soaked blouse.

Ken was ahead of me. He always is. "Nolan—get away from her."

I didn't understand. He grabbed me by the arm and yanked hard. "Get *away from her*."

I scrabbled back, finally realized what he meant. The gas was building up so very fast that there was only one thing that could happen to the body containing it.

There was a tearing sound as the buttons on her shirt gave way.

Then a darkening as blood trickled out of a line across her belly—the pressure from inside so dreadful that it was causing the flesh to split. Or so I thought.

But then something emerged from the line.

This was so very wrong that it took a second to credit that it was really happening, that it wasn't just a trick of the light, the eye misinterpreting the slow spread of dark blood.

But no, something was coming out.

It was leathery, like a bat's wing, but bigger.

It seemed to thrust out like an elbow. Then more of it was released. Another arm, or wing. A hunch of back.

Finally a head. The creature wasn't even that big. The size of a small hawk, though scrawny and sinewy, and with a skull that was bony and elongated.

The thing finished digging its way out. It flopped off the glistening mess of Gemma's belly and onto the ground, turning its head, assessing its environment.

I stared at it, openmouthed, frozen. Pierre and Molly were the same. But Ken stepped over in one fluid motion and kicked it with all his might.

It flew right across the room and crashed into the wall. He strode over there and was by it in seconds, heel raised.

"Wait," I said.

I stood with him and looked down at it. It had already gotten itself back onto its clawlike feet, and was unfurling wings dripping with Gemma's blood and tissue.

"It's a fucking pterodactyl," Ken said.

"Kill it."

He stamped on its head, and then again, and again, until it was dead.

FROM THE FILES OF NOLAN MOORE:

PETROGLYPH FROM THE THREE RIVERS AREA, NEW MEXICO

CHAPTER

41

I'm kind of dumb sometimes and notoriously slow on the uptake, but I generally get there in the end. You may think you would have been faster but it's different when you're lost in the middle of it and far more aware of spilled blood and broken intestines and the danger of starvation than you are of abstract ideas. I was waiting for my back brain to nudge me—knowing, somehow, that it finally had something to bring to my attention—when Pierre spoke.

"What the *hell* just happened?"

He was looking to me for an answer rather than Ken, but I wasn't there yet. He could tell I was thinking, and he waited patiently rather than repeating the question. I was long done with considering Pierre annoying.

Meanwhile Molly rounded on Ken. "Where did you go?"

"Hmm?" Ken sounded as if wheels were turning in his mind, too.

"I asked where you'd been. You said 'just looking.'"

"Yeah, well, that's what it was."

"Really?"

Ken looked at me. I nodded. "All right," he said. "Just before... before what just happened happened, Nolan and I saw something."

"Something?"

"Kind of, well, a creature."

"*In here?*"

"Yeah."

"What was it?"

"Not sure," I said. "I didn't see it clearly. I doubt Ken did, either." Ken shook his head. "But it was big. With teeth. When it realized we'd seen it, it disappeared."

Molly was staring at me now, horrified, her eyes wide. *"Disappeared?"*

"Not, like, vanished. It backed off into the dark. We went looking for it. When we heard you shouting, we thought it must have gotten around us and come back here."

"So . . . so what the *fuck?*"

"We don't know, Moll," Ken said.

"But how did it get *in here?*"

"I don't think it did," I said.

"What do you mean?"

"This morning," I said slowly, as the idea laboriously translated itself into words. This morning seemed like a long time ago. It was back when Gemma was alive. Before she'd become that object lying on the ground between us. "This morning. There was a mosquito, right? I slapped at it."

"So?"

"And Pierre—you saw a bug in the night. And maybe there's a whole restricted little ecosystem in here and bugs are no big deal, but it's kind of strange that we didn't see any in the hours after we first arrived. And then this morning . . . Gemma felt something brush against her leg. But the way she described it made it sound like it wasn't big. Domestic cat-sized, or a small dog. Right? Then something came up to me in the dark after I'd been talking to Feather. I didn't see it and so I can't swear to it, but I'm sure it was larger than that. But *not* as big as the thing Ken and I just saw."

"So Gemma got it wrong," Pierre said. "It was dark. She was already getting sick."

"True. Or . . . maybe they're all different things."

"Nolan, I don't understand what you're getting at."

"Come with me," I said. "All of you. From now on, unless there's a very good reason, we stick close together at all times. Okay?"

Pierre and Molly mumbled assent. I grabbed the light and led them to the corridor over on the left side.

Ken and I stood a foot back from the ledge over the pool where twenty-four hours previously the two of us—and a woman who was now very dead—had taken a swim. Molly and Pierre were behind us. I held the light up so everyone could see.

The surface of the pool was now entirely covered with the greenish-black algae, or whatever it was. It was thicker, too, at least an inch in parts.

The room was much hotter than it had been before. A mist over-hung the water. It smelled . . . It didn't smell like water. There was an organic, meaty undertone.

Ken was nodding. "It's got to be, hasn't it?"

"I think so," I said.

"For God's *sake*," Molly said. "*What?*"

"The spheres," I said. "The ones that were on pedestals but are now all in the water. You saw what they looked like."

"Yes, so?"

"The largest was at the back. Much bigger than the others. Dark gray, a matte surface. I'm thinking that was carbon. And we saw another that looked like copper. And iron. There will have been potassium and magnesium, and calcium and others. Some of those spheres were pretty small, remember. Trace elements."

"What about oxygen and hydrogen?" Ken asked. "Those are the big guys, right?"

"From water in the pool. Plus that plant stuff could now be break-ing down carbon dioxide."

"Nitrogen?"

"The atmosphere. And for all we know one of those balls could have contained a stock of it under pressure."

"Sodium, and chlorine?"

"A ball of salt. Bromine and some others are probably bound into compounds, too."

"Are you guys just going to stand there listing all the chemicals there are?" Pierre asked.

"No," I said. "Only about twenty-eight of them."

"Why?" Molly said. "Why those?"

"They're the ones you need to create life."

We stood staring out over the portion of the pool visible within the lamp's glow.

"But how would it *work*?" Molly asked.

"You got me. I know—you'd expect to see a bunch of wires and computers and stuff. And for all we know, maybe there's a ton of that hidden under all the rock. But we don't even know how to do what we're suggesting is happening here. Couldn't get it started. So whoever put this together knew stuff that we don't. Maybe you can make rock function that way, too. Maybe this whole place is a giant computer."

"And it's been sitting here all this time? But . . . then why did it start working?"

"We went into the pool. Maybe that was enough—skin cells sloughing off, triggering a reaction."

"Or blood," Molly said. "Remember? When you and I went down to the end in the night. There was a smear over that megalith in the middle, with all the symbols on it."

"Christ, yes," I said. "Gemma. The scrape on her arm."

"You think that was it? Some of her blood getting in the water? Her DNA?"

"Maybe," Ken said. "Or maybe that rock isn't an inscription after all. Maybe it's a console. I mean, the way it's right there in the middle—could be, right?"

"And Molly—you noticed that none of the symbols repeat. And we couldn't figure out why that would be—what message or text would have each letter or word appearing only once. *That* could be why. Because it's not a text. It's a *list*."

"A menu system," Ken said. "Press a symbol, and that's what it makes."

"Right," I said. "Except that more than one of us ran our fingers *all over it*. I'm going to guess we pressed almost every single icon. The simpler, smaller things appear first because they're faster to make. It'd already started when Molly and I were in the water last night. Which is why our skin was itching like hell first thing today. And then..."

"This morning," Molly said, sounding nauseous, "Gemma drank some. Which already had...that thing growing in it."

There was a pause while we thought about that, and about how the creature growing inside Gemma might have gained sustenance. What it must have been feeding on as it got larger and larger.

"Nope," Pierre said firmly. "I don't believe any of this. None of it is even *possible*."

"Find me another explanation and I'll be happy to listen," I said. "Until then, this isn't a ceremonial site. It's a machine. And you understand that kind of thing far better than I do, so we could use your help."

I saw Molly staring glumly into the darkness, and added: "You too, Moll, obviously."

"I got nothing," she said. "Except this. If you're right, and this place is making all these things, it means the creature you saw didn't have to find a way in after all. And that means there's no way out."

CHAPTER

42

Pierre considered for a minute.

"Wait here," he said.

"Weren't you listening earlier? We *stay together*."

"Okay, well I want to check something."

We followed him back up the passage, across the main corridor, and into the room opposite. He walked straight up to the pyramid carved out of the floor and put his hand on it. "It's warm. Really warm. I thought I felt it on another one earlier, but I wasn't sure."

"Yeah," Ken said. "I noticed that, too."

I went to touch the cool wall of the room, and then returned to place my hand on the pyramid. There was no question it was significantly hotter, especially at the apex.

"You must know about pyramids, Nolan," Pierre said. "What's the deal with them?"

"A bunch of people have said a bunch of stuff, for which there's no scientific evidence. There was a fad in the seventies about the shape focusing positive energy. People made them out of wood and slept inside. Plus the Egyptians were kind of into them, as you may be aware. There's wingnuts who've claimed the big pyramids in Giza were an ancient power plant."

"Right. And didn't we tape you saying something a couple days

239

ago about how some people think the Egyptians made it to the Grand Canyon?"

"But like I said at the time, I don't see it."

"It doesn't have to be them, though," Ken said. "It could be someone else using the same technology. Or maybe the Egyptians themselves were only ever going through the motions, obsessing about the shape because they were misremembering something that had existed long before their civilization—and it was actually some *previous* lot who made it here."

"*What* technology, Ken? It's just a *geometric shape*."

"Which is very *warm*. Unlike all the other rock in the place. Like you said two minutes ago—find me another explanation, and I'll run with it. Otherwise..."

"Okay, fine. But does it help?"

"We could try to stop them producing energy?"

"What—all of them? Including the ones we saw in the rooms on the other side of the ball, before we got trapped here? And how? And with what? Punching them with our bare fists?"

"All right—we got anything else?"

"The spheres in the pool," Pierre said thoughtfully.

"What about them?"

"The pyramids, whatever they're doing, basically that's magic as far as we're concerned. We can't do anything about it. But if it's those balls being in the water that mean this place can make things, then..."

"...let's get the balls out of the water," Ken said.

We stood together back at the pool. I'm not going to lie to you—getting in there felt like the least appealing prospect in the world. It wasn't only about the slimy plants on top, or the fetid, organic smell. It was Gemma, of course. What had happened to her. Though paradoxically I knew that a large factor in why we were even trying this was to avoid thinking about her death.

"Okay, so how do we do this?" Ken said.

"We have to avoid getting the water in our mouths. Which should be fine because it's not deep. But having it on the skin probably isn't a great idea, either, if we can avoid it. It was itching like hell this morning, and it wasn't anything like this developed when Molly and I went in last night."

"All right," Ken said, stepping right up to the edge. "So how do I do that?"

"Seriously? You're not going in there, Ken. You are the least aquatic human I've ever seen."

"Bollocks. I go in pools all the time."

"I know. I've seen you, in Florida. You spent all afternoon in a floaty thing, consuming a series of strong alcoholic beverages. I had to help you out in the end."

"You're a picky bastard, Nolan. And the way you cite past events, just because they 'happened,' is really annoying."

"I'll do it," Pierre said. "Nolan, give me your jeans. Ken, your sweatshirt. I'll put them on top of my clothes."

"That's not going to make a difference. It's still going to soak through the cloth. And get on your hands."

"It'll help a little. And I'll do it fast."

"No, it's going to have to be two of us," I said. "Those balls will be heavy even if they've started to dissolve."

"This isn't going to *work*," Molly said. "How are you going to find them? There's hundreds of square feet of floor under there, and you can't see any of it."

"They'll be down at the other end."

"Unless the floor slopes this way. And why are we *doing* this anyway, Nolan? You're putting yourself at risk, for what?"

"Because, love," Ken said, "sooner or later something that's come out of this pool is going to get hungry. We've got enough to deal with already. Stopping it getting worse is all we've got."

He pulled off his sweatshirt.

Pierre wore Ken's clothes on top of his. I wrapped Molly's shirt around mine. There was no point in my trying to get into her jeans. I tucked mine into my socks, and Pierre did the same. I was aware it was likely to make no difference.

I perched on the edge of the pool. I still didn't want to do this. I believed it was the *right* thing to do, the smart and forward-thinking thing, that it made sense to play a long game in the hope there actually was one. But I still didn't want to do it.

I reached out my foot and shoved at a portion of the mossy plant material. It resisted, then broke away. The water beneath looked clearer than it had earlier in the day.

"Maybe all that cloudy crap was a stage one," Ken said. "And it's now forming into bigger things. Like the plant stuff."

"That'd be good." My skin was itching in anticipation, however, and I was trying not to wonder whether it was possible for water to get into the body via the skin's pores.

"If you're really going to do this dumb thing," Molly said, "head straight for the carbon ball. Everything that lives on Earth is carbon-based, right? Get that one out of the pool and you've pulled the plug."

"That," I said, "is smart thinking, Moll. You win."

I lowered myself down into the water. It was warm, the temperature of a moderate bath. Body temperature, I guess. My entry stirred the water around, but it stayed clear.

I walked out a few yards holding the light, to give Pierre room to follow. I'd given Ken my phone but they were keeping the screen turned off for now.

By the time Pierre had waded up to where I was, my clothes were already wet through. We needed to do this fast.

We walked farther into the pool, heading toward the middle on the grounds that's where the balls were likely to be, assuming they'd rolled off the platform at the end in a straight line. "Keep an eye on how far the water comes up your chest," I said.

"Why?"

"That'll tell us if there's a slope. If so, then the heaviest ball will be closest. I think. Yes?"

"I guess. If not?"

"It's going to be right at the other end."

We kept going. The plant material resisted being torn, seeming almost to knit up again after we'd passed through, though that was presumably merely the effect of currents bringing it back together in our wakes. I realized I was unconsciously keeping both arms up and well clear of the water, even though when we found the balls we were going to have to reach down into it to lift them. Each time I believed I'd thought something through, a few seconds later I realized I'd missed something incredibly obvious. That worried me.

It scared me, in fact.

"Nolan?" Pierre spoke quietly, apparently in an effort to prevent the others from hearing. I remembered the way sound had carried across the water when I'd been in here before, however, and pitched my voice even lower.

"What?"

"I just felt something."

"A ball?"

"No. It brushed against my thigh. I think it was a fish or something. But..."

"But what?"

"It felt kind of...big."

"Just keep moving."

We advanced, a couple of yards apart, taking our little pool of light with us. About twenty feet from the end, my foot stubbed into something. It was hard and heavy but moved a little. "Wait. I think we've got one."

Pierre came over and moved his foot around until he found it. "Oh yeah. Okay."

I used my elbows to shift the plant stuff aside, and we looked down at the water. It was clear enough that I could see a sphere. Its diameter was about the length of my foot, meaning it was one of the smallest ones.

"Now what?"

"Eyes shut. Mouth shut."

"What about nose?"

"Shit. I don't know."

"How about we each close our own nose, go down with one hand on opposite sides of the ball, lift it together?"

"Pierre—that's going to be really hard."

"I don't want that water in me."

"Neither do I. Okay."

We maneuvered around so we were facing each other. I balanced the light on a thick and unbroken section of the plant material and gripped my nostrils shut with my left hand. "Fast, but not too fast—or we're going to fumble it. On three."

We nodded at each other: one, two . . .

And dropped at the same time.

Finding the ball was easy—my hand landed right on it. I slipped my fingers underneath, gave it a beat, and then tried to lift. Pierre did it half a second before me.

It slipped out of our grasp.

We surfaced. "Crap," Pierre said. His voice was shaky, and I didn't blame him. Being under the water felt really dumb. "Seriously, Nolan—are we sure this is worth it?"

"It was your idea, dude."

"Yeah, but what the hell do I know? I'm just the guy who points the frickin' camera."

"We're doing it. Try again."

We did the same thing, at the same measured pace, with the same result. This time when we surfaced I heard Ken shout.

"You two okay?"

"We're fine. It's not going well, though."

I wiped each eye against the corresponding shoulder. Pierre did the same. The plant material now surrounded us in a circle. It was hard not to feel like it was closing in.

"We're going to try this one more time," I said.

"Okay."

God, he looked young. I didn't know Pierre's exact age. Twenty-six, thereabouts. I'm sure he would have been embarrassed to know how much he looked as though he needed reassurance from someone who had experience. A grown-up. A dad.

But I wasn't one of those, and it was looking increasingly unlikely I was ever going to be. The best I had for him was a smile and a wink.

"You know what?" I said. "Screw this."

And before he could move, I clamped my eyes and mouth shut, tilted my head forward, and dropped.

I got my hands around the ball immediately. It was heavy, though. Very heavy.

I yanked at it with all my strength and it did come up, but I lost my balance and found myself keeling over to the right, the ball slipping out of my fingers.

Then Pierre's hands were on it, too.

We burst up out of the water coughing and blinking, the ball wedged between us. It was very, very heavy.

"You okay?"

"I think so," he said. "This looks like copper, right?"

"Yeah." I remembered seeing this sphere the night before, admiring the smoothness of it. The surface was matte now, however, and markedly pocked in places.

"So now what?"

"We take it down to the end."

Pierre pulled his shoulders back, causing the ball to move smoothly into a firm grip between his arms. He clasped his hands to hold it there, tendons standing out like cords in his arms and neck. We slowly headed together toward the platform. I was aware of my feet knocking against other balls below—we were walking through a field of them now.

Dropping full-body into the water had screwed any chance of making a precise judgment on whether the level was coming higher up our chests, but it didn't seem like it was. Which should mean the carbon ball would be right where we were headed.

245

Pierre got into position against the end of the pool, steadied himself, and between us we hefted the copper ball up onto the platform. I had my hand ready to hold it there, and then gave it a gentle shove back.

It didn't go far, but it seemed like it would stay. "One down, twenty-seven to go."

"Like Moll said—let's find the carbon."

Within a couple of minutes we'd found a couple of smaller balls, and we got them successfully up onto the platform using the one-hand-each technique. We even started to fall into something of a rhythm, doing what had to be one of the weirdest tasks I'd undertaken in my life.

"Wait," Pierre said. "I think I've found it."

He had. And how did we know? Because once you pushed the plants aside, the top of the sphere was only just below the surface of the water. It was far more uneven than the balls we'd dealt with so far, suggesting that a lot more of it had dissolved off. But...it was still *massive*. Of course.

"I...kinda forgot it was this big."

"Yeah," I said, feeling incredibly dumb. "Me too. Can you even move it? At all?"

He waded around to the other side and braced his hands against the ball. Gathered himself to give it a shove.

And then disappeared.

CHAPTER

43

He was there, and then he wasn't—dropping below the surface so fast it was like he'd blinked out of existence. I called out his name but I knew he hadn't slipped. I dived under.

It was dark, with the light from the lamp still balanced above barely penetrating. The water was clear, however, almost back to the way it had been the first time we entered the pool. I glimpsed something on the bottom—not a ball, nor one of the pyramids I knew were there somewhere, but an aggregation of material: as though a portion of the plant matter had sunk and started to build into something else. Maybe that's how it worked. I didn't have time to care.

The dark ball of carbon loomed in front. Pierre was thrashing around next to it. At first I couldn't see why.

He made it to the surface, gasped for air—but was immediately whipped back under.

Something was wrapping itself around his legs.

A dark, twisting shape.

As I swam up, I saw another of the same thing, reaching around his waist. I experienced a flashback to something I'd seen painted on a wall—like a spider, but all its legs pointing in the same direction.

I got to Pierre and grabbed his arm. It took him a second to realize it was me. He reared back, trying to fight. When I saw recognition in his eyes I moved in closer, grabbed him around the waist.

Then I felt the sticky, muscular contact of something trying to wrap itself around my arm—something far more powerful than me, pure strength wrapped in flesh.

My feet went out from beneath me as another tentacle grabbed my ankle and yanked it.

Panic fell like a curtain. I kicked out spastically, driving both legs back and forth, not trying to strike anything in particular. I felt Pierre doing the same.

I had no air left now and my head was starting to sing, some deeply scared part of my brain urging me to open my mouth and gasp.

Then Pierre was pulling ahead.

I kept kicking, wriggling, trying to roll.

I felt something on my arm and thought it was another tentacle but it was Pierre, one leg still held fast, but trying to pull me along with him.

Our eyes met, and I nodded:

One—two—

We both slammed out with our free legs. I felt mine plunge into something giving. The grip around my other leg was momentarily less tight and I wrenched my knee up toward my chest, pulling it away. Took a glancing blow to the face as Pierre did his own kicking, scything his foot down again and again. I turned to move out of his way and felt myself suddenly free.

I jammed my foot down against the floor of the pool. The impact jarred my knee but gave me enough momentum to drive myself up and get my head out of the water.

I gulped air and threw my arm around Pierre's chest to pull him away from the thing under the surface. His head breached, too, mouth already open, coughing water, and I knew then that if the water was still bad we were dead men swimming, but it didn't make any difference. You keep fighting anyway.

It's hard, kicking sideways underwater. The water doesn't want to let you. But I kept at it, pulling Pierre with me, and then suddenly there didn't seem to be any resistance.

I fell forward, decided to go with it and turned it into a dive, pulling myself forward under the water as fast as I could and trusting Pierre to do the same.

I passed over several more of the creatures on the bottom, the last far larger than any of the previous. I stopped and drove my foot down into it, and then again.

Then I thrashed and gasped my way to where Ken and Molly were standing shouting at the other end. They yanked me out so fast I barked my shins on the ledge.

I rolled out of the way so they could do the same for Pierre, and lay there coughing, panting.

"What the hell happened?" Ken said.

"Squid," Pierre gasped. "Huge big-ass squid."

"*Seriously?*"

"Did it look like we were screwing around?"

"There's other things growing under there," I said. I was rubbing at my lips with one hand and my eyes with the other, trying to get the water off. But I could taste it in my mouth, the mineral tang. When I coughed it was wet and phlegmy. Some had gotten into my windpipe, too, and into my ears and nose. "This place is nowhere near done making stuff."

Ken stood over me. "How much water got inside you?"

"I don't know."

"Fingers down the throat, mate."

I didn't think it was going to make any difference but I did what he said. I knelt over the pool and stuck my index and middle fingers as far down my throat as I could. After a while I managed to get my gorge to rise in a vomit reflex, but nothing came out except a long trickle of spit.

"Okay, so not much," I said, falling back against the wall. My stomach muscles had locked, feeling empty and torn.

Ken made Pierre do the same. He managed to get a mouthful of water to come back up. He stayed on his hands and knees afterward, looking out into the room—and specifically at the faint glow right at the other end.

"Shit," he said. "We left the light."

"You know what? I'm not going back for it."

"Did you get the carbon ball?"

"No, Moll," I said. "It's still *massive*. The four of us together wouldn't be able to move it—ten people couldn't. And that's where we got attacked. That entire plan was screwed from the get-go. I don't know what we were even thinking of."

"So let's get out of here," she said. "I don't want to be sitting waiting when the next thing climbs out."

We limped back along the narrow corridor. As we turned into the wider passage a sound echoed down along it. Long, mournful, keening, split into several notes.

"Christ," Ken said wearily. "That sounded like a wolf, didn't it?"

"No," I said. "It sounded like two."

"So what do we do?"

"Main room."

"Which is where the sound *came* from, Nolan."

"Maybe—or it could have just echoed through there from one of the other tunnels. I don't want to get trapped down a corridor with no exit, do you? Especially the corridor where anything new and bigger is going to arrive."

"Good point. All right, well, let's be big and loud."

And so we coughed and talked and made strange pointless noises as we advanced up the passage, my phone on and held above my head. We stopped at the entrance to the main room. We couldn't see or hear anything, and so headed for the middle.

"Oh, Jesus Christ," Moll said, turning away.

We'd disturbed some creatures by returning to the main room. They hadn't finished what they'd been doing. Ken and I looked at what remained of Gemma. But not for long.

"Things are getting hungry."

Despite what we'd said about being trapped, we headed down the passage toward the big stone ball. Maybe because it was the closest thing we could do to leaving. The idea of being stuck in this place with other creatures had been unnerving enough. The knowledge that they were getting to a point where they needed sustenance was far worse.

They weren't the only ones. We split the last two granola bars and shared the remaining mouthfuls of water. Nobody suggested only eating or drinking half this time. That way led to dividing and dividing until we were down to crumbs and molecules and eventually lost in homeopathic memories of food. There was no point in going there. We needed far more than what we had, not even less.

We finished it all.

There was nothing left now.

CHAPTER
44

Yes, we were scared. But the body—especially when its most basic needs are not being met, and it is becoming desperate—has a way of closing the shutters, conserving energy when it can. It switches to low-power mode.

One by one the others fell asleep, or passed out, slipping sideways into a state where awareness was turned inward, wandering the internal halls. The distinction between sleep and wakefulness was becoming less and less clear. Time, too, was ceasing to have the usual depth of meaning. When I glanced at my phone and saw it was 9:43 p.m., the numbers looked arbitrary, like shapes left in sand by the swish of a dog's tail.

Part of this was the fact it was permanently dark and we had no mealtimes or sleep periods to make sense of the slow onward march of minutes. But also this place felt sodden with duration. It had existed for longer than any of us had the ability to comprehend. How long had we been in here now? Twenty-four hours? Thirty-six? Either was so minuscule in comparison with the site's age that in the grand scheme of things it would be rounded down to zero—as would our entire lives. No matter how long we managed to last out, statistically we wouldn't have been here at all.

This realization didn't help my mood, and so I let my mind wander, not trying to push my thoughts in any particular direction. Being at the end of the passage with my back to the big ball reminded me of the last time I'd sat here, talking with Feather. Assuming that was her real name, of course. Assuming *anything* about her was real, from the hippie clothing—and in retrospect, wasn't her outfit maybe a little *too* perfect, right down to the ankh necklace?—to claiming that if I put my mind to it, I had all the information I needed to work out what was happening.

I kept blinking and opening my mouth wide to stretch my face, keeping myself awake, believing one of us should keep watch. The amount of Gemma's abdomen that had been missing when we returned from the pool made it clear that it wasn't going to be long before the things abroad in this place became hungry enough to regard us as a foodstuff worth tackling, even while we were capable of self-defense. I wasn't sure how much of a fight we'd realistically be able to put up, but starting from a position of fast sleep seemed a dumb tactical move. Not least because if I'd been right in thinking I could hear not one, but two wolves, that might be the case with some of the other...

My thoughts braked suddenly.

They skidded, as if I'd blown past a mental stop sign and knew I ought to back up. I could tell I was half-asleep by the way it felt like I'd been driving through my mind, watching ideas go by like the view out of a car window.

But part of me knew I was awake, and had just thought something to which I needed to pay attention.

There's a story here.

An arc.

Hadn't Feather said that? Something along those lines? I believed she had. I was pretty sure. And I belatedly realized I'd interpreted the last word as the term I'd heard in a thousand meetings in LA. Partly because of the word "story" before it. Because that's what I used to do.

But she hadn't meant it that way. She'd been giving me a clue. She'd been spelling it differently.

She meant "ark."

I sat up straight, far more alert now.

Of course. An ark—where the animals went in, two by two.

I couldn't begin to understand how that worked, but I'd seen the evidence with my own eyes and I was done questioning it.

And maybe . . .

I was aware I was engaging in exactly the kind of speculative thinking Gemma had mocked back at the trailhead, before this whole disaster began—that style of *is it therefore perhaps possible that two plus two equals seven?* faux-reasoning that'll take you anywhere you want to go if you're not careful. But right now nobody was keeping score.

And maybe . . .

Maybe that's the way it had actually been.

Perhaps at some point in prehistory something like this had been discovered before. An ancient people had stumbled upon a similar machine, hidden deep in a cave, and triggered the same process. Maybe the paintings in the gallery beyond the smelling room were even a record of this.

And instead of going in, two by two, animals came *out*.

And maybe this had happened somewhere in the Middle East, too—because hadn't Feather implied there was more than one of these sites?—and was such a head-spinningly strange event (even to people with a less science-dominated grip on what's supposed to be possible and what's not) that it became enshrined in a myth as a cautionary tale . . . for long enough that a mangled version was eventually wrapped into the collection of stories, history, and legends that became the Bible.

An ark. And what else was part of that story? What was, in fact, the defining theme of it?

A flood.

It was coming on quickly now, a rush of things I knew or had at least read more than once and should have been able to put together much earlier—and perhaps might have, if they'd seemed in any way related before.

The Hopi Indians, like a lot of cultures—as I'd told Gemma, at tedious length—cherished a flood myth. I couldn't remember the specifics of it, but I realized I didn't have to. It was right there in my hands.

That's what Feather had meant.

On the night before we climbed up into the cavern she'd borrowed my phone and looked through my notes. The only problem was that there were a thousand pages cached onto there and I didn't have time to sift through all of them.

But then I realized I didn't need to. Partly because I already understood now where this was going. Also because the app readily presented me with a history of which files had been opened most recently. What she'd looked at.

And yes, she'd read documents on the Hopi. Which wouldn't previously have struck me as significant—we were in Hopi territory, after all, and she'd asked to look at my note stash after I'd been talking about Newspaper Rock—but now that information alone was enough to take me the final steps.

The Hopi believe the world we live in is the gods' fourth run at it. The first attempt was erased by fire. The second was wiped out when two minor gods left their posts at the axes of the planet, causing the spin to tilt, provoking an ice age.

The next world was notably more advanced than the previous two, in which humans had lived with the animals or in small villages. This third version was their Atlantean age, with a far larger population and more advanced civilization—but of course it went to pieces. The people created a "giant flying shield" called a *patuwvota*—which naturally some have interpreted as an aircraft or alien spaceship—and used it to attack a foreign city. They retaliated, and it all kicked off.

Seeing this, the boss god Sotuknang decided to get eschatological once more and brought down a flood. But the good guys—the ones "with a song in their hearts"—were allowed to survive, and given another chance in a further world. Instead of being uniformly perfect like the previous ones, the Fourth World (called Tuwaqachi) was going to be possessed of height and depth, hot and cold, lush and barren areas, a more challenging environment—the idea being to keep the turbulent humans occupied with staying alive, rather than attacking each other. While it was being prepared and the planet was still flooded, the worthy were assisted by Anu Sinom—the "ant people." These beings escorted the remaining Hopi to a place where they could wait out the transition, and meanwhile prove their piousness and fealty to the gods.

That place was a system of caves.

Of course, the legend didn't say where it was. But the Hopi, heirs to the oldest-known Native American tribe, the Anasazi, had an ancient custom of trekking hundreds of miles from their current homes all the way to . . . the Grand Canyon.

Why?

And why did some of the figures on Newspaper Rock strongly resemble the paintings we'd discovered in the adjunct to this complex—pictures that Feather claimed were fifty thousand years old? I had no proof that her information was trustworthy. But I had no proof to the contrary, and I'd spent enough time looking at reproductions of Neolithic cave art to believe they seemed convincing. Not least because the Lascaux paintings hadn't even been discovered until 1940—thirty years *after* Kincaid found this cavern, which had never been entered since.

Neither he nor anybody else *would have known what to fake*. Which meant they *had* to be real.

What I didn't understand was why the Palinhem Foundation would want to locate a place like this. It wasn't out of intellectual interest, that's for sure. Feather had sounded triumphant, evangelical. Then I saw the last document she'd looked at.

The Hopi Prophecies.

An ancient list of nine signs that were supposed to portend the ending of the Fourth World, in preparation for Armageddon and rebirth in the Fifth. There are those who believe that—with liberal interpretation—most have already been fulfilled. The First Sign mentions the coming of the white man. Others perhaps prefigured railways, catastrophic oil spills, the Internet, and 1960s countercul-ture.

Only the Ninth had not yet been deemed to have come fully to pass, as it involved a blue star appearing in the heavens and crash-ing to Earth. Other elements of that Ninth Prophecy, however—the "white man battling against people in other lands"—well, yeah, that's a known thing.

You could choose therefore to believe we were on the brink of ful-filling the prophecy, waiting only for that blue star/meteor/spaceship to push us over. You could believe this if you were a little crazy, and if you *were* a little crazy, then you might want to get ahead of the curve and preemptively claim the place to hide out.

A site waiting patiently to repopulate the Earth.

You would try to find the ark.

I knew my reasoning didn't stand up straight yet. It didn't feel wrong, though.

It felt *very far from wrong*.

I heard Molly's voice, quiet. "Oh dear God."

Head still deep in my notes, I looked up from the phone to see her staring up the passage toward the main room. I angled the glow from my phone screen to make it brighter.

Something stood at the edge of the glow, remaining mostly in shadow.

It was about the size of a young horse. It had a clump of algae on one bulky shoulder, and its hide was still wet. It stared back at us cu-riously, angling its head.

A single dead-straight and pure white horn protruded from its forehead.

It turned and walked away into the darkness.

Molly didn't move a muscle. "What...was that?"

"A unicorn," I said.

CHAPTER

45

We woke the other two. We discussed it, very briefly, and the consensus was firmly in favor of *not* following the animal Molly and I had just seen. We were plain terrified now.

"Come on, Nolan," Ken said, and even he sounded freaked out. "You're now badly in the realm of made-up shit."

"Maybe not," I said. "The weird thing about unicorns is that the Greeks never mentioned them in mythology. Only in their natural histories. They didn't think unicorns were legendary. They believed they were real. And the thing we saw was only fairly horselike. Who knows, maybe it was a young Elasmotherium."

"Which is?"

"Was. Northern European style of rhino. Which some people think may have outlasted the most recent ice age and overlapped with humans, maybe even giving rise to stories of reclusive unicorns."

I took them through the thoughts I'd just had, the ideas I'd mashed together into a possible explanation for this place. Molly immediately began asking questions and making objections, while nervously glancing up the passage. Pierre stared at me like I'd started talking in a foreign language.

Ken, bless him, simply went with it. If Satan himself turned up at Ken's house—wreathed in sulfur and lightning bolts—Ken would give him a hard time for not bringing enough wine/cigarettes/vodka but otherwise tell him to pull up a deck chair and make himself at home.

"This ball, though," he said. We were beside it, huddled close together, apart from Pierre, who was standing a couple of yards up the passage keeping an eye out. "Assuming you're right, Nolan. Bonkers though it sounds. Why trap everything in here? If this is the machine that reboots life on Earth, you want it all to be able to get *out* of here afterward, right?"

"To which there's three possible answers."

"Christ, you and your fucking brain. Can't there just be *one* answer to any given question, and it always be good news?"

"First is . . . the ball wasn't supposed to be triggered. It was a last-resort defense in case the site came under attack, and it's just bad luck Gemma stood on the thing."

"That idea's shit. Next."

"Second is there *is* a way out, but we haven't found it yet. Best bet for that is the other end of the paintings room."

"Which *we can't get at*. That idea's shit, too."

"Third is there's some way of resetting the physical environment, once the things created in here are ready to leave and populate the cleansed Earth. Of moving the ball and reopening the passage."

"How?" Moll said. "Turning the whole place off and on again?"

"Don't see that helping us either way," Ken said. "I'm always happy to take a stroll down Woo-Woo Lane with the Anomaly-meister, but I don't think moving the ball's the answer. It's a very heavy thing at the bottom of a slope. Physics is not our friend on this one."

"I know," I said. "The third answer sucks, too. I'm handing the Talking Stick over to somebody else."

Nobody said anything for a while.

"What if there's another trigger?"

Pierre spoke as we were gathering ourselves to cautiously head back up the passage, for no better reason than it didn't seem like a great idea to be trapped with nowhere to run, should it come to it. Which it was increasingly feeling like it might.

"Not for, this ball," he said. His speech was losing normal patterns, words clumping in odd ways. I'm sure mine was, too. "What if there's a fourth answer? Something else we can move by pushing something or stepping on something or whatever?"

"We haven't seen anything like that."

"No. But we've been poking around in the dark, only looking for ways out. We haven't rigorously checked every corner of every room. Like it's a *Tomb Raider* game or something. Because, you know, it kind of almost is."

Molly shook her head. Her voice was a dehydrated croak. "Pierre, there's a hundred rooms. And God knows how much corridor. With . . . random *things* roaming them."

"And the logic's not secure, either," I said. "This could be a failsafe designed precisely to stop people like us from unleashing the process before the proper time, or from doing it in the wrong order. Feather implied there could be more than one site like this."

"She *did*?"

"Sounds like the permafrost expedition that Kristy's on could be wandering into similar territory. Or was deliberately sent there, in that hope."

"Shit," Molly said. "I hope she's okay."

Molly has never met Kristy. She's heard almost nothing about her from me, and I would imagine little from Ken. I felt absurdly touched that she would care. "Me too."

"Nolan," Pierre said. There was a faint tremor in his voice. "It'd be cool if you could stop proving there's no way out, okay? I kind of need the idea. Even if it's wrong."

"Sorry," I said. "And, yes—it's possible the ball's there to seal the site while it's in Genesis mode, and there's some way of releasing this shit into the wild at the right time."

"I don't think so," Molly said. "There's nothing to eat here. I'll bet most of the rooms in this place were originally designed for storage. Like, grain and stuff. They're *empty*. How were these things supposed to survive without food? We found the place by accident at the wrong time, when it wasn't ready for action and hadn't been stocked with food and freaking Ant People, or whatever, and we triggered a failsafe. We're *done*. And *we're the only food in here*."

"*Molly*," Pierre snapped. "Seriously. Shut the fuck up."

"We have got *one* proper light and one small one and no idea how much power is left in either of them."

"I've still got the camera light."

"Great. So what do we *do*? Grid-search thousands of feet of floor and wall, stepping on every inch and pressing anything we can find? How long will that take? Plus there are fucking *wolves* in here. And saber-toothed tigers. And they're going to get hungry, too."

"I still think the paintings room is our best bet," Ken said. "Or...well, there is that other pool room."

Molly and Pierre turned to him and said: "*What?*"

"It's crystal clear," Molly said.

She was lying on her front, hanging over the pool, holding the light down close to it. Ken stood at the back of the group, keeping an eye on the corridor behind us.

"Yes," I said, "but—"

"Don't 'but' me," she said. The more tired she got, the more Molly was turning into team mom again. A mom who was moreover done with taking her kids' crap for one afternoon and in need of a weapons-grade alcoholic beverage, stat. "You drank from the other pool and you were fine. A few hours ago, you and Pierre ended up with postgenesis soup inside you, with the water clear again, and you both seem okay, right?"

"We need to drink, Nolan," Ken said. "Or we're done."

Just talking about it was causing us to look hungrily at the pool—gaunt, drawn faces half-lit.

"It may have been Gemma's blood that kicked the other pool into action," I said cautiously. "I'm tired enough to speculate that ancient ideas of blood sacrifice could even be a mangled memory of a process just like this. Give the gods blood, and they will provide...weird stuff. In fact—"

"What?"

"The trigger plate. The one that made the big ball roll. She'd dripped blood onto that, too. Maybe *that's* what kicked this whole thing off, instead of her treading on it."

"Could be, mate. And something else struck me earlier. Those three letters chipped in the wall next to it."

"What about them?"

"Little extra nick at the end? Maybe it wasn't the start of another letter. Maybe it was an apostrophe."

"Huh?"

"Maybe instead of a name, whoever put them there was trying to write 'DON'T'—as in 'Don't screw around with the pool down this corridor, because it will fuck you up.'"

"Don't care about any of this," Molly said. "I need to *drink*."

"Do we have anything made of glass?"

"Why?"

"It's the least reactive thing in water."

Molly dug in her backpack. "No," she said, though she kept digging. "Oh." She held up a small glass pot. "There's this."

It was her empty lip balm container. "Got a tissue?"

She found one and handed it to me. I used this to wipe the residual balm out of the jar. She rooted around in the bag again, and came up with some tweezers.

"Would this help keep your fingers out of the water?"

"Not only that." I got out my cigarette lighter. When the jar was as clean as I could get it, I held it with the tweezers and sparked up a flame. I played it methodically over the inside and outside of the little pot, producing a not-unpleasant smell from a burned smear of balm. It made me realize how long it had been since I'd smelled anything but cold rock and endless dust. Something sweet, and warm.

"It's not perfect," I said.

"Close enough," Ken muttered. "Get on with it. I don't want anything coming up behind while we're trapped here."

"Wait," Pierre said.

He was standing at the end of the ledge overhanging the pool. He had the camera on his shoulder and the strong, hard, white light above its lens was directed straight across the space in front of us, revealing for the first time that this pool room was significantly larger than the other one. Much wider, and higher, and far, far longer.

"Fuck's sake," Ken said.

He sounded more exhausted and defeated than I'd ever heard him sound before. Than I'd heard *anyone* sound, ever. Because not only down the end but along both sides were vast tiered platforms, holding hundreds of metal spheres, *thousands* of them—all of them far larger than the ones we'd seen before—stretching back, rank after rank, into the darkness.

While I was staring at these I heard a little splash, and looked down to see that the lip balm pot had slipped out of the tweezers, and was now sinking to the bottom of the pool.

CHAPTER

46

We stood looking out over the water until Pierre turned off the light, and then sat and stared into blackness. Nobody gave me a hard time about dropping the pot.

Ken and I shared a cigarette. There were only two left now. Just after I stubbed it out, a long, howling growl echoed down the corridor. It didn't sound like a wolf. I don't know what it sounded like. The kind of thing people heard a very, very long time ago, prowling outside their cave in the night. The kind of thing that made people afraid of the dark. It didn't seem like whatever made the sound was close. That yielded little reassurance. We had nowhere to go. It would find us sooner or later.

Pierre turned the camera light back on and directed it up the corridor. For the first time I noticed that there was a flat and polished section on the wall there. In the middle was a single large pictogram. It looked familiar—the one with the short horns—and I knew where I'd seen it: on the console rock in the other pool room. The light went past it and found Ken, and I saw he was looking thoughtful.

"What's on your mind?"

"What did Feather say? Before she left."

"I told you."

"Tell me again, Nolan. As precisely as you can remember."

"She said Dylan was dead, or told me again. She said the thing about an arc, which I'm now thinking she meant another way. As discussed. That's it."

He shook his head, frustrated. "Something else."

"There really wasn't."

"There *was*, Nolan. It nipped at me even at the time, but there was other crap going on and I blew past it. Fuck. Think. What was it?"

I closed my eyes. This made me feel lost and nauseous. I half opened them again. I couldn't recall anything else. I could barely remember the things I'd already mentioned. "There's nothing else, Ken."

"Paintings," Pierre said. "Didn't she say something about the paintings?"

And then there it was. "Actually, yes. She said they were fifty thousand years old. That's all."

"That's it," Ken said quietly.

"What?"

"You mean," Molly said, "how would she know they were that old?"

"No," Ken said. "Well, yeah. There's that. But roll back further, Moll. You, me, and Nolan were there in that cavern. We saw the paintings, and then the light died on us before we could get to the end. But what happened when we got back to the main room? Why did we hurry back?"

"Because...shouting," she said. She was frowning with concentration, like someone in eighth-grade algebra keen to show she was following along. "We were in the fissure on the way back and we heard Gemma shouting."

"Right. So we ran back in here and dealt with the clear and present danger. Then what?"

"We ate," I said.

"And then?"

"Ken—can you just say the thing, whatever it is?"

"No. I need you to walk it through for me. To make sure I'm not missing something. After we ate, what *then*?"

"Fuck's sake, Ken. You and I went to check out the pool straight after, thinking we'd try the water despite the risk. We bailed on the idea because of the algae and when we got back that's when Gemma dropped her bombshell about Feather's phone and the photo on it. We were deep into that when we heard Feather clapping. The end. So?"

"And we talked to her and she pretended to go, and then later *you* talked to her . . . And *that's* when she mentioned the paintings. Right?"

"Right."

Ken grinned at me. It was tired and lopsided, but it was real. "Come on, Nolan. Get there yourself, you muppet."

I looked at him, frowning—and finally it dawned. "Shit," I said. "Are you *sure*?"

"Not a hundred percent, but bloody close. It's why I made you remember it step by step."

I was silent for a moment, thinking back through the sequence of events again as rigorously as I could. "Christ."

"Exactly."

"Please, you two," Molly said. "*Stop doing this.*"

"Feather knew what we'd been doing because she'd been listening behind the rock during the day," I said. "Staying quiet. Eavesdropping on everything we said. Right?"

"Okay, so?"

"But we never mentioned the paintings."

Molly blinked at me. "What?"

"Pierre," I said. "When did you first hear about them?"

"When you and I went to check out the smelly room, and found the crap on the floor had melted."

"None of us told you about them before?"

"No."

"Are you *sure*?"

"Absolutely sure."

"So," I said. "Given she could not have overheard us, how did Feather know about them?"

266

"Oh," Molly said. "Oh."

"You're still only halfway there," Ken said, however. "Who *knows* what that bitch knows, or the people she works for. She talked about another site like this in Alaska. Maybe there's others around the world. Could be they've *all* got cave paintings. That is not the point."

I frowned. "Well then, what is?"

"It's not that she knows about the paintings," Molly said, evidently a step ahead of me now. "It's that she knows that *we've* seen them."

"And how would she know that, Nolan?"

"She...she could have assumed," I said. "We'd been exploring. She just assumed we'd found them."

"Is that the way it sounded?"

"No," I admitted. "She told me the age as if answering a question. A question she'd overheard."

"Which you asked..."

"...when we were there."

Pierre looked back and forth between us. "But what does that mean?"

"It means you can get from the other side of that ball, to the other end of the paintings cavern," Ken said. "That's the only way she could have been in position to hear us, the only way she could know we'd found them."

"It means there's a way out," I said. "Maybe."

"It's the best we've got," Ken said, standing. He staggered, badly, veering back into the wall as if very drunk. Tried to right himself, but staggered again, and this time toppled heavily to the ground.

"Fuck," he said. He looked old for a moment, lying on his side, trying to get up. Pierre and I went to help. And we both immediately keeled over onto our sides.

It would have been funny, except it wasn't.

All three of us eventually got upright. Then Pierre and I reached a hand down to Molly, who'd simply watched all this, goggle-eyed. She took them and we pulled her up, gently.

"If we're going to try this," she said, "I think it needs to be soon."

267

"No," Ken said. He looked something like his usual self again, but exhausted and drawn. "It needs to be now."

Then, from a distance—but closer than last time—came the sound of a low, rumbling growl, mixed with a keening howl.

"Or even sooner," he said.

CHAPTER
47

Five minutes later we were in the stinking room. It was noticeably warmer than before and the smell had gotten worse, unbelievably. More open in texture, fresher, making it easier to work out what it reminded you of. The deeply, offensively rank odor of something two days into rotting—like a dead seal on a beach, or a rat caught in a trap in hot sun, but multiplied ten-thousand-fold. It assaulted the eyes and stomach like a living entity, making you retch until you coughed and your stomach heaved.

Despite this, Pierre waded out into it for a few yards before retreating with the rest of us to the doorway. "It's more liquid than it was."

"You think?"

"Definitely," he said. "Earlier it was like molasses. It's looser now."

"Still pretty thick, though," Ken said. "And we don't know how deep it is down the end, do we?"

"The room's only thirty yards long," I said. "We can make it that far."

"Maybe."

"Of course we can."

"Look," Ken muttered, "I can't fucking swim, all right?"

"*Seriously?*"

"I grew up in London in the 1970s and I'm not a masochist, Caliboy. Life on land only got started in the first place because all the

269

fish decided to get the fuck out of the North Sea because it was too bloody cold. Assuming," he added, "that evolution...is even a thing. Which, judging by what's happening here right now, it may not be. Christ."

"It's fine," I said. "We'll get you across."

"How?"

"Basic life-saving technique," Pierre said. "I swim on my back, arm around you from behind, pull you along."

"Fuck's sake."

Pierre nodded decisively. "Two minutes," he said, turning toward the main room.

"Where are you going?"

"The drives are in my pack."

"Drives?"

"Hard drives. The footage of everything we've seen in here. I'm not going without them."

"Okay, but Jesus—we discussed this," I said. "We *stay together.*"

Which was still a sensible policy, and we were all keen to get a break from the smell, too...

But it was a mistake.

It was clear from the state of Gemma's remains that something had visited her again in our absence.

I reached for my backpack but realized there was nothing in there I needed. Ken and Molly made the same call about their own packs. The lighter we were traveling, the better. We quickly loaded the portable drives into Pierre's bag.

"How waterproof are these disks?"

"Not very. I'm thinking I'll take the pack across first, holding it up above my head, then throw it up into the fissure. That'll give me a chance to assess the liquid, too, and check if there's anything we need to know about below the surface."

"Like what?" Molly asked nervously.

"Just pyramids. Most of the rooms here have got them," he said.

"And they're getting hotter, right? Maybe that's what made the gunk in there loosen up. We don't want to trip over one. Or get burned by it, if they're even hotter now."

"Okay, good thinking," I said. "Let's put the phones in your bag, too."

As we were doing that, there was a sound. The one we'd been hearing for the last half hour. Much louder this time, however, and coming from the corridor that led to the original pool. A kind of a grunting noise, but with a whispering texture around the edges.

It wasn't good. It wouldn't have been good if we'd heard it in the middle of a sunlit meadow. Trapped in a pitch-dark abandoned ancient anomaly half a mile underground, it was really very not-good indeed.

"What the *hell* is that?" Molly whispered.

"I don't know. But it's not wolves. It's too deep, too loud. Too big-sounding. To be honest, I don't want to find out."

The sound came again, but from a different corridor.

"There's two of them," Ken said quietly. "They're grid-searching, looking for us. Let's go. Now."

Molly, Ken, and I stood in the corridor outside the room. There was a brief whispered debate about whether it'd make sense to divest ourselves of clothes while crossing, sending them ahead in Pierre's backpack, to stop us taking the appalling smell with us afterward. The opposing view—that we wanted as little skin contact with the gunk as possible—won out, not least as the only thing we'd have to wipe the crap off with after the crossing was...our clothes.

Molly positioned the camera on her shoulder and directed the light down the room. It reached far enough to catch the edge of the fissure, giving Pierre a straight-line course.

"Be careful," Ken told him. "And if you feel anything moving under there, come the hell back out."

Pierre nodded, held his pack up above his head, and started to walk into the liquid.

"It's still thicker than water," he said as the level got above his knees. "Though—" He stopped talking abruptly and retched. "Holy *crap* it smells bad."

But he kept going. The depth increased rapidly. Within another minute it was up to his waist. Then his chest. He was making near-constant coughing and retching sounds now.

"Okay," he said, when he was halfway across the room. "I'm going to have to start treading water now. Or not water. Whatever this stuff actually is."

He paused, adjusted his angle, and moved forward again. He kept the hand holding the pack aloft. He dropped the other into the liquid and started walking. After a few moments it became clear from the movements of his head that his feet were no longer touching the bottom, and he was treading water, using his hand as a paddle to laboriously pull forward.

It was very slow, the liquid still thick enough to make progress tough.

"Are we even going to be able to do this?" Molly asked me. "I've got swim game, but that looks hard."

"We'll be fine," I said. There was nothing else to say. I heard Ken breathe out heavily behind me, however, and knew what he'd be thinking. That he was not light, or fit, and it was going to be extremely challenging for Pierre to swim for both of them. "We'll be fine," I said again.

We watched Pierre slowly progress toward the end of the room, Molly holding the beam of the camera light steady, until his head and arm became the only things we could see. At one point he seemed to lose rhythm, and his head sank closer to the surface, but he recovered and kept going.

Then there was a grunting sound as he wrenched his right arm out of the liquid.

"There," he said. He sounded a long distance away—much farther than the length of the room. There was a thud as his backpack landed in the fissure. "Done it."

"Good work. Take a minute before you come back."

"Oh yeah," he said. He was panting hard, and sounded exhausted. "I'll be doing that, trust me."

And then there was a really bad, loud sound, from the direction of the main room.

The three of us jumped and swung around in that direction, Molly unthinkingly bringing the beam of light with her.

For a fraction of a second I saw something, only about thirty yards away up the corridor.

A shape, momentarily lit. Not as tall as a man, only five feet high, but twice human breadth. Muscled like an ox. Hands like spades, totally out of proportion, spatulate fingers red with Gemma's blood.

A huge, bald head, thick with bone.

By the time Molly whipped the beam across where it had been, the creature had slipped back into the darkness. It hadn't gone far, though. You could hear it breathing.

"There's two of them," Ken said. "Turn off the light."

Molly flicked off the beam. Everyone listened.

Two things, breathing in the darkness. Heavily. As if struggling to push air in and out of noses and chests still thick with the nutrient soup they'd crawled out of.

One made the sound again. The sound we'd been hearing. It was guttural, throaty. Over a couple of seconds, it changed in pitch three times. It wasn't language, but it was communication of some kind. Not with us. With the other one.

They were planning how to attack.

"They're coming closer," Molly said. She sounded very unhappy and very scared.

Swishing footfalls on the stone floor. A low, rumbling growl. Deeply buried parts of your heart, soul, and most ancient DNA know exactly what that sound means.

Molly and I took a step back into the room.

Another growl, louder now.

"Go," Ken said.

"What?"

"We don't have time for Pierre to swim back for me. I'll lead them away down the corridor."

"Fuck off, Ken," I said.

The creature nearest us made another sound. Not a growl. More like a roar. They had us cornered and they knew it. They were coming for us now.

"You hang around and we're *all going to die*. Seriously. I'm done. We're almost out of cigarettes anyway."

"Don't be a—"

"Molly!" he shouted. "Just *do it*."

"But—"

She didn't want to, but she was very used to doing what Ken said and in that beat of hesitation he grabbed the camera from her with one hand and with the other shoved me, hard.

I tripped over the lintel and fell backward into the room, winding up full-length on the floor. Ken flicked the light on, and for a moment was lit, grinning, from underneath. He winked, looking for a moment so much younger.

"It's been fun, mate," he said. "Really. But you're still a twat."

Then he ran away up the corridor.

I scrambled to my feet, pushed Molly hard behind me, so she went skittering across the floor and into the liquid. Through the pitch darkness, I heard a thick, gloopy splash.

"Go," I shouted to her.

"What's happening?" Pierre called.

"Come get Molly. Help her across."

"What's *happening*?"

I turned to where I thought the doorway was but was hurled backward by a thudding swipe, sharp nails tearing across my chest, shredding through my shirt.

I landed six feet back in the liquid and barely got half a lungful of air before my head was sinking under the surface. It was the thickness of dishwashing fluid and very warm. I didn't sink as fast as I would have in water but I had no idea of where I was, or how far I was going to drop.

After a few seconds I felt hands yanking at me and let them pull me in a direction that turned out to be the right one because a couple of moments later my head was out. I gasped in some air before becoming aware that the room was now full of noise.

Molly and Pierre were screaming at me to come with them. The creature at the end was full-body roaring now, chaotic with blood-hunger.

"Ken," I panted. "I'm going ba—"

"No," Pierre said. He kept pulling, and Molly did, too.

"You heard him," she said to me from between gritted teeth as they pulled me out of my depth and farther toward the other end. "You *heard* what Ken said. He said to go. That thing's going to kill you if you go back—and I'm not letting that happen. I'm *not letting it happen.*"

The creature roared again, but wasn't advancing as quickly as I would have expected—as if wary of the foul gunk we were half drowning in, unsure how to deal with it. It was wading toward us, though—you could feel movement in the liquid. There was only one of them in here, I was sure of that even in the darkness.

Ken had led the other away, giving us half a chance.

I still tried to fight Pierre and Molly but I was winded and confused as to which direction to go. Maybe I even knew in my heart of hearts that I had to leave it.

"You *asshole*," I shouted, and tried one last time to get them to let me go, but my voice was thick with tears and I don't think they could even hear what I said.

None of us knew we were at the far end until our flailing arms smacked into the rough wall. Molly got out of the liquid first and up into the opening, and she hauled me after her as Pierre pushed my legs from underneath, somehow fit enough to still be treading water.

Then we were crowded together in the mouth of the fissure,

coughing; too out of breath to do anything except suck huge lungfuls of air—lungfuls that were acrid with the thick, noxious smell.

"I'm going back," I croaked.

"No, you're not," Pierre said. "You even try, and I'll knock you out."

"Fuck you," I shouted. "Ken is my—"

Then we heard it.

We all heard it, cutting through the roars of the creature at the other end. A shout, or scream. It was high-pitched, awful, human. It came from outside the room we'd just crossed, from back in the main room. He'd gotten that far, at least.

Then it stopped. Cut off suddenly.

The creature that had pursued us went silent, and then after a moment we heard it moving quickly away, back toward the corridor, leaving the room to take its share in the spoils.

"Come on, Nolan," Molly said gently.

Pierre found his backpack and picked it up and they pulled me into the fissure with them and we left.

FROM THE FILES OF NOLAN MOORE:

ENGRAVING FROM THE LONDON MAGAZINE, MAY 1766

CHAPTER

48

We squeezed our way along the crevice. Pierre went first. I went in the middle, using my phone to give us some light. Molly was at the back, and though I heard her doing her breathing thing a couple of times, it seemed recent events had blown her disquiet at claustrophobic darkness out of the water. I guess that'll happen when you've been reminded that there are far worse things. Eventually we emerged into the gallery. We stood a moment, catching our breath.

"That doesn't look good," Molly said.

She was talking about my chest. There were deep gashes across it, an inch apart, from the claws of the thing that'd nearly taken me down. They were bleeding heavily. I looked at the mess with indifference. It didn't matter and there was nothing I could do about it.

"Ken gave us no choice," she said quietly.

"I know. And when I see him in heaven, I'm going to punch him in the face for it."

Molly's chin was trembling. She pursed her lips defiantly. "Actually, I hope it's hell. It'd be much more his kind of thing. And you'd adapt fast enough."

I was surprised into something like a laugh. I started to speak but couldn't work out what I could possibly say.

Pierre meanwhile looked upon the paintings for the first time. You can read people's thoughts sometimes. That's not a magical or super-natural ability. You merely have to know them. I saw him thinking that he had to capture these things, get them on disk—as well lit and pho-tographed as he could—so others could see them. So that the world would know. Then I saw him remember he didn't have the camera, and who'd last been holding it, and firmly drop the entire line of thought.

He walked along the wall, however, holding his phone up high and looking at each in turn. "Mosquito," he said. "Bug. Coyote or wolf. A horse with a horn. The squid-thing that nearly got me. And that . . . That's what Gemma had inside her."

It was the picture I'd noticed the first time, something like a bird, but with an odd, bony head. "I guess."

"But there's millions of species on Earth," Molly said. "A hundred buttons isn't enough."

"Maybe you can combine them," I said. "String together se-quences or something. Or this is the starting set, and then evolution takes over. Don't know."

The light passed across a picture I hadn't seen before, right at the end, past the hands. It was stylized, hard to discern, especially in the feeble light of a phone screen. It wasn't something that had been found in the fossil record, that's for sure—unless the archeologists involved had elected not to mention it on the grounds that it would be likely to freak people out.

It was exactly like the figure I'd pointed out to Gemma on the picture of Newspaper Rock. Short horns. Built like a bear, bulky and powerful across the back. Its shoulders were bunched, gripping hands directed downward.

Short horns. Like the pictogram I'd spotted in the first pool room, and then as the only available option on the wall outside the much bigger one half an hour ago.

"Let's get to the end and see what there is to see," I said. I unthink-ingly left a beat, used as I was to leaving space for someone else to speak, either to back up what I'd said or else suggest a—usually better—alternative course of action. Or swear. Or talk about cheeseburgers.

The regrets kept coming in waves, deeper each time. If only we hadn't lost time looking at the bigger pool, trying to work out a way of getting a drink that in the end didn't happen anyway. If only I'd gotten his point about Feather overhearing us more quickly. Or he hadn't made me slog there. If only we hadn't gone back for the hard drives.

I realized I wasn't going anywhere useful, and I would end up being a liability to the others if I kept swirling around the vortex. The past is full of if-onlys and they're all bullshit. You only think that way when it's too late. You only if-only, as Ken would have said, when you're already screwed.

So I shoved them all to the deep back of my mind and we hurried to the end of the room.

Soon after the point we'd reached on our first visit, the gallery tapered in rapidly from both sides. After another ten feet it ended abruptly in a narrow crevice—this distant end of the room, like this entire space, showing no sign of the workmanship so evident throughout the rest of the complex. There was no way through the crack. I shoved my hand into it and found an extra pocket of space beyond, but my fingers reached the end of that, too. There was no way forward.

There was a dull crunching sound under my feet when I moved, and I turned the light down in that direction.

"What . . . are they?" Molly said.

I squatted down. "Bones."

"From . . ."

"The last people who got stuck in here, presumably. The ones who made the paintings. While they waited to . . ."

There were five skulls that I could see. Five full skeletons. I'd just trodden through more Neolithic bones than had ever been discovered in the rest of the world, put together. Bones of the beings that had huddled together here at the end of this cavern, waiting for the end. Recording what they'd seen, until they ran out of energy. Until they starved and died.

"What now?" Pierre said. He hadn't said a word about Ken since it happened, but he didn't have to. The underlying panic in his voice said it all. Suddenly the ground beneath his feet had disappeared, and he knew it, and he wasn't sure that I represented a viable plan B. "What *the hell now?*"

Molly took the phone from him and pointed it upward. This showed a sheer, narrow wall of jagged rock, stretching up into darkness. "It has to be up there," she said.

"Or we're just plain wrong," I said. "And Feather overheard it some way we've forgotten or she wasn't answering my question after all."

"That idea sucks," she said, handing the phone to me. "And I'm bored with things sucking."

She squared up to the wall. Found sufficient hold with both hands to start inching her way up, using the wall opposite to patch together a half-assed chimney climb. She was breathing hard before she'd even gone a few feet. She looked very different from the girl who'd confidently made her way up the canyon wall when we'd spotted the entrance to this place. Skinnier, beyond exhausted, someone at the end of her resources but giving it one last try because that's what you do, rather than in any hope of success.

I wished we'd drunk some water from the bigger pool, with our hands if necessary. It was hard to see how it could have made the situation worse. But that was another if-only.

"See anything?" I realized this was a dumb question as soon as it was out of my mouth. The source of light was still in my hand. I held it higher, hoping I wouldn't be called upon to do any fast thinking soon.

"Nope."

Pierre rooted around in his pack and pulled out the remaining flashlight. This about doubled the height of the wall we could see, to perhaps twenty feet. No opening was visible. To my inexperienced eye there was little in the way of handholds, either. There was no guarantee there would be any way out of here, of course—and the former inhabitants of the bones around my feet evidently hadn't found one. This wasn't a video game, some tough but resolvable puzzle constructed for recreational amusement. There didn't have to *be* a way out. Even if Feather genuinely had overheard us this way, it didn't mean there was a way up or down from whatever speculated opening might be above.

I kept this thought to myself.

Suddenly Pierre turned his head. "What was that?"

"What?"

He held a hand up for silence.

I heard it then. A howling, yipping noise, echoing from the fissure at the other end of the gallery.

"Sounds like coyotes," Molly said, voice matter-of-fact but straining with effort as she kept heading upward.

"Fuck. Can coyotes swim?"

"Oh yeah. They'll get across that room easily. And they'll attack just about anything if they're hungry enough."

I grabbed the light from Pierre and told him to start climbing.

"But you're not going to be able to—"

"Just do it, Pierre. I'll be right behind."

Molly started flapping out with her hands, grabbing at anything that might serve as a hold, moving as quickly as she could. Pierre started up the wall. There was no question he was the better climber, and still pretty strong.

I alternated between watching what he was doing—in the laughable hope of replicating his moves—and glancing toward the other end of the gallery. The snarling sounds were getting closer, echoing strangely from the fissure. It sounded like there were more than two throats involved. Maybe things didn't only leave this ark two by two after all. Maybe once it was activated, it kept going. A first pair, and then further pairs, until the balls of elements were used up—in the smaller pool, and then the vastly bigger one, and perhaps others we hadn't found—until it had produced a sufficient population for the creatures to start reproducing by themselves. To repopulate the Earth.

"Light, Nolan!"

I redirected it upward again. Molly was more than twenty feet up the wall now. "I see something. There's... There's an opening up here! There's an *opening*!"

"Great. Keep going," I said as calmly as I could, knowing that with the panting and the pounding of blood in her ears, she had no idea how close the animals were to us.

"I see it," Pierre said. "Nolan, start climbing. We can take it from here without light."

Maybe they could. I wasn't so sure about me. I'm not a climber. Especially not in the dark. But I guess you play these things through to the end.

I stuck the light in my mouth and reached out for the holds that I'd seen him use. I pulled up off the ground, and immediately slipped back down again.

The coyotes—assuming that's what they were—weren't howling anymore. That wasn't because they'd given up and turned around. They knew they'd found something worth pursuing. They probably even knew, in that spooky way animals do, that their prey wasn't in a position to run.

They were closing in, coming forward in the darkness.

I could hear feet trotting along the rock floor now, and I smiled to myself, sensing that—whether it be heaven or hell—it was likely I was going to get a chance to punch Ken in his spectral face a lot sooner than I might have hoped.

"For God's sake, Nolan!" Pierre shouted, breaking me back to awareness. "*Climb*."

I tried again on the handholds, using all the strength I had. I felt my fingers slipping once more but reached up and grabbed, and then again, pulling up and up, getting my right foot onto the lowest ledge. Got a few feet higher but then felt myself losing it again, toppling backward, not sure I could do anything about it, as the scrabbling paws got closer.

I threw my hand up and found another hold but it wasn't enough to keep me tight to the rock. I felt myself starting to fall and tried to twist in toward the wall, hearing Molly shouting down at me, no content in her words, only urgency.

I thought I was going to tumble to the ground but I felt my back thud into the opposite wall and realized I'd gotten far enough up to use it like a chimney. I reached behind with one hand and pushed up with my feet, inching up, trying to get far enough from the floor that I couldn't be jumped at.

I twisted around to look below at the exact moment something launched itself up at me.

The beam of the light in my mouth slashed across the slavering face of a coyote, or something like one, leaping up at me. Its jaws were wide and rife with teeth. It had an extra eye, not quite centered, in its forehead.

"Oh dear God." My voice was muffled around the light.

"What?" Molly called, panicky.

"Never mind."

The next lunge, from a different creature, nearly reached me, and in trying to turn away I slipped—but only a couple of inches. I pulled and shoved and inched my back up the wall, in a cacophony of howls and strangled barks—until I heard Pierre shout at me to shove off from the back wall and throw my weight in his direction.

I did, and felt his hand grab me firmly around the wrist. He pulled as I pushed up with my feet. My wrists scraped across a jagged edge and I knew I was almost there.

Molly started pulling now, too, but then there was a deep, shuddering thud—something that reverberated through the rock as if a meteor had landed on the Earth's surface high above. If they hadn't been holding me I would have tumbled straight down the wall again.

I scrabbled up over the edge and into another fissure.

"What was that?" Molly asked.

I shrugged and headed onward, trying not to think about the owners of the bones below, or how close they had been to finding a way up. And maybe out.

CHAPTER

49

The fissure we found ourselves in was taller and wider than the one between the smelling room and the gallery. Though apparently natural, and far from straight, in the dim light from the phone it showed signs of having been worked. I found this reassuring, insofar as I was capable of experiencing that emotion, because it suggested a route of sufficient importance to have merited the effort.

All three of us were stumbling now, using our hands to support ourselves along the wall as we lurched as quickly as we could along the tunnel. There were further distant thudding noises. It was hard to be sure, but these felt as though they were caused by impacts at a level below us.

"Is that what it sounded like? What you heard in the night?"

"Yes," Pierre said. "Similar, anyway. It's the balls dropping into that bigger pool, isn't it?"

"I think so. The site is stepping up to phase two."

"Which means more of those things are going to appear," Molly said.

"Lots more. The console in the first pool room implied a hundred types. We haven't seen anywhere near that number. The bigger pool only had one option on offer. Could be that's something else."

"What?"

"Something bad, with horns. I don't know. *I don't know.*"

"Are you ... okay?"

"I'm fine," I said. That wasn't true, of course. I was in an increasing amount of pain. The gashes across my chest felt like they were burning hot. Either that or very cold. I wasn't sure. Nerve endings in tearing discomfort, either way, and the sensation was spreading down from the slashes into the muscles of my stomach wall, burying itself deeper. I didn't see any point in sharing this information.

"I don't believe you," she said.

"Let's keep moving, Moll."

It's not easy to maintain a sense of direction in a dark tunnel, especially when you're doing your best to run, but it seemed to me that the fissure struck out at an angle for a long while, and then started to pull back around, curving in a gradual arc.

Then it was straight again, very straight. Both the walls and floor became much smoother, too.

"Have we been here before?"

"I don't think so," I said. I couldn't be sure, but it didn't feel like we'd curved around enough to rejoin the corridor off the main passage on the other side of the stone ball. "Pierre—you never made it to the end of either of those corridors before the ball, right?"

"No. So this could be ... Oh."

In front of us, the tunnel split into two.

"For God's sake," Molly said. "So which way do we go?"

"One way, together," I said. "And if that's not the right one, then we come back and go the other. Together."

"But *which*?" Pierre asked. He sounded worse than scared now. He sounded truly desperate. "Which *way*, Nolan?"

"Right," I said.

"But how do you *know*?"

"I don't. It's trial and error. It's okay, Pierre—we're going to get out of here."

"I don't think I can take much more of this," he said. "I need to see some real light. I need some *real air*."

I led us down the right fork, somehow confident it would be the correct one. But after curving harshly for about thirty feet, it dead-ended. No sign of anywhere to climb to. It simply stopped. In a site this complex, this was far beyond my comprehension. It was hard to believe they'd run out of time or energy. This side tunnel meant something. Just not to me.

And either it was my imagination, or there was something happening now, too. When you touched your hand to the wall, it felt as though it was vibrating.

"Christ," Pierre said. "You *said this was the right way*."

"I was wrong. It's not the first time."

We lurched quickly back to the fork. As we arrived there was a massive thud, far more resonant than any of the ones before. It sounded like something very heavy indeed.

"We've *got to get out of here*," Pierre said. "If it's making hundreds or thousands more of those things..."

"It'll be okay," Molly said, though she didn't sound like she believed it. "Pierre, it'll—"

"Seriously, Moll? What *single part of this has been okay*?"

"All the bits where we haven't died," I said, planting a hand on each of their backs and shoving them up the other tunnel.

The tunnel started off straight but then bent markedly to the right. It kept going, too. And got wider, until we could trot along three abreast.

"Stop," Molly said suddenly.

"What?"

"There's light ahead."

Her eyes were better than mine. I hadn't noticed it against the glow from the phone screen, weak though it was. When I turned it off I saw a soft light in the tunnel ahead.

We were still and silent for a minute. Heard nothing.

"It's her," Pierre whispered. "It's Feather—coming back around to the gallery room."

"So what do we do?"

"It's three against one," Molly said, her voice hard. "And I really kind of want to talk to her."

I nodded. "Okay, so. Very, very quietly."

They dropped back a pace and let me go first. Moving slowly and carefully made me more aware of the cramp in my stomach. The muscles were locking up. Could just be a spasm, the muscle wall twisted at some point in the last hour, accentuated by the fact my stomach had basically received three mouthfuls of food in the last two days. Hopefully it was that. If not, it was something from the claws of the thing that swiped me, or the gunk still smeared over me.

There was barely any sound from our feet on the floor, but I held my hand up every few yards, and we froze, and listened. Nothing— except for the low vibration I'd noticed, and which I still wasn't entirely sure existed outside my own head.

Another few steps—still nothing.

But gradually it became clear there was a doorway ahead, a perfectly rectangular opening. Whatever was causing the glow lay beyond.

We crept closer and closer until we had no option but to commit, and stepped up to the edge of the room, and then into it, down a short flight of three steps—the first real steps, it struck me, that we'd seen in the entire site.

It was immediately clear that the space was devoid of people. But it wasn't empty.

Molly came down after me. "What the hell...is this?"

CHAPTER

50

The room was large and perfectly square. The ceiling was low. A path led directly across a flat, open space. In each corner stood one of the stark pyramidal shapes we'd encountered throughout the complex, but much larger: about four feet high.

How could we see all this?

Because the room glowed.

I don't know how else to describe it. The light didn't come from any particular source. There were no fixtures on the walls or ceiling or floor, no torches or other forms of illumination. Light simply hung like a cloud within the space, a muted opalescent glow.

"How is this even possible?" Pierre asked.

"I've no idea. It's not something we can do."

"You mean, modern technology?"

"Now or ever."

We walked into the center of the room. There was a frieze on the floor, split into equal halves by the path, taking up the entire space. Portions were raised by about an inch. The edges were sharp, as if laser-cut, far more precise than anything we'd seen in the rest of the structure. The shapes within it were rigidly geometric—some large, yards to a side; others smaller. Some had tiny points of light within their boundaries. Again, not actually *in* the stone. The glows didn't appear rooted to the rock itself, but as if suspended an inch above the surface. There weren't many lights. I counted six in the left half, seven in the right, thirteen in total, widely spread. Most were a dull amber color. I turned to face the left portion.

There was one in the upper left quadrant of this that was a deep, rich red. It was this that enabled me to finally find the pattern.

"It's a map," I said.

Molly frowned down at it. "Of what?"

"The Earth. Reduced to basic land masses. Look."

Once you'd seen it, the shapes fell into place. They showed the continents and the world's major islands, simplified to stylized geometric figures. Done that way out of an artistic impulse, or maybe even to allow for gulfs of time long enough to involve continental drift.

She pointed at the tiny rich red light. "So that's us?"

The glow was about a quarter of the way in from the left in its quadrant, about three-quarters of the way down. The approximate site of the Grand Canyon within a heavily simplified North American continent. "I think so."

"And the other lights are sites like this?"

"They must be." I held up my phone and took pictures of both halves of the room. One of the amber lights looked like it could be in Egypt. There was one in a rectangle that was presumably Australia. Another deep in the heart of Russia; one in France. One in what was probably Israel.

Then I noticed one of the lights was up in an area that could be interpreted as the far reaches of Alaska.

"Shit. Yes, they are."

The light there was the same dull amber as the others. But would it stay that way? Would they all? Or had we started something even bigger than we'd realized—something that would now arc out across the entire world in an avalanche of destruction?

"Nolan—look. At the other one."

I looked back at the light that seemed like it must indicate our position. It had started flashing.

"Why's . . . it doing that?" Molly asked.

It was pulsing at a rate of maybe once every two seconds, smoothly transitioning from off to on and back again. "I don't know."

Pierre was looking twitchy. "Let's go."

"But this could be a control panel. We might be able to stop this thing from happening."

"It's far more likely we'd just make things worse," Molly said, staring at the light and sounding scared. "As with every single other thing we've done."

"We have to *try*," I said, and stepped off the path and onto the frieze, heading straight for the flashing light.

"Nolan—no!"

But nothing happened. I walked straight over and stamped on the light. When I removed my foot, the glow was still there, pulsing like a tiny inaudible siren. I tried again, and again, stamping down with increasing frustration and panic.

Pierre put his hand on my arm but I shrugged it off. "There's got to be something we can *do*."

He pulled at me, harder.

"Let's go," Molly said. "Nolan. *Please*."

"It's not working," Pierre said. "Come on."

Molly led the way to the other side of the room, moving fast. As we ran up the matching set of steps I noticed a cavity to the left of the doorway. Lodged in there was a narrow slab of stone. There was a groove across the top step.

That gave me reason to hope, but I decided to keep it to myself for now. Pierre caught up with us as we stepped out into the corridor beyond, which led left and right instead of continuing straight ahead.

"Now where?"

"Right," I said. "And this time I'm pretty confident."

"Why?"

"When we first got here, to this level of the site. On the other side of the stone ball. You went exploring down the other corridor by yourself. You found a doorway blocked with a single sheet of stone, yes?"

"Yeah, I think."

"I'm hoping this was it."

I turned on my phone, noticing the battery icon was now in the red. We ran along the corridor, passing doorways of a style I was sure we'd seen before, curved at the top. The air felt different, too. Less stale. Less dead.

After a hundred yards we encountered another corridor, crossing at right angles and noticeably wider. "Yes," I said.

"Is this it? Really?"

It was hard to be certain. A rock tunnel in near-dark looks very much like every other near-dark rock tunnel you've ever seen—and God knows we'd seen a lot. But on the opposite side, a couple of yards down, was a doorway like the one we'd just come out of—surely to the corridor we'd first explored when we'd emerged here after the ladder. "I think so. Oh thank God."

"There's one way to check," Pierre said.

He turned left and moved into the darkness. Stumbled but kept going. Molly and I followed. It wasn't far. About sixty feet, if I remembered correctly.

It didn't take long before we hit a blank wall. This wasn't like the one we'd seen before the map room, however—a point where the builders had stopped tunneling. This wall was uneven. It had been created by cementing an opening shut with rocks and mortar.

It was the bricked-up end of the corridor we'd encountered two days ago. And the other side of it...

...was the world.

"Okay," I said, scarcely able to believe it. "We're in the right tunnel. The first one we were in when we climbed up here. So we just have to go back to the shaft and..."

I realized Pierre wasn't listening. Instead he was kicking at the wall. Kicking hard, time after time.

"Pierre..."

"I've got to have some air."

"You'll get it when we've climbed down the shaft."

"I need it *now*. Nolan, I can't wait anymore."

I tried to put my hands on his shoulders, to calm him down. "Pierre, I get it. But—"

"I can break the wall. We can get out that way."

"*What?* Of course we can't. We can't climb down hundreds and hundreds of extra feet of canyon wall in the dark. Or maybe you can, but I can't. Certainly not now."

I tried again to grab him but he shrugged me off. His skin was hot, his eyes wide.

"Leave him," Molly said.

"No."

"Leave him, Nolan. Leave him here in the dark. I'm done being in this place. I'm going out the way we know."

She walked away.

"Pierre," I said, as calmly as I could, "I want to get out of here as badly as you do. But this isn't the way. Like Moll says—we *know* how to get out. Let's just do it."

But he wasn't listening. Maybe he couldn't even hear. He'd been solid the whole time. Thoughtful, dependable, always ready to do the right thing. He was done with that now, done with keeping on keeping on. He'd run out of being that guy.

And I was running out of being that guy, too.

I tried one more time to lay my hands on him, to again talk him down. He kept kicking at the wall, though it was clearly achieving nothing.

I did the only thing I could do. I believed he'd come to his senses soon. Sometimes you need to let the spastic energy out, let the panic fly.

And sometimes maybe you have to say screw the other guy and look after yourself.

So I turned and walked away.

Then I heard Molly scream from up ahead in the darkness, and shout out in fury.

I ran along the tunnel, phone held up in front of me.

"Feather," I said. "Let's talk."

But then I saw Molly. She was rigid, eyes wide, an arm wrapped tight around her throat. And it wasn't Feather's.

"Hey, Indy. Weird situation you've got yourself into this time, hey?"

It was Dylan.

CHAPTER
51

I stopped dead in my tracks. In the near-darkness it was exactly like seeing a ghost.

"Feather... said she killed you."

"Fake news," Dylan said cheerfully. "It's an epidemic, man. So—where are the other dickheads?"

"Dead," I said, angrily and very loud. "Ken and Gemma and Pierre are dead. They died *on the other side of that fucking ball.*"

"Well, I'd be lying if I said I gave a shit," Dylan said. "And, hey, saves me doing it."

"But... why did Feather say *you* were dead?"

"To keep you on your toes. Or off them. Without me there's no way home, right? Very dispiriting. A real will-sapper. She's all about the psych stuff, that girl."

"Where's she now?"

"Out of here. With my phone, because apparently you've got hers. Reporting back to base. Mobilizing Palinhem—or the ones we trust, anyhow. And about time, because once we thought you'd found the right place she was only supposed to sit tight and observe until it was confirmed. Which she did. But she also *talked*, hey."

"Not much."

"So how come you're here, instead of trapped back there?"

I didn't say anything.

"Right, Indy. She made a mistake. Doesn't matter. I'm here to clear that up. It's what I do."

"You're with Palinhem as well?"

"Of course. My father and grandfather, too."

I realized something. "It was you, wasn't it. You and Feather. You met in the parking lot of the hotel, a couple of nights before we came down here."

"And you nearly found us. But didn't. Story of your life."

"Wait—your *grandfather*? But...the founder, Seth Palinhem—he only died ten years ago, Feather said."

"God, but you're dumb, man. There was no such guy. You need a story to explain why a foundation's got so much money to spend, that's all. In reality it's older than your stupid country. Than *any* country. Feather's born and bred to it, too, but she had a shine for you, Indy. She's got big ideas and might have tried to wrap you into them. I don't have that problem. I know my place. My job is not to reason why."

"Then what—"

"It's to make sure things happen nice and clean. Make sure all the sheeple out there, the ten billion dumb assholes of the world, never understand what's going on, never suspect what's being done in their name. You do *not* take risks with the mission. You tie up loose ends. You tie them up *hard*."

He moved his other hand out from behind his back and placed the barrel of a handgun firmly against Molly's temple. "So let's get that done."

I was ten feet away from him. Even if I'd been faster and fitter and less broken there was no way I could get to him before he pulled the trigger. There was no point even trying.

For a moment I felt that car crash swell of relief that comes when the worst is happening all around you, right now, and you can stop bracing yourself for it.

I breathed out slowly and held my hands up.

"Okay," I said. "Okay, Dylan—you win. I'm not going to come at you. You know that."

"Ya—because you're weak. All fucking talk, man."

"Maybe. Also because I know when I'm beat, and Molly is my friend, and I'm not going to be the cause of her death. You'll have to do the deed by yourself. But what I don't understand is why this is so big a deal."

"Seriously? It's the biggest deal there is, Indy. It's how we start again. How we reboot that big fuckup out there."

"Reboot what?"

"Planet Earth. It's not the first time. The other cycles—everything was lost. *Almost* everything. A few pockets escaped the flood. Cleanup crews that survived. Their DNA is supposed to collapse once they've done their job but somehow last time they made it into legend and the next human bloodline. The giants you're forever talking about—it's *them*. Echoes in the blood. But that's why the last reboot *didn't work*. You talk all the time about 'anomalies'—and ya, I've seen your dumb show—but you don't get it. *Mankind* is the anomaly, jackass. *Humans are the fuckup*, the thing that got mangled and messed up. This time we're ahead. This time we're going to run the game."

"*What* game?"

"The game of *life*. When the Ninth Prophecy comes fully to pass and all is wiped from the Earth, we'll be safe, in position to make sure it's *clean* this time, and ready to lead the way into the next epoch. It's time, my friend. This is a planet of dead men walking. And you helped us find the switch on the electric chair."

"One of several, according to the room we've just seen. Why?"

"One of these machines isn't enough to repopulate the world. This one should trigger all the others."

"But how would that even work?"

He shrugged. "I don't know, man. I don't know how gravity works or why bees dance or how sharks can smell blood in the water from miles away. Do you? No. It still happens." He nodded at the slash marks across my chest. "You got lucky. But only because they were barely out of the pool. And there's worse to come. Much worse. The things we remember as demons."

I remembered the pictogram by the big pool. The one that seemed to show something with short horns.

Dylan saw the look on my face. "Oh yes. Mankind didn't make that shit up. They're real. We know that in our back brains. And I'm not worthy, Indy. Those guys are the *hard-core* cleanup crew. Hundreds of thousands of them. Millions. Flooding the world at once, killing every living animal. No way to fight. No chance of escape. Wiping the planet clean."

There was a distant thud, from way back in the complex. It didn't distract Dylan, however. It was depressingly clear that he was focused on his task.

"It doesn't have to go this way," I said. "Look, Molly and I... we don't care about any of this. We just want to stay alive. Let us go, and we'll disappear. For good."

He shook his head.

"Seriously," I said. "Who would even believe us?"

"You're done, Indy."

I saw in his eyes that even if this weren't his job, he would have been happy to do what he was going to do.

I heard another thudding sound, very faint this time. "Please," I said. "Look. Kill me if you have to. But let Molly go."

He laughed, good and loud. "You're not the hero in this movie, man. You don't get to save the girl."

The thudding sound was a little louder now. I only needed a few seconds more.

"There's nothing I can do?" I said, sounding as desperate as I felt. "*Nothing* I can say to change your mind? Or offer you? Nothing at all?"

He shook his head, tightening his forearm still further under Molly's neck, pressing the gun harder into her temple.

She was staring straight ahead. The monster had finally come for her in the dark, and she knew she wasn't going to escape this time.

"You've always thought too small, man," he said. "Fuck the body shots. This is the knock-ou—"

Molly blinked with both eyes. I stepped to the side and killed the light from my phone.

And Pierre ran past me like a freight train.

I didn't see him slam into Dylan. I heard the guy get off a shot—his reactions were fast—and after that the grunt of a sudden impact, the scrabbling of feet, a shriek from Molly.

When I had a bead on where most of the noise was coming from, I ran over and threw myself into it.

At first I was probably hitting Pierre as much as Dylan, but then I worked out who was who and started punching as hard as I could. Pierre was hitting him, too, but then Dylan sank his teeth into my forearm, so I elbowed him in the face, grabbed him around the throat, and slammed his head into the ground.

While Dylan continued to resist, punching me in the stomach again and again, Pierre grabbed Dylan's shoulders and was helping me lift his head up and smack it back down again. We kept going until there was no resistance, no fight coming back.

Only as we stopped, panting, did we realize that we'd both been shouting, screaming at Dylan, or each other, or something.

Pierre fell back. I remained with my hands locked around Dylan's throat. "Molly? Are you okay?" I said finally.

"I'm okay."

"Find the phone. I dropped it."

I heard her shuffling around in the darkness behind me, sweeping her hands over the rock floor. "Got it."

She turned it on, came back to where I was. Stood over me and shone the light down.

Dylan was dead. He was very dead. It was awful and horrifying and it was something that I had done. The hair on the top of his head—hair that I remembered noticing, about two million years ago, was starting to thin—was attached to something that now bore only passing resemblance to the shape of a human skull. One eye was half-open. The other wasn't. They were no longer in line with each other.

I let go of his throat. My hands ached.

I heard an intake of breath from Molly. I assumed she'd only just caught sight of the full extent of the unpleasantness. But it wasn't that.

"I'm fine," Pierre said.

But he wasn't. He'd been shot.

CHAPTER

52

M olly helped me lift Dylan's torso so I could get his shirt off. Then it took us several minutes to tear the shirt apart, yanking at it like two exhausted old people, and find a portion that wasn't covered in gunk. Pierre tried to help but I told him to sit still and stop bleeding on us. Eventually we had something that could serve as a bandage.

The bullet—the only one Dylan had time to fire before Pierre slammed into him—had hit Pierre in his right shoulder, then seemed to have glanced off the bone, thankfully without continuing into his rib cage. So, yeah, it could have been worse. On the other hand, it was a total mess. A bad, churned-up mess, and bleeding freely.

And we had a long way to climb.

Molly had done first aid at some point in the past and so I held the light and mainly let her get on with it. While she fashioned a second piece of shirt into a basic sling, I pushed myself to my feet and shone the light up the corridor. But it didn't seem like Dylan had brought anything up here with him. No sign of a bag or even water.

When Pierre was as bandaged as he was going to get, he stood up. He swayed a little, but rested his other hand against the wall. Caught his breath.

Molly looked at him dubiously. "How's it feel?"

"Fine."

301

"Pierre," I said.

"Yeah, okay, it hurts. What do you want from me?"

"Can you climb?"

"Yes."

"Effectively?"

"What the hell else am I going to do, Nolan?"

I stood in front of him. "Listen, Pierre. You've just done the single bravest thing I've seen anyone do, ever. You saved my life. Molly's too."

"I didn't."

"Yeah, you did. Are you serious? Dylan was done talking. I was looking that guy in the eyes and I know we were about to be only the most recent in a long line of people he's killed. There was *nothing there*, Pierre. No fear, no indecision, no qualms. If you'd stayed safe, back in the darkness, like anybody else in the world would have done—like I would have done, if I'm honest—then ten seconds later we'd have been sprawled on the floor with holes in our heads. You stopped that by being ridiculously, *stupidly* courageous. By being dumbass brave."

Pierre looked away. I reached out, grabbed his chin, yanked it to face me again. "But now you're done," I said. "You don't have to do it again, okay? I'm telling you not to. Because the next thing is getting down that shaft, and I'm not letting you try it if you don't think you can. Because it'll be dangerous to you, and dangerous to us, and *I'm done losing people*."

I had no idea I was going to shout that in his face until it had echoed flatly against the tunnel walls.

"Okay," he said quietly.

He stepped back, rotated his head around his neck. Lifted his right shoulder experimentally. Winced, but did it again. Extended his elbow out, and then back.

"Hurts like hell," he said. "But nothing's tearing. Or not tearing worse. Feels kind of like after a dislocation."

"You've dislocated your shoulder before?"

"I've played a lot of beach volleyball, dude. It happens."

"So you think you can climb with it?"

"I'm sure I can. And I'm sure of something else. It hurts plenty now, but soon it's going to start hurting a lot worse. I'm good to go, Nolan. We need to do this right now."

My phone was down to ten percent battery and I couldn't hold it and climb at the same time anyway. So I took the last remaining lanyard light instead. No way of telling how much power remained. No way of doing anything about it.

We decided to have Pierre lead the way. There was an argument that Moll, as the person in least pain—and with both arms functioning properly—should go first. But Pierre was firm on the subject. He was, he pointed out, the person most likely to fall. He didn't want anyone below him if that happened. We couldn't argue with that logic so we helped him over the ledge into the shaft and made sure he had a solid grip on the first of the handholds with his good hand.

"You sure about this?" Molly asked.

He didn't answer. He started down.

Molly went next. When she was in the shaft, I hung the light around her neck. She looked up at me. We knew what we were leaving behind, and who, and that there wasn't anything that could be said about it. Not now.

I sat on the ledge for a minute to give her clearance. I could hear more thuds in the distance. The machine doing whatever it was supposed to do. Maybe they'd be heavy enough to trigger some seismological measuring system in the area and people would come investigate. Probably not.

Most likely everything Dylan had spoken of was going to come to pass, as it had been foretold.

Still. At least it wasn't completely and utterly my fault.

I don't even know how Pierre did it. I assume he was able to use his hampered hand to at least grab a lower hold each time he moved his good one down. I heard a few grunts and a couple of times when he wasn't able to stifle a sharp, pained intake of breath. Otherwise he just climbed. We moved quickly, maybe too quickly. Pierre evidently realized he wouldn't be able to keep this up forever, that his good arm would tire, and there was only one possible outcome if that happened. There was a risk, also, though, that going fast would just bring this on sooner.

Molly climbed silently and steadily in his wake.

I descended in a cloud of if-only. I knew how dumb it was but I couldn't stop. When the here-and-now sucks that badly, you can't help retracing the steps that got you there. Going backward down the shaft only made it worse—as if we were retreating into a past where, had I but possessed the sense to think ahead, there might have been a different path.

If you start unpicking the threads the garment falls apart, however, and it's hard to tell which were the most important seams. Sure, there was the evening when I decided it'd be worth trying to find Kincaid Cavern. But before that there was not really paying attention when Ken said we had a new sponsor—just thinking, great, more kudos, and hopefully more money than the dumb books I'd been working on. Which I needed because the job I did before hadn't worked out. Which I needed because I wasn't with the woman I should be with. Which happened at least partly because I came out of a bar in North Hollywood—not especially drunk—and decided to go talk to Kristy's friend about the email she'd sent. I swear to God I did not intend the evening to go the way it did, at least consciously, but there are covert machineries in our minds and souls, and they take us places we don't know exist until we find ourselves stranded there, exhausted and aghast at ourselves.

You can tell yourself *if only*, but the truth is you never know about the big things until it's too late. It's always the wave you don't see coming that will knock you down.

What the hell was I going to tell Ken's wife?

It was going to have to be me. I owed him that. I knew her, a little. We'd had dinner together a number of times. They met back when she had a walk-on in *The Undying Dead*. That had been the high point of her acting career but now she helped run an animal shelter and a homeless literacy program. She was smart and calm and a good person and I knew that Ken took her advice on most things. Or listened to it, at least. I also knew she felt he should stop fucking around with webcasts and low-rent conspiracy nuts and work harder at getting back into the movie business—and that she regarded me with suspicion, both professionally and personally (like I said, she's smart).

I didn't know, because of course Ken hadn't said, how they'd parted on the morning he'd driven the Kenmobile around to pick us all up and embark on this disaster. Had he given her a quick peck on the cheek? Or a real hug, and an "I love you"?

No idea. But I was going to have to tell her.

And it was my fault.

Down and down and down and down and down.

I gave up trying to mitigate the pain across my chest and stomach. I told myself it was merely an infection or a muscle spasm exacerbating the low-level discomfort I'd felt ever since Gemma nearly fell off the canyon wall.

Down and down and down.

"It can't be far now," Molly said. Her voice was slurred.

"We're going to get there."

I realized she'd sounded that way because she was crying, but I didn't have anything else to say.

And I also didn't tell her—because it wouldn't have helped, or made any difference to our present course of action—that for the last ten minutes I'd been pretty sure I could hear noises from above me. Not thuds this time.

The sound of something climbing down the shaft after us.

Climbing fast.

CHAPTER

53

I knew we were approaching the bottom when I heard a grunt and then a crashing sound.

"You okay?"

"Yeah," Pierre said faintly. "Lost my grip at the last minute. I'm okay. Just . . . Yes, I'm okay."

We heard him shuffling back out of the area at the end of the shaft. "Clear," he said.

Molly dropped down the last few feet. Then I followed. We stood crowded together on the rock ledge.

"Air," Pierre said. His voice was barely more than a croak now. Both his bandage and the sling were soaked through with blood. "Real, fresh air. I can smell it."

"Let's go get it."

"I need a minute," Molly said. She was panting hard.

"No, seriously, keep going."

She was about to snap back at me but stopped. Cocked her head and listened. "What . . . is that?"

"I don't know," I said. "But it's been coming awhile and it's moving a lot faster than we were."

Molly dropped off the ledge first. Half turned her ankle on landing, swore feebly and nearly fell over. But got herself quickly in position to help Pierre as he scrabbled down after her, letting out a yelp of pain. Then I descended, making both of them look like mountain goats.

"Run," I said.

They ran. Molly in the lead, the light around her neck bouncing shadows off the rough walls. Pierre did a decent job of keeping up. I was moving at barely more than a fast shamble. My entire torso was rigid now and felt cold as ice.

Soon I heard something arrive at the bottom of the shaft behind me. It made a noise. A low, resonant sound that echoed around the tunnel. I couldn't tell for sure whether it was the same noise we'd heard from the things that had attacked us—and slashed me—in the bad-smelling room upstairs, but I thought it sounded different. Bigger.

"Come on!" Molly shouted.

They started to get ahead, to pull away from me, and that was okay. I wanted them to. They had a decent chance to escape and I could make it better.

Another growl and now I was pretty confident it was of a different kind than the one the ogre/troll things had made in the site above. It was deep but had greater texture to it. There was more articulation in the sound, a variation in tone—as though, under the right conditions, it could be bent and twisted to render speech.

It was loud enough this time that Molly stopped running. She turned. "Nolan!" she screamed. "*Run!*"

"I can't," I said. "And there's no point."

Even if we managed to get to the ledge, to the hole in the canyon wall, to the fresh air and the big world outside, we were still hundreds of feet up a rock wall. You can't climb down something like that with a thing after you. Not when you're exhausted and in terrible pain.

Molly gave Pierre a shove and told him to keep going. He didn't, of course.

They both came back for me.

And so they were by my side when the thing finally came into the range of the light from the lanyard, twenty feet away.

"Oh, Jesus Christ," Molly said.

We saw its limbs and body first. These answered the question of why the height of the passages in most of the site was well over that required for humans.

It was nine feet tall.

It was naked, and its skin had a burnished quality, like a dark hairless hide. It was broad-shouldered and very powerfully built, but basically in human proportions. It had stubby horns coming out of the top of its skull but these were not neat or symmetrical—there were three of them, twisted and gnarled like winter branches. They were a weapon, something that could be thrust into the belly of another animal and then twisted to effect immediate evisceration.

Its face was nearly human, though the jaw was massive and the features large and coarse. And there was something else about them, too.

"No," Pierre said. "Shit no."

The hair hanging down to the creature's shoulders—bunching up as it raised its huge hands—was a dark, rusty red. That could have been natural, the way this creature was supposed to be. But the arrangement of the face...

It wasn't female, so it wasn't exact or even close. But it could have been a cruel caricature of Gemma's brother, if she'd had one, a terrible sibling the family kept hidden under the stairs and never spoke of.

"Her DNA was in the blood in the p—"

That's all I got out.

The thing we'd encountered in the smelling room had been round-shouldered, squat. There had been a rotation to its movements, a lumbering quality that you might have hoped to have been able to avoid if you were faster and better on your feet than I was.

Not this thing. It came in hard, fast, and straight, with clinical precision and ferocious speed.

I barely knew it was upon us until Pierre had already been swatted out of the way—sailing back into the dark.

Once he was dispatched I saw the thing's eyes flick between Molly and me, then back again, swiftly making a judgment (possibly wrongly) that I was the second-biggest threat.

Those eyes had ten times more depth than Dylan's. This creature wasn't human but it possessed equal and perhaps similar intelligence. An enlarged, souped-up, weaponized version of us. The end-times cleanup squad.

It started to lower its head, arms out wide.

Pierre hadn't moved or made a sound since he'd been thrown from the fight. He'd been counted out of the equation for now, possibly for good. I was next on the creature's list.

But Molly ran straight at it, pummeling it with her fists. It felt the blows. It wasn't impervious, but it wasn't troubled. It tore her off with one hand, unfurling the motion to sling her down the tunnel past me.

"Go," I told her. "Just go."

Molly was pushing herself back to her feet. She looked me in the eye. "Do it," I said. "Get out of here, Moll. Please."

She nodded, took off the light, and left it on the floor. Then she grabbed Pierre and started trying to haul him away. He was moving, but slowly. She kept at it. Molly Mom wasn't going to give up, I knew that. Good for her.

I turned back just in time to see the thing's fist coming toward my face. Managed to twist my head enough to stop it smacking me front-on. Instead the blow caught my ear and the back of my head. The impact threw me straight across the tunnel to crash into the wall.

The creature did not immediately pile into me after I landed on the floor.

It waited. It judged the situation.

I tried to stand. Got halfway, but my legs collapsed under me. My ears were ringing. I tried to stand again and made it farther this time, but then a swinging blow from its other fist caught me in the temple and I was down again.

Down and nearly out.

The clanging in my head was so loud now I could barely hear. My vision was doubled and darkening. It felt like all the pains in my body were joining together.

And deep in the shadows, beyond the thing standing over me, I saw movement and knew another one of them was coming. Out of the ark, two by two...And then many, many more.

An army unleashed. The end of the world.

It kicked me, a crunching impact to the rib cage that had me crashing into the wall once again. The edges of my vision were folding in now as shadows came flooding into my mind, turning my thoughts upside down, breaking continuity like a movie cut up into single frames.

I knew I was right to do this, to have stayed behind. Not just because I'd given the other two something closer to a fighting chance, but because I'd spent so long running from things that didn't work or that hurt. Turning and facing this one had always been doomed to failure, but sometimes failure is what happens next. What happens last.

Another kick and everything was broken in my head. Nothing connected anymore. Time itself was malfunctioning and I couldn't tell the difference between what was happening now and my memories. I had a flickering recollection of lounging in the bar back at the hotel, a brief delicious illusion of the sensation of a cold beer going down my throat. A momentary snapshot of the view from my balcony back in Santa Monica.

A memory of Kristy looking across at me when we were out walking in the woods somewhere, years ago, with the crooked half smile that meant there was nowhere she'd rather be.

I even thought I heard Ken's voice, making fun of my shirt one last time.

The creature reached down and pulled me up by the throat. It was not monstrous; that was the worst thing. This was no chaotic blow from an uncaring universe, no car crash or landslide. This was a living, intelligent thing, as I was, and it was going to do what it had been created to do, and carry on doing it. For once in my life, I was going to be first.

It pulled back its fist, and I noticed that it had a thumb and five fingers, rather than four. It was a real-life actual giant and it was going to kill me, and unless unconsciousness claimed me first, I was going to be there as that happened. I was going to die in real time.

It opened its mouth, revealing that it had two rows of teeth. The better to eat me with. It stared down at me with eyes that were hazel flecked with green, as Gemma's had been.

Then the right side of its head exploded over my face.

I heard five more shots.

As I lost consciousness, pretty sure it was going to be for the last time, I experienced a strange vision.

It was of Ken, standing grinning over me. "Stop dicking around, Nolan," he said. "It's time to go."

Then darkness.

CHAPTER
54

I wasn't out long. Five minutes, they said. It seemed longer. It felt like a million years, and like returning from a very great distance. There was a brief phase where I was apparently conscious but in no pain, as though everything to do with the body was an optional extra that I didn't need to be concerned with. It was nice that way.

Then it wasn't, and everything hurt. Very badly.

My ears were still ringing. I tried to open my eyes but couldn't seem to move the lids.

"He's concussed."

The voice was Molly's. That disappointed me, because I thought she'd probably know what she was talking about, and if she believed I had a concussion she was most likely right. On the other hand, it presumably also meant I wasn't dead.

"Nah. He's just a tool."

That was enough to open my eyes.

Ken was sitting opposite, his back against the wall of the tunnel. His shirt was torn, there was a big cut up his arm, half his face was covered in grime, and he was missing a shoe. Other than that, frankly I've seen him looking worse.

"Seriously," he said, exasperated. "Why'd you leave the gun up there, you muppet?"

"I didn't think I was going to need it," I said, hauling myself into a more upright position. "And, you know, fingerprints and shit."

"Oh," he said. "Yeah, fair point. Well, whatever." He winked. "I stand by my decision to pick it up."

"Me too. But... *how are you still alive? How?*"

"No one's more surprised than me, mate."

"But we heard you..."

"Covered this already while you were snoozing. The executive summary is that yelling out like an injured thing was the best idea I could come up with to draw those creatures away from you all. And it worked. Bit too well, if I'm honest. Suddenly they're both haring after me and I'm running but bottom line is it's dark, I have no idea where I'm going, and it's seeming increasingly likely I'm on my way to meet my maker, which is not an encounter either of us would be likely to enjoy. Anyway, so I'm pelting down the opposite corridor and they're getting closer and I realize I'm nearly at the end and have nowhere to go except... The room with the original pool in it. So I do the only thing I can do, which is run down there and jump in.

"And you know the funny thing? They can't fucking swim, either. Worse than me, even. Who's going to have taught them, right? So I went to the end, scrabbled up onto that platform. As I'm watching them I grabbed the smallest of the balls you and Pierre got out, and dropped it down onto the console thing. Smashed it up like a beauty. Anyway, so they're thrashing around in the water still trying to get me and I see they're getting their shit together disappointingly quickly. So I jump back in and get back to the other side and go running back the other way. They follow. So I'm back to square one. Except..."

"What's that smell?" I said.

"Exactly. Come on—stand up."

He and Pierre pulled me up to my feet. My legs felt woolly and insubstantial. Molly was standing a couple of yards up the corridor, looking tense.

"Hey, Moll," I said groggily.

"We should go," she said. "We have no idea what else is coming down that shaft."

"She's right," Ken said. "But okay, look."

He pointed down at the giant. Portions of its skin were sloughing off, rotting down to a black, thick liquid. The rest was darker than it had been, too. The smell, though as yet mild, was the same as we'd encountered in the room upstairs.

"What's happening to it?"

"Got me, mate. But it's happening upstairs, too. One of the things after me had killed one of the wolves prior to that, and the remains were doing exactly the same thing. And something else. That big ball? It started moving."

"*What?*"

"Very slowly. But it was starting to come back up the passageway. I have no idea how, but whatever. Those little pyramid things are getting hotter and hotter, too. I put my hand on one and it was actually pulsing. I think the site's being reset, Nolan—like they're preparing to film the whole sequence again. Take two. When I was in the pool room, there were new balls up on the platform at the end."

Pierre stared at him. "From *where*?"

"Dunno. Out of the wall. Or dropped out of the ceiling. There were a lot of thuds going on. Anyway, I get to the room that smells and it's drained out—and you know what? I'm wondering if all that gunk was in fact the remains of creatures from the *last* time this happened. I got across and up into the fissure and the rest is history. Somehow, whatever runs this thing knows it got triggered too early. It's turning itself off. Winding everything back. You saw the map room, right?"

"Saw it and took pictures."

"Nice. You're a pro, Nolan. I've always said so. Well, sometimes. Once, maybe."

"Was one of the lights flashing when you came through? Quite slowly?"

"Yeah, but no. It was going really fast."

"Please, guys," Molly said. "Let's *leave*. So far we've only gotten rid of *one* of the cleanup crew, remember?"

"I emptied the gun into it, too," Ken said. "So, yeah. No more bullets. Moll's right. It's time to vacate the premises."

I looked at him. "I'm glad you're not dead."

"Yeah, me too, mate. You still got that cigarette?"

I pulled out the pack. Inside was the unsmokably broken remains of the last Marlboro Light. "Oh."

"Fuck's sake. Wish I hadn't bothered to save you now."

We made it to the end of the corridor—Molly supporting me around my waist, Ken doing the same for Pierre, who'd gotten a twisted knee when he was thrown down the tunnel by the giant.

We stood for a moment at the opening, looking out into the night. The air was cold and fresh and pure. There were stars. There was moonlight.

I had something like a panic attack when it came to starting the climb. A full-body *I can't do this* reaction. It didn't last long. I had to do it.

"We're going to take it slow," Molly said.

I hadn't voiced anything out loud, wouldn't have thought anybody could have known what was going through my head. But she knew.

Pierre went first. Me second, then Ken and finally Molly. In our current states, every single one of the men was more likely to fall off the wall than she was, and we knew it.

It was the middle of the night and dark but it was a different kind of dark. It was the kind of dark where you know there will be light at some future time.

A few minutes into the climb the side of the canyon seemed to shake as if something deep within was finally triggered, and then a wall of fire burst out of the cavern entrance above us. We waited, clinging onto the wall, in case anything else happened afterward, but it did not.

315

We climbed down slowly, ten feet apart. It took a long time. It took forever. I had to keep stopping every few yards to catch my breath, to refocus my attention on the rock in front of me. There was water at the bottom, I knew. I had no idea how safe it was to drink the Colorado River but there was no question it was going to happen.

We climbed in isolation but we climbed together.

We made it down.

CHAPTER
55

The dinghy was tied to a rock at the bottom, for which I was very grateful. We clambered and half fell in, and then leaned over the edge and—mindful of not overdoing it—got some water in our mouths. And over our faces. It was very, very cold. It tasted of the outside. It was unbelievably awesome.

The river was flowing fast but we realized we didn't even know how far we had to go to reach anything passing for civilization. Molly's GPS device was back up in the main room of the complex: after so many hours of it being useless, she'd forgotten to add it to the hard drives in Pierre's backpack. My phone ran out of battery and died as I tried to use it. Even if we'd known the right place to head for, we were in no shape to make a six-hour hike up to the top.

We sat staring at each other, goggle-eyed at this latest realization, and when Ken suggested trying to make it back to the beach we'd last camped on and setting off in the morning, nobody disagreed.

Molly and I took the oars and Ken untied us. After a hectic period of almost capsizing the boat as a result of near-total ignorance of how to work a dinghy, we got it together and started floating down the river. It felt like emerging from a spaceship onto the waterway of some new, unknown planet.

After about twenty minutes the general shape of the outcroppings on the right bank began to look familiar—and then yes, the beach was there, a hundred yards away.

We used the oars to direct us toward it. I couldn't tell whether my stomach and chest muscles were hurting a little less or maybe I wasn't actually feeling them anymore, but trying to move fluently—shoving against water that felt like it was actively fighting our attempts to change course—made it clear they weren't working properly. Ken saw I was struggling and stood up to come over and help.

And that's when the big raft came sailing silently out of the darkness behind and rammed straight into us.

I landed in shallow water, on my head. My face, in fact, smacking down into the stones under the surface with a crunch that had me seeing stars. Again.

When I got up to hands and knees, still trying to work out what the hell had just happened, I saw that Pierre had landed worse. He was unconscious, head half-under the water.

I grabbed his good arm and hauled him up onto the beach. He spluttered, pulled in huge breaths. Molly was already on the shore, turning to look back at the river.

The raft was jammed up against the rock on the side of the beach, where it had overturned the dinghy.

Feather was standing on it.

"You people really don't give up, do you," she said as she jumped down onto the gravel. She was holding a chef's knife—the knife, presumably, that Dylan had used to make our food.

"Dylan said you'd left to bring in Palinhem."

"They're on their way. In the meantime he was supposed to kill you if you got out, which is the only thing he's actually any good at. Clearly he failed. Is he dead?"

"Yes."

"Good. He was an asshole."

"Is . . . is what he told us true?"

"I've no idea what he said. He's just a field grunt. Or was. He wasn't

THE ANOMALY

supposed to say *anything*. I simply need you three remaining problems resolved so matters can unfold in the manner of my choosing."

"*Your* choosing?"

"Of course," she said. "You don't think I'm going to let the old fools at Palinhem actually run this, do you? All they do is hide. They've spent a thousand years navel-gazing and have forgotten how to *act*. I found you. I found *this*. It will be for me and my associates to govern."

"It's not going to happen," I said. "You failed. The site's resetting."

"I don't believe you, and I don't have time for this. I'm sorry, Nolan. You're the anomaly in this situation. You have to go."

"Three?" Molly said. "Shit, Nolan—Ken!"

I realized he wasn't on the beach with us. He wasn't in the dinghy, either.

"Go!" Molly shouted.

"You're not going anywhere," Feather said, advancing on me with the knife. "This is the end of it."

She slashed out at me, the movement measured and assured. I know nothing about knife-fighting but even I could tell she knew what she was doing.

I took a hurried step back, turned my foot on the pebbles and started to lose my balance. She side-kicked me in the chest, right where the gashes were.

Half a second later I was flat on my back and Feather was standing over me. "Webcasts season two, episode five," she said. "'Is There an Afterlife?' You're about to find out."

But Molly came running in from the side and tackled her, sending the two of them sprawling in the pebbles.

"Go!" she screamed at me.

I ran to the water. Saw—or thought I saw—a head bobbing in the river, forty feet downstream. I wasn't even sure in the darkness but I didn't know where else Ken could be so I threw myself into the water.

*   *   *

319

I've never understood people who are scared of flying. I mean, okay, there you are, defying gravity, tens of thousands of feet above the ground in a machine that may be a couple of decades old and flown by a person who for all you know could be...Fine, maybe I do get it. But large bodies of water have always unnerved me far more. The ocean, specifically. It is huge and restless and strong and it owes us nothing. Weak as I was and with a head swirling with concussion, I felt much the same about the river.

It felt as if it was moving more quickly than before we'd entered the site, too. Maybe because of the rain. I hoped so, because otherwise it seemed like I was going to be dealing with rapids and I simply didn't have what it took to win that fight.

I headed for the center line on the grounds that'd give me a better chance of glimpsing Ken's head again—assuming that's what it had been—and the water would be traveling faster there.

And yes—there it was, still thirty feet ahead of me. It was definitely Ken: He had his head tipped back, trying to gasp in air, and was thrashing about with both arms.

He went under, then reappeared—barely breaking the surface this time. And he was farther away.

"Swim, you *bastard*!" I shouted, but he couldn't hear, and he couldn't do it anyway.

I put my head down and kicked, pulling through the water with my arms until I was closer to the middle of the river and starting to move more quickly.

Ken's head popped up again but now I could hear him choking, coughing water up out of his lungs. His arms were barely moving at all.

I stopped trying to fight the water, relinquishing any attempt to influence the path it had in mind for me. I hadn't been making much difference anyway. Instead I kicked and used my arms to lift my torso, keeping a fix on Ken's head.

But then it was gone again.

And this time it didn't come back up.

I dived, going under the surface crooked, immediately bent around by a strong side current. It was pitch dark under there, swirling with bubbles, incomprehensible.

There was no way I could hope to find him. I was not even certain that I'd be able to find my own way back to the surface, turned around as I now was.

It was so very dark, black-green, and felt again like one of those places where there never was and never would be the promise of light. It seemed to be getting colder, and even darker, the void creeping in from the edges of my mind again.

A darker patch.

Ahead, a blacker black within the darkness.

And then it was more visible, as we turned a corner in the river and enough moonlight penetrated to make out the shape properly. I struck out for it, knowing I didn't have much air left, but that even if I could get to the surface to top up there was no chance of then finding again what I could see ten feet in front of me now.

A shape, floating swiftly downward, arms up over his head, legs pulled out in front by a competing current. Eyes open. Trying to keep his mouth shut.

I kicked and pulled myself through the last yards and got an arm around his chest from behind. I hoped he'd be able to help, just a bit, but his mouth was cracking open and air leaking out, and I'm not sure he even knew I was there.

I looped out behind me with the other arm, pulling against the water, kicking out spastically until I smacked a foot into something below—and I knew, with absolute certainty, that one of the aquatic things from the pool up in the site had somehow gotten out ahead of us, that there was a hidden waterway connecting the two and it was now here in the dark depths and ready to pull us down with it.

But then my other foot connected, and from the way it slid I realized it was scraping the bottom of the river instead.

My lungs were bursting and my ears full of a high, singing note that was getting louder and louder, but I shoved my feet against the rocks below, one after the other, until my head crested the surface.

Ken's came up with it and he was coughing and spluttering but still alive, and I kept driving my feet down, leaning back against the water, again and again, until suddenly more of me was out than in and I was stumbling backward. We fell together against the rocky side of the river.

I tugged my arm against Ken's chest, snapping it hard—provoking a gush of water out of his mouth, and more coughing and retching. I was coughing, too, burning wet barks that felt as though my guts were coming up.

And then we were only panting, chests hitching up and down, slowly bringing our breathing back to normal.

"Cheers, Nolan."

"You're wel—Oh *shit*," I said.

"What?"

"Molly."

I pushed Ken around to go in front in case the opposing current got the better of him. We kept close to the bank, grabbing any outcrops we could find, pulling our way around stubby trees when they forced us into the river, fighting our way upstream as fast as we could.

Finally we turned the bend and saw the raft tilted up, still half-over the dingy. We ran up onto the beach, legs giving out underneath us.

"No!" Ken shouted.

There was a figure lying on the ground.

A woman was kneeling astride her, holding up the knife for one more hack into the figure's chest.

She looked up as she heard us coming, eyes bright and wide in a face splattered with blood.

"That's enough, Molly," I said.

But she brought the knife down into Feather one more time.

FROM THE FILES OF NOLAN MOORE:

NES OF GIANT

FOUND IN SO

Giant Skeleton Unearthed.
VALPARAISO, Ind., June 3.—While the steam shovels of the Knickerbocker Sand Co. were loading sand at Dune park, on the shore of Lake Michigan, they unearthed a well-preserved skeleton seven feet two inches in length, and is supposed to be that of a member of an early tribe of Indians. It was found nearly thirty feet under ground.

SKELETON UNEARTHE

Produces Bones of Ma
ed to Have Been Mound
Builder.

Preserved S.
inct Tribe H.
Chan:

Giant Skeletons
Found in Florida

Indianapolis, Ind.—The comple
of one of Indiana's oldest i
said by Dr W. N. Logan, sta

Tampa, Fla., July 28.—(AP)—
Giant Indians who roamed Florida

GIANT INDIA

Diicovery of an Extr
eton Near Fond

Fond du Lac, Wis., J
—An Indian skeleton w
farm of Matt and Josep
south of St. Cloud. St
nothing strange in fin

BONES IN
IDIAN MOUNDS

J OLD GRAV

Professor and Stu-
ts Excavate His-
rical Hills Near
Stoddard

ns of Giant Warriors Un-
earthed in France.

STRANGE SKELETONS FOUND.
**Indications That Tribe Hitherto Un-
known Once Lived in Wisconsin.**
Special to The New York Times.
are much larger than the heads of any
race which inhabit America to-day.
From directly over the eye sockets, the
head slopes straight back and the
nasal bones protrude far above the
cheek bones. The jaw bones are long
and pointed, bearing a minute resemblance to the head of the monkey.

KELETONS UNEARTHED

ins of Giant Aborig-
Discovered; Weapons
and Utensils Are
Buried

Lived 25,000 Years Ago B
Have Died Fighting—Ar.
Found in

iscovery

GIANT SKELETON

Found in Bed of Sand in Northwest-
ern Ohio—Man Was Eight
et High.

FIND HORNED MEN'S SKU

narkable Discovery by Arch:
in Susquehanna Valley.

ns (Pa.) Dispatch to Philadelphia Record.

he archaeologists who are traversing
Suspuehanna River to the bay visiting
of Indian villages and digging up

**BONES OF PRE-
HISTORIC GIANTS**

Relics of By-gone Race May
be Exhibited at
Jamestown.

O., Aug. 14—While
sand for building on,
TON

ayton, O., Nov. 25.—The skeleton
a human giant was found in the
el pit east of the city by W. C.
the owner of the pit. He found
asured about nine feet in length.
skull was six times larger than
of the average Caucasian. Pro-
ors Metzler and Foerste of the
Steele High school believe the bones
are those of a member of the primeval
race.

CHAPTER
56

F ive days later I woke from a dream.

I won't describe it in detail because much of it was muddy and confused and because other people's dreams are always boring, like their coincidences. Both gain resonance through their roots in the individual's history and character: Unless you're that person you simply won't get it, or understand why a dream might feel like it enshrines insights or judgments out of reach to the conscious mind. I'll give you the gist. It had been the same three nights in a row. It was quite direct. I'm a pretty simple guy.

I was somewhere utterly dark. There was a sense of a dreadful secret, something I'd done that would color everything forever. Though I could see nothing, I knew I was in a tunnel, and there were two directions I could choose to go.

One led to the outside, to escape, to freedom.

The other led back to the bad thing.

I wanted to go the first way, of course. I started crawling that way in the fetid dark. But I realized there could be no release in that direction, no future worth inhabiting, unless I dealt with what was behind. So I laboriously maneuvered myself around in the cramped, dusty passage and set off in the other direction, back toward the bad thing. I crawled and crawled, squeezing myself into the ever-tighter and more claustrophobic tunnel into the past.

But I couldn't find it. The bad thing wasn't there anymore.

Except . . . it was, really. It was just farther. It would always be farther. Always just out of reach.

Because what's done is done.

I woke for good a little before five a.m. Though it was not yet dawn, my bedroom wasn't fully dark. Since returning to Santa Monica I've left the drapes wide open at night.

I put on sweat pants and a hoodie and made a thermos of coffee. Rounded up my cigarettes and a lighter and went for a walk. A few minutes from my apartment will get you to the promenade along the beach. At that time of day there's nobody around but lunatic joggers taking pre-pre-meetings via earpieces and homeless people spread-eagled on the grass or determinedly shoving a shopping cart loaded with their inexplicable possessions. The previous morning—when I'd woken at a similar time, after a similar night—I'd turned right, toward the pier.

So this morning I went left, toward Venice Beach.

I walked slowly. I hadn't appreciated until I got back to LA just how many parts of me were hurting, or how much. Not only from blows or collisions with tunnel walls in the closing stages, but additional discomforts right back to the spasm incurred when Gemma nearly fell off the wall on our first ascent to the cavern. Too many aches to count. You don't notice the toll life's taking while it's happening. Only when it stops.

I'd also lost seven pounds, and it'd been several days before I was anything like hydrated again. For thirty-six hours I'd labored under a dangerously high temperature, too, feeling as though there was something literally burning in my veins. It's possible that was the case—that the claws of the thing that had gashed my chest had been carrying microorganisms from the pool. The fever got so bad that I considered going to the doctor, though I suspected any antibiotics they dispensed would have little chance of tackling bacteria that had presumably never been seen before. So I sat it out, wrapped in a blanket and sweating, and finally it started to fade.

I'm not sure it was a case of my body winning. It's equally likely the same thing happened to those microscopic invaders as to their much larger counterparts in the tunnels. Their programming failed, or the balls Pierre and I managed to get out of the pool led to systemic failures down the line. They died, fell apart, decayed.

Perhaps obsolescence was built into them. Perhaps it's built into all of us.

I felt a little better this morning, thankfully. The body was doing its thing in the aftermath—repairing damage, restoring equilibrium. The equilibrium of a man in his forties doesn't exactly make you feel like a young god, but I'll take it. I'll take it gladly.

The mind tries to do the same, to return to balance, and part of this is a conscious process. I had thought back over what happened, many times. Portions of the experience in the canyon were already hard to access with clarity. Points of detail, the sharp edges of real things happening in real time, get sanded off in recollection. You wear them out. This is a normal function of the brain, the thing that enables us to stay sane after trauma. Exhaustion and dehydration amplify the effect. Parts of those days felt as dreamlike as what I'd encountered in the night.

But I knew they hadn't been a dream.

The portions that most occupied me will not surprise you. I had not anticipated that I would ever look down to see my hands gripped around the throat of someone whose existence I had brought to a halt. Nor that I would have to gently pry a ten-inch chef's knife from a woman's hand, blood dripping from it onto the coarse sand of a hidden beach. After Ken helped Molly to her feet, and Pierre limped over, the four of us stood in a silence that was long and profound.

Then we had to make a decision about how to proceed.

After a long discussion we loaded Feather's body onto the dinghy and took it back upriver. Then Molly and I hauled her up the wall to the opening of the cavern. Feather had been slight of build, but no dead person is ever light. Bodies, like past life events, turn into black holes, sucking the gravity of the future into themselves.

We made it, barely. It took forever, pulling and pushing the body a foot at a time, and it was very, very tough. We laid her out in the antechamber cave inside the cavern, and though she had not only meant us grave harm but tried hard to bring it to pass, the knowledge that we were going to leave her there was still dreadful.

But what was the alternative? Neither burying her on the beach nor throwing her in the river was safe. The only other option was taking her with us when we struck out down the canyon the next morning—a far longer and more arduous journey—handing both her and ourselves in to the cops when we reached civilization.

Molly was all for doing this, and Pierre, too. She'd tried to kill us, they said. We were in the right. The police would see that. Ken and I weren't so sure. Of course hiding a corpse felt terrible. But even if we claimed we'd come upon the body of a stranger, our own battered state would provoke an investigation, with us as the prime suspects. A check at the hotel would reveal that Molly had booked five rooms, too. The only chance we'd have of escaping from the situation would be to tell the truth—including about what we'd found.

Again, Pierre and Molly were all for this. Couldn't see why we wouldn't, in fact. Get everything out in the open. Tell the world. Shed a light.

Perhaps you have to be a little older to realize some things should remain in the dark. That the world at large isn't ready for them, can't be trusted with their care, and they need to be kept hidden. At any cost.

After we'd climbed back down to the dinghy there was further discussion, which I eventually put on hold by saying at least Feather's body would be safe there. If we decided we needed to go the other route, we could tell the authorities where she could be found.

We dozed away the remaining hours of night, and next morning set off up the river. We hiked back up the canyon wall to the top. We got back to the hotel and retrieved our belongings. We came home.

*　　*　　*

I'd thought I had been comfortable with the decision we'd made in the canyon. As the days slowly passed back home, however, it became clear that I was not.

There were two bodies lying in darkness. Three, if you included Gemma, or what was left of her—assuming anything except dust remained of her and Dylan, after the purifying fire the site had unleashed upon itself. Gemma's death had not been our fault but that only made it worse. It doesn't matter how deep you bury an incriminating letter in the trash, it's still there. It doesn't matter how far you push a body back into a tunnel, either. That's still there, too.

Even if it has been destroyed, it's still there.

You know this already. You'll have bodies stashed in tunnels of your own. Things you've done, mistakes you've made, secrets you hold—the guilt you carry for moments that stick out in your past like black stars in the firmament of your inner life. The outlier occurrences. The anomalies. The events you look back upon in disbelief, wondering how the hell they could have come to pass, and if they can be made to fit in a story you are prepared to own.

But the truth is you get where you're going not through the long, forgettable years of sticking to the path, but through the moments when you wander off it. It's the things that don't make sense that reveal who you are inside.

The anomalies make you who you are.

That realization will not make you feel any better about them. Time may help you turn a blind eye, but guilt is the stain that never goes away.

In the last twenty-four hours I'd become aware that part of my mind—one I hadn't used very often since the afternoon I'd walked all the way to the beach from Hollywood and decided I was done with being a screenwriter—was working at the story of what had happened. Rewriting it. Seeking a way of bringing it to a different conclusion.

Eventually—just before I'd gone to bed the night before—I believed I'd gotten an alternative narrative straight in my head. A way of making it appear as though I alone had been responsible for what happened to Feather and Dylan and Gemma, without having to mention what we'd found in Kincaid Cavern.

I would write it down, email it to Ken, and tell him to stick to the script and make sure the others did the same.

Because it was true. If I hadn't dragged us all out on that expedition, three people would still be alive. And the four people still living wouldn't have to get up every morning with those deaths in their minds, wondering when payment would come due—either from God, or someone much closer to home.

Perhaps there are people within whose lives that guilt can be accommodated.

Mine isn't one of them.

At the far end of the promenade, where it runs out and turns to beach, I stopped for a cigarette, sitting on the low wall facing the sea. It was still early and there was nobody else in sight. I smoked, gazing vaguely down at the sand.

After a few minutes something dropped onto the ground in front of me. For a moment I couldn't work out what it was.

I picked it up.

A necklace. With an ankh on it. Something I'd last seen hanging around Feather's neck, when Molly and I laid out her body in the entrance to the cavern.

A man sat down near me on the wall. I didn't turn to look, but I could tell he was very tall. He didn't say anything.

"So now what?" I asked after a while.

"There will be no repercussions." The man's voice was deep but modulated. "From us, anyway."

"Why?"

"What would it gain? Damage done to the site has more than likely rendered it nonfunctional. Congratulations, Mr. Moore. You managed to break the most important thing ever found."

"But Ken only smashed the console in the smaller pool."

"The larger pool creates those that come before—the ones that clear the Earth in preparation for a new beginning. To unleash them without the others would be planetary suicide. All evidence of what occurred has been removed. We have sealed the cavern."

"Kinkaid tried that."

"It has been done far more thoroughly this time."

"But there are others, right?"

"Yes. We discovered a room at the site. It seemed like it might have been a map. It was dark, lifeless. Did you see it?"

"We may have."

"Were any markers lit on it? Indication of where other sites might be?"

"No," I said. "It was just dead rock."

"I don't believe you."

I turned my head to look at him. I saw a man, and yes, he was unusually tall—but not so much that people would stand and point. His face was big and bony, but again, within normal parameters. You'd have to have witnessed the creature I saw, the one who nearly killed me in the final run out of the cavern, to glimpse the genetic ghost of something not human in it. To anybody else, he'd just look like a basketball player.

"Okay," I said. "Does that change the situation?"

"Not for now. I'll put this in a way you'll understand. It's always cheaper to not make the movie. And it's generally better to not kill people. Unless they talk."

"Who'd believe us?"

"Nobody. But we've spent a very long time keeping this quiet. Our mission and purpose is not only to find, but to then keep it hidden afterward. Now is not the time for renewal, and it must never be within one man or woman's power to take matters into their own hands. This needs to be secret. Keep it that way."

"Sounds good to me," I said.

"Be careful, Mr. Moore. Turn your attention from this, forever. And make sure we never have to meet again."

He got up and walked away.

*   *   *

I sat a little longer, looking out at the ocean. After a while I realized that although there had been moral heft to the decision I'd come to about the deaths we had been involved in, a portion of what I'd felt had been provoked simply by fear. I'm not proud of that, but neither will I deny it.

I didn't write the email to Ken.

And that night I did not dream at all.

CHAPTER
57

A couple of days later Ken and I were sitting across a table in the courtyard of #ColdBruise, a dumbass new hipster bar/ restaurant in Santa Monica. We both agreed it was even more annoying than the previous dumbass hipster joint it had replaced, but it had a nice terrace and included a wide range of alcohol among its wares and so it was good enough for me. For now—though I knew the effect was bound to wear off as the injuries and memories faded—pretty much anywhere was good enough.

I'd called Ken as soon as I got back to my apartment and told him about the meeting I'd had with the man on the promenade. We'd discussed what it might have meant, and whether we had any reason to trust him.

Our holding conclusion was probably yes.

We'd discussed it further over lunch without changing that position. We'd talked about many things and were not yet done. When Ken got back from visiting the john for about the fifth time, he looked serious. "Here's a thing, though. Yesterday I discovered that entire section of the canyon has been declared off-limits, for the foreseeable future, due to 'seismic activity.'"

"The balls dropping could have triggered a response."

"Yeah, maybe."

"What? You think the Foundation got the area closed?"

THE ANOMALY

"It's not out of the question. And here's something else."

He put a sheet of paper in front of me. A printout from a well-known website specializing in offbeat news, describing how the battered remains of a strange creature had been found in the canyon. Except it turned out to be an exceptionally convincing model, lost by a film crew who'd allegedly been shooting a sci-fi/horror movie in a cavern nearby.

"Bullshit," I said. "They planted that. You know damned well that the things *we* saw weren't special effects."

"Of course I do, mate. But this is out there now. Anything we say is going to be laughed at. And here's another thing: I sent them an email last night."

"Who? This website?"

"No. The Palinhem Foundation."

"Why, Ken? *Why* would you do that? Did we not agree that we'd keep our heads down?"

"We did. But after a couple of drinks I thought to myself—and this is a direct quote—'Shit on that.' I'm not spending the rest of my life looking over my shoulder, wondering if someone's going to creep up on me in the night and bash my head in. Okay, the guy you met seemed to push back that possibility. But I'd like a little more confidence."

I'd had the same thought, but hadn't done anything about it. "So?"

"So I dropped them a line. I said the Kincaid Cavern expedition was a bust, sorry, we didn't find anything."

"And?"

"Wasn't expecting anything fast, because I sent it after office hours. But just before midnight I get a reply. From some bloke I've never dealt with before. Saying never mind, it happens. But as a result of internal budgeting changes, they are no longer able to sponsor the show."

"No shit. So what do we do now?"

He shrugged. "I dunno. I'm taking the wife to Palm Springs this weekend. When I get back, you and I should talk. Pretty sure we can scrape together enough for another season on YouTube."

"But do we even have a team left? How's Molly?"

"She's all right," Ken said. "I saw her again yesterday. She's still got a thousand-yard-stare thing going on, but a lot less than last time. She'll be back to the Moll we know and love before long, don't you worry."

"I hope so."

"I know it. With the interpersonal skills for which I do not receive anything like enough credit, I even talked to her about the thing. Asked if she was dealing with it okay."

"What thing? There's a lot that could encompass."

Ken glanced around. Though the courtyard wasn't crowded—it was midafternoon, and we'd been there awhile, sampling the place's many craft beers in strictly alphabetical order—he dropped his voice. "The thing involving her and the great big knife, you tool."

"Oh."

"I told her that she'd had no choice. That she shouldn't blame herself."

"And?"

"She looked me in the eye and said she hadn't lost a wink of sleep over it. That she'd killed the monster in the dark and that was that. Mean anything to you?"

"Maybe," I said.

"All right, well, whatever. She's fine, basically. Or will be. She sends her love—though it looked more like 'guarded affection' to me, with a hint of revulsion—and said to tell you that she's found you a replacement shirt. So, yeah—I'd say she's still on board."

"What about Pierre?"

"Talked to him again this morning. He needed minor surgery on that shoulder, and he's still depressed about his disk drives."

"They're definitely screwed?"

"Yeah. His backpack wound up in the river, didn't it. Plus apparently half of the drives had got flattened at some earlier point, so...Sorry, mate. We've got none of it. Not a single frame. Evidence-wise, none of it ever happened."

"What about Pierre himself?"

"He sounded okay but...quiet."

"Dylan," I said. "We did it together."

"Yeah, and I blew half the head off a...We've all of us had a very unusual time. Which, from a legal point of view, it's preferable no one ever knows about, even if the evidence has been removed, as that guy implied."

"It's not just that."

"I know, mate. I am not immune to guilt. Or nightmares."

"I've been back and forth over it in the last couple days," I said. "Bottom line is Feather and Dylan drove the play, and it came down to us or them. I'm glad it was us."

"Very much my take on the situation."

"Gemma, on the other hand..."

"Ah, well, there's another thing I need to tell you. She's different. And her people need to know. So...I did something."

He looked sheepish. I wasn't sure I'd seen him look that way before. "What did you do, Ken?"

"Got in touch with the site she worked for."

"*What?*"

"I was only going to see if I could get contact information. Maybe try to work from that to finding out about a boyfriend, relatives. Someone I could let know, subtly, somehow. I talked to her editor. All she had was an email address and a PayPal account. So after that I hired a bloke I used a few years ago, when a wanker agent was trying to fuck me over about...Never mind, long story for another time."

"What kind of bloke?"

"A private investigator. Told him to dig up whatever he could find about her."

"And?"

"Parents both dead—cancer and a car accident. No brother, sister, other relatives. A few friends, but none of them very close. She was all about her work, one of them said. My guy tracked down her apartment, gained access. Just being thorough."

"Christ, Ken."

"I know. But there was nothing to see anyway. Tiny place. Clothes, few bits and pieces, couple pictures of what he assumes were her mum and dad. Only other personal thing was a big poster above her desk. Looked old, like she'd had it awhile."

"What was it of?"

"The Earth, from space. Some writing across the bottom, in Sharpie. 'Make a mark—Love, Dad.'"

We sat and looked at each other for a while, knowing that because of us, she would not.

When the next beer was nearly done, Ken glanced at his watch.

"You supposed to be somewhere?"

"No," he said. "But I can't waste the whole day talking to a wanker like you. Come have a cigarette with me, then I'm going to fuck off home."

We stood out on the sidewalk, smoking, withstanding wounded glares from passing health nuts and perfect people.

"Any luck with those pictures?"

"No," I said. When I checked my phone the day after getting back to Santa Monica, it turned out the only photographs I'd taken inside the complex—of the two sides of the map room—hadn't come out. Instead of showing the frieze on the ground, there was only a dark, speckled gray fog. "I've put them through every piece of software I can find but there's just nothing there. I don't think that was a normal kind of light in that room. Far as my phone was concerned, we were in darkness."

"Ah well. We know what we know."

We did, even if it was going to have to remain a secret. Because we had zero evidence. Because of the warning I'd received. But mainly because of acts we had been forced to undertake in the closing stages, extreme events that bound us in silence. We'd fallen from grace together. It's a long fall.

But we knew some things. And I was starting—in notes I was

writing straight into a heavily-encrypted website, not even stored locally on my laptop—to join the dots. I'd begun to wonder if the tattered remnants of ancient and anomalously advanced civilizations on Earth might be evidence of previous occasions when there had been a cleansing of life from the planet. I'd considered the idea that the skeletons of greater than human height found in America and other countries—and the way giants crop up in our oldest myths and legends—might be proof of interbreeding between remnants of a population of cleanup beings and the next human line. Because doesn't it say in Genesis that "there were giants in the earth in those days; and also after that, when the sons of God came in unto the daughters of men, and they bare children to them"? Yes, it does. And perhaps I'd even sat on a wall in Venice Beach and had a conversation with a piece of evidence for this.

The data is not in, and someone, somewhere, does not yet believe it's time to wipe the board and start again. I don't know whether that's because that person or culture still has faith in us, despite the violence in our hearts and the mistakes we seem intent on making, or if they're working to a subtler agenda than we can begin to comprehend.

But look at the world, and the state it's in. I'm not sure we've got much time left to prove the worth of the current round of the experiment.

"So we'll chat when I get back," Ken said. "But in the meantime, think about an idea for a replacement episode. I've got one, in case it helps. Seen a couple mentions in dodgy forums online to some bunch called the Straw Men."

"Who are they?"

"No idea, mate. No one's sure if they even exist. But might be worth a look."

"Sure," I said. "I mean, how bad can they be, right?" Then I realized Ken was looking shifty. "What?"

Over his shoulder I saw someone halfway up the next block, coming toward us.

"What the hell is she doing here, Ken?"

"You two are always going to be on the same road," he said. "I'm just reminding you where the car is."

He winked and walked away down the street.

Kristy came up to within a few feet of me and stopped. She looked poised, beautiful, self-contained—but also nervous. I'm sure I looked the same, except for the first three parts.

"Hey," I said.

"Hey."

"How was the Alaska thing?"

"Stupid cold. And we didn't find much."

"Bummer."

"Life goes on."

"Well, you know what they say. It matters not whether we find. Only that we continue to—"

"Shut up, Nolan," she said. "And buy me a drink."

We walked together back into the courtyard, and we stayed there for a very long time.

ACKNOWLEDGMENTS

A huge thank you to my literary agents, Jonny Geller and Jennifer Joel, and Kate Cooper; my editors, Wes Miller and Sophie Orme, and to Miriam Metoui; to Ellen Goldstein-Vein and Lindsay Williams for their efforts and enthusiasm, and to Luke Speed; to Stephen Jones and Adam Simon for friendship and support; to publications and writers like the *Fortean Times*, Bill Corliss, and Charles Fort, for reminding people how weird the world is, and how little we know, and how much there is still to find out; to Tes and Eleanor; and to Paula and Nate.

ABOUT THE AUTHOR

Michael Rutger is a screenwriter whose work has been optioned by major Hollywood studios. He lives in California with his wife and son.